THE POET'S WIFE

THE POET'S WIFE

JUDITH ALLNATT

ISIS
LARGE PRINT
Oxford

First published in Great Britain 2010
by
Doubleday
an imprint of Transworld Publishers

Published in Large Print 2010 by ISIS Publishing Ltd.,
7 Centremead, Osney Mead, Oxford OX2 0ES
by arrangement with
Transworld Publishers
a Random House Group Company

British Library Cataloguing in Publication Data
Allnatt, Judith.
    The poet's wife.
    1. Clare, John, 1793–1864 - - Mental health
    - - Fiction.
    2. Authors' spouses - - Fiction.
    3. Mentally ill - - Family relationships - - Fiction.
    4. Large type books.
    I. Title
    823.9'2–dc22

        ISBN 978–0–7531–8644–2 (hb)
        ISBN 978–0–7531–8645–9 (pb)

Printed and bound in Great Britain by
T. J. International Ltd., Padstow, Cornwall

X000   000   039   3000

For Janet: friend in need
and friend in deed.

The lunatic, the lover and the poet,
Are of imagination all compact

Shakespeare

Contents

Part I — July 1841

CHAPTER
ONE

Names in Wood

After four years away, I found my husband sitting by the side of the road, picking gravel from his shoe and with his foot bloody from long walking. His clothes were crumpled from nights spent in the hedge or goodness knows where, and he had an old wide-awake hat on the back of his head like a gypsy.

"John," I said. "Are you coming home?"

When he heard his name he looked up at me, as if curious that I knew it, then held out his shoe as if to show me its parlous state: its sole loose and hanging from the upper. I bent and put it back upon his foot as gently as I could, for his stocking was brown with blood from many blisters. He watched my face with a look of puzzlement and when I stood and reached out my hand to help him up he refused it, levered himself up by his own efforts and began to walk away. His short figure and limping gait were so pitiful as he set off again along the empty road that my heart followed straight after him.

I turned back to Mr Ward and Charles, who were waiting in the cart, but they looked as nonplussed as I. Not wishing to lose him again, I followed down the road, calling, "John! Wait!" and when I reached him I caught his hands fast in mine.

He pulled them away as if I had burnt him, saying, "Are you drunk, woman? Leave me be!" and continued to shuffle along with his shoulders set as if he had been mortally offended.

Although my heart hurt to find him so estranged from me, when I had been missing him and thinking of him these past four years, I fell into step beside him and we walked awhile, until he seemed to forget that I was there. Soon we had gone such a way along the road that Mr Ward had to click his tongue to the horse and follow us. A strange procession we must have made to anyone watching: a broken-down journeyman, a woman trying to stop from wringing her hands and a cart stopping and starting behind them.

As we came to a place where tall elms grew on either side, shading the road, John's pace slowed even further and while still in the sun he stopped, as if loath to go on.

"Is this the way to Glinton?" he asked me, as if noticing me for the first time.

"It's the way to Northborough," I said, trying out the sound of his home to see if it would ring in his ear with any echo of the past.

He looked at me blankly. There was no glimmer of knowledge in his bright blue eyes, though I searched them with my own and willed him to see his own Patty before him.

"Is this the way to Glinton?" he said again.

A sigh escaped my lips, for I knew very well why he would hanker so for Glinton and it affected me deeply. "Yes," I said. "Glinton is near Northborough. It's on the same road."

Mr Ward drew the horse in and the cart stood beside us.

"Are you tired?" I asked. "Why not ride awhile with us?"

He looked ahead at the shadows that the trees' branches were casting on the road. It was full summer and they were thick-leaved, their shade deep. He took the arm I offered him. His hand was sun-browned and grimy against the paleness of my skin where my sleeve fell back, yet my arm was strong and firm, whereas his hand gripped tight as a baby's fist round a finger as he climbed up into the cart, so weak was he from long journeying.

Charles, whose eyes had been round as plates through all this strange exchange, moved along the wooden bench to make room for his father and stared in a most unseemly manner. He looked as if he would say something to greet him, but I shook my head in case he receive the same blank stare as I had and be hurt.

Mr Ward flicked the rein and we set off, John safely between Charles and myself. John took off his hat and held it on his knees and I took the chance to observe him.

Although he had been away from us a full four years, beneath the stains of the road he looked, if anything, younger. His cheeks were plump and his slight frame

5

had filled out as if he had had good food and regular. His hair was still fair with no trace of grey, while I myself had a little at my temples, although it did not show much among the brown. He was wearing different clothes from those he went away in: a dun coat of good cloth, though lightened by dust and smeared with grass stains, and a yellow neckerchief. For the first time I noticed a bundle in his pocket, and knew from its square-cornered and lumpy shape that it was books tied in a handkerchief. At this I could not forbear to smile, for only John would come away on a journey of nigh on eighty miles with no bottle for drink but with books for company.

We trotted on for a while, John staring at Mr Ward's back, which was indeed all he could see from where he was sitting. Suddenly he tapped him on the shoulder so that he glanced round.

"Aren't you from Helpstone, my native village?" he said. "You look uncommonly like Mr Ward."

A broad smile grew on Mr Ward's face. "Indeed I am the very same and this is your wife, Patty, and your son, Charles."

John looked quickly side to side at us, then back to Mr Ward. "I thought at first that you must be his brother," he said.

Mr Ward bellowed with laughter. "Come, John, have I changed so much?" he said. "My brother isn't half the man; I could pick him up under one arm by the time I was ten year old." And we all laughed, for indeed it was true, his brother looked nothing like him, being red-haired and slim-built and cause for talk in the village when he was born.

We proceeded then in greater comfort for a while and I told John the news from Helpstone, our old home, with John nodding and smiling as if he remembered all and it was dear to him. Presently, Charles took his collection of pooty shells from his pocket, a handful of glossy shells some whorled in brown and green, some tiny and a whitish grey. John admired them as a good father should; my hand stole across and covered his and he did not push it away.

We began to pass through country close to Helpstone and I pointed out the places that would please him such as Royce's Wood, where the orchises grow, and the windmill at Barnack that stands so tall and proud with the flat fields all around. Small things too, the Brimstones fluttering in the hedge flowers, eglantine and woodbine, hoping by this to draw him back to early memories as a stepping stone to the present. Indeed, a dreamy look did come into his eye and by and by he gripped my hand and turned to me.

"How is Mary?" he began.

My tongue dried in my mouth and I pulled my hand away. The old fit is still on him, I thought. "She's been dead three years," I said. "You know that, John."

He shook his head. "That can't be, for I saw her this twelvemonth walking in the wood in Essex and with cornflowers in her hair."

At this I fell silent, for I knew very well that she was dead and buried in Glinton churchyard, but I shivered at the thought of her walking abroad and wondered, as

I often have, whether it is possible for the living to long so much for departed souls that they can conjure them to appear before them. Such, I knew, was the longing of my husband.

Fearfully, I asked him, "Did you speak to her, John?" I saw Mr Ward's back stiffen as if he felt my discomfiture.

John shook his head and smiled. "She slipped away from me and hid behind the trees for me to follow and catch her, as she did when we were children."

"And did you . . . catch her?" I asked, though it was hard to do it.

"No, for one of the keepers came for me and she wouldn't show herself then but kept herself hid."

John's mention of the keeper brought me back from my own concerns. "Surely they treated you kindly, John?" I said. "Dr Allen would have made certain of that."

He frowned. "Yes, if you think following a body and poking and prying into all his affairs is kind enough."

I thought that, from what I'd seen, the following was probably to watch over him and make sure that he did himself no mischief.

John fidgeted and turned to look behind him as if he expected a keeper to come trotting after us any minute. After scanning the road, which was empty save for the nodding flowers and grasses and the small flocks of birds that scattered to the hedges as the cart passed by, he settled back in his seat.

"I gave them the slip," he said, "and went a-visiting Mrs Pratt and Mrs Fish's daughter at the Owl and Miss King, who I lent my Byron to . . ."

Mr Ward turned round to glance at me and I felt my colour rising. "But Dr Allen fed and clothed you and tried his cures?" I said quickly.

At this second mention of Dr Allen, John fell silent and rubbed his chin, with the look of a boy caught stealing peas.

"You didn't tell him you were leaving," I said flatly. "You must write to Dr Allen directly when we get home."

Charles looked up, hearing in my voice the tone I use when chastising the children, for, to tell the truth, John's remarks about one mistress and then another had stung me further. All were silent for a while.

At length, Charles fished in the pocket of his breeches and offered his father a sycamore key. Taking one himself, he held up his father's hand level with his own and showed him the game of dropping them to see which should twirl best and take longest to reach the floor of the cart.

I couldn't help but smile inwardly at this show of comradeship with his father, as if both should side together against a strict parent, and so I let them be, hoping that John would become engrossed in the game and we should pass Glinton without mishap.

All was quiet and peaceful save for the clop of the horse and the clatter of the cart-wheels as we passed over the ruts. As we came out of a stand of trees, Glinton spire appeared in the distance, needle-sharp and white-gold in the bright sunshine. John opened his mouth to speak and I quickly turned away, as if keenly interested in the view in the opposite direction, though in truth it was nothing but a field of oats.

Nonetheless, the more I looked away from the spire, the more I felt the desire to look again. Such is the power of a vertical object in a horizontal landscape; it draws the eye as the pole draws a compass. Though I would not look round, I could feel John's eyes drawn to it, and I thought bitterly of this village where Mary Joyce had lived and gone to school alongside John. I fancied his heart as a compass needle drawn always back to Mary, just as a traveller, befogged in the fen, always scans for the thicker shape of the spire or listens for a muffled peal of bells.

I wished that there was another road we could take, out of sight of the spire, but it is visible for miles around, its tapered point pricking the very clouds. I thought of the orchard at home and how John liked to sit there beneath the apple boughs in the evening, and how sometimes I would join him when my tasks were done, and wished that we could be transported there in the twinkling of an eye rather than at a trotting pace. At this, a sigh escaped me, as, in truth, what I wished for was to fly not just across the fields and woods, but back in time to when John was not so ill and could still be relied upon and showed me tenderness. It would have been better if I had not allowed myself such musings, for they brought such feelings up into my heart that I fear I began to lose my patience.

As we approached the turning for Glinton village, John broke off from his game with Charles and pulled at Mr Ward's sleeve. "Turn here," he entreated. "Turn here. This is where I want to go."

Mr Ward looked askance at me.

I said, "But we're going home, John, home to North-borough, where all your children are waiting for you."

He set his face with that stubborn look I know so well and said simply, "I want to see Mary."

My patience was breached and all my feelings of frustration with him welled up, the flood loosened by this slight to his own children. "For God's sake, John, your own kin are waiting that you haven't seen in four years!"

At this, he stood up, nearly unseating Charles, and made as if he would get down from the cart and recommence his footsore wanderings. I pulled him back down and waved my hand to Mr Ward to continue straight on. "We're going home," I said, "and if you cannot believe me that she is dead, I will track down the newspaper and you can read it with your own eyes."

We had passed the turning and he twisted round to look back at it as if all his joy lay down that road. Mr Ward clicked his tongue to the horse and we continued at a smarter pace until the turning was out of view. John reluctantly turned away and sat straight again. He put his arm round Charles as if for comfort.

"It is true, John," I said in a gentler manner.

"It is a lie," he said and stared fixedly at Mr Ward's back.

Is it possible to be jealous of the dead? She is gone; her bones lie in Glinton churchyard, six feet deep, with the earth pressing on the lid of her coffin. Yet I know in John's mind she walks and talks as fresh and scented as a flower after rain.

I know she is dead; I mind well enough walking to Glinton a year after her death to see the grave for myself. The thought, even now, gives me a guilty shiver. What was I thinking? I need not pretend. I know very well that I was thinking that even after the newspaper report of her death, even after the neighbours' tales of her funeral, I still had to see for myself where she was laid to rest. I remember I set out early on a summer's morning, my dress soaking up the dew as I walked the field's edge. The vision crossed my mind of my John as a child walking to school at Glinton from his home in Helpstone and Mary walking her shorter walk to the schoolroom, which was in the vestry of the church, and now I was walking to Glinton from Northborough and it was as if the three of us were all walking towards the spire and would all converge at that point to face one another. It was as though I had slipped through time into a place where I had no business — John and Mary's childhood.

On reaching St Benedict's at Glinton I entered through the gate, walked a little way into the centre of the churchyard and looked up at the spire. It loomed over me, its height dizzying, its tapering point drawing the eye imperiously to heaven. The sturdy weathercock, from this distance, seemed a flimsy thing as it swung in the slightest of breezes. It is said that its six-pound weight balances on a single glass marble and I wondered that it should still hold there in the face of wind and weather. Though worn pea-green it never has blown down, but in a storm is said to spin back and forth, as if our Maker plays with it a little, allowing it to remain because the spire has been raised by mortals in his praise.

Though the stone of the building shines golden in the early-morning sun, the gargoyles at the roof corners grimace horribly. All save for one, which turns its back and shows its nether regions. I had heard before of this gargoyle, which is said to demonstrate the mason's opinion of the low payment he had received. Children point at it and lewd youths snigger and mutter the word "arse" behind their hands, but looking at its grossness it seemed to me to speak of man's beastly side and to be set there to remind the parish of their sinful thoughts and the pains of damnation the Church says are set aside for those who cannot control them. I turned my eyes earthwards and began to walk the paths of the churchyard.

I found her grave; the stone still new and white, the hummock still rounded, not flattened by the falling-in that time wreaks on the dead. The inscription read *Mary Joyce, died 1838, age 41*, the lettering etched deep and clear, with carved oak boughs crossed above to make her resting place a bower. And it is true I felt the pinch of jealousy even then, for I knew that if John were there to see it he would weep. I tried to bring thoughts of the Lord to my mind and to imagine her at peace at last with her hands across her breast and the marks of pennies on her eyelids. Then I thought on the facts of the case: that she had died by fire when a cinder had caught on to her cotton dress and there was no one there to help her, and that her body was fixed after death with her hands plucking at herself in an effort to tear off her burning garments; and I felt a terrible pity thinking of her in her casket in the very shape of her agony and I was awfully ashamed. I hurried towards the church to seek some peace within.

I entered the church porch and stood at the dark oak door, unsure whether to try the handle, it being a Saturday and no sign of clergy present. With a shock I saw that, on either side of me, what I had at first taken for two rough-hewn pillars were in fact two huge stone figures. A man and a woman, they stood facing into the porch. The woman was in a long shift and wimple and with her hands clasped in front of her. The man carried bow and arrows and a horn: a forester. The figures themselves were imposing as they stood taller than I, but chiefly I had drawn in my breath because they *hadn't any faces*. Mask-like, where their faces should have been there were only blank ovals of stone, their lineaments blunted by time and now marked only by small random pits in the surface. As soon as I recognized these signs of weathering I realized that the figures were tomb tops, brought in from outside to stand there like sentinels. They faced each other, expressionless, their judgement on those who passed over the threshold kept secret and unmarked. With a shiver I moved forward, grasped and turned the iron ring and entered the church.

I slipped into a pew at the back, put my head down and closed my eyes tight to pray. I breathed in the smell of damp and old wood and, although no prayer would come, the coolness calmed me. All was silent and the air felt as though it had not been disturbed for some days. At length I rose and went slowly towards the vestry. I was sure that no one else was in the church, but I felt eyes upon me as I walked up the aisle and, glancing up, saw that not only angels but also hobgoblins and beasties were sculpted holding up the corbels. I didn't know of which I was more afraid, the demons or the angels, but unable to stop myself I stepped aside and went in at the vestry door.

I had not realized that the vestry was still used as a schoolroom, so where I had expected to find only cassocks and candles I faced instead the very scene that I had imagined in my dreams so many times. At the far end, sun streamed in through an arched, leaded window to fill the whitewashed room with light. Two rows of stools and desks faced a larger desk with a chair set behind it. Beneath the window was a large oak chest, the wood black with age and the lid with thick iron hasps. The room smelt of candle wax and ink. I walked to the large desk and stood facing the room. I rested my fingertips on the cold wood and it was as if the room was filled with childish giggles and whisperings and John and Mary were sitting at the back with their heads bent over the same book. As though in a dream, I walked along the row of desks to the back, my skirts brushing against the tiny stools, and as I went I read the angular, scratched letters on the lids — *Peter Thresher 1798*; *Tom Wildern of Glinton*; *Sarah Missell will be catched* — until at last I found what I knew I would, and in a familiar hand that had taken the time to add curlicues to the letters, *John Clare loves Mary Joyce*.

John Clare loves Mary Joyce; it ran like a refrain in my head. I ran my fingers back and forth across the surface as if I would rub it out. *But she did not marry you*, I thought in bitterness, and then, far worse, *and now she is dead*. I pulled my hand quickly from the wood.

As if there must be worse still to come, I began to wonder what lay in the oak chest — maybe school books with notes passed between them? — and once I had started to wonder, I needs must open it and see.

There was no key in the lock but the hasp hung loose and I saw that all I need do was pull it free and lift the lid. The metal was bumpy and dark with rust and the lid heavy, but I put my shoulder to it and heaved it open. Inside were many fusty books with dates upon the covers, which afterwards I thought to be the parish records, but at the time I had eyes for only one book and that was big and black, its pages edged in silver and its title tooled in brightest gold. The words "Holy Bible" seemed to burn out of the black and I dropped the lid of the chest. The noise echoed in the roof like a clap of thunder and I picked up my skirts and ran down the nave, out of the church and back along the path as if I had the finger of God upon my back.

As I passed through the churchyard gate, my shawl became entangled in the latch and my fingers shook as I picked the knot apart to let me free. The gate clanged shut behind me and I fancied the gargoyles laughing at my struggles and walked away fast, back the way I'd come. A woman at the pump gave me good morning but I had not the breath to answer her so I nodded and

16

walked on. She looked at me curiously and I made myself slow a little and find a sedate pace more becoming to my age and stature.

As I escaped the village and gained the quiet of the field track, my heart began to slow at last and the whisper of the oats and the nodding of the poppies began to calm me and give me leave to think. Well, I thought, I have done a bad thing in coming here today and I have had my punishment. The old adage has it that those who listen at keyholes find out no good and I had listened at the keyhole and heard the voices of a world in which I had no part.

I realized, with a heavy heart, that a dead woman is a fearsome rival, for over time her absence will surely smooth out all her faults and the rosy glow of memory illuminate her virtues until she becomes the very epitome of a lost love. I am a handsome woman, many have said it: I have straight and regular features, clear grey eyes, thick hair and a firm figure, but I am forty-one summers old and each year adds another line, a little grey.

Mary, though, will always be untouched by time. John can call her to mind like a magic lantern show: the smocked twelve-year-old playing jacks with him after school; the sixteen-year-old with a mouth as sweet as blackberries; the twenty-year-old he hankered for and whose father would not let him near. She will never be over worn with tiredness, never sharp-tongued, never ill or pale, never stale-breathed or with the sweat of labour on her. She will never be old.

CHAPTER
TWO

Return of the Prodigal

When Mr Ward brought us home he said goodbye kindly to John and accepted my thanks as payment enough from one old neighbour to another. He wished me good luck. At first John seemed at least a little pleased to be back. He went straight to the garden and walked for a while with Charles, exclaiming at each new discovery of remembered flowers, the hollyhocks he grew from seed and the lavender full of honey-bees and smelling sweet this time of year. He was disappointed in the yews, though, which have been let to grow out of the shapes he cut them in, their spheres and pyramids blunted by his four-year absence from overseeing the boys in their clipping.

I fetched a pail of water for him to soak his travel-worn feet and he sat on the garden seat where the heat from the house wall warms your back and the small flies dance around the eaves above, coming and going from the thatch. The youngsters were all still out at work, or in the fields, so the house was empty save for Parker, who came as fast as his stiff joints would carry him to greet his son. They fell upon each other's necks and clasped tight, Parker patting him on the back and marvelling at how he had thickened out to fill his jacket to the seams. John even teased him back for his loss of hair atop, asking him if he'd borrowed from his crown to get his long whiskers.

They sat together talking of the orchard and how much of our crop had been lost in the June drop and with Parker bemoaning the fate of our vegetable plot, which has become overgrown despite my best efforts to pull what weeds I can. John managed to converse, albeit in fits and starts. I marked that every now and then he would break off and mutter a phrase or two, repeating "God bless them" or "keep them all from evil", as he used to do before he went to the asylum, but this being said quietly and Parker being a mite deaf, the conversation seemed to go along quite smoothly. Charles sat at their feet, throwing pebbles at a flowerpot and glancing up at John to make sure he had seen each time one found its mark. And thus the afternoon wore on until the others returned.

We heard the youngsters and Eliza in the lane beside the house before we saw them, as Sophie let out a shriek and Eliza, trying to keep the peace, remonstrated with William for pulling her hair. They rounded the corner of the house, Sophie still holding her head, William wearing a scowl and Eliza putting her frame between the two. The argument sputtered to a close as they saw their father, then Sophie ran to him and held him tight, but William hung back a little, looking at his boots, for he and John had not parted on good terms.

Eliza waited her turn to embrace her father. She blushed with pleasure as he exclaimed over her womanly bearing.

"You are become a beauty, Eliza," he said, "with your skirts to the floor and your back held so straight."

I could see that he would find a great change, for when he had left for High Beech Eliza had been a thin fifteen-year-old with her blonde hair in a tidy ponytail; now, at nineteen, she had blossomed into a young woman with a trim figure and her hair swept up and pinned in place. Sophie, too, had changed from a chubby eight-year-old to a slender young lady of eleven.

John was wet-eyed, quite overcome with the joy of seeing his children again. He turned to William, who still stood with his hands in his pockets. "What, William, no embrace for your father?" he said. "Or are you too much the man?"

William stepped forward and put out his hand and John took it, then clasped his elbows and drew him into his arms. "Ah, William, William," he said, "if you knew how I have thought of you and worried for you these four years." He let him go, then said to me, "Has he been a help to you, Patty?"

I smiled and nodded, although, in truth, finding William is usually hard enough, never mind persuading him to his chores once you have found him. Nonetheless, I nodded for the sake of peace and John seemed satisfied with this.

By evening time, Freddy and Jack had returned. There was great joy in the house at their father's homecoming and we were able to sit at our board, a family once more. Freddy asked John why he hadn't written to let us know he was returning but he only smiled and said he hadn't known himself until he set off. Jack, looking at his travel-worn clothes, asked how he had come all the way from Essex and was amazed at his reply that he had put one foot in front of the other.

I had been used to sitting at the head of the table with Charles and William nearest either side, the one for answering his constant questions and the other to keep under my eye, but with John back I moved into Anna's old place. John noticed at once and asked if Anna were not coming home.

"She is married, John," I said. "Freddy wrote to you to give you the news. Do you remember?"

"Married?" John said. "My little flower is grown and gone?"

"She is Sefton's wife now," I said, "and at present they are staying at Helpstone, at work at the haymaking."

John nodded thoughtfully. "It doesn't seem possible, my first-born child! She used to love Mrs Barbauld — do you remember, Father, Mrs Barbauld's lessons for children? I used to have to read it to her again and again."

Parker smiled his gap-toothed smile.

John continued, "Do you remember, Patty, when she was so ill as a child? It was one thing after another, the cough, then the measles. Then our neighbours lost a son and a daughter both in one day when they thought they had recovered . . ."

Sensing the start of one of John's agitations, I took up the serving spoon and began to fill his plate with potatoes and broad beans. He held my arm and said in great earnest, "She is well, my little Anna? You are hiding nothing from me?"

"She is well and happy and married," I said firmly, and he let me go and started to eat.

Through all of this talk of Anna I marked how Eliza sat with a downcast look. She had not been herself since the wedding and was always pestering to visit, despite my strictures that she should leave the newlyweds to themselves for a while.

Perhaps she feels a little abandoned, I thought, for the two girls had been close companions since childhood, being only a year apart in age and used to sharing everything from story-books to combs and petticoats. I remembered how, as girls, they used to walk out together to the market or the fair, when I could spare them. I would hear them whispering in bed afterwards, chewing over which young lad had said what and to whom and what he might have meant by it. Sometimes they would shriek with laughter, as young girls do when unobserved and with no need to bother with decorum, and I would smile to myself, remembering my own girlhood and its freedoms. With a pang I wondered whether Eliza was finding it hard to forgive Anna for leaving her alone at home with the chores and only her ma for womanly company.

She sat, taking no part in the conversation, toying with her food. Something was certainly troubling her, and I would have to think further on it, for here was a puzzle that a mother needs must unravel.

"Eliza," I said, "could you see if Grandfather would like some bread?"

She leant close to Parker's ear to ask, then cut a thick slice of barley bread, took off the crusts and passed it to him.

Parker, who faced John from the other side of the table, smiled on us all and asked what we all wished to know. "Well, son," he said, "tell us how you made your way home to us; it must be eighty mile or more from High Beech."

John finished his mouthful, for he had been eating at speed and had almost emptied his plate by the time I had served the last dish.

"I got my way from the gypsies who had made their camp in the wood," he said in good humour. "I was going to travel with them on Sunday, but when I went back they'd upped and gone. There was nothing left of them but an old hat, so I clapped it on my head and just set off on Shanks's pony."

"Was there dangers on the way?" asked Charles, round-eyed.

"No more than two saucy drovers who called me 'gypsy' on seeing my hat. After that I stuffed the crown with leaves to make it stand up more respectable and hoped that no one would detain me."

"But where did you sleep?" Sophie asked anxiously.

"Well, here is a riddle for the first night," John said. "I slept on a bed as soft as a cloud . . ."

"A hay-rick," said Sophie quickly.

". . . With a pillow strewn with flowers . . ."

I smiled at this, for in shaking out his jacket I had found the three-fold leaves of clover along with twigs and grass seeds in its creases and its pockets.

"Like pom-poms . . ."

"I know, I know," said Charles, fidgeting in his seat.

". . . And a smell as sweet as honey."

"Clover!" shouted Charles. "You slept on clover!"

John laughed. "Indeed, I did. I found some clover trusses in a shed and lay down with my head pointing north, so that I should be in the right direction in the morning, and slept a honeyed sleep." He rubbed his chin. "It was not so good on other nights, though. One was spent between a wall and some elm trees, where the wind whistled through so sharp I had to move on and find a house porch to curl up in, and another night I slept in a dyke bottom."

"What did you eat?" asked William, interested in spite of himself.

"For three days I ate nothing but grass and tobacco," John said. "But then some neighbours, from where we lived at Helpstone, passed in a cart and gave me money and I feasted on bread and cheese and ale and was no longer hungry, only crippled and foot-foundered, and that was how your mother found me." He looked at me and my heart went out to him, for I fancied that, although he had been at first half-crazed and had not even recognized his own wife, he had come to see me now as his rescuer and I was thankful.

Parker nodded. "Well, we are glad to have you home," he said, "and must tell you what news we have. Anna, of course, is wed. Eliza . . ." he patted her arm, "is needed here and is a great help to her mother and to me, but I fancy perhaps a little out of temper with being at home so much."

24

At this Eliza looked fixedly at her plate.

"Come, Eliza," I said, "your grandfather is only teasing you a little."

"Well, I don't care for it," she said, but low enough for her grandfather not to hear. Nonetheless her face was sour for all to see and Parker looked at me askance.

"Take no heed," I said. "She's not herself today. Freddy and Jack are working for Mr Potter," I said, and began to busy myself pouring out the ale.

"What are your duties?" John said to Freddy.

"Apprentice carters helping with the horses," Freddy said through a mouthful of potatoes and continued to fork his dinner in as if it might be taken from him.

"The boy still has a good appetite, I see," John said. "D'you mind him, Patty, in that little sealskin coat he had as a child? And his face as rosy as an apple?"

I smiled and nodded, for, truth to tell, I could say nothing, the picture of those happy times came up before my eyes so clear and sharp: Freddy setting off through the fields with his podgy hand in John's and his little red bonnet on his head. They would return, with Freddy carrying something held carefully before him: plants dug to fill our garden or birds' nests with eggs to blow.

"Jack has just joined Freddy at Potter's last month; he's taken to it well and has a real love for the horses," Parker said, "but the pay is pitiful little." As he said this he looked not at Jack but at William, who snorted and busied himself tearing off another piece of bread. "We're still very short with eight mouths to feed,"

Parker said pointedly, "and some birds as could fly but still have their little beaks ever open."

John looked sharply at William and the colour began to rise to William's cheeks.

I broke in quickly, for I could see where the turn in the conversation was leading and had no wish for an argument on John's first night home. "It would be good to have your advice on the use of our plot, John, when you're feeling well enough. We still don't have sufficient money for a cow to make any use of our little pasture and I've only been able to fill a part of the ground we have in the garden for lack of good seed."

At this, John began to mutter again under his breath and Sophie's eyes grew as round as pennies.

"Keep them from evil, keep them from evil," John intoned and rocked forward and back in his chair.

"John," I said, "perhaps you would like some more beer? Pass your father's cup," I said to Sophie, but she seemed unable to move.

"What is it, son?" Parker said. "We shouldn't have burdened you with talk of no vittles, with you so exhausted after your long journey."

"I suppose you'll say this is my fault too," said William, looking somewhere to the left of his grandfather's face, as if talking to the pans that hung behind him would somehow grant immunity from a response.

Before Parker could answer, however, John took a deep breath full of effort and seemed to rouse himself to sit more upright and still in his chair. Pushing his plate away he said, "And how are my other family?"

This stopped all in their tracks. The young ones exchanged frightened glances. William laughed and, finally out of patience with him, I reached over and slapped his hand. Parker was saying "Eh? What's that you said, son?" Eliza, God bless her, seemed to gather her wits and started clearing the plates with as much clatter and fuss as she could muster.

"Can we get down from the table?" Sophie asked. I nodded grimly. William left first, shoving his stool back with a grating noise and holding his hand, which, I saw with a pang, had a red mark upon it. Freddy helped Eliza and the others trailed out, looking woebegone.

"Will someone tell me what has happened?" Parker said.

"John and I are going to sit awhile in the orchard," I said. "We need to speak together."

I set two stools down where John and I were wont to sit in better times, under the biggest apple tree in the orchard. The grass grew long and tussocky as we had no sheep to crop it, but a three-legged stool will always find a level and I sat and gestured for John to do the same. I judged it best to let things settle and so we sat looking out through the fruit trees to the low sun spilling over the flat fields.

At length John sighed. "I wish we were at Helpstone," he said. "It's not like home here."

I thought of our old home at Helpstone with its two rooms that, at the worst while all the children were young, nine of us had shared: how my temper was so short with them all under my feet and how too many in a bed meant that if one caught the cold then we all did. Here there was room for the boys and the girls to sleep in separate rooms and for John and me to have our privacy. Behind us in the garden foxgloves were busy with bees and hollyhocks spread their evening scent. To me, it was a very Eden.

"The fields are all gilded in the sun," I said.

John stared at them for a moment. "No woods. Level and featureless," he said. "Where is the end of them? They could go on for ever." He rested his chin in his hands.

"The children are happy here and there is more room and ground for a cow, if we could only save enough to get one."

He looked aslant at me without moving his head. "And neighbours who hate us and envy us that room and think we are Lord Milton's lapdogs and favourites because we have this cottage."

"That is not so, John," I said, stung by the suggestion. "We pay rent the same as all."

The ferocity of John's scowl silenced me. "In Helpstone there was the Close brothers and the Billings brothers for drinking partners, and William Bradford at the Blue Bell and the Royce family and Otter the fiddler for merry times and old Mr Crowson and the Misses Bellars and Large . . ."

I held up my hands.

His voice dropped lower. "And there were other things: the crowfoot among the brambles in Crossberry Way, the hollow tree I stood in when I was a child, as if in a pulpit, the old walnut where we hung a swing and used to swee, the crooked stile, the woodbine at the garden gate . . . all my friends, all my friends."

"But there are different beauties here, John," I said, gesturing first towards the fine ash tree that grows at the back of the orchard and the little grove of ash saplings beside it that Parker tends to, and then sweeping my hand to take in the apple, plum and cherry trees around us. "And the garden has asters and China roses and all your favourites."

He bent and picked up a hard green apple from the grass and turned it over in his hand. "I would rather have the furze on Emmonsales Heath than the garden here," he said, "and teasel burrs and shepherd's purse than any garden flowers."

I tutted at this despite my good intentions to keep patient, for it seemed perverse to miss the very weeds from our old environs and shepherd's purse was to be had a-plenty here just as well as there.

"It was not all plain sailing in Helpstone," I said, looking at the apple as he turned it over and over like a hermit's bead. "Remember when the Golden Russett tree failed and, with no apples to sell, we couldn't raise the rent?"

I pointed up into the branches above us where Bramley apples glowed like pale green lanterns in the shade, clustered in twos and threes so close together that you'd barely be able to slip a penny between them. John gazed up into the thick-leaved canopy but made no answer. Then he bent forward and set the apple he held back down upon the ground. He stared at it for a moment, then moved it an inch or so to replace it exactly in its original position.

I remembered how disoriented John had seemed when we first came here. So wedded had he been to the home of his childhood that he lost sense of time when the sun was in a different quarter of the sky, and his appetite and sleep had suffered. I wondered if his stay at the asylum in Essex had wrought a similar befuddlement, for everything there would have been different again and John may have longed all those four years for his old home and not this.

So my voice was gentle when I spoke again. "Perhaps it is the past you long for, John." For, in truth, I could well understand that feeling, as sometimes the longing for the time of our closeness in courtship, or for the holding of babies we had lost, caught me as sharp as a knife between my ribs. I sighed and laid my hand lightly on his back. "But a clock will not run backwards," I said. "We must plough the field we have and look to a new crop with hopeful hearts."

He looked towards me and his eyes were wet and shining, so that I could not help but put my arms, which had ached so long to hold him, around him and clasp him tight. He smelt of hay and sweat and ale and his body felt sturdier and more solid than when he went away, the jacket filled out with no puckered fabric at the shoulder. I laid my head against his and, for a moment, it felt like a homecoming, but he made no move to return my embrace. He patted my arm, as you might some aunt or uncle when you wish a greeting to be over, and I sat upright again upon my stool and let my arms drop. How I longed for him to turn to me, to hold me and call me once again his Patty of the Vale!

The light was fading and the fruit trees cast their bushy shadows in long ovals across the grass. Beyond the hedge I heard the children trooping back and a blackbird, disturbed by their progress, flew low and chattering across the orchard to alight on the fence and bob its tail angrily.

"It was a long journey," I said. "You must be very tired. Perhaps a night's sleep will raise your spirits."

I stood and picked up my stool, intending to go and see the children safely to bed, and John followed me. As we entered the house the sound of fiddle-playing issued from the kitchen and Parker struck up "My true love for ever", a gentle ballad and one I like well. I turned to smile at John and bid him come and listen, but he stood at the doorway to the parlour, staring in at his bookcase, which fills the whole of one wall, being more than a man's height and around ten feet wide. He had it as a present from a patron, the editor of the *Stamford News*, Octavius Gilchrist, and at first I feared that seeing it would make him sad, for when that kind friend had passed away John was very much affected. He went in and ran his hand first along its oak side, then along a row of books, lingering here or there upon a favourite or pulling one out a little way with a muttered exclamation.

I followed him into the room. "They are all still here," I said, "and have been well looked after." John took no heed of me but slid out from the shelf a volume of Thomson's "Seasons". It was the first book he bought as a boy and, having read it all afternoon in a field with his back to the wall of the Burghley estate, he had walked on home composing the first of his own poems that he thought worth committing to paper. He ran the flat of his hand across its cover, then traced the title again and again with his thumb. However, when his eye fell upon his desk he didn't open the book but laid it aside. He pulled the desk flap open, sat down before it and rifled through the contents until he found pen and ink.

"I must set it all down," he said, as much to himself as to me.

"Do you not think it better to wait until morning?" I asked. "When you're rested and the light is good again?"

But already he was filling his pen. He patted his pockets and drew out first some scraps of newspaper with scribbled pencil notes along the margins, then a little octavo notebook, which he opened and smoothed flat in front of him. Then he looked round at me as though waiting for me to leave. His eyes were bright and his hand, holding the pen poised above the paper, trembled a little.

"It's late, John," I said, although I knew that when his writing fit was on him this argument would carry no weight. Then, thinking of a way to curtail the fit and turn it to good effect, I asked, "Will you write to Dr Allen, to let him know you are safe and thank him for his care?"

"I'm not writing to any Dr Bottle-Imp now," John said. "I need to get it all down on paper before I forget."

"All of what?" I asked.

"All of my journey, of course," he replied. He turned his back on me and began to write.

The light was waning in the window above the desk and John huddled over his notebook as if he was warming his hands on his words and did not want to share the fire. In the other room, Parker played a mournful air and my last chance of persuading John to come and join with his family floated out into the garden on each sweet, heart-wringing note. By the time I had unbraided Sophie's hair and brushed it out, and seen that Charles washed properly and did not merely pass a cloth across his forehead, and helped Parker to mount the stairs and to remove his boots, which he could no longer easily reach down to, the light was fairly much gone. When all were abed, I tiptoed through the dusky hall and looked in again on John. He had lit a candle and placed it next to his notebook on the open flap of the bureau, so that it was sheltered by the upright portion of the desk from the draughts of the casement window.

The flame burnt steady and illuminated his features in a golden light. The fine set of whiskers that complemented his high cheekbones and long narrow nose, and his sensitive mouth, which moved a little as he formed the words on paper, were all as familiar and dear to me as ever. His hair was receding now where once it had curled about his temples and the height this lent to his forehead gave him an even more studious look. His face was a little plumper than when he left us for High Beech and this, at first, suggested health, but there were new frown lines between his eyebrows and his eyes had a sad and haunted look.

"All are abed, John," I said. "Will you bring the candle up now or shall I have to light another?"

He glanced up for a moment. "Go on ahead. I shall be up presently," he said.

I withdrew quietly with a heavy heart, for I had hoped that he would want to hold me in his arms again and I longed for the comfort and warmth of my husband in my bed.

I retired to our room and lit a candle to undress by. As I slipped between the cool sheets the puff of air almost put the candle out. It guttered, making the shadows of the rush chair and the ewer and basin on their stand jump against the whitewashed wall. Then it burnt clear again and I kept it lit, though we could ill afford it and it was poor company. I listened to the noises of a summer night — the squeaking of young owls in the ash tree and the tiny scurryings in the thatch above — and watched the hours melt in a pool of tallow.

At last, John came upstairs, placed his candle next to mine, undressed and piled his clothes upon the chair, then spat on his fingers and snuffed both candles out. I felt his side of the bed go down as he climbed in but sensed rather than saw him in the inky darkness. Tentatively, I reached for him and my hand met the bare skin of his shoulder. I ran my hand down to his elbow, then to his hand and clasped it; at last he returned my squeeze with a pressure of his own. I took his hand and placed it on my nightgown at my breast and he moved closer, until our bodies touched along their whole length. Then his mouth was on mine and his arms round me and we fell into that sweet and practised dance that we knew so well after many years married.

All was over very quickly, for years of abstinence meant that passion burnt like powder rather than a taper, and we both fell back, exhausted, on our pillows. We lay facing each other and though I could barely see his face I heard his breathing and knew that he was still awake.

"John?" I said, for I wished that he would whisper those endearments he was wont to do, and call me by my name. He said nothing, but took a lock of my hair between his fingers, stroking it and twisting it in his hand, then brought it to his lips, then let it lie. I reached to touch his face and found his cheek wet with tears. Whether these were tears of joy or relief I did not ask, for it was enough to know that I had moved him. I dried them with the back of my hand and settled to sleep with my hand curled at his chest and hoping that, through our bodies rather than our words, all had now been set to rights between us.

I woke, hours later, with the noise of the birds calling from their woody roosts as the sun got up and spilled a pinkish light across the sill. John had rolled away from me on to his side and I raised myself on my elbow to look fondly at his sleeping face. He was so deeply asleep that he didn't stir as I pulled the blanket up over his bare shoulders.

If I woke very early it was my normal habit to allow myself a half-sleep until the clock downstairs chimed seven and the others needed to be woken, but today I did not want to sleep again. I stretched out in the bed like a cat by the fire and felt my body pliant, every fibre relaxed and rested. I thought of our courtship in the fields around my home near Pickworth and felt as young and bonny as I had been then in my blue gingham gown. I remembered John in his olive-green coat, pointing out a fritillary here and a cluster of cowslips there, picking a harebell to tuck into my breast or helping me gather lily-of-the-valley for my garden. I remembered him showing me a pettichap's nest with a clutch of tiny eggs, beside the road, not inches from the passing wheels of carts yet still intact. Such things did not seem miraculous to me then, when I was buoyed up by youth and love.

John would set down all the wondrous things he'd seen with me, or when out walking on his own, then write his verses and bring them to read to me next time we met. He had such clear sight of all he looked upon that, when he read of the landrail's summer cry or the hare that squats in the green corn "like some brown clod the harrows failed to break", you'd think, "*Just so: that is the very nature of the thing*," and almost clap your hands in delight.

He used to tease and keep the verses writ especially for me until the end and ask me, "Do you not want to know what I have set down about you, Patty?" until he would make me blush. Then he would take a paper from his breast pocket, perhaps a scrap of newspaper or

the wrapping from a block of sugar, or any bit of paper
he could salvage at his lodgings, and sometimes he
would say, "What is it worth, Patty? Is it worth a kiss?"
and sometimes I would refuse him until he had read it
and I was pleased, and sometimes I would kiss him
straight away and then blush after it. Some were such
pretty things like:

Of all the days in memory's list,
Those motley banish'd days;
Some overhung with sorrow's mist,
Some gilt with hopeful rays;
There is a day 'bove all the rest
That has a lovely sound,
There is a day I love the best —
When Patty first was found.

When first I look'd upon her eye,
And all her charms I met,
There's many a day gone heedless by,
But that I'll ne'er forget;
I met my love beneath the tree,
I help'd her o'er the stile,
The very shade is dear to me
That blest me with her smile.

Strange to the world my artless fair,
But artless as she be,
She found the witching art when there
To win my heart from me;
And all the days the year can bring,

As sweet as they may prove,
There'll ne'er come one like that I sing,
Which found the maid I love.

And though there have been hard times in our marriage since and bitter hurts at times, I find I have it still by heart.

So, as I lay turning over these memories that were lent an extra shine and vividness by my loving feelings towards John, just as pebbles have bright colours when passed over by the brook, my mind turned to John's writing of yesterday evening. I began to wonder what manner of thing he had set down about his journey and his feelings at returning home, and the old desire to know what he had written of me returned with all the sharpness of my nineteen-year-old curiosity, but there John was, as fast asleep as a worn-out puppy. With a thrill of pleasure, all at once I realized that I need not wait for John to awake. Now that I had learnt my letters properly from Freddy teaching me alongside Charles, I could go downstairs and *read it myself.*

No sooner had this thought occurred to me than I must turn it to the deed, and with a joyous feeling of pride in my new-learnt skill of letters I slipped from the bed, put my woollen shawl round my shoulders and went downstairs and into the sunny parlour.

The bureau was closed up with the key in the lock and for just a moment I hesitated, a memory of dark wood and the smell of the church hovering at my shoulder, but I shrugged it off, turned the key and sat down at the open desk.

Inside, tucked into one of the upright compartments, was the octavo notebook with the pen still between the pages where John had left off his writing. The covers of the book were well worn, as though he'd carried it with him a long while, and the page edges were thumbed and torn. I took it out and laid it on the desk flap; it fell open and I put the pen aside.

The notebook was not one that I had seen before and was almost full, so I saw that John had procured it at High Beech and had been keeping up his writing there. The pages were covered in tiny script, not elegant like the hand in which John writes his letters, but scribbled and sloping down the page towards the right, at odds with the straight horizontal grain of the creamy paper. The left-hand page was densely packed, the lines as tight together as the bristles on a brush, and seemed to have been written in haste, judging from the number of blots. At the top was a short paragraph and I bent close to make it out.

My own writing is almost printing, the letters rounded and compact, whereas John's is ornate, with loops and adornments, so that at first I could make it out only slowly and with my finger following the words.

With a shock I read: *Returned home out of Essex and found no Mary — her and her family are as nothing to me now.* Here was the same old conviction that Mary, who was childless, had a family, but at least I could take heart from the words following, that John might finally be beginning to accept her death. Then I read on and saw *How could I forget?* and my heart began to misgive.

The rest of the page was taken up with the story of John's journey, how he came to set off and who he met along the way, but on the following page was some writing divided into verses with a horizontal line between, as was John's practice. Slowly, with my finger under the line, I read the first two lines:

I've wandered many a weary mile
— Love in my heart was burning —

My heart was gladdened by the words, despite my remembering the sorry picture John had made at the side of the road when I found him, for I felt joy that he had missed me so and that he had come home. I read on:

To seek a home in Mary's smile,
But cold is love's returning.
The cold ground was a feather bed,
Truth never acts contrary,
I had no home above my head,
My home was love and Mary.

My heart seemed to still in my chest. I stared at the words, my finger stupidly following along the line again as I moved my lips to sound them out, although I knew that I had made no mistake. "My home was love and Mary": the bald statement struck me with the force of a blow.

I had no home in early youth
When my first love was thwarted,
But if her heart still beats with truth,
We'll never more be parted.
And changing as her love may be,
My own shall never vary;
Nor night nor day I'm never free,
But sigh for absent Mary.

Nor night, nor day, nor sun, nor shade
Week, month, nor rolling year,
Repairs the breach wronged love hath made:
There madness — misery here.
Life's lease was lengthened by her smiles
— Are truth and love contrary?
No ray of hope my fate beguiles —
I've lost love, home, and Mary.

I clasped my shawl closer over my thin nightgown and held it tight at my neck. I thought of John's touch on my body, the same hand that, minutes before, had penned these lines, his lips on mine that had sounded out the rhythm and the rhymes.

How foolish I had been to let myself believe for a moment that his driving force had been a longing for me and the company of his children. As I looked again at the events of yesterday, I realized that he had never even tried to hide the truth. His steps had clearly been bound for Glinton; indeed, he had almost upset the cart when we had passed the turning, and he had asked after Mary again at the table, in front of all the children

... I had been in his arms and he had never once uttered my name.

From above me came the creak of boards and the sliding of the chamber-pot as Parker rose to relieve himself, then the sound of the bed springs as he returned to his bed, as was his habit. It being a Sunday, I would need to wake the children to break their fast and dress for church.

I stood the book back up in its compartment and sat for a few moments with my elbows on the desk and my hands to my cheeks. In the pigeon-hole next to the notebook were some sheets of paper meant for letter-writing. With bitterness I thought of my previous intention of writing to John at High Beech and how I had been practising my letters to make them clear and legible. Like a child, I had anticipated with delight John's amazement at receiving a letter from me in a fine hand. My heart ached at my foolish thoughts. I felt empty as a well shaft, hollow and dark.

Outside, the business of the day was starting. The birds were piping their songs to one another as they fetched grubs for their young. Some drovers passed by on the road, their nailed boots sounding on its stones and their coarse jokes and laughter ringing.

Soon I would have to go and wake the household, but I would leave John to sleep, for I could not act the part of lover, and our joining last night seemed as unreal as a dream. He had taken my hopes and trodden them underfoot and I did not know how to restore them. Not since losing our last child had I felt so weary.

CHAPTER
THREE

A Cutting

Leaving John and Parker still abed, we walked to our old village of Helpstone to attend church, as I hoped to talk to Parson Mossop, who had been a good friend to our family all the time we lived there. I shepherded the family through the churchyard and into the church, checking them for tidiness as they filed into their seats.

News of John's return seemed already to be spreading as the congregation came in and there were enquiries as to his health from some and nudges and whisperings in the pews from others. The children and I sat in a long line near the back and heads turned now and then as the news proceeded forward and was picked over as eagerly as a tray of cakes.

When Mrs Carter heard it from Miss English, she craned her head round so far I thought it would come right off. However, the stir died down towards the front as the churchwarden's wife takes little interest in tittle-tattle and, stiff as a guardsman with eyes front, stops any disturbance reaching the gentry in the best pews.

To my joy our good friend Parson Mossop was there, sure enough, to conduct the service and my spirits rose at the prospect of speaking to him afterwards. Being a well-built man, his tread on the steps to the pulpit was heavy, causing the wooden boards to creak and Sophie and Charles to snigger. I gave them a sharp look and for once I could not help but be glad that William had slipped away to the fields at the sight of his Sunday clothes laid out on the bed, as he would certainly have laughed loudly and drawn the eyes of the whole congregation at once.

Then all fell quiet as Parson Mossop looked over the assembled company, his broad face smooth, save for the lines at the corners of his eyes, which always hinted at a smile to come. He said the bidding prayer and moved on to the first lesson, which was "The wheat and the tares". I had heard it many times, and so did not attend fully, but instead said my own prayer in thanks for the parson's part in securing our cottage in Northborough through writing to Lord Milton on our behalf. It is true that others had applied before us, but none had been promised it and, though there are still those in the village with sour faces, I cannot help but be glad that we got it and be ever grateful to the reverend.

He has always had a fondness for John through his liking for John's poetry and the two of them being of an age, although you would not know it now, the parson's hair still curling thick and brown, whereas John's is scanter and his face more lined with trouble. If anyone other than me knows the sources of those troubles and the tale behind every line, it is the parson, for he has seen John both in his fit and out of it. I mind the time some years ago in Helpstone when John went visiting across the road at the vicarage, to be introduced to a friend of the reverend's, and became ill while there, first fancying he saw strangers peeping in at the window and then becoming distressed at visions of hideous spirits moving about in the ceiling of the parlour. The parson was the very soul of kindness and sent his friend to walk in the garden with his sister, Jane, while he calmed John and brought him home to me. That was a bad time with John afflicted with evil dreams and sweating fevers and all manner of strange fancies. He thought that his friends bore enmity towards him and he would not be argued out of it. Still, I must remember that at length it all passed off and I had my own John back again for a while, and pray that his latest fancy of another wife and family will do likewise.

On either side of me, Jack and Freddy's deep voices repeating the creed, as they followed the lead of the parish clerk, brought me back to myself and I joined in the responses, the murmurous sound filling the church and echoing away with the last amen. Then there was a welcome release from stiffness as we rose to our feet and rustled through the hymn-books to find the first hymn. The musicians in the gallery behind us marked the parish clerk blowing his pitch pipe and played the introductory verse of "God of the Morning, at whose voice/The cheerful sun makes haste to rise" on clarinet, bassoon, serpent and trombone, before the choir and congregation joined in. "God of the Morning" is a good, stirring hymn and Sophie and Charles sang it with gusto, though not without some pulling around of the hymn-book they were sharing.

I took little note, however, as I was watching Eliza. She looked well in her Sunday dress, which, although a little short in the sleeves, gathers tightly at the waist and shows her tidy figure to good advantage. At first I was filled merely with a mother's idle admiration, reflecting that her hair, where it showed beneath her bonnet, was still as pale a gold as when she was a child. She follows John in this respect and in her delicate features and grey-blue eyes she resembles John as he was in his youth, whereas the other children in our Sunday line all have my brown hair with golden lights and the oval face and straight nose of the Turner family. My reflections were broken when she lifted her head from her hymn-book and I saw her face more clearly. Her cheek was flushed and her eye bright and she looked upward at the vaulted roof as she sang, as though willing it to open to let her fly to some other place. As the hymn finished and her eyes dropped again to her book, I saw her set her jaw as though she would clamp inside her the feeling that the music had raised, and as we all sat again, I saw that she gripped her book tight.

Parson Mossop began the sermon, which was earnestly given but dull, the reverend not being of the disposition to scare his audience with tales of hell-fire and retribution, which, while being unpleasant reminders of one's shortcomings, do at least aid the attention and add a little spice to the proceedings. I willed the time away, eager to speak to him and to enlist his help.

At the end of the service, as was his usual custom, Parson Mossop gave the blessing and led the congregation out, then waited just outside the church porch to shake the hands of the parishioners and wish them good morning. I hung back, keeping the family busy in straightening their dress and tidying the prayer books so that we would be the last to leave. At last the others had all departed, though not without some curious backward glances, and we emerged into the sunny churchyard.

Parson Mossop's large hands clasped my own warmly. "How are you, Patty?" he said, searching my face, and suddenly, despite my urgent desire to speak, I found that no words would come and I could only nod. "The family is looking well," he said, looking from one to the other of the children. "Perhaps they'd like to go on ahead?" The youngsters didn't need asking twice, Charles almost breaking into a run even before reaching the church gate and Eliza hurrying right behind him.

"I hope Miss Jane is well?" I asked, remembering my manners.

"Very well indeed," he said. "Now, I hear from Mr Ward that John is back home again, and walked all the way! Tell me how you find him."

I recounted a little of the tale of John's journey, at which he marvelled, then asked, "And how is he in spirits?" at which my whole sorry tale slipped out and I told him of John's conviction that he be married twice. Parson Mossop listened, nodding as I went along, and when the musicians began to emerge carrying their sheet music and instrument cases he led me to a seat against the warm church wall. Beside us an ancient yew cast a dappled shadow across the frass of dry brown clippings strewed across the path and a pigeon cooed from deep within its shady branches. I told him of John's desire to visit Mary at Glinton, and when I tailed off he sat leaning his elbow on the arm of the bench with his hand to his mouth, tapping the knuckle of his forefinger against his lip.

"You say he doesn't just remember her as a sweetheart but thinks himself twice married," he said, "though he knows it is against God's law. That must be a cause of distress to him and such tensions will exacerbate his illness."

"I haven't seen any sign of it pricking his conscience," I said, "but it is certainly a cause of distress to me, for there is only room for two in a marriage bed."

"Now, Patty," the parson said, "it is no good getting angry. If you are so tart with John it will only lead him further into his delusion. You must tame that temper of yours."

"I cannot help it," I wailed, "when I find verses to Mary in his notebook that he's written when not even home half a day." I stopped and flushed.

Parson Mossop said nothing, but he looked at me with that enquiring expression he has.

I said, "Well, yes, I know I should not have looked at John's private papers," and sighed.

"He is still ill," the reverend said gently. "We must bear in mind all the time that he did not come home because he was cured but simply discharged himself from Dr Allen's care. In fact, to set out on a journey of eighty miles, on foot and with no map or provisions, is an irrational act, which further proves the disturbed state of his mind."

We sat for a few moments, each pondering John's journey. Encouraged by our silence, sparrows flitted from the yew to peck over the twigs and pebbles on the path and flutter dust over their wings. The sun was growing closer to its height and beat down upon us, making my skin prickle under the stiff material of my Sunday dress.

"So, what is to be done?" I said in a small voice. "Must I send him back?"

"Do you want to, Patty?"

I shook my head. The reverend placed his hands on his knees and sat more upright. "Then, what we must do is fight irrationality with the rational," he said. "We must present John with incontrovertible proof that what he believes is not, in fact, the case. If he believes that he has another living wife, we must show him evidence that Mary is dead."

"I have told him so many times," I exclaimed, "but he simply sets it aside and takes no notice!"

"But he will impute motives to you that he will not be able to impute to me," he said, patting my hand. "He will think that you tell him this out of jealousy." The reverend rubbed his chin. "We will show it to him in black and white," he said. "I can obtain a copy of the newspaper report; someone in the parish is sure to have it and I will place it in front of him. He will not be able to discount the evidence of his own eyes so easily." He stood and offered his hand to help me to my feet. "I will ride over this afternoon and we will set events in motion to turn his attention back to his family where it belongs and thereby hope to effect an improvement," he said, nodding all the while as if much pleased with the plan. He walked with me to the gate, opened it and rested his hand upon it. "Never fear, Patty," he said. "He will return to the real Mrs Clare."

Then he bade me farewell and returned to disrobe and close up the church, leaving me to walk home in a mixture of fear to witness John's reaction to the tumbling of his house of cards and a lightening of spirits as a little hope grew in my heart.

Parson Mossop and Miss Jane arrived by gig in the late afternoon and, after asking Sophie to fetch a pail of water from the pump for the horse and showing Charles how to tether the reins to the fence, I showed them into the parlour, where John was once more at work upon his writing. He rose from the desk and welcomed them both, offering Miss Jane his chair, while I went to fetch the stools from the kitchen. The house was quiet as Eliza and the menfolk were reading in the orchard and the children stayed outside, taken up with the novelty of the horse. Only Parker remained indoors, napping in a chair, his fiddle propped up against the table leg.

When I re-entered, Parson Mossop and John had fallen into their usual gentle banter.

"I can see you're knocked up by your journey, John," the reverend was saying, with a smile and a glance at

John's ink-stained fingers, "but maybe we'll see you at church next week?"

"I'll not be there next week, nor the week after," John replied, "but I'll read my Bible and think on it as I always do."

Parson Mossop nodded. "That is commendable and one can always receive benefit and instruction, but it is good to worship together too. There's nothing like a good, rousing hymn to lift the spirits and a well-planned sermon to turn one's thoughts to the Almighty."

John snorted. "Dry as dust. A walk through a pasture and the song of the willow-warbler is more to my taste. I'd rather read God's words written in a green hand."

Miss Jane looked pained on her brother's behalf, but Parson Mossop laughed loudly. "Well, I must be content that you find your solace out of doors," he said, "and rely on Patty here to keep you on the straight and narrow path." He made himself more comfortable on the stool, which, in truth, was too small for his large frame, and began again. "The children will be glad to have you home?"

At this, John smiled and began to speak of each child in turn — how they had grown and changed and learnt since he had been away. I fetched a jug of cool water from the kitchen pail and some oat cakes and offered Miss Jane some refreshment and we talked quietly of old friends and neighbours in Helpstone while the men continued, but I with one ear always open for how their conversation progressed.

"Your family is a great blessing and does you credit, John," Parson Mossop was saying.

"I have not seen them all yet, though," John said. Thinking that he meant he had not yet seen Anna, as she was married and away at the haymaking, I took little note, but he went on: "My second wife, Mary, has children too to think of and I have not yet been allowed to visit her."

Seeing me look up sharply, Jane's tale of visitors at the Blue Bell in Helpstone trailed to a close.

Parson Mossop rubbed his nose. "I think you are mistaken in this, John," he said gently. "It is Mary Joyce, your childhood sweetheart, of whom you speak?"

John glanced across at me as though challenging me to say anything. "Childhood sweetheart, lover and wife," he said, then leant forward towards the parson. "I have two wives and two families to keep, you see," he said in a low voice, "and it is a terrible worry to me how to feed them all."

Parson Mossop held his gaze. "I'm afraid I have some very sad news for you, John. Wife or not, it pains me to tell any man that he has lost someone he loves." He reached into his waistcoat pocket and brought out a small piece of printed paper, folded into four, and held it on his lap. "Mary has passed away," he said.

John looked from the parson to me and back again, frowning, but the reverend laid his hand on John's arm. "I know that it is hard to accept a parting," he said, holding out the folded paper to John, "but it is better to look such things in the face than to hide our eyes."

Slowly, John's fingers closed round the slip of paper and his eyes dropped to it. He unfolded it, spread it out upon his knee and began to read. Despite my own hurt feelings, my heart went out to him. He blinked two or three times and his brow furrowed, like a child who puzzles over his lessons. He glanced up at Parson Mossop and took a breath as if he was about to speak, then looked down and commenced reading from the beginning again.

"It is from the newspaper of the fifteenth of July 1838," Parson Mossop said, his eyes never leaving John's face.

John turned the paper over as if he sought the date upon its back.

"I'm truly sorry," Parson Mossop said.

"It says no one else was there when it happened and so no help to hand," John said, looking from one to the other of us. "How could that be?" His voice rose. "And what will happen to the children?"

Parson Mossop leant forward on his stool towards John so that their knees were almost touching. He gripped him by the elbows, holding him as if he feared he might leap to his feet and run from the room. He held him firm as if to stop a rick-cover from being taken by a wind that might blow it who-knows-where.

"There was no one there because she was not married and had no children," he said, making each word sound out. "The paper says this clearly: 'Mary Joyce, a single woman, spinster of the parish of Glinton'."

John shook his head. "This was while I was at High Beech, you say?"

Parson Mossop nodded. "It happened three years ago." He let go of John and slowly sat back.

John's shoulders slumped and he felt in his jacket for a pocket handkerchief and then passed it across his face. Jane got to her feet and poured some water into John's cup and handed it to him. He began to sip from it, and his colour returned a little. "I am a widower, then," he said, looking askance at Jane, but she merely laid her hand upon his shoulder. "Or a bachelor?" he said, redirecting his gaze to the reverend.

"You are husband to Patty and father to your family here," Parson Mossop said firmly. "You may grieve for a former love but you must put behind you the fancy that Mary was your wife and look to the future now."

At this I rose, thinking to embrace John, but as I reached for him he drew back from me and said, "You should have sent word to me at High Beech."

I stood helplessly in front of him. "Do you not remember, John? Freddy wrote to you of this when it occurred."

John looked at me strangely, as if he thought me a liar. "You should have come yourself," he said.

The parson looked surprised at this and opened his mouth to speak, but I spoke first. "How could I come, John? We have barely had enough to eat; where would I find money for a passage? Was I to walk and leave the children to starve for a week? I would have been taken for a vagrant and locked away. Who would have cared for the children then?"

Parson Mossop gave me a warning look. "Patty could not have left the children and wandered eighty miles to find you. It wouldn't have been safe: a woman alone on the road. Nor should you wish it."

"She should have come," John said stubbornly. "Four years I was at that place and never a visit from either of my wives." He scowled at me.

"Patty would have come if it were possible," Parson Mossop said, "and the other matter we have already dealt with." He leant forward and gently took the piece of paper from John's hand. John stared at his empty hand and fell silent.

Parson Mossop tucked the paper back into his pocket, watching John's face all the while to see if he would speak again, and at length when it became apparent that he would not he rose to his feet and took his leave. Jane picked up her reticule and gave John "Good day", but John returned only the slightest of nods. We left him sitting with his face turned to the wall and I led them from the room and out into the garden, where we paused beside the house to speak.

Parson Mossop said, "Well, Patty, it will be a hard path, but that is the first stile mounted and crossed."

"I am sorry for John's curtness," I said in a low voice, aware that the open parlour window was not far off. "He blames the bringer of bad tidings as if you made the news yourself."

"Think nothing of it," Parson Mossop said. "It has no doubt been a great shock to his system. Should I get Dr Skrimshire to visit next week? I trust he has had none of the shivering and ague that he used to suffer?"

I thought of the time when John was so ill with fever that the doctor had him cupped and a seaton passed through the skin of his neck to draw out the bad blood. "No," I said quickly, "there is no sign of fen-fever; it is a malady of the mind alone at present, I feel."

Parson Mossop nodded. "As you think best. Let's hope that there is no return of those symptoms or of the mania that led to his committal. He seems peaceable at least."

"I'll guard against the fen-fever by making sure he sleeps at home," I said. "It was when he wandered too far from home before and slept outdoors in the night vapours and prey to the biting insects that these fevers came."

"Indeed, indeed," Parson Mossop said as we began walking to the gig. "But you must let me know, Patty, if he becomes unmanageable as he was before he left for High Beech. Don't struggle on alone this time, eh?"

As he went forward to talk to Sophie and Charles and admire the knots that Sophie had braided in the horse's mane, Jane dropped behind. She opened her reticule and drew out a green velvet purse, a soft pouch closed with a silver ring. She pulled the material from the ring and took out some coins. "Here," she said, pressing three pennies into my hand, "for the children."

I thanked her and put the coins carefully into my apron pocket. Charles held the horse while Parson Mossop helped Miss Jane up into the gig, then climbed up in front and took the reins from Charles. Then, with a click of the tongue and a slap of the reins on the horse's rump, the parson set it off at an ambling pace and they rumbled off down the lane towards Helpstone. We watched them until they were out of sight.

Sophie looked curiously at my apron pocket where the coins pulled the corner down and I wished with all my heart that I could promise her the buns and toys and ribbons that she craved; but the money had to be added to the tin behind my pans on the pot-shelf for the rent, where it would rattle with the little that was already there.

When I returned to the parlour, John was back at his desk, sitting with his head in his hands, with a jumble of notebooks, papers, pen and ink before him. I didn't approach him but began quietly tidying the room, carrying the stools back to the kitchen and gathering the cups on to the tray.

Without looking up, John said, "Why were you whispering with the parson?"

"We were not whispering," I said. "It was kind of the Mossops to visit; you could have given them a fonder farewell."

John turned his head sharply. "I dare say you asked them to visit to bring me the newspaper. I doubt the parson just happened to have it in his pocket."

I stopped with the tray in my hands. "I did ask him," I said. "I admit it freely; we thought it best that you saw the newspaper. I know it will have come as a shock . . ."

John swung round in his chair. "As I thought, the two of you in cahoots, plotting and planning and pretending to have my interests at heart."

"There was no plot!" I said indignantly, my colour rising.

"You didn't tell me he was expected," John said. "You keep things from me."

"I had no opportunity to tell you."

"Why didn't you visit me?" he said, changing tack. "In all that time no friends came, and that was hard enough, but to be there for years without wife or bedfellows . . ."

It came into my mind to list all the Mistresses Pratt and King that, by his own lips, he had mentioned visiting and lending books to but I bit on the words.

"There was no money, John," I said flatly instead.

"Mary would have come," he said; "if she'd been alive, she would have come. She was ever true to me."

Despite my promises to Parson Mossop my temper began to rise. "She did not come in the first year when she could have," I said, regretting the words the instant that they were spoken, "and I have always been a faithful and true wife and held you ever in my thoughts."

John snorted. "I see you're as sharp-tongued as ever and you lay claim to what cannot be proved. Four years alone, and never a sly look or a lingering of hands? Never a meeting in the woods or a tumble in the hay?"

I gasped. I was stung most of all by the way his words seemed to take our own courtship and twist it to something tawdry and cheap. Of necessity, we had met in the fields and the woods and I held those memories sweet and our love-making natural and good. Now, it seemed like a fine cloth dragged in the dirt, all smattered and torn, and I knew that this had been his intention. I felt myself begin to shake with anger.

"How dare you accuse me of faithlessness!" I said, setting down the tray with a clatter. I went to the desk and pulled the little octavo notebook towards me. "Look!" I said. "Look at what is written here!" and I turned to the pages where Mary's name was writ so many times and jabbed my finger at the lines. John stared at me, aghast. "Not one day home and yet hankering after another woman like a moonstruck calf! Shame on you for judging me by your own standards!" I took up the pen that lay leaking ink among the papers and struck it, top to bottom, right through the page with the poem to Mary, leaving a thin dark line that bisected it and petered out into a scratch at its foot.

John let out a cry and seized the book by the corners and I let it go. "Now see what you have done," he said and looked up at me with such an expression of reproach that I burst into tears of anger and frustration and stepped back, with my hands to my burning cheeks.

We stared at each other, and I felt the moment when we could have said sorry and made our peace, when one of us could have leant forward and touched the other, slip away like a wisp of cloud on a summer's day.

John hardened his gaze until he looked at me as though I was a stranger, then turned his back and, muttering under his breath, took from a drawer a large quarto book with marbled covers and laid it over the rest and beside the notebook.

"I will make a fair copy," he said, picking up the pen and smoothing the quarto book out flat, its creamy expanse untouched as fresh snowfall, ready to receive John's imagined romance, each letter clear, formed with care, word perfect; whereas reality was messy: a marriage he saw as dog-eared and tattered at the edges, too well thumbed to matter.

I wiped my eyes on my apron. "A fair copy," I repeated. "A fair tale is all it is, John," I said, thinking that those times of his boyhood with Mary borrowed their loveliness from the passing of the years as any common hill is blued by distance into mystery and longing. "What you set down is what you wish could be again, but never will."

CHAPTER
FOUR

Moon through Glass

I have been trying to put John's hurtful words out of my mind. He is not himself and says things that are hard to square with my own knowledge of our past or with the man he used to be, which is his own true self. Maybe by thinking on a little of our history I will be able to recapture how we once were together, for those memories are the jewels that I take out from time to time and turn side-to-side to make them catch the light.

The first time John saw me I didn't even know that his eyes were upon me. I learnt only later that, seeing me going home to Walk Lodge through the fields near Tickencote, John had climbed a tree to get a view of me and follow my progress to seek out where I might live.

It is strange to think that I was all unaware of the man who would later be my husband and in fact my thoughts were quite elsewhere. I had been at Pickworth with the family of Thomas Butterworth, a shoemaker my father thought a good match for me. I was walking home feeling excited and uneasy all at once. I was nineteen years old and flattered by the attention from a family who my parents said were of equal, if not better, standing than our own and impressed by the ladies' lace collars and thin china, and by their careful manners that made me feel an honoured guest.

Thomas, however, I found unsettling. He had an intense expression and rarely smiled. As he drank his tea I tried not to look at his hand, for his forefinger and thumb were bent and greatly calloused from cutting leather and stitching with waxed thread. As yet, we had only walked out together and had not touched in affection, but I felt none of the desire for him to take my hand that the other girls spoke of feeling for their young men, and found myself carrying a basket or a handkerchief or a posy of flowers whenever we met, so that the situation would not arise. He said little but stared a great deal.

John, on the other hand, was full of words to woo with. He was working at Casterton as a lime-burner and though his hands were roughened by labour and ingrained with chalk they were finely shaped with long, delicate fingers. I used to love to watch him play the fiddle at the Flower Pot Inn at Tickencote, where folk would dance. His fingers moved so fast and dextrously across the strings and in the dimness of the candle-light his whitened hands seemed to glow like a conjurer's gloves as he filled the crowded room with music that whirled the dancers round.

But I am running ahead of myself . . . On this day I knew none of this, for there was only a girl of nineteen in a violet-sprigged dress and a man of five-and-twenty climbing to the top of a pollarded tree to get a better view of her. I think of him there, high above the jibes and jokes of his work-fellows down below, one arm round the nubby end of a branch where the whippy shoots spring anew, catching the small breeze of a summer's day against his face. He told me that I had walked across the pasture quite near where they were sitting in the shade of the hedge, playing cards, but that I was too deep in thought to pay any mind to them and that it had been this dreamy abstraction that had arrested him. That I should be so unconcerned to walk past three fine young fellows that I gave not even a glance seemed touchingly artless. From the tree he noticed that my hair shone golden brown and my hat hung by its ribbons on my back, I having pushed it off in the heat. He told me that my slender figure clothed in mauve and violet was pleasing as I moved across the green field, all brightened by the sun, and he felt a lifting in his heart. "I was in love at first sight," he said.

I see that day now as if there were a silken thread from him to me, spun ever thinner as I walked away, until at last I climbed a stile and, following the path on the other side of a high hedge, I passed from view and the thread broke. What chances there are in life! John still knew nothing of who I was or where I lived and I knew nothing at all of him. If he had never seen me again I could be even now a shoemaker's wife with fine linens folded into chests and meat on the table. Well-shod, no doubt, and maybe even grown to care for that poor, misshapen hand, but lonely for some conversation beyond wooden lasts and soles and heels.

A few weeks later, in the evening, I was walking along the Stamford road with some friends on the way home from Tickencote. We saw in front of us, heading the same way, a group of young men, one of them carrying a fiddle and wearing his Sunday coat. The coat looked new; it was a soft olive-green in colour and fitted well, so that the young man cut a dash among his companions and was clearly dressed for a performance.

There was a deal of glancing behind at us by the young men and a deal of looking at our feet and make-believe earnest conversation among us, although Annie Carson, who was always prone to laughter, kept nudging me with her elbow and giggling every time one of the young men looked round. At length their pace grew so slow, what with pausing to cut a hazel stick from the hedge and then again to point out something in the field — though it looked to me like an ordinary field of barley — that we needs must catch up with them.

John immediately fell into step with me and at first I thought him odd, for he glanced at me and said, as if solving some great puzzle, "Ah, they are violets on your dress." Unsure how to react to this self-evident observation, I smoothed down my skirts and remained silent. He seemed to recover himself then, and asked my name. I told him that my given name was Martha Turner but that I was always known as Patty. He asked where I was going and where I was from and I asked the same, and about his fiddle-playing. He let me pick a few notes and showed me the bow, telling me the stringing was made from the gut of a cat, at which I quickly handed it back to him and he smiled, saying he could see I was tender-hearted. The conversation went along very nicely and all too soon we found ourselves at the fork in the road toward Pickworth, where I must turn off towards home. I remember how my heart leapt as he handed both bow and fiddle to one of his friends, urging him to take his place, and asked if he might accompany me home. Annie's eyes were out on stalks. I thought on my mother's advice to decline a young man's advances politely and firmly, but my heart beat so loud that it drowned out her voice in my head and I found myself thanking him for his trouble and the two of us turned off alone down the lane with its hedges full of dog roses, while the others took the broader road towards Stamford.

I forget some of the particularities of the words we spoke that day, for it was four miles to home and we talked all the way. He told me of his home at Helpstone and his family and of his great fear that they might lose their cottage through rent arrears and his parents be sent to the workhouse. His work at the lime-pits was dusty, choking labour, but it had enabled him to send money home and to buy a coat. I must have looked askance at such an extravagance in his straitened circumstances and he blushed and began to explain. He said that he wrote poetry and hoped to raise himself and his family through publishing his verse and that the coat was an important part of his plan to look at least respectable as a man of letters.

"From my experience of booksellers, a man in a cowherd's smock or with the dust of the lime-kiln seeping from his clothes cannot expect to be seen as a poet," he said.

"It is a very fine coat," I said shyly, breaking into a wry smile.

"Indeed it is," he said, holding out his arm for me to feel the cloth, and I touched him lightly on the sleeve, without even thinking.

I said little at first but listened intently, for I was taken with his frankness, though surprised that he should tell me all so easily when we were not long acquainted. I was not used to such openness, for in our circles worries and feelings were always hidden behind a mist of manners and I was unsure how to respond to a man who laid his heart bare as a snail out of its shell, tender and uncockled.

The lane was deep and quiet; the sun was waning and began to dip below the hedgerow and the flowers twined through it filled the shady space with a heady scent. Fresh earth was spread here and there around the hedge roots where new rabbit diggings disappeared into the banks and from time to time the occupants would hop leisurely to and fro across the lane in front of us, reassured by our slow and steady pace which deviated neither left nor right and caused them no alarm. We walked slowly in a green world, the only sounds our muffled footfalls and the last of the day's birdsong.

Little by little John drew me out to speak about myself and my family, of our cottage near Pickworth, my father's farm and his plans to take on more casual labour. At this John's face fell, and I rebuked myself for inadvertently drawing attention to the difference between his lot and my own and turned the conversation back to his poetical aspirations.

At length, we left the lanes and climbed the stile that led to the common. Still deep in talk, we followed a sheep track between the furzy hummocks he called molehills, which gave way eventually to a large cow pasture, where we crossed into my father's fields down into the woody dip towards Walk Lodge. Our steps slowed as we reached the trees and petered to a stop before we reached sight of the house.

"Well, Patty, I hope that I may see you again?" he said, and I nodded and smiled as he suggested that he call the following Sunday after midday. I remember he drew near me and my heart quickened in confusion. My uncertainty must have shown in my expression, for he stopped, his eyes searching my face. Gravely I held out my right hand and he took it and held it and I found that I was loath for him to let it go. Then we said our farewells and I walked away, this time feeling his gaze upon my back as he watched until I was lost among the trees. I walked on lightly, unwilling to break a twig or rustle the leaves in pushing past too close, as though if I tiptoed through silence I could keep the feeling of his hand on mine humming through me like a plucked string.

As I entered the dim hall of the cottage, the sound of voices reached me from the parlour, where I found my family sitting comfortably: my father studying his accounts, while Mother and Polly worked at hemming some sheets, the light being now too poor for any finer needlework. Mother asked after Annie and her family and patted the seat beside her, but I said that the long walk had given me a tired headache and that I would turn in for the night. Polly looked up from her stitching with a question in her eyes, but I gave a tiny shake of my head and bade them all goodnight.

I went directly to my bedroom and lay down very still, my hands spread on the counterpane. I felt within its cool smoothness every raised embroidery stitch and slub in the fabric, as though my finger ends had been awoken by the touch of his hand.

I lay there until I heard my mother coming upstairs and saw the light of her candle advancing underneath the door, then I jumped up and began to undress, moving noisily round the room so that she would not come in to sit upon the end of my bed and talk. The light paused beside the door. "Goodnight, Patty," Mother said and I gave her a "goodnight" in return and waited for her to retire.

When the house was quiet I opened the casement window, for it's unlucky to look at the moon through glass and I felt that I must weave what charms I could round me, as if I carried something precious that must not be broken. Still in my shift, I looked out upon the night. Long shadows streamed from the trees across the grass and my mother's white foxgloves shone pale and blue. The moon was full and bright, its corona soft against the deepening ink of the sky. Though I have never told John, and perhaps now I never will, I felt my heart to be as big and luminous as the moon, as if its brilliance would surely shine out of me for everyone to see, as if its light were strong enough for both of us to travel by.

The week passed slowly and my everyday tasks of feeding the chickens and collecting the eggs, cutting fresh sweet-peas for the house and baking pastries for my mother's visitors were performed as if in a dream. Polly and I were engaged in embroidering new napkins and tablecloths, but I made so many mistakes that a whole corner design had to be unpicked. My mother had said that they were to replace our table linen that had become a little thready, yet she constantly asked me whether the design pleased me and drew my attention proudly to the quality and whiteness of the cloth, so that Polly whispered to me that she thought the work was to be for my marriage chest. At this I pricked my finger so badly that it bled upon the tablecloth and I was roundly scolded by Mother and sent to soak the cloth directly. Polly followed me and asked if anything was troubling me, but my secret felt too new to tell and I was still hugging it close to me. Instead, I said that I felt too young to be thinking of marrying and that the thought of my wedding chest had startled me. While I stood sucking my finger she found the soda for me and rubbed out the mark in the cloth. "I'll miss you when you're wed," she said.

On Sunday I made an excuse that I would visit Annie again and after clearing the cold meats from the table I forced myself to go slowly about, finding my gloves and hat. Once in the wood I hurried through the trees until

I reached the far edge, where I paused to pick pink campions from among the flowering nettles and cow parsley, all the time searching the horizon of the pasture for an approaching figure.

A long, low whistle broke the silence and I straightened and turned right to look along the tree line and saw John coming towards me. He shook my hand. We walked back together the way that he had come, then skirted the edge of the cow pasture, saying never a word but exchanging shy smiles until we came to the common and sat down upon a grassy molehill, the turf close cropped by sheep and rabbits.

"I lost my way last Sunday," John said. "We were talking so hard that I paid no mind to the route we'd taken and was quite wandered in my return." He laughed.

"You got to your lodgings before darkness, I hope?"

John shook his head with a mournful expression. "I followed the wrong track across the common and found myself quite mazed, so I sat down beside a field of wheat . . ."

"Ah, that would be Mr Blake's field," I said.

". . . And I wrote some poems." He leant forward and took my hand. "About you."

I felt myself blushing scarlet at this attention and he loosed my hand and felt in his breast pocket. He drew out some sheets of paper and before I could say another word he began to read.

The first poem was a pretty thing, almost like a song. It described me as an "artless maid", which made me feel both admired and vexed that he thought me childlike. The second poem was a ballad that told of a "labouring swain" who persuades a shy girl to accept his company on the walk home. I smiled at the beginning, but as the verses went on to describe him praising her beautiful eyes and her hesitation "between the *Yes* and the *No*" I frowned, feeling that he had read me too clearly and was speaking too frankly, and when, at the end, the boy clasped the girl and kissed her I could listen no longer.

"But that didn't happen!" I said.

At this, the colour rose to John's cheeks too and I realized too late that what he had written was what he had ardently wished had taken place. However, he recovered himself and said mildly, "It is a poem; it is not about facts, but feelings."

The tone he adopted, of a teacher with a pupil, offended me further and I put my arms round my knees and said, "Then, a poem is a very tricksy thing and does not tell the truth."

John looked out across the common and I followed his gaze. The afternoon sun lit the rolling mounds and the yellow gorse flowers and turned the bare, packed earth of the sheep tracks into shining paths winding like tiny streams across the scene. "It might not tell the literal truth," he said thoughtfully, "but that doesn't mean that the truth isn't in it." He gestured towards the scene before us. "If I say to you, this day, this place, this time is golden, would you know what I meant?"

"I suppose so," I said slowly. "It is beautiful and the sun has touched it."

He turned towards me, leaning forwards on one arm. "It is more that that. Golden says truly that it is a treasure," and he kissed me lightly on the lips. He drew back a little, watching my face, and I saw myself reflected in his grey-blue eyes.

"Can I make the poem true, Patty?" he said playfully, moving nearer and slipping his arm round my waist, and I kissed him for answer and the sun beat down upon us, and I felt that I too was turned to gold, my very veins molten as my body cleaved to his, and I felt that although his hands caressed me skilfully there was a trembling in them too and I broke away and sat upright with a gasp and began straightening my hair and gown.

John leant back upon his elbows, watching me intently, and I felt tears coming to my eyes as though I was a silly girl who didn't know the ways of love.

Quickly he smiled and said, "You know what they say about the gorse?"

I shook my head.

"They say when gorse is out of bloom, kissing's out of fashion."

"But it's always . . ." I started, then realized his meaning and began to laugh.

"Here's one I'm sure will please you," he said. "'Tis only about summer and what we see around us." He looked away from me, out over the common, and began to speak:

How sweet when weary dropping on a bank
Turning a look around on things that be

E'en feather-headed grasses spindling rank
A-trembling to the breeze one loves to see
And yellow buttercups where many a bee
Comes buzzing to its head and bows it down
And the great dragon flye wi' gauzy wings
In gilded coat of purple green or brown
That on broad leaves of hazel basking clings
Fond of the sunny day — and other things
Past counting pleases one while thus I lye
But still reflective pains are not forgot
Summer sometime shall bless this spot when I
Hapt in the cold dark grave can heed it not

He broke off and turned to me. I looked askance, for I liked the way the scene was painted so wondrous exactly but thought the sudden turn the poem took at the end might be another way of wooing, as if to say, "Time is short and we should make the most of it while we have youth and breath." However, he didn't reach across to clasp me again but instead looked thoughtful for a moment, then shrugged, as if shaking off a dream and coming back to wakefulness.

"Shall we walk awhile?" he said. He jumped to his feet and held out his hand to help me up.

John walked on the grass so that he could stay beside me while I took the narrow sheep path. Sometimes, though, when bushes or brambles would force him on to the path and we would go in single file, he would keep turning back to me as if to check I was still following. As we walked, I asked John how he had found his way back to his lodgings at last the previous Sunday.

He laughed. "I almost didn't reach home at all. I waited by the wheat field until the moon was up, but I was no better off because the little remembrance I had of the lie of the land bore no resemblance to the scene under moonlight."

I thought then of the feeling I'd had as I looked out into the moonlit garden, my glowing certainty, all unaware that John, befuddled and lost, had gazed on the same moon.

"What did you do?" I asked.

"There was a line of land that shone bright on the other side of the common, and I thought it to be ground that had been beaten bare by cows in this hot weather."

"You thought there would be a farm where you could ask your way?" I said, taking a few quick steps, for John's stride was longer than my own.

"It was no farm land," John said, "but a river, and coming upon it as the moon was covered for a few minutes by cloud I almost stepped right in, and if it hadn't been for a bush that I caught hold of I could, even now, be floating down the river and out to sea!"

He pulled such a comic, mournful face that I laughed and said, "Come, you would only have had a ducking!"

He shook his head as if in sorrow and said, "I am no swimmer," at which I felt sorely vexed that I had made light of his misadventure and touched his arm in my concern.

He stopped on an instant and clasped me tight, saying into my ear, "Yet here I am back again: you see what risks I'm willing to take for you."

He tried to kiss me, but I saw the mischief in his eye and leant back from him, saying, "Shame on you, John Clare, for lying again," for even I had been taught to swim as a child by my father, it being a county of rivers with the Gwash and the Welland running through farm land and fen, and it seemed unlikely that a country boy who would catch sticklebacks almost as soon as he could walk would not have learnt it.

He laughed and said, "But I slept in a hedgerow all night, my Patty of the Vale, and woke cold and hungry with the dawn; is that not worth a kiss?" and I relented and we were friends again.

Those times were sweet, those days of courting when we were not to know of the difficulties that lay ahead. I think of them now and wish myself back to that laughing girl while our love was still a secret and grew stronger with each meeting. Our walks grew longer, first to Turnpole Wood, then out to Tolthorpe Oaks, and our words and loving became more ardent, so that by the time I confided in Polly my heart was set upon him. I thought, then, that John's was set as firmly upon me and that, despite my parents' wishes regarding Thomas Butterworth, the strength of our mutual attachment would prevail with them and they would see where my happiness lay. It makes me sad to think how something as simple and right as love can become complicated and twisted about by the words of others, and by distrust and misunderstanding.

I look back now at our courtship and it seems to me that John and I were fated to miss our moment. A distance seems always to have been interposed between us at a crucial time. I think of John's realization of love, watching me across a green field while I was walking away from him. What would have happened if he had called out to me and walked with me that first time, and John had been a rival to Thomas while the idea of that match was still a seedling in my parents' minds and not a rooted plant?

And I regret my shyness. I think back to our first parting at the edge of the wood and I wish that the magic of the lane had held a little longer, that I had still felt safe and secret and that we had embraced. That was the time; that was the moment at which there should not have been an arm's length between us. Had we held each other then we would have been hand-fasted, as some choose to be at their wedding day: joined as sure as if our wrists had been bound together. I think of us on that first night, both gazing at the same moon, and the distance between us seems not just a few fields, but the arc of the whole night sky.

CHAPTER
FIVE

Ghosts in the Hedges

John and I have hardly spoken these last few days since our exchange of words after Parson Mossop's visit. The days have fallen into a regular pattern. I carry on the same routine that I had before his return, following the usual round of washday and baking day, pressing and stitching. Sometimes Parker tries to interest him in the garden and leads him out into the sunshine and points out the cornflowers and snapdragons. John bends to look and nods and smiles and hurries on to the next, as if he thinks, "Well, things will grow without me to look at them," and would fain get back to his work.

Mainly, he shuts himself away in the parlour to write, emerging only for his meals. He says that he is writing a great work: that since the fashion has moved on from rural rhymes and there's no longer any market for them, he must now write such things only for his own pleasure. Instead he pins his hopes on a new *Don Juan*, written in the style of Byron's great poem. Despite the fact that his publisher knows the turmoil of John's mind and was the very person who arranged for him to go to High Beech, John convinces himself that when the work is finished it will be taken up and will solve all our problems.

When I take a drink in to him I always find him intent on his work, his thinning hair sticking up on top where he leans his forehead on his hand, with his elbow on the desk as he writes. I place the cup beside him, but he doesn't look up and sometimes when I return to take it away it is sitting where I left it, still full, untouched.

At first I was glad of his distraction, as I feared further outbursts, and at least it has allowed the house to run peaceably, but it is hard for the children, particularly Sophie and Charles, who covet their father's attention.

Today, I had to wash clothes. I had put it off through three days of close, cloudy weather, but today looked to be set fine enough for the drying. I sent the children to fetch water from the pump. William is as strong as an ox and takes two buckets, but he is clumsy and spills half before he reaches the house. Sophie is more painstaking and leaves hardly a splash on the path, and Charles, bless him, fills his bucket half full and still has to hold the handle up at his chest in front of him to manage it, his legs being too short to be able to carry it at his side.

Eliza and I were soon in a lather as the coolness wore off the day outside and opening the scullery door did little to abate the heat from the fire where the water was heating, or the steam which was suffocating and made my dress stick to my body and my hair stick to my brow. I was up to my elbows pounding the men's shirts with the dolly-peg while Eliza mixed more soap and the air grew heavier still with the dust from the shredded lye and powdery soda.

William began to moan that he was hungry and to run a spoon up and down the zinc surface of the washboard, making a horrible grating noise. Sophie and Charles grabbed handfuls of soapsuds and clapped their hands high to make suds fly out in blobs at each other's faces, until Charles crawled under the table, squealing, and knocked into the empty buckets and sent them rolling round my feet.

I saw William catch sight of my face and quietly slip away. I hauled Charles out, caught hold of Sophie's wet hand and marched them into the parlour to John.

"I cannot get the washing done," I said, standing both of the children in front of me, knowing that he must have heard the hullabaloo coming from the scullery. He held one hand up towards me as he finished writing his sentence, then laid down his pen and looked at the children.

"You should be helping your mother," he said mildly.

"We carried the water in," Sophie said.

"We were only playing," Charles said.

"Nonetheless I can't get through the washing with soap flying in my face, buckets rolling around my ankles and the floor a muddy mess for the clean clothes to trail into," I said.

John held out his hands palms down and pressed the air as if I were some shrill genie that he would push back into its bottle. Then he turned to the children with a softer face and said, "Shall we go for a walk? Shall we go across the fields as we used to and see what we can find?"

"You'd best go out towards Maxey, then, where there are fewer new hedges and no one to take you for a poacher," I said. I left the children in his care, rolling my sleeves up a little further as I went.

Eliza had finished making the soap flakes and put a plate over the bowlful to keep them dry until needed. I smiled at her as if to say we would get through the task all the faster now and she gave me a wry look in return. We set to rubbing and wringing, with me washing and Eliza rinsing in the smaller basin. Together we began slowly turning the pile of grubby labour-stained clothes into indistinguishable twists of sodden cloth lying beside the shifts and the girls' light dresses in the wicker baskets. At first we worked without talking and I savoured the quiet of the empty room, the only sounds being the sloshing and trickling of the agitated water and the hiss of the kettle and pans as the next batch of clean water came to the boil. I glanced at the pile of clothes still on the table. "We should be done by midday," I said. "And there is bread and a little cheese that I had from Mrs Gayton in return for Charles keeping the rooks from her peas."

Eliza nodded. "The walk will give them an appetite."

"It'll do your father good to get some fresh air," I said a little tartly, but noting the look of alarm on Eliza's face at the opening of this subject I softened my tone. "Perhaps there will be some calm in the fields for an unquiet mind."

Eliza bent her head over her work and I watched her slender hands with their elegant, tapered fingers move deftly from one garment to the next. Although they would be brown and roughened at harvest time, it grieved me to see them in water so long, for it is very bad for the hands: my own are always chapped and red after washing day and my wedding ring feels tight.

"Here," I said, "change places for a while," and I handed her the dolly-peg and took the shirt she was rinsing from her, saying, "Save your hands for your young man." Much to my surprise, for I had said it only in jest, she flushed to the tips of her ears. She sought to hide her confusion by applying the dolly with such vigour in the tub that she might have been mashing turnips and I feared for William's shirts, which, having come down already through Freddy and Jack, were none too robust in the seams. I remembered the look of longing on her face at church and said nothing, hoping that she might confide in me. After a spell I ventured, "I hear there's to be a fair this Saturday back at Helpstone, with stalls around the Butter Cross and fiddling and dancing in the evening."

She looked up then and said quietly, "Will Anna be there?"

"I don't know. I imagine she and Sefton will go together, as they're over there for the haymaking anyway," I added as gently as I could, knowing that Eliza would miss going arm in arm with her sister to such an entertainment, as they always used to. Now, with Sophie being so young, Eliza had no one to pick through a stall of ribbons with or to sit with until called on to dance.

She looked crestfallen.

"Perhaps Peter Guest might need a partner?" I said mischievously, as he had been sweet on Eliza when we lived in Helpstone and I had often seen him offering to carry her basket. Eliza, however, just shrugged and offered no comment on Peter or any other potential dancing partner. She turned away to wrap a cloth round the handle of the kettle and move it off its hook over the fire as it hissed steam and the lid began to jump.

"Well, maybe Sefton will be working and Anna will be going alone. Why don't you and I take your father over to the haymaking tomorrow so he can see Anna? You could ask her yourself about Saturday then."

Eliza's back stiffened and she stood for a moment holding the kettle before her. Then the heat from the handle reached her through the cloth and she put it down with a clatter and a muttered exclamation.

"What have you done?" I said, dropping the clothes back into the tub. "Have you burnt your hand? Let me see!"

Eliza thrust her hand deep in her apron pocket. "It's nothing," she said. "It'll be good to see Anna."

"It will," I said, and my heart lifted at the thought of seeing that dear face and those kind grey eyes again, for Anna's presence is like a sheet of clear water, calming to the mind and cheering to the spirits.

Eliza began to shift the bubbling pots down on to the hearthstone. "Father will be glad to see her," she said, keeping her voice light.

"As he was you, and glad to still have daughters at home to make a fuss over him," I said firmly, for Eliza was wont to feel that Anna, being the firstborn, put her in the shade a little with her father. I took one handle of the tub and said, "Help me carry this out, there's a dear."

She took the other handle and we lifted the heavy tub full of dirty water down off the table, then Eliza backed through the door with me following. The metal clanged against the door jamb as we went but we lifted it clear and carried it to the side of the house, where there was a weedy patch of earth. It was our usual habit to tip the stale water here where the soap could do no harm to the flowers, and we were well practised at swinging and tipping it both together, but today Eliza turned her end a little late and the water splashed on the baked earth of the path, wetting her shoes and stockings and the hem of her dress.

"Ups-a-daisy!" I said and laughed, expecting her to tut and fuss at the dirty splashes. Instead she stood quite still, looking down at the marks on her dress without comment, as if her thoughts were far away and the dress nothing to do with her.

"You seem very distracted today," I said crossly.

"Sorry," she said, coming back to herself. "It's the heat."

"Go and fetch some more water," I said relenting, "and have a long draught while you're there to cool you down. And see where William's got to!" I called after her.

I went indoors to refill the tub and when Eliza came back she said that there was no sign of either boy or bucket at the pump.

"Humph! Playing hookey again," I said. "Although why he has to take my best bucket with him is quite beyond me."

Eliza and I looked at each other and said at the same moment: "Fishing!" I pursed my lips, for William rarely caught anything but would potter about all day with a hazel stick and a piece of string with a worm on a bent pin tied to the end of it. I pictured him rolling up his breeches to wade out into a cool stream or sitting on the upturned bucket, his hat over his eyes, and felt vexed that Eliza and I should be toiling away in the stuffy kitchen. I rolled my eyes heavenwards, then lifted another pan of hot water from the fire and tipped it into the tub. Eliza added a little cold water and a cloud of steam rose up between us.

We worked on together for the rest of the morning. The conversation turned to happenings in the villages: Mrs Carter's new hat that she bought in Stamford and was said to cost a whole shilling; the thickening waist of Daisy Cardwell, who people were saying had eaten the green apples; and rumours of the railway coming to Helpstone and a huge cutting to be made through the little remaining common land.

Eliza chatted along with me when I opened a subject but started none herself, leaving me still puzzled at her strange mood and, when we had finally finished, glad enough to leave her to prepare the meal while I took the clothes baskets outside.

84

The day was still fine with small clouds drifting in a blue heaven as though the very sky had been rinsed clean. I lifted each garment and wrung them a little tighter before unrolling them and shaking out the worst creases and spreading them on the bushes and hedges to dry. Soon the garden was peopled with ghostly figures: white shirts with outspread arms; dun-coloured carter's smocks billowing a little as the breeze caught their hems; shifts and drawers woven through with twigs to stop the flimsier material catching the wind and flying away.

In the last basket were the girls' dresses, made of light cotton that would dry quickly. As I laid Sophie's tartan printed frock and Eliza's green sprigged gown upon the hedge and spread out the skirts, a vivid picture sprang unbidden into my mind: me, at nineteen, gathering a gown up quickly from the hedge at Walk Lodge. It was during the time when John and I were courting, his first visit to the house. He had come earlier than expected, no doubt over-eager to be punctual when meeting my family for the first time. Polly, seeing him coming across the cow pasture, came to tell me and I ran into the garden to gather up my blue gingham gown. Clear as day, I saw myself unpicking the sleeve from a thorny twig and pressing the cloth to my face. I remembered the smell of fresh air and sunshine; it was not quite dry, yet I ran with it into the house and put it on, knowing that it was more becoming than the dress I was wearing. The memory came upon me so sharply as I stood back from the girls' dresses, bright against the green of the foliage, that I sat down quickly on the garden seat.

The meeting between John and my family was an uncomfortable affair. Father and Mother sat at head and foot of the table, with Polly and me on one side and John on the other. Although the day was hot, John was unwilling to take his coat off and seemed to shrink down inside its high collar. The more Mother and Polly tried to make him welcome, filling his china cup with tea and pressing cakes and fancies on him, the more he seemed to hide away inside the coat. Father had little to say until he had finished his first cup. He stroked his beard and looked round at us all before starting.

"You are a lime-burner at Casterton, I understand," he said flatly, as a statement rather than a question, so that John did not know how to respond other than to nod his agreement, and said never a word about his poetry or his future hopes. "Indeed," said Father, tapping his fingertips together and looking at John from under his brows. "And is this your usual employment?"

"I was at Burghley House before that," John said.

"As gardener," I added quickly.

"Ah! A horticulturalist!" Father said. "So you were involved in devising the planting. Flower gardens or kitchen gardens?"

"It was mainly digging, weeding and scouring out the fish ponds," John said.

Father fell silent. John lifted his teacup and it clinked against the saucer. He put it back down without taking a drink.

"John writes poetry," I ventured. "He hopes to get up a subscription for a book."

"So that people promise to pay for the book in advance?" Mother asked.

"Exactly," said John, rather too loudly. He shuffled in his chair. "A bookseller told me that is how it's done."

"What are your poems about?" asked Polly, giving my hand a squeeze under the table.

"Birds and beasts, the life of the country — things that I see around me every day."

"And people will pay to read about what they can see with their own eyes?" said Father.

"Well, let us hope for the success of your plan," Polly said quickly.

"It hardly seems promising," Father muttered behind his napkin as he dusted the crumbs from his beard.

"Have you ever been apprenticed for a trade, John?" Mother asked.

"I was once to be apprenticed to a solicitor," John said, "but I was just a lad and so tongue-tied I was sent home again!" He looked at my mother as if expecting the smile of sympathy for his shyness that he would have found from his own family, but, finding none, ploughed on: "Then I was to be set to learn with a stonemason, but my parents couldn't afford the 'prentice fee . . ." he trailed off.

"That's a great pity," Polly said and smiled at him. "You could have engraved verses you had written."

"Cobbling is a useful trade," Father said heavily, looking directly at me.

I wished that I was sitting next to John and could touch his hand. I knew that comments such as my father's, ones that criticized his poetry, affected John deeply. As a stick swung idly by a boy leaves behind a trail of broken grasses, so another's scepticism cut John's spirits and left them drooping.

"One of John's poems was printed in the *Stamford News*," I said, with a little lift of my chin.

"Is that a fact," Father said, and returned to buttering his bread.

When the meal was finally done John excused himself, saying that he must walk the nine miles to Helpstone that night as he needed to take some of his wages home. Mother asked solicitously enough after his family before saying farewell and agreed that I could walk a little of the way with John to set him back on the right road, but as the door closed behind us I heard my father's booming voice saying, "A lime-burner? With three at home to feed? They'd be on the parish before the year was out."

John seemed not to have heard, however. In fact, once outdoors he straightened his shoulders as if shrugging off a burden and, as soon as we entered the shade of the woods, took my hand. I squeezed it firmly and he led me deeper into the shade. Instead of taking the quickest route through the woods to the pasture, we turned along a track that led among beech and sycamore and soon wordlessly sank down to sit with our backs to the bole of a tree. The dappled sunlight fell across my skirts, overlaying its regular pattern of blue and white checks with a shifting, random pattern of light.

"Are you cold, Patty?" John asked, putting his arm round me.

"I am a little," I said, for in truth the slight dampness of the dress was chill against my skin now that we were out of the sun.

John took off his coat and put it round me, then enclosed my shoulders within his arm once more. I moved up close and placed my hand against his chest.

"You said nothing about your love poems," I said, teasing him a little.

"It didn't seem the right company," he said, but the words that were meant to be playful had a hollow tone and I felt indignant that my father should leave him feeling trampled and low. I lifted my face to his and he kissed me, at first half absent-mindedly, as if his thoughts were still elsewhere and sad, but then, as I raised my hand to touch his face, we kissed more ardently and he slipped his arm inside the coat and encircled my waist. The carpet of last year's beech mast and sycamore seeds crackled beneath us as we pressed closer together and the anger that I felt on John's behalf shifted subtly to something fierce and strong.

"Do you love me, John?" I said, stilling his hand that lay now against my breast.

"With all my heart," he said and kissed my forehead as if to seal a pact. And I believed, and do believe still, that at that moment it was true and that something good and perfect passed between us, a promise that I thought stronger than any ring, so that when we kissed again and he laid me down with his coat beneath me I made no demur but clasped him tighter, wondering at the warmth and heaviness of him and the softness of our living flesh moving against the dry, dead seed cases beneath us.

I smile even now when I remember that first time, how I gave a gasp of surprise as I realized that his loving was not like the rough fumblings of a carter's boy that was all my experience before that date. Rather, he was practised and careful to make my first pain easy, so that when I stiffened and made moan he murmured to me and stroked my hair and was gentle until it had eased. He sought my pleasure and there was give-and-take between us, so that when we cried out together the birds rose in alarm from the trees around us in a clatter of applauding wings, as if our joy had lifted us out of ourselves and become embodied in flight.

We laughed then as the birds circled and returned to settle again and I buried my head in his shoulder as if I would breathe him in and keep the breath for ever. He rolled away and I reached for his hand. We lay together for a while, looking up into the moving leaves that hid and showed the dazzle of the sun by turns. A phrase from the Bible came into my head, "*and Adam knew Eve*", and I understood it for the first time. I felt no guilt but only gladness that we had been like those first two in the Garden.

"I should go back," I said, without moving. John lifted my hand to his lips and laid it down again and I smiled at him. "No, I *must* go back; they'll wonder what has kept me," I said, sitting suddenly bolt upright and pulling my clothes straight again.

John got to his feet and straightened his own while I fumbled with the buttons and ties of my dress. "Here, you have twigs in your hair." He came close and began to tease out the frassy bits one by one.

I put my hand to my head and found that the complicated loops and curls that I had arranged in honour of John's visit were all awry, with strands loosened and a tangled surface where once all had been smooth. "I can't go home like this," I said and tears began to well up in my eyes.

He kissed me and shushed me and picked out every leaf fragment from the mess, but the combing and pinning of it was beyond him and I could only pat it and pin it as best I may.

"You look beautiful," he said when I was done. "Fit for a dance." He shook his coat out and carried it over his arm. "Are you hungry?" he said.

I nodded, wishing that I had eaten more at table, but I had been in such a state of nervous agitation over John's visit that I had eaten hardly a thing. He reached up and pulled a branch of the beech tree down towards him, then searched through the foliage to find the young, tender leaves and picked them off one by one. "Poor man's bread-and-cheese," he said, holding them out to me. I took one but held it in my palm, seeing anew the delicate tracery of veins and the regularity of its serrated edges. John laughed, put a handful into his mouth and began to chew. I nibbled gingerly at the edge. It was papery and pungent with a peppery taste, a little like parsley, and John picked me some more. We set off, retracing our steps back to the main path and then out again to the sunlight.

"You must tell them that you walked all the way to the road with me," he said. He brushed a stray lock of hair from my face and I tucked it behind my ear and began to search for a pin to secure it. "Tell them that we fell in with some friends on the way," John said, "and all went along together."

We kissed long and slow at parting and promised when we would meet again.

Then I set off on my way and he on his and never did I want more to turn round and match my footsteps with those of another.

As I reached the last stretch of path towards home, Polly was coming to meet me.

"I thought I'd better find you before you came in," she said. "Father has been shouting and is writing a letter to the Butterworths."

"What does he mean by it?" I said, feeling the blood drain from my heart.

Polly simply shook her head. I reached out and took her arm to steady myself and she looked at me more closely and sighed. She smoothed my dress collar and began quickly to unpin, re-twist and pin up my hair. "You are set on him, then?" she asked and my look gave her all her answer. She took my hand that was still closed around the beech leaves. "Is he in earnest?" she asked. "Has he given you a love token?" She opened my hand and looked at me in puzzlement, for there was no silver ring or glittering pin but only a handful of leaves, crumpled and crushed, with dark creases leaking sap. She closed my fingers back round them, tucked my arm through hers and led me home. "I will say I'm sick to my stomach," she said, "from eating too much rich food and that I need you to take care of me. Then you need not sit with Father."

I have those leaves still. They are wrapped in a handkerchief at the bottom of my marriage chest. They are skeletons now, golden brown: a mere tracery of veins with all their flesh become air. I haven't looked at them for many years, fearing that in the unwrapping they would fall apart to powder. But I think of them sometimes. They are both precious and fragile, a filigree of gold as insubstantial as a dream.

CHAPTER
SIX

Eel Pie

I was woken from my musings by John returning with the children. As they came round from the lane at the side of the house Sophie and Charles were arm in arm, laughing and staggering, chanting, "Left! Right! Left! Right!" as they marched along on three legs, Sophie's left ankle being tied to Charles's right by means of John's handkerchief. In her other hand, Sophie trailed a bunch of wild flowers, their heads nodding at the path.

"Halt!" John called like a sergeant major as they came level with me and the children stopped smartly. Sophie gave me the flowers and tried to drop a pretty curtsy, which took Charles down with it, so that they landed in a heap on the ground, helpless with giggles.

"'Tenshun! 'Tenshun!" shouted John. "Posy delivered: mission completed! Discipline in the ranks. Let's be orderly!"

I helped the children to their feet and bent to pick apart the knot that had tightened with pulling.

"Quick march, quick march! We must set off again," John said. "We must cover all the fields before dark sets in."

I looked up at him and saw that he was flushed and breathless and he glanced around as though ready to set off again in any direction. Quickly, before the children became alarmed I said, "Soldiers can't march on an empty stomach, Sergeant. Perhaps you'd like to take some vittles first?" He hesitated for a moment and that was enough. "Sophie, take my lovely flowers and stand them in some water and tell Eliza to bring our bread and cheese out here." I moved along the bench. "Won't you sit down, John?" I said. "You've had a long march and could do with a rest."

John flopped down on to the bench, throwing his legs out straight before him in a comic posture of exhaustion, and patted the seat for Charles to sit beside him.

"When I was in the militia the sergeant made fun of my coat for the amusement of the other soldiers," John said to him. "It was too big, me being just a lad."

"What did you do, Pa?" asked Charles.

"I knocked him down," John replied, laughing and swiping first one fist then the other through the air to demonstrate. "I split him into chops . . ."

I laid my hand on his sleeve. "John!" I said, glancing at Charles, "settle now. Show a good example to the boy," for Charles was sitting on the edge of his seat, aiming an imaginary rifle at the washing spread to dry and making explosive noises with each shot.

Eliza came out with a tray laid with a barley loaf, a little cheese cut thin and a pitcher of small ale, and Sophie followed behind, carrying a chair. Parker, still tousled from sleep, brought up the rear. Sophie set down the chair in the sunshine and Parker sat down with a grunt. "I woke up with all the shouting," he said mildly. "What was all the noise about?" but John's attention had finally been taken by the arrival of food and he was munching enthusiastically on a crusty piece of bread.

I breathed a sigh and took a little ale myself, for the washing had been thirsty work and I was relieved that I had so easily headed off one of John's agitations, the slight he had suffered at the hands of the militiaman being a common refrain with him before he went away to High Beech and prone to lead him into imagining himself ready to take on all-comers.

As we talked and ate together in the sunny garden, with the smell of warm flowers and fresh laundry infusing the still air, I started to feel peaceful. I looked round fondly at my family: at Parker chimbling cheese in tiny pieces, Eliza like a little mother serving us, Charles and Sophie picking daisies to make a string and John with his eyes closed and his head thrown back to catch the sun upon his face beside me and safe in the midst of us all.

"Does anyone have a tale to tell?" I asked, remembering other days when we had sat together and told stories for our amusement.

Charles and Sophie both turned expectantly to John, then Charles said, "Have you got one, Pa?"

John said, "Hmm," opened his eyes and scanned round the garden, then up at the bright sky and finally ran his eye over the orchard, where his gaze came to rest on the plum tree that stood in the hedge close by the road. "Is that a good place to plant a plum tree?" he asked the children.

"No," said Charles promptly. "The Peakirk boys steal them."

"The branches hang right over the road, so it's easy," Sophie added.

"What do the Peakirk boys want with our plums when they're still hard and not ready to eat?" said John.

"They use them in their catapults," Charles said. "Especially the hard green ones."

"And how do you and Sophie see them off?" John asked.

"Well . . . we have catapults too," Charles said.

"Hmm," said John, "so I dare say the crop on that tree comes only from the topmost branches, the guardians being as prone to stripping it as the marauders."

Sophie nudged Charles with her elbow and frowned at him.

"The very worst place for a plum tree, then," John went on, "and strange, given that all the apples, crabs and cherries are well within the orchard borders. Well, how do you suppose it got there?" he said.

"Someone dropped a plum stone," Charles said.

"Or the hedge was moved after," Sophie added.

John sat up and leant towards them with his elbows on his knees. "Neither of those things," he said. "The answer is stranger by far."

Parker shuffled his chair closer to be able to hear.

"That tree," John said, "grew originally many miles from here on a farmer's land over by Tickencote." He shot a glance at me and I smiled and nodded as if to back up his story.

"The farmer loved plums and would have liked them in a pie, but instead he was saving the best of them to pick and sugar and keep for his children's Christmas feast: lovely juicy plums glowing like jewels among the leaves. But . . ." John paused and looked around to make sure he had the children's full attention, "in the woods near by there lived a monstrous crow, who liked plums just as much and would come and dine upon them until it had stolen a whole pie-full away. The farmer set a boy to watch, but he ran away to play with his schoolmates and another plum was gone. He hung pots and pans in the tree to clatter when the crow landed, but it was canny and soon found its way to the branches that were clear, and that was another plum gone. Finally, in desperation, the farmer painted the branches with lime, thinking that when the pans rattled he would then come out from his house with a gun and kill the pesky crow where it had stuck fast to a branch." John paused. "Was it a good plan?" he asked Charles.

"Did he shoot it?" said Charles as he nodded.

John shook his head. "He waited and waited and the crafty crow sat in a tree just out of range, until eventually the farmer had waited so long that he fell . . . fast . . . asleep," he said, letting his head fall forward on to his chest. "Then down swooped the crow and began pecking and a-picking at another juicy, ripe plum. When it had finished, it spread its wings to hop along the branch and take another but found it was stuck fast!" He pulled a comic face and flapped his elbows up and down like a chicken until Charles started to laugh.

"Well, it flapped and it flopped, it flopped and it flapped, until the branches of the whole tree jiggled up and down and clattered the pans and woke the farmer. Down comes old Giles, a-swearing and a-cursing and a-pointing his gun, and the crafty old crow can see that he'll soon be in a pie along with the plums, so he flaps and flops harder and harder and the tree sways side to side and the pans clatter so hard they drop right off. Then up by the roots comes the tree — and crow and tree and plums all take off into the sky!"

At this Parker began to laugh and Sophie's mouth became a round "O".

"The whole tree?" Charles said.

"The whole tree," John repeated seriously. "Then flap-flop, flap-flop, the crow flew across the fields and molehills, over the river and Lolham Bridges and past Helpstone, with the tree and its twisty roots trailing down from its gnarly old claws that were still stuck fast to the limey branch. Then just as it flew over Glinton church steeple, a few drops of rain fell. All the people who were coming out of the church looked up and wondered to see a tree flying by overhead and some were afeared and ran back into the church, and some were excited and said it was a sign, and some tried to follow it, but the hedges and houses got in the way and they lost sight of it and it disappeared!"

"What happened?" asked Charles.

"Well, the rain rained harder and harder until all the lime washed clear away," John said. "The old crow gave a hearty caw and sailed away into the clouds, never to be seen again, and the tree plummeted down and landed smack bang in the middle of the hedge."

All heads turned to look at the tree where it grew with a stretch of hawthorn either side of it. Then Parker began to laugh anew and I joined in and soon we were all laughing and Charles was looking from one to the other and saying, "But what about the farmer's children and the sugar plums?" and that just made me laugh all the more, until I thought I would burst my dress at the seams.

John kept a poker face. "Their misfortune is our good luck," he said to Charles. "Now you and Sophie, if you can keep the Peakirk boys at bay, shall have the sugar plums this Christmas," and he ruffled Charles's hair and turned to me and smiled.

Although I knew that when John became too excitable sometimes he could not govern his moods, I could not help but feel my heart gladden to see him in such good spirits. Parker suggested that they walk down to the orchard to take a look at how the fruit was coming along and they all went off in a party, but for Eliza who loaded the tray and followed me indoors.

No sooner had Eliza set the tray down than there was a knock at the door. On opening it I found a stranger dressed in a tightly buttoned coat and a wide top hat, a sheet of paper with writing on it in his hand. He was a man of about five and thirty, with a florid face and of a stocky build. He held himself very upright and his bearing and expression immediately suggested to me that he was some kind of official. My mind flew straight to William.

"Yes?" I said. "Is anything the matter?"

The man removed his hat and tucked it into the crook of his arm. "Is this the residence of John Clare?" he asked and glanced down at the piece of paper.

"Who is enquiring?" I said, folding my arms.

"My name is Mr Garth. I'm here on behalf of Dr Allen of the asylum at High Beech, Essex."

From the orchard I could hear Charles and Sophie at play. I hoped that Parker and John would pause there too and would be leaning on the gate, looking out over the fields and talking over the ways of the world, as was their habit.

"You had better come in," I said and hurried him inside. I offered him a seat at the kitchen table and asked Eliza to join the others in the orchard. "Try to keep your father occupied outside for a while," I said to her under my breath, for I feared that if he saw the asylum man he would imagine himself followed and tracked down and would not react kindly to it.

Despite my trepidation, hospitality demanded that I offer our visitor refreshment. I took his hat and placed it carefully aside, saying, "You must be tired after such a long journey. Will you take some ale?"

He accepted and, having taken a long draught and mopped his brow, asked if he might take off his coat. I took it and laid it across Parker's chair. It was of a good cloth, though a little frayed at the cuffs and smelling masterly strong of pipe tobacco.

"You are Mrs Clare, then, I take it," he said, after passing the back of his hand across his lips. "John is not here, then?"

"You know my husband well?" I said quickly.

Mr Garth nodded. "I am an attendant at Leopards Hill Lodge, High Beech, where your husband has been staying. I have been closely involved in his care and have been sent by Dr Allen to find him. He left Essex over a week ago and Dr Allen is naturally concerned."

"He has been home," I said hurriedly, "but he is not at home now."

"Aah," said Mr Garth, giving me a long and searching look. "You know that he didn't officially discharge himself?"

I said nothing.

"Dr Allen thinks it best for him to return and continue his treatment at High Beech, where he can receive proper care."

"He will be well looked after here," I said.

He looked pointedly at the remains of our meagre meal upon the tray, where some hard crusts of bread and a few crumbs of cheese remained, then glanced round the room as if appraising its dirt floor, the disorderly wash buckets and the ashes of the fire that had not yet been removed, and finding all wanting.

"He walked a long way to return to us," I said simply.

"But what can you offer him?" Mr Garth asked. "We have good food to sustain him, proper sanitation, warm baths, gardens where he can find peace and seclusion. He can live like a gentleman." He raised his hands as if offering a gift.

"It is not his home," I said.

Mr Garth sighed and rubbed his head. "How has he been since he returned?" he asked.

"He has been calm in the main," I said guardedly, for I didn't want to go into his fancy about Mary or his suspicious imaginings of plots between Parson Mossop and myself. All this, I felt, was private. "Yes, calm," I repeated.

He gave me a look that was plainly sceptical.

"Well, he was a little ebullient today when playing with the children, but I was able to settle him," I conceded.

"He has not been Byron, then, since he's been at home?" he said. "You would say that he has been himself?"

"What do you mean, Byron?" I said.

"Sometimes he has imagined himself to be the poet Byron, and sometimes Jack Randall, the boxer, and it is difficult to say which is the harder of the two to deal with," he said.

"In what way? What form do these fancies take?" I asked.

"When he fancies himself Byron he rewrites the famous poems, sometimes in a shocking, bawdy fashion, and when Jack Randall he becomes a veritable pugilist and issues challenges to all and sundry to step up to the mark and fight him."

I looked at him, astounded. "He never thought such things while he was at home," I said. "What can have induced him to entertain such ideas? This is surely something he has learnt from other poor souls at the asylum."

Mr Garth shrugged as though unconvinced.

"He always strides round the orchard when composing his verses," I said, "and at times he can be violent in his language if he feels an injustice has been done, but he has never thought himself another person or aimed a blow in anger."

"He is more malleable here than he is at High Beech, then," he said. "He has been quite unbiddable at times: wishing to walk when and where he likes and not come in for mealtimes or at evening time. At High Beech, inmates of a decided nature must be accompanied by attendants."

I remembered then what John had said about his dislike of the "keepers" and realized that Mr Garth was just one such keeper, set to follow and watch John, but whether this was to restrain and order him or to protect him I was yet to establish.

"John is used to freedom," I said. "He has the fields and woods to roam at home; perhaps he can be forgiven for wanting to escape the confines of house and gardens? Surely you followed him too closely?"

Mr Garth laughed and said, "High Beech is not like that, Mrs Clare. There are no iron bars at the windows and there are acres of woods and fields to wander. Your husband had to be supervised because his wanderings were of quite another kind."

I felt myself flush at what he implied. I picked up the tray and moved it to the dresser so that I could turn my back on him and he would not see my face.

"He is prone to bothering the ladies at Springfield, the women's quarter," he said. "At the Easter Hunt, which the patients were allowed to attend as an

104

entertainment, he followed a young woman, then stood close up to her and would not be easily persuaded away."

I turned back to face him. "Then, it is a good thing that there are no houses full of women here," I said tartly, for what he had said had caught me on the raw.

"I beg you to reconsider," he said. "John can become quite . . ." he searched for a word ". . . unpredictable when he's crossed. His language is sometimes not for the ears of the fairer sex and he fancies himself something of a boxer . . ."

I thought of how I had seen John earlier in the day, with his family round him and the faces of the children as they listened to his story, and despite all that Mr Garth had said I could not but be hopeful that home might effect a recovery.

"Nonetheless," I said firmly, "I will try him at home for a while."

Mr Garth sighed and rose to his feet. "I hope you won't regret it," he said. "Dr Allen's offer will remain open, I'm sure, should John prove too much to handle."

I picked up his coat and hat and handed them to him. "Please give Dr Allen our kind regards and tell him that John will write soon," I said, and showed him out to the lane, where he said he would set off on foot for Stamford, intending to catch the coach to London and thence back to Essex the next day.

I returned to the garden and began to gather in the washing. For the moment, the concentration needed to disentangle the cloth from the twigs relieved me of the necessity of thinking any further about the interview with Mr Garth and the repetitive action of folding the clothes and placing them in the wicker basket soothed my troubled spirits.

It was now late afternoon and I began to wonder where William was and to feel a return of my earlier annoyance as all the bread and cheese had been eaten and I was hard pressed to think what to give him to eat when he returned. It's his own fault, I thought. He will just have to do without — and serve him right for making off before his water-carrying chore was properly done.

Over in the orchard I saw Parker and John turn to look across the field and Sophie and Charles running over to the gate. As if conjured by my thoughts, there was William coming across the field with my best bucket carried low as if full of something heavy. I left off folding and walked down to the others to meet him, muttering under my breath.

When I reached them, all were crowded round the bucket and William stood with his hands on his hips and a wide smile on his face. I looked over the top of Charles's head at a bucket full of the filthiest water and mud I'd ever seen. "William . . ." I started, as I turned to go and catch hold of him.

"It's eels, Ma!" said Charles. "Look!"

Sure enough, as Charles moved aside I saw that the contents of the bucket were in motion, a squirming mass of brown water and eels.

"Where did you catch them?" I asked William, my tone changed from thunder to sun in an instant, for here was our dinner, and fresh meat to boot.

"Down the Welland through High Borough fen," said William. "I'd been trying for ages, but the water was too deep and they could hide away in the middle where I couldn't reach them!"

"The water's down a bit now, though, is it?" said Parker.

I looked in fascination at the movement of the eels, the way a wave seemed to ripple along their length. I could almost believe what some folk say: that eels are the spirit of the restless water come to life and are the wavelets made by the wind on the water bodied forth.

"Do they grow in the mud like flies in cow-pats?" asked Charles.

William laughed. "No, stupid, they come from eggs, like birds do."

John, too, stared into the bucket but seemed aghast at the eels' frantic squirming and let out a sound of disgust. "A nest of snakes!" he said. "Serpents and offspring of vipers."

Sophie drew near to me and held on to my apron.

"They're not snakes, my love, just eels," I said, and squeezed her shoulder.

"Do you know how to gut them, William?" Parker asked, having heard nothing of John's comments.

Eliza gave a little scream and Sophie stepped away from the bucket. I took Sophie firmly by the hand. "You girls can come and help get the washing in," I said. "We'll leave this to the menfolk. Bring them to me prepared for the pot and I'll make a pie."

As all moved away to their allotted tasks, John still stood staring into the bucket. He looked pale and his lips moved as he muttered to himself. I drew nearer and heard him repeating, "Devils and snakes. Devils and snakes."

"Come," I said, "come inside now and rest." I took his arm and he let me lead him away.

We left the girls attending to the remains of the laundry and went inside, where I sat John down in Parker's chair and brought out from the sack some potatoes to go with the pie. I filled a pan with water, put a peeling knife and a potato into John's hands and started on another myself, catching the peelings in a paper on my lap. I talked all the while to John of the garden and the children and how much we had laughed at his tale of the crow, for I judged such talk would calm him. He did not answer me but scraped a few tiny parings of skin from the potato, placing each one carefully in my lap, and every so often stopping and looking round or sniffing the air.

At length I laid down my work and asked him what was the matter.

"He's here," he said. "The keeper is here."

"There's no one here but us," I said as calmly as I could, for my heart had started banging at my ribs. Remembering how agitated John had become at my merely talking with Parson Mossop, I feared him finding out about the visit from Mr Garth.

"He's here somewhere," he said. "I smell his tobacco." He jumped to his feet, the knife falling from his lap and jangling as it hit the hearthstone, and the potato rolling away under my chair. Then he pulled open the door to the stairs and pounded up them. I rose to my feet, not knowing what to do or whether to call the others, and stood there all undecided. I heard John go from room to room and the sound of doors being flung open and beds shoved about, then he clattered down the stairs again and emerged, breathless, into the room.

He grabbed my arm and pulled me with him to the parlour. "Where is he?" he said, looking round at the empty room. "How long has he been gone?" He crossed to the window and peered out, then took to his heels and ran outside into the lane with me following behind.

The lane was deserted. In both directions not a man or beast stirred and over the scene hung the heaviness of a late afternoon in summer.

"I'm ready for you!" John bellowed to the empty road and the empty fields. "Come back here and fight like a man!"

"John," I said "Shh . . ."

He wheeled round and stared at the next cottage, fifty yards down the lane, as if he thought a score of robbers were hidden there. "I'm ready for 'em!" he shouted. "Jack Randall's ready to meet any customer in the ring or on the stage," and he puffed out his chest and raised his fists in a fighting pose. "A fair stand-up fight, a one-minute round!"

From the cottage, Mrs Walker and her children came hurrying to the gate and then quickly withdrew again.

"Come on, you customers! Has no one the pluck to step up to Jack Randall?" John bawled at their retreating backs.

"There's no one you need to fight, John," I said.

I tried to pluck at his sleeve, but he shook me off and ran down to the Walkers' gate, which he rattled and shoved. Mrs Walker's face appeared at the upstairs window, peering out beneath the thatch.

"Parker!" I called. "Boys! I need some help here!" for I saw that I could not manage him on my own and was afraid that soon someone would send out for the constable.

William and Parker came out on to the lane further down by the orchard and ran towards John from behind, then circled him carefully on either side. William looked wide-eyed and scared.

"What's all this, son?" Parker said, approaching him with open hands.

"Won't you come inside with us now, John?" I said. "Look, your father has come to fetch you home."

John was staring round from one to the other of us. "I'm Jack," he said, "Jack Randall . . ." He backed up against the Walkers' gate. "Leave me be," he said gruffly.

Parker took another step towards him and John looked down at his hands, which were dirty and bloody from gutting the eels. He shuddered and recoiled, all the fight suddenly gone out of him. "Nebuchadnezzar, the King of Babylon, has eaten me up," he said, looking straight at me with an expression of such appeal that my heart ached. I held out my hands to him, but he wouldn't take them and remained with his own pressed against the gate behind him. "He has thrown me into

110

confusion," he whispered, shaking his head. "He has swallowed me down like a big snake."

William came forward slowly and stood in front of him. He put one hand out and gently touched John's shoulder. "Pa," he said, "won't you come home now? I've got some bird eggs I want to show you. I got 'em today before I went fishing." He looked up at me and I nodded him on. "They're white, with a red fleck," he said, moving his hand down to under John's elbow. "You see, I don't rightly know what they are."

John let his shoulders drop and looked at William as if beginning to listen.

"White with a reddish fleck," William said again. "Three of them. Won't you come and look at them for me?" and he helped his father step away from the gate.

"They could be nuthatch eggs," John said.

"I found them in a hole full of leaves, in a tree," William said.

"You didn't take all, did you, William? You did leave some behind for the hen bird, so as not to stop her song with a broken heart?"

"I left half and I was quick and careful. I took them up in leaves so that none should break and my smell shouldn't drive the hen away . . ."

They moved slowly towards the house, William's straight, sturdy frame supporting his father's, John shuffling and leaning on his boy's arm.

Parker and I looked at each other and both of us were near to tears. He reached over and, bloody or not, I took his hand and squeezed it, then we followed on, hand in hand.

CHAPTER
SEVEN

Meadow Flowers

The next day, John sat at breakfast with his porridge untouched before him until I put his spoon in his hand. His spirits were downcast, as though a storm had swept through him and blown itself out, to leave a desolate landscape of flattened corn and broken branches. The family was subdued and talked little and in hushed voices. I was tired too, having watched over John until the early hours as he muttered in his sleep and sometimes started up, complaining of a chill that began at his feet and moved up to his head, and a numbness in his limbs. This made me fearful that he might fall into a fit, as he had done on occasion in the past, once even in the street in Stamford with poor little Sophie running hither and thither for help and catching at the arms of passers-by. However, at length he fell into a fitful sleep and I knew that the episode was over.

When John had eaten his porridge, Parker suggested that he come for a stroll with him, saying that the light and air would do him good.

"Which way are you going, Grandpa?" asked Eliza, and I remembered our plan to visit Anna over beyond Helpstone at the haymaking.

"Maybe you could go out along the Helpstone road and we could all come along?" I said, my spirits lightening, for seeing Anna was the best tonic for John that I could hope for.

John looked up at the mention of his old home. "I should like that," he said, and it was settled.

Eliza and I bustled about, clearing up. We sliced bread and packed it into a basket, and Sophie and Charles were dispatched to pick wild strawberries while we filled pitchers with cold tea for the journey. I set the dish with the remains of the eel pie in a basin of cold water in the coolest spot in the kitchen and the thought that there would be a meal waiting for us on our return made my spirits lift further, as if it were a holiday. Quietly, I took thruppence from the tin and put it into my pocket. When we reached the Blue Bell I would get a pitcher filled with beer and we would have something to take to Anna and Sefton to quench a labouring thirst, haymaking being hot, limb-aching work.

We set off mid-morning, planning to arrive for the mowers' midday break, and soon got clear of the village. Small clouds were awash in the huge over-arching sky of the fens, their edges slowly fraying before a warm westerly breeze. John complains that the landscape here is featureless: flat fields stretching in all directions, broken here and there by low hedges, a lone white house or a straggle of trees. In winter it is true that it can seem grey and oppressive. But in summer the openness seems to me to be airy, the wide pastures are easy on the eye, the breeze stirs the wheat fields to soft

113

movement and in the weeks leading up to harvest all is blue and gold and a vastness of air and light. Even the fen drains, which are deep and steep-sided and so treacherous in winter, are, in summer, lined with wild flowers. Grass tracks lead across brick bridges that are wonderfully built to describe an exact semicircle over each stream and as you cross you look down on banks nodding with kingcups and crowflowers.

Eliza carried the pitchers, I took the basket and Charles and Sophie went on ahead, kicking a stone between them or picking grasses to hold between their thumbs and blow to make the hooting of an owl.

John walked slowly, matching his pace to his father's, Parker getting along with the aid of a sturdy thumb-stick cut from the hedge. It gave me pleasure to see John out in the open air once again and hear Parker humming the old songs under his breath. As we left the edge of the fens the fields became smaller and the skyline was softened by gentle slopes and woodland. John paused often to stare at the landmarks of his childhood or to peer into the hedge to seek out a songbird and seemed to find satisfaction in each rediscovery of the treasures of his native land.

"Father is better today," Eliza said to me as John stooped to pick larkspur from the hedge bank.

"He is always better out of doors, I think," I said.

John turned the delicate flower between his thumb and forefinger and then tucked it into his buttonhole.

"He notices everything, even the smallest flower or insect," Eliza said.

114

"The small things distract him from the larger; they make him look around and forget himself for a while."

Eliza looked puzzled.

"I don't mean 'forget himself' in the sense of forgetting his manners," I said.

"Or like yesterday," Eliza said, pulling a face.

"Nor like yesterday."

"You mean he forgets his worries?" she ventured.

I smiled at her because she was thinking as a woman, not a youngster, and this pleased me.

"More than that even," I said. "Your father has a gift that isn't given to many; he sees beauty where others would simply set their foot." I paused to think how best to explain this further. "He told me once that the feeling he experiences when he looks at the sun on water or the shape of a favourite tree or the old stile he played on as a child is one of kinship, as though all things are connected."

Eliza laughed. "As if he hasn't got a big enough family!" She was quiet for a moment, then added, "Parson Mossop would say he is seeing God's hand in all things."

"He would, I'm sure, and your father would agree, but Parson Mossop says it with the weight of the Bible in his hand, whereas your pa feels it as a oneness with field or flower that lifts him out of himself, like thistledown floating free from its stem." I put the basket down for a moment to rub my hand where the wicker handle had scored my fingers. "And I envy him that," I said, picking it up again and shifting it to the other hand.

"But he's sometimes so miserable!" Eliza exclaimed. "If he finds such joy in the world about him, how can he become so angry or so sad?"

I shrugged. "It's his nature; he's always been . . ." I searched for the word, ". . . mercurial. Perhaps it's just the nature of a poet?"

"We will have to take him out." Eliza lifted her chin in determination. "Take him for walks, so that he has no opportunity to become despondent. Or upset."

I glanced at her and saw again the look of worry that had crossed her face when she had come running last night, having heard the hullabaloo. She had found us all gathered round her father and William unwrapping the bird's eggs and putting each tiny one in John's hand as if he were a child.

"I'm sure that would help," I said and patted her arm. "I'm sure it would."

In Helpstone we stopped at the Blue Bell to fill the pitchers anew and to ask which hayfields were being mown today. Having obtained directions, we managed to get Parker a lift on a wagon that was taking provisions out to the workers and he was glad of it. We walked on until we met the long wall that stretches for miles along the roadside and marks the boundary of the Burghley Estate. The walking being easier on the road, we carried on there until we came level with the hayfields, then John helped each of us across by giving us a leg-up over the wall. The children scrambled over as quick as squirrels, but there was much laughter at my attempt, with John pretending I was too heavy.

116

"Come and put your shoulder behind her, Eliza," he called. "The days when I could lift your mother over the threshold are long gone!" So with Eliza shoving me from behind I was able to get my foot to the top of the wall and the children reached up to help me down the other side. When everyone was over, John pulled himself up, scuffing his boots on the way, then jumped down, out of breath, on to the soft grass.

"You can still climb a wall, then," I said, smiling.

"I had plenty of practice with this one when I was a gardener here." John dusted his hands down on his trousers. "They used to lock us in the garden house at night in case we stole the fruit, but we used to skip out of our lodgings once the overseer was gone home and go to Stamford for the evening." He winked. "A meeting with Old John Barleycorn is a great inducement to nimbleness."

He looked out across the estate and we all turned to follow his gaze. Three fields away the mowers were working with their backs to us, a line of men moving rhythmically together across the field, blades glinting on the back swing. Some way behind them, a more ragged line of women and older men were raking the hay: pulling it into long parallel swathes that snaked across the field, following its contours and running east to west, so that the sun would travel over them all day. In the distance the domes and tall chimneys of the big house rose above the landscape, pale and shimmering in the noonday heat.

We walked across the fields until we came to where the mowers were working, then paused at the gate. The

117

gang of men, some stripped to the waist, swung their bodies in time, leaning into the circular sweep of the scythes, their hands on the double curve of the snaiths, keeping the long blades level and parallel to the ground. Every so often a man would stop to take a whetstone from his pocket and run it along the shining steel to get a keener edge, then he would move quickly forward to fall into step and resume his place in the line once more.

I spotted Anna among the group that followed on behind, raking the hay into windrows. She had on my old straw bonnet to keep the sun off, and when she paused at the end of a row she laid down her rake, put both hands to the small of her back and stretched in a movement that was so familiar to me and so dear that I had to stop myself from calling out to her.

Anxious not to distract her and bring her to the overseer's attention, we filed along the hedge to rejoin Parker and settled ourselves in the shady spot he had chosen, underneath an ancient hawthorn. The grass here was already short, the headland having been cut first to allow the strip in the shadow of the hedge a longer drying day. As I spread out my dress under me and sank down on to the soft, green stems, their sweet smell rose up to meet me. Sophie and Charles, echoing the actions of their elders and helped by Eliza, drew the wisps of feathery grasses that had been missed into two piles, which they called their nests, each vying to see who could make the biggest, softest heap. Parker sat with his back against the hawthorn and busied himself with lighting his pipe, but John remained standing, his eyes never leaving Anna as she worked.

At last the overseer gave a mighty shout and the gang moved to the side of the field to pile their tools together, then dispersed in chattering groups to find their own shady spots. I waved to Anna and she broke away from her group of women and came towards us. John opened his arms wide and Anna, recognizing him, quickened her pace until, almost running, she met his embrace with her own, her hat falling to hang at her back and her eyes tight shut as she threw her arms round him.

"Dear, dear Anna," John said, and kissed her on the forehead. He held her hands and took a step back to look at her.

She said, "When did you get home? Are you well? Are you home to stay?" the words tumbling over each other head-over-heels.

"He's been home these five days," I said, "and dying to see his grown-up, married daughter."

"Well, here I am," she said, embracing each sibling in turn, "and not so different, as you can see."

When she came to Eliza she hugged her, but Eliza didn't offer her cheek to be kissed. I felt a little vexed with her for seeming cold to Anna, who, after all, had done her no wrong but only got married as it's natural for a girl to do. Eliza should surely have grown out of such sulks. Anna hesitated for a moment, but then took her hands and said, "You're looking uncommon pretty, 'Liza, with your hair all in curls."

Eliza's hand went to her head self-consciously.

"No, it suits you," Anna said. "Mine is like a bird's nest after all the haymaking — you'd think I'd combed it with the rake." She laughed and pulled at one of many strands that had escaped her simple twist. "Will you plait it for me when we've eaten dinner? I don't manage it half as well as you used to do."

"It would need combing out and starting from scratch and I have no comb with me," Eliza said.

"No matter," Anna said warmly. "I should only get grass in it again by the end of the day. We shall sit and gossip instead and I'll tell you all the news from Helpstone."

At last she came to me and I folded her into my arms and rocked her side to side on her feet. "Your little house is kept well-aired, never fear," I said. "I've been round every day to open the windows for a while and to water the vegetables."

"Thank you. I'm glad my little seedlings are well looked after," she said with a smile as I let her go.

I looked at her closely. Her sleeves were pushed back and her dress loosened at the neck for coolness. Her forearms and chest were browned by the sun, with just a line of white showing where the cloth had been pushed back further as if this was the hottest day yet.

"You're brown as a cob-nut," I said, touching the side of her face, "but maybe a little thin?"

"Nonsense! I'm very well, Ma," she said and, taking John's hand, drew him down to sit beside her.

I began to delve into the basket. "Well, you should eat," I said, pulling out the hunks of buttered bread and passing them round.

Someone in the group closest to us began to play a mouth organ and the others joined in, singing "Nobody cometh to woo".

A group of men walked by us and Anna called out, "Andrew, where's my husband? Can you tell him that my family is here?"

Eliza looked up quickly, then blushed as one of the men stared boldly at her. He clicked his tongue as he might do to call up a slowing horse and Eliza bent her head and rummaged in the basket. Anna remonstrated. "Shame on you, Jack Cowley," she said quietly, "and you with a sweetheart of a year or more! Now, look, there's my husband. Do something useful and fetch him over here for me, like the good fellow I know you are."

The man smiled and turned to where Anna was pointing. "Sefton!" he bellowed. "Over here!" Then he followed the rest, who were drifting away in the direction of a band of laughing girls. Sefton raised a hand in reply but didn't immediately break away from his group. A firkin was being passed hand to hand and Sefton waited for his turn, then threw back his head and took a long draught, before taking his leave of his fellows with much back-slapping and rib-nudging. He walked over at a leisurely pace. I noticed that his hair, already fair, had lightened in the sun to near straw and even in a week of haymaking his shoulders seemed broader and his confident stride longer — maybe, I thought, with just a hint of swagger.

He nodded to John and to Parker, murmured, "Ladies," to us, then flopped down beside Anna with a

121

wide grin that took in the whole assembled company. "Thirsty work," he observed with a sideways glance at the neck of the pitcher that protruded from the cover of the basket.

"Help yourself," I said, smiling in spite of myself as he put on a face of comical pleading and made the eyes of a spaniel puppy. He uncorked the pitcher, tossed the stone marble in the air and caught it, took a long swig, then looked round as if to say "Who is to have it next?" He made as if to pass it to Anna, then snatched it away at the last minute and called over to Charles, "How about Charlie boy? I hear he's a drinking man!" At which Anna gave his arm a shove and, laughing, told him to behave himself.

Sefton twisted round to face Eliza. "How about the young lady?" he said, proffering the pitcher.

"No, thank you," Eliza said.

"Aw, come on, 'Liza," Sefton said. "It'll bring colour to your cheeks."

"She's got colour enough," observed Parker as poor Eliza began to blush again, this time the flush rising to the roots of her hair.

Sefton passed the pitcher to Anna, then, glancing round at the group who had just started a rousing chorus of "The Maiden's Welcome", he sprang to his feet.

"If you won't drink, then maybe you'll dance!" he said and described a deep bow to her, flourishing an imaginary hat.

Though still red-faced, Eliza stared straight at him for a moment, before gazing pointedly away into the middle distance of the field. I looked at her closely and my brow furrowed, for what I had seen in her glance had not been shyness, as everyone else seemed to assume, but a flash of anger.

"Stop teasing, Sefton," Anna said mildly. "Sophie will dance with you, won't you, Sophie?"

Sefton reached down to Sophie, who took both his hands and was duly whirled round and round until her feet nearly lifted clear of the ground. As they came to a dizzy halt, Sefton stumbled backwards in a pantomime show and deposited Sophie back on to her grassy heap.

"My turn, my turn! I want a whirligig!" shouted Charles, and Sefton picked him up under the armpits and spun round and round until his body swung out in a straight line and one of his shoes flew off and went bouncing across the field. Charles squealed and, once Sefton set him down, set off dizzily to retrieve his shoe, his weaving gait making us all laugh.

"You've set his brain in a spin," I said to Sefton as he sat down again beside Anna and slipped his arm round her waist.

"You should take more water with your ale, Charlie!" Sefton called out.

"How is it going along?" John said, his hand making a sweep that took in the fields behind us that were already cut and those in front and to the left, a vast swathe of green land and hedgerows.

"We've hardly made a dent in it yet," Sefton said. "Overseer says that when we get to that ridge," he pointed to where a line of trees marked a field

123

boundary, "we'll still only have got in the fodder for the horses."

John nodded. "Twelve teams, the marquess had, when I used to work here."

"And a stable block as could house the village," Parker added, breaking off from drawing on his pipe. He picked a shred of tobacco from his tongue and spat absent-mindedly into the hedge.

I gazed across the fields at the house — no, palace I should say, for house is too small a word. Its stone was pale gold in the bright sunlight and it stood four-square in the landscape like some great citadel, with more windows than I could count to. Its lofty central spire was topped by a pennant and the ranked columns of its chimneys clustered thickly at the corner towers or stood like half-built temples in the centre of the vast flat roof. Small octagonal towers were topped with domes the shape of half an onion placed cut side down, their stalks pointing skywards. A balustrade ran round the edge of the roof and for an instant I imagined myself up there, standing at it, heat striking up from acres of stone behind me. How far would I see? Tallington, Helpstone, Stamford, the whole county spread before me, clear as a map, and the dots of colour that were the groups of men and women in the fields, our little group a bright spot next to the green smudge of a hawthorn tree.

Charles limped back over and sat on my knee to have his shoe put back on, the laces being so frayed that once they were loose of the eyelets they were difficult to thread back through.

124

John was still speaking of his time working at Burghley. ". . . A huge table," he was saying, "long enough for forty people, for the staff, you see. The kitchen was as big as a hall, with a high vaulted ceiling and the copper jugs and fish kettles filling the dressers, and copper pans hung all along the walls, ranged from the smallest to the largest, so the cooks could find them." His face took on a dreamy look. "In the candle-light the copper glinted and winked at you like a thousand little flames."

"Did you eat at that big table?" Charles asked.

John laughed. "I ate there once after I was called to see the marquess on account of my poetry, and very grand it was too. But when I worked there, no, I just delivered the vegetables twice a day and dallied on the doorstep, rubbing the toe of one muddy boot on the back of my shin in case the cook should notice my dirty feet and call me 'clod' and box my ears."

"You liked the work, though," Anna ventured. "Being out-of-doors?"

"That was the good part," John said. "The garden master kept everything most orderly and there were rows of carrots and onions stretching as far as you could see. It took all day to hoe them."

"Was he kinder than the cook?" asked Anna, though I knew she had heard these stories many times before.

John snorted. "Hardly. He felt his own consequence a great deal and wore white stockings to show he need not get his own feet dirty. The head kitchen gardener was the worst, though!"

"What did he do?" said Charles, ignoring my attempts to show him how to lick his fingers and thumb and pinch the laces to a point so that they would pass through the eyeholes again.

"He could swear like a soldier and shout fit to burst his waistcoat," John said. "Once, I left some wild flowers in among the leeks — yellow poppies, they were, and the petals were as thin and smooth as silk. I hadn't the heart to root them out."

"What happened?" said Charles.

"He swore so long his face went dark as beetroot, then he kicked the flowers out and docked my wages."

Charles looked over at the house. "Is he still there?" he said, as if afraid of a bogeyman.

John shook his head. "Long in the ground," he said. "He pickled his liver through too many visits to the Hole in the Wall. His wife used to send me to fetch him home but I was too scared to go into the inn, so I used to sleep outdoors and turn up again in the morning when the row was all over."

Parker leant forward and placed the flat of his hand on John's back. "Why didn't you tell us at the time, son?" he said. "We would have had you home, and managed somehow."

John gave a lopsided smile. I thought of what he'd told me in the past: that when he'd slept in the lee of the park wall, too scared to go either forward to the inn at Stamford or back to his lodgings and the wife's wrath, he'd often woken covered with hoar-frost, the whiteness on his clothes and hair powdering as he staggered to his feet.

It was after many such freezing nights that he first experienced the episodes of numbness that overtook him on one side of his body and that led on sometimes to fainting or a fit. I remembered his words from the previous night as he shook with an ague despite all the blankets that I heaped upon him. He had looked at me with his eyes darkened by their widened pupils. "The frost is on me, Patty," he said, "like a winding-sheet." Recalling this, I shivered, despite the heat of the day.

"I won't have to work there, will I?" said Charles.

I tied his shoe-lace in a bow and pulled it tight. "No," I said firmly. "You keep learning your letters like a good boy and maybe you'll be a clerk in a nice warm office." I patted his behind as he scrambled to his feet. "The only dirt on your hands will be ink."

Charles wandered over to Sophie and Eliza, who were sorting through Sophie's pile of gathered grasses to plait the longest stems into a garland. Sophie was chanting their names as she separated them: "Timothy, meadow-fescue, cocksfoot, rye . . ."

John and Anna were still talking of the old days at Burghley, and Sefton, perhaps growing bored, unlinked his arm from Anna's and sauntered over to Eliza and the children. Eliza looked up quickly, then resumed her threading of yarrow and devil's bit through the plaited grasses, bright splashes of white and violet-blue on a vivid green ground. She inclined her head to the work, showing Sefton a studied indifference.

Sefton bent forward to look into her face. "Are you coming to the fair on Saturday?" he asked with a broad smile.

Eliza made no answer.

He turned his attention to Sophie, picked out a buttercup from the pile and held it under her chin. "Look, Charles. Sophie likes butter," he said, tilting the flower to shine sunlight on to her skin.

Charles lifted his head up to receive the same treatment. Sefton tickled him as if by accident with the stem and Charles clamped his chin down and started giggling. "Do Eliza," he said, pushing Sefton's arm away. Before Eliza could speak, Sefton reached across and, with the back of his fingers, lifted her chin. Eliza sat absolutely still. She looked up into Sefton's face as he moved closer and twirled the flower below the white arc of her throat.

"She does like it," Charles said, peering from behind Sefton's arm. "She does like butter."

Quickly, Sefton leant across and whispered something into Eliza's ear. Then, without waiting for an answer, he got up, letting his hand rest for a moment on her shoulder as if it were part of the same movement of rising to his feet. Eliza looked after him as he walked away as though there were words on her lips that she couldn't say. She touched the place at her throat where his hand had been, then brushed the grasses from her lap, rose and strode away along the hedge line. Sophie gazed after her for a moment and then picked up the abandoned garland and began to join it to her own.

As Sefton walked towards us he glanced over his shoulder at Eliza's departing back, then came on with a small smile on his face that I didn't quite like. Just then a shout went up as the overseer broke away from his group and strode towards the line of standing grass, hailing the workers to return from their noonday break.

"Back to work, then," Anna said, planting a kiss on John's cheek.

"Sefton," I said, gesturing to Anna, and he held out his hand to help her up. She pulled herself to her feet and stumbled against him, laughing and using his arm to steady her on the uneven ground.

She said her goodbyes, promising to visit as soon as haymaking was over and they were back in Northborough. "Where's Eliza?" she said when she had hugged everyone else. We scanned the field and spied her talking to a group of girls on the far side of the meadow.

"Tell her goodbye from me," Anna said, busying to replace her bonnet and lay the wide head of the wooden rake over her shoulder, "and that we'll meet her at the fair."

I glanced at Sefton, who had also followed my gaze. "She may not be able to come," I said quickly, though it hurt me to do it. "I may need her at home."

The overseer gave another bellowing shout and the straggling workers picked up their pace and moved towards their allotted spaces.

I embraced Anna closely and noticed again how slight she felt beneath her clothes.

"You look after my girl," I called out to Sefton as they walked away together to take their places.

It was pleasant in the shade and we sat on for a while. As I took in the whole scene, something about the widening stretch of green between Eliza and Anna caught at my heart. I thought of the girls growing up together, and clear as anything a picture of John measuring them against the door jamb at Helpstone came into my head: two little girls in smocked aprons taking turns to stand against it and John cutting notches in the wood and writing initials and the date in pencil beneath, Eliza's "E" following the "A" an inch or so behind each time.

They used to play together for hours in the garden. John kept stock doves for a while and the girls would feed them crumbs to try to entice them close enough to touch. Anna tamed one so that it would take food from her palm, but Eliza was afraid of the bird's sharp beak and pulled her hand back, making the bird flap and flutter and stalk away.

"No. Like this, 'Liza," Anna would say, then Eliza would push Anna's guiding hand away and there were tears of frustration, a bag of crumbs thrown down, and she would hide her face in her apron. Anna was at a loss following these outbursts, for she was a patient, confident child who would meet obstacles with equanimity and work out ways to get round them. She would suggest something else: that they search for the old frog that lived in the stones at the base of the well or that they make a midsummer cushion. Parker would cut a piece of turf and make a box for it and soon Eliza would come to see the pansies and cornbottles Anna had chosen to push into the grassy square and add more flowers of her own.

Generally they would make up quickly and all would be sunny again, but if they were to disagree badly and

Eliza got in such a hip that she would speak to no one, I would take them along Crossberry Way to pick blackberries, or down to the stream. Half an hour of scooping out holes with a stick or an old spoon and trying to catch minnows in cupped hands would always put Eliza back in temper, for here was an activity in which she could excel, being quick-sighted and having dextrous fingers. She had an eye for pattern too and would make a complicated series of tiny dams and runnels with little stones. When they were finished to her satisfaction she would call Anna to see her put in a leaf or twig and they would stand back to watch it float and bob on the water running through from one tiny pool to another. If Anna admired her handiwork Eliza would determinedly say nothing, but her eyes would light up and we would have smiles for the rest of the day.

Their best games were ones where age was no advantage. They had a model village sent them by a friend and admirer of John's. It had a little wooden church and houses and tiny farmhands, thatchers, milkmaids and housewives, and even ducks for the pond, all carved of wood. They would take a figure each and make the two talk to each other, and the exchanges between them used to make me hide a smile. One of them started, "How are your children, Mistress Smith?" to which Eliza replied, "They are all run away to sea and good riddance too, for they fight something terrible. How is your gout?"

When they were a little older we managed to send them, in the months outside harvest time, to a dame in the village to gain a little book learning alongside the skill of lace-making. The old lady was very poor, as she was on her own. All the girls complained that her house was awfully cold in winter and I would send my two in extra flannel petticoats and both with a basket each containing a brick that had been heated overnight in the embers of the fire, for them to put their feet on while they worked. She was a hard task mistress and would make them say their lessons again and again, while they sat bent over their lace-maker's cushions. Eliza took to it well and mastered the art of repeating her multiplication tables at the same time as clicking the bobbins. She took great pride in her work and would lay it out to show us. I would admire the detail and intricacy, saying she had made something fit for a queen, but it was John's voice that she was listening for and only when he smiled and said her handicraft was good would she carefully fold it away in a clean white linen cloth, as if saving his praise along with it. Anna, however, found it difficult enough to make lace without having to recite at the same time and said that splitting her mind in two gave her a headache. John laughed at this and told her that she would still be his dear girl even if what she produced was a tangle of knots.

When the old dame died, Eliza could already do quite complicated patterns and earned by the piece, selling handkerchief corners and pillow lace to a draper's shop in Stamford. Anna, though, had to give it up, for she has a long back and couldn't stand the constant stooping over the hard cushion and her headaches worsened along with her handwriting. I realized then that her eyes had been overstrained by the close work and rued the day that I had ever sent her to the dame school. At length, she gave up book learning altogether and helped me in the house. I was mighty glad of the extra help, as by then there were the three boys and Sophie, and baby Charles on the way.

When, eventually, machines started to be used for pillow lace and Eliza's draper said that he could buy all he wanted from a workshop at a fraction of the price, Eliza joined us in keeping house. She was once more frustrated with the sense of lagging behind, for Anna had become a practised hand at breadmaking and cooking and knew what should be cleaned with bicarbonate of soda and what should be polished with a cloth dampened with milk, whereas Eliza had it all to learn. I was happy to teach her: with a good-sized family, the round of washing and ironing, tailoring and mending, digging and hoeing, getting windows cleaned and floors swept, meals on and off the table and pots washed never lets up.

She has become a good housewife and I couldn't manage without her now that Anna has gone. Sometimes I wonder, though, if she misses the skilled work she used to do. It must feel a little like biding time at home with us at Northborough, which is too small to provide any entertainment and has so few families that there are no young people of her own age save those that are already wed. I have been trying to send her on more errands in the hope that she will come across old friends in Market Deeping, but recently she has been sometimes so quiet and subdued: she seems reluctant to go and, when she does, is home again so quickly that I know she hasn't dallied to chat with anyone at all. When I try to open the subject of meeting new people, she quickly closes it again and says that she is quite happy as she is, but I cannot help but feel for her, especially now that Anna has a household of her own.

I sighed, and began gathering up the pitchers and the papers that the food had been wrapped in. Anna and Sefton had returned to work. The group of girls Eliza had been talking to were making their way slowly towards the line and Eliza was heading back towards us. I raised my hand in a cheery wave and she raised hers in return.

By the time I had re-packed the basket, work on the field had resumed for all and the sounds of the swishing scythes and the click of the whetstones travelled to us across the meadow. The men and women moved in their respective parallel lines, separated by a wide band of green. The ranked, blank windows of the Hall stared out over the fields as the mowers toiled, small as emmets in a green world.

CHAPTER
EIGHT

Hay Carts and Iron Horses

When Eliza returned she pointed over the fields behind us and we turned to see the hay carts trundling in, each one pulled by a shire-horse and laden with men and women, who swayed with the motion of the horses' steps and jounced and bounced together when the huge cartwheels hit uneven ground.

One stopped at the headland and all the passengers climbed down, save two men who gathered up armfuls of two-tined pitchforks from the base of the cart and passed them down to the people below.

"Can I go and see the horses?" Charles said.

"Can I too?" asked Sophie.

The other two hay carts continued further into the field, one stopping a third of the way over and the other two thirds, so that the field was divided into three.

"They're going to be busy," I said. "It's probably best not to get in their way."

"Please, pleeeease," Charles said, tugging on my arm. "Eliza will come with us, won't you, 'Liza?"

"Oh, all right, then," I said. "If you go on ahead with Eliza you can give them a pat when they stop. We'll follow on after."

The children started off with Eliza; I picked up the basket to follow after.

John plucked at my sleeve. "I wish you hadn't let them go," he said. "You know how dangerous carting hay can be. I told you about Thomas Drake, remember?"

I did indeed remember, for John as a youngster had witnessed Thomas Drake slip and fall from a loaded hay cart and break his neck. He had told me that the sight of the man's pallid face and his eyes, emptied of life, had stayed with him and given him nightmares of open graves and charnel houses for many weeks afterwards.

"They will be perfectly safe with Eliza," I said firmly. "This is just a morbid fear that lingers with you, John," but he had already begun to follow them across the field. I sighed and, hefting the basket up on to my arm, hurried to catch up with him. "Look," I said, "they won't be climbing in the carts. Anyway, there is barely any hay in them yet."

The carts were moving slowly along the windrows, stopping every few yards for the workers to pitch the hay up on to the wagon, whereupon the man aloft piled it evenly so that it would be stable as the load increased. As yet, no cart had hay reaching above its wooden side.

Nonetheless, John quickened his pace, trying to reduce the distance between him and the children as if he wished to snatch them up and swoop them away. Eliza had caught up with Sophie and they were walking together, deep in conversation, but Charles ran on

136

ahead lickety-spit until he came through the gate and into the field. He bent to pull some handfuls of long sweet grass from beside the gate post, then ran on again towards the nearest wagon. Sensibly, he crossed the line of hay that the labourers were pitching and went behind the cart, giving a wide berth to the sharp prongs of the pitchfork tines. I was struggling along with the basket, trying to catch up with John, but when Charles disappeared behind the cart and was no longer in view it proved too much for John and he began to run.

"John! Wait!" I shouted, for I could see from my more oblique angle what he could not: that Charles was safe on the far side, at the horse's head, and was holding a bundle of grass flat on his hand for the great beast to take, just as I had taught him, and that the driver was bending forward to say something to Charles.

I became acutely aware of every detail around me. I saw the other labourers stand back as the last bundle of hay was pitched into the cart.

I saw John, assuming that the cart would now move forward and that his son was somewhere in the way, start waving his arms and shouting, "No! Look out! Stop!"

As if the world had suddenly slowed in its turning I saw the carter swivelling in his seat to see what the noise was, and, with the reins still in his hands, pulling the horse's head round so that it shook its great neck, jangling the heavy brasses, and began to move forward, pulling the weight of the cart behind it. I heard the cry "Whoah!" go up from the labourers and saw the carter trying to rein in the horse. As I dropped the basket and took to my heels myself, I saw a flash of colour through the horse's legs and a gasp went up from everyone.

My heart pounded at my ribs as I ran, and I saw the carter get control of the horse again and draw it to a halt some yards further along the row; the horse stamped its huge feathered front legs and blew down its nose a snorting breath. From behind the cart a man appeared, carrying Charles, thank God, against his chest. Everyone gathered round, exclaiming, and John took our boy, still clutching a handful of grass, from the man and clasped him tight, holding his fair head against his shoulder. As I reached the group he was thanking him, and the driver, looking white, was still swearing under his breath.

John turned to me. "You see!" he shouted. "Whatever were you thinking of? He could have been trampled underfoot!"

"What do you mean?" I said. "It was you, running at the horse like that and shouting! You frighted it, coming up from behind with all that noise."

"Don't talk such rubbish, woman," John said. "The child should never have been let go in the first place."

There was a stir among the labourers and the one who'd snatched Charles up shifted from foot to foot. I buttoned my tongue and reached for Charles, who was looking from one to the other of us. As John passed him to me he scrambled to the ground and ran to stand with Sophie and Eliza. I took a deep breath. "Thank you," I said to the man. "You've been very kind. Come, John, we must get home," and I made to lead him away. John brushed me off and strode away towards the gate, leaving the rest of us to wait for Parker, who was struggling along, trying to manage both basket and thumb-stick, and who now approached with a puzzled look on his face.

I nodded my thanks and apologies again to the company and the carter, took the basket from Parker and followed the others with as much dignity as I could manage. I felt John's rebuke that I had not behaved as a good mother should as sharp as a bee sting, for I had been caring for the whole family these last four years without a husband's support and playing the part of both mother and father.

I had nursed Sophie and Charles through their childhood illnesses, done my best to discipline William and keep him on the narrow path, and gone without in order to feed the others when Jack broke his leg and couldn't work. I had dug, sown, hoed and harvested, washed and mended, cooked and baked to keep them fed, clothed and respectable.

I knew my children inside out, their strengths and weaknesses and what they could and couldn't do, and I knew that Charles was perfectly safe around horses. As long as no one else made them bolt, I thought, as I laboured across the field, my ankles prickled by the hay stubble and my aching arms bitten by the tiny insects disturbed by the mowing.

The sun beat down on us and we walked in single file just inside the wall, though it afforded little shade. John led the way and by mutual consent we set out on the walk to the estate entrance, in consideration of Parker whose wall-climbing days were long over.

As we toiled along in the heavy heat Parker lagged ever-further behind, so I stopped and waited for him to catch up. We went on together at a slower pace and I explained what had happened with Charles and the horse and John's reaction.

He frowned. "It's true it was a terrible business when Thomas Drake died. He was a grown man, you know, churchwarden, well known in the village, and John only a lad with barely a hair on his chin." He paused to take out his handkerchief from his breeches pocket and wipe his face, his bald crown and the back of his neck. "It was the work of a moment, apparently. One minute he was atop the load on the cart, laughing at some quip made by his partner; the next . . ." Parker sighed. "It must have seemed to John that if it could happen to Thomas, a man in his prime, snuffed out like a candle, it could happen to anybody."

"It would have been a shock for anyone," I granted.

Parker nodded. "But with John, such things work on his imagination and plague his dreams. Afterwards he grew morbid, fearing hobgoblins and will-o'-the-wisps from the fen, ghosts in the churchyard and all the old flim-flam that's talked late at night in an alehouse."

"Well, at forty-eight years old it's time he grew out of it," I said, more sharply than I'd meant, for I still smarted from his harsh words to me in front of strangers. "I just wish he could hold his tongue a little. Whatever he thinks, he says straight out with no thought of how it will be taken."

Parker gave a wry smile. "I think we both know that John gets more outspoken as he grows older." He looked ahead to where John was striding out at a pace that none of us could hope to match, the set of his shoulders stiff and stubborn. "He feels everything too deeply. He's like an onion without its skin. Unprotected." He looked at my downcast face and took my arm. "Well, you know what happens if you pierce an onion. It'll have you in tears over the slightest scratch." He sighed. "It's just so with the fearful: they attack most viciously when they're most afraid."

Ahead of us, John had finally stopped to wait for us at the entrance to the estate and the others had caught up.

"Will you forgive him, then, Patty?" Parker said as we approached.

I made no reply, but seeing my family gathering together once more my heart softened and yearned for harmony between us. When we reached them I set the basket down and passed round the pitcher so that we could finish the dregs of the small-beer. I found a few strawberries rolling among the leaves in the bottom of the basket and when no one was watching I picked them out and put them into Charles's hand and saw his face brighten.

As we rejoined the road back towards Helpstone, my eye was caught by a plume of smoke rising from a field on our left just inside the hedge.

"Whatever is that?" I said, for the smoke was behaving most strangely — not rising in a continuous column as one would expect on a still day, nor yet billowing as if someone were flapping at a fire to put it out. Rather, it came in regular spurts as if being puffed out by huge bellows.

"It's a dragon asleep under the hedge," Parker said mischievously to Charles.

Charles looked askance at me.

"It is not," I said firmly.

"Snoring," Sophie said.

"Sophie . . ." I warned.

"Waiting to eat little boys who don't share what they've got with their sister," she said, making a grab for the last of the strawberries.

"It smells sulphureous," John said. "Phew! Bad eggs," he added with a wink to Charles.

By this time we were almost level with the field and could see that the gate was open and the smoke was coming from a spot just a little further on. We walked on at a smarter pace, for we were all curious to know what was happening in the field, and as a group we turned in at the gate and then stopped in a huddle.

At the edge of a field of straw stubble was a huge machine. It had six wheels, each one as tall as a man with a boy on his shoulders. On a platform slung between the axles stood an engine and two enormous drums, with the thickest chain I have ever seen wound round them. The whole was topped by a sloping roof and through this protruded a tall, black metal chimney, from which the smoke came in great huffs. Charles took one look at it and grabbed on to his father's leg, and, truth to tell, the engine made such a racket, such a puffing and clanking, that I too took a step back, for fear that it would imminently explode.

A man appeared from behind the monstrosity, carrying two empty buckets. He set them down and gave us a cheery wave.

"It's Toby Bainbridge, the blacksmith from the estate," John said, and we all pressed forward to greet him. I saw from the black dust in the bottom of the buckets that they had been full of coal.

"What do you think? Isn't she fine?" said Toby, as though the machine were a mare or a prize heifer.

"But what's it for?" said Parker.

For answer Toby led us round to the other side of the machine, John firmly holding Charles's hand. He swept his arm across to take in the whole field before us: "Ploughing," he said.

We could now see that the chains, which all this time had been slowly moving, extended the breadth of the whole field and passed round another, smaller, carriage with pulleys on the other side. The whole contraption was being used to haul a plough, which, guided by a ploughman in his usual cotton smock and battered hat, was moving through the earth like a knife taking a curl of butter. It turned a single furrow, the dug earth dark as tea-leaves against the pale stubble. At the other side of the field a further ploughman and a carter looked on. A water cart was parked beside the engine, its horse taking advantage of its redundancy to pull mouthfuls of fresh leaves from the hedge.

"Well, I never," said Parker, "ploughing in a July like this! The earth's baked as hard as ship's biscuit." He tutted in disbelief. "It must be a master powerful engine to plough three-horse land in July."

Toby stood with his hands on his hips, surveying the field with a broad grin on his face. "'Tis a Heathcoat and Parkes steam plough," he said.

"Aah," said John. "I read in the newspaper about the trials up in Lancashire. Bog land, wasn't it? Up at Red Moss?"

"That was the first trial. It went on to Lochar Moss in Scotland later but, sadly, it never came back," said Toby, his gaze all the time following the motion of the plough. "They dug two ditches to drain the land it was to sit upon, but it came too close to the spongy edge and tipped sideways and, well, that was that."

We all turned to look at the mammoth machine, thirty tons or so of worked metal. I imagined its slow descent into the bog, the great gulp of air displaced as it sank beneath the morass, the impossibility of ever reclaiming it.

"Blimey!" said Charles.

"How long does it take to plough an acre?" John asked thoughtfully.

"Just under the two-hour mark," Toby answered.

"Two hours!" said Parker. "It's a marvel."

John was shaking his head. "It'll put our men out of work," he said. "There will be tilled fields and no money for the bread that's grown in them."

Just then the ploughman gave a shout, "Landfast!" and seemed to struggle with the plough, which must have hit a stone or an old tree root. The chain, already taut, pulled even tighter. Toby rushed over to the engine, checked its gauges quickly and pulled a lever down to give the engine more steam. Instinctively I

144

drew Sophie and Eliza back from the thing and gestured to John to do the same with Charles.

Toby leant sharply on the lever to open out with all the steam he had to try to release the plough. I feared that the chain would break under the strain and recoil like a whiplash. I pushed Sophie behind me and shut my eyes. There was a shout, "Clear!" from the ploughman and when I opened my eyes again the ploughshare was once more moving away from us, and Toby was wiping his hands on his jacket.

Parker said, "I can see you need a cool head for the job."

"That's what His Lordship said when he asked me," Toby said. "'Tis a responsible job and it needs a steady-going man to do it."

Still feeling shaken, I asked, "Aren't you worried that the chain might break?"

Toby grinned. "It's true the chain does break sometimes, or the strain flips the plough out of the earth, and then the ploughman must be very nimble!"

I shuddered. "And what if the boiler becomes overheated?" I asked. "Might it not . . .?"

Toby gave a bellowing laugh. "I've been a blacksmith this thirty years or more," he said. "I've learnt to respect the element I work in." He held out his arm and pushed back his sleeve. His hands were covered by small marks where the skin was smooth and shiny as glass, while on the pale inside of his arm a dark-red patch extended from wrist to elbow: such a weal as made me suck my breath between my teeth.

He ran his finger down the scar and touched the raised twist of skin at his wrist. "I slipped," he said, "and my arm touched the anvil." He glanced at the huge cylinders behind him. "You have to check the boiler plate for rust or fracture lines." He fumbled at the fastening of his shirtsleeve and I helped him. "Mind, my eyes aren't as good as they were," he said. "It's a relief to work without metal that's white-hot. You get so as you have it imprinted on your sight even in sleep."

The plough had now reached the pulley at the carriage on the far side of the field and the other ploughman and the water-cart man joined together to manhandle the heavy plough round the pulley and into position for the home run, leaning on its long handles to swing it over and into the next furrow line.

"Nine inches deep, it ploughs," Toby said. "None of that shallow ploughing that boys do after late nights at the alehouse; better yields and more food for all."

"More food for those with wages in their pockets," John said stubbornly, and although I stiffened, sensing that John would grow belligerent on this subject, I did agree and was proud of him for speaking out.

"You blame the landowners, then?" Toby said, half joking. "You are a rebel and a Whig now, eh, John?"

"I am neither, sir," John replied, "but that doesn't mean what is happening is right."

"It's progress, son," Parker said mildly, meaning to smooth over the disagreement, but John dashed his hand against his leg, saying, "Progress be damned! What is behind it is the same thing that fenced off the heath, so that a man cannot pasture his cow nor collect his kindling, nor even walk straight across it to get from village to village, but must wind and wend and go long ways round." He jabbed his finger at the air to emphasize his points. "It's the same thing that ripped out the old trees and tore down the stiles and turned the very streams in their courses so that our three common fields and Emmonsales Heath could be parcelled out instead of shared, and old tenants thrown off their land to make way for upstarts who can pay the higher rents!" He took a deep breath, then blew it out again. "Pah! Progress! It's nothing but another name for greed!" He scowled at the approaching plough as though he would halt it in its tracks and turn it to rust.

Parker scratched his head. "You have a point, son," he said.

Toby opened his mouth to reply to John, but John held up his hand. "It's true what I've said. Take our friends the Turnills. They farmed at Helpstone for generations past and paid their rent in corn and chickens. Suddenly it's to be ready cash, and when they haven't got it they're turned off their land without compensation."

Toby remained quiet, for he, as well as the rest of us, knew the Turnills and the decline of their fortunes, and others, like the Jacksons, who had less to start with: a few strips of land and a beast or two. They had ended at the poor house. We all stood silent, watching the steady approach of the plough, bearing down towards us.

At length, John spoke again, but this time in a dreamy tone. "As a boy I used to love to plough," he said, "even if it meant getting up in the dark and blowing on my thumb-nails to get life into my hands. Once the sun was up, the dew sparkled on every blade and leaf and there was nothing but the plod of the horse and the singing of the birds. You could fancy yourself the only man in the world." He sighed. "You could walk free from all the troubles that congregate like flies on meat wherever men gather together."

As the plough grew close and the ploughman hailed us, Toby made preparations to move the whole engine a few feet further along the headland, ready to plough the next strip. He climbed up on to the platform and checked the winding gear and steam gauges again. The plough arrived along with the men and John and Parker stood aside while they detached it from the chain to allow the engine to move forward. Round the rims of its tall wheels ran an endless track, a jointed band of metal that spread the heavy weight and stopped the wheels digging into the earth and sticking fast. On one of these tracks a dandelion had stuck and as the huge bulk began to creep forward Charles watched, as if hypnotized, the weed's slow progress up the back wheel, along the sagging stretch under the roof, and down the front wheel, where it was squashed flat as a thruppenny bit into the ground.

Toby halted the machine and jumped down again. Deep, straight tracks were imprinted on the earth, the stubble pushed down into it. Charles picked up the dandelion and showed it to me. It was dry as a pressed flower, all the juice squeezed out of it. We wondered over it and Charles put it away in his pocket to add to his collection of curiosities: smooth stones and pooty shells, a pencil stub and a tinder-box. We said our farewells and left the men to their work. As we made our way along the road the puffing and mechanical clanking gradually faded until it was no more than a faint hooshing, clinking sound and the tang of sulphur was replaced by the smell of woodbine and wild garlic from the hedgerow.

CHAPTER
NINE

The Ash Grove

That evening, when all my chores were done and the family sat reading or dozing or playing at pontoon, I slipped out while the light was still good and went down to the orchard. The evening air cooled my face, which was hot from kitchen work. There was not the slightest breeze and the apple trees pointed their long shoots to the sky, disturbed only by the occasional shake of a leaf or two as a sparrow entered or left the branches. The ash tree at the far side of the orchard towered above all, thirty or forty feet high and in full leaf, with a tall oval crown; it cast a deep pool of shade across the ground. Around its base many little ash plants grew, some shoulder-high, some as yet only up to my knee: new life shaken from the clusters of ash-keys that hung thickly there each year. Parker, who normally liked all to be shipshape and tidy, far from rooting them out, tended these treelets as if they were his offspring. One spring he had got Freddy to dig up the plants with the strongest growth, then cut off most of their length and all of the side shoots save one, and replant them with the stub of trunk under the ground and the side shoot as the new sapling.

I had no understanding why Parker would want to grow a tree on its side or what he was up to. When I asked him his reason for growing a thicket of ash that would eventually be wholly impenetrable, he would tap the side of his nose and say that I should wait and see and that he had a plan to bring in a little money. So I left well alone and didn't question him further, only sometimes commenting to please him that such and such a plant was doing well or that such and such another had a blighted shoot that might need cutting away. Over time I had become attached to the scheme despite being unaware of its end, so that when John returned and questioned the need for a nursery of ash that wouldn't yield firewood in our lifetime I found myself joining Parker in its defence and John had shrugged and been persuaded to indulge his father.

As I walked down among the saplings, enjoying the coolness of the shade and the softness of the grass beneath my feet, I started to look over the plants in my usual fashion. I stooped to each one and lifted the new shoots to check beneath and pick off any tiny insects from the underside of the long, pointed leaves. As I fell into the rhythm of the repetitive action, my mind wandered through the day and my thoughts came to rest on Anna. There had been something different . . . something that made me uneasy. She had seemed cheerful enough, but I felt concerned that after working from seven in the morning she had such little appetite. She had shadows under her eyes. She seemed thin. Perhaps she hadn't been eating well for a while? She was exactly as I had been when . . . The thought that

151

had been at the back of my mind, eluding me, suddenly took shape. Of course, I was sure if it: she was going to have a child. I stopped what I was doing, my hand still holding a tiny twiggy branch. Sure enough, it was only to be expected; they were newly-wed and, as it says in the service, *marriage is for the making of children*, so why did my heart beat so wildly and why did I not know whether to be sorry or glad for Anna?

I tried to catch my quick thoughts and lay them out for inspection. My first-born child was, in turn, to have a child of her own. It made me feel both proud and fearful at one and the same time. My little Anna grown to be a mother! I prayed that all would be well with the baby. Memories of my own two lost little ones rose up before me: the empty place in the bed where they should have lain, the cold touch of my pillow wet with tears. Quickly, I closed my mind against the familiar pain, shutting it back into my heart like a box that must always stay closed, but other fears rose in its place. Anna was so slight, her figure still more girl than woman . . . the birth might not be straightforward . . . already she didn't seem well. Northborough was so small, no midwife lived here . . . I took a deep breath to calm myself. It was clear what must be done: I would attend her, and Eliza would help. I clenched my jaw. I had borne nine children, not all of them easily, and three had come too fast for help to be at hand. I would think back to my own labours and I would know what to do.

I let the green pointed leaves slip through my fingers, each one perfectly formed, then moved to the next plant, a taller sapling, which grew straight and strong but had one broken shoot. I nipped it off in case it should infect the whole, leaving a pale bark-stripped mark.

My mind flew back to my own first discovery that I was with child. I tried not to overlay what would surely be a joy for Anna with my own experience, which was far from joyful, yet the memory once started would not be stemmed and flowed over me, carrying me along.

I had not wanted to believe it. John and I were not even betrothed; it was not possible! And yet my treacherous body tired and paled, my hand flew often to my mouth at the farming smells that were once familiar and ignored, my head turned away from the plate of good cooked food set down before me. I pretended that it wasn't so, choosing to believe my own lies to my family that I had been too long in the sun, had suffered a sleepless night, had spent too long doing fine needlework — anything that would allow me to plead a headache and retire to my room and out from under my mother's eye. All the while, I knew in my heart what had happened. I even knew when I had fallen for the child.

A mossy bank beside a slowly winding stream. The sun on our heads and the sound of the water making us languorous. Kingcups and cushioned ease. A kiss for a poem and another for itself. Shoes and stockings taken off for toes to feel the silk cool of water weed.

An eagerness grown week by week after the first time, to touch, to taste, to hold. Our legs still chill from the water, our hands and bellies hot. John silhouetted above me, the sun blinding behind his head and shoulders as I pulled him into my arms and hid myself in his shadow. Losing myself utterly and yet knowing that I had been found. Trusting him.

Afterwards, the brightness of the sun fell upon our limbs, whitening them and painting the moss a verdant green; beside my face, each tiny filament glowed as if charged full of sunlight. I felt different: my limbs heavier, my blood as slow as syrup. I felt as if inside me something had opened, like the trumpet of a flower, open to the bee. I said nothing to John, not knowing how to explain the feeling nor wanting to seem a silly girl, but kept my wonder to myself and simply kissed him and laced my fingers between his as we lay.

It was only as my body changed and the sickness started that I realized what had taken place that day, and became afraid of what it would mean.

Two months passed and still I had told no one, neither John nor my parents. Then, as the cold weather came in, John's employer, Mr Wilders, had less gardening work for him and cut his wages. There was nothing for it, he had to go home to Helpstone and I had missed my chance to tell him. The period that followed was one of the worst times of my life.

I shook my head, as if to dispel my thoughts, and, leaving the saplings, walked through the deep shade of the ash where the starnels were now gathering to roost with a great fluttering and chattering noise. Reaching the fence that bounded the orchard, I looked out over the level pasture where distant cattle gleamed pale and moved like slow ghosts, or stood horned and heavy-headed, chewing the cud. The sky was red at the horizon, etching the sparse lines of trees in black straggles on the level landscape.

I sighed as the memories returned, tenacious as the gnats that danced in the twilight in front of me and could not be batted away.

John's visits had become less frequent, but this didn't worry me at first. Helpstone was a fair step and he had told me that a bookseller in Stamford was interested in publishing his poems and that he was busy pursuing this. He was trying to canvass support among the gentry and looking for a patron who would perhaps get up a subscription for a volume. I welcomed this development with joy as I knew that it would make John happy and because I hoped to be able to soften my parents' feeling towards him before the result of our amorous connections became obvious. I remembered his sweet words to me and thought of him working hard to raise himself in the world so that my father would have no reason to oppose a marriage.

Then, one day, on an errand for my mother in Market Deeping, Polly and I were at the grocer's, waiting to buy candles and tea, when Sarah Eaves and Jane Woodman came into the shop and waited behind us. They had always been unfriendly to me when we were at school together, calling me a dunce because I couldn't master my letters, so I hoped that our quick

155

"Good day" would be the start and end of the conversation, but they were not put off so easily.

"I hear your young man is quite the poet," Sarah said.

"With verses in the newspaper," added Jane, nudging Sarah's arm and sniggering.

I glanced quickly at Polly to see if she knew of this and Sarah caught the glance as quick as a terrier is on to a rat.

"Patty doesn't read the papers," she said.

"Nor yet perhaps his letter," said Jane, and they laughed again.

"Why, what do you mean?" I said. "What letter?" though Polly was plucking at my sleeve to draw me forward to our turn at the counter.

"The letter as says what is hard to say face to face," Sarah said. "Or that's what folks are saying Helpstone way."

Polly was holding the bag open for the shopkeeper's wife to tip in the measure of tea, but at this she twisted round with a look fit to freeze lightning.

"Sarah Eaves!" she said. "Your tongue was always as loose as a sheet on a line. Say what you know straight out or hold your gabble."

Jane began to look in her purse as if wishing that she could shrink to a Tom Thumb and hide in its corners, for Polly is fearsome when roused.

Sarah, though, stiffened her shoulders and poked her head forward towards us. "Why, Betty Sells," she said. "Everyone knows John Clare has been going with Betty Sells again ever since he went home."

156

The shopkeeper's wife tutted and took the bag from Polly. As if in a dream I watched her twist and secure the packet. I felt as if my blood was draining to my boots and I leant upon the counter.

"Absolute nonsense," Polly said, looking Sarah in the eye.

"Fetch a seat for the young lady, Mr Darnley," the wife called to her husband, and he came out from behind a curtain at the back of the shop carrying a stool, which he passed over the counter to Polly.

She helped me down on to it, as my legs would scarcely bear my weight. I had heard the name Betty Sells linked with that of one lad after another, she being both pretty and free with her favours.

Sarah had blushed red to the roots of her hair under Polly's fierce gaze but still managed to say, "'Tis not nonsense. 'Tis the talk of the villages," before turning on her heel and walking out of the shop.

Jane did not follow her at once but stood looking at me strangely, her eyes wide with curiosity as, overcome by a sick, faint feeling, I lowered my head to my knees. Then I saw Polly's dress in front of me as she stood between me and my tormentors and bent to place her hand on my back, and I heard the shop bell clang as Jane pulled the door shut sharply behind her.

I could hear the shopkeeper muttering to his wife; odd words seemed to drift by my muzzy head. The names "John Clare" and "Betty Sells" were linked together in their talk and the man used a word I didn't know: "Cyprian". The wife shushed and tutted at it, but I caught the man's voice again, saying "more than willing" and "for the price of a pair of gloves", and then I understood.

And this was only the beginning. The following Sunday, I was to meet John. I stood waiting at the stile where we usually met, stamping my feet to keep out the cold and damp. It was November and no longer good weather for walking out. In my head, I rehearsed what I would say. I would tell him my news: that we had fallen into the trouble that only marriage could mend. I would trust in his reassurance of love; his arms around me would show me that his heart was still mine. He would kiss away my tears and whisper the promises that would be my spell to ward off fears and false rumours.

He did not come. I paced and stamped, and stamped and paced, my shawl clutched ever tighter round me as the cold bit. I waited hours. I watched the shadows of the furze bushes lengthen and the watery sun sink down towards the copse until its edge brushed the trees and I knew he would not come. I pulled my shawl up over my head, so that anyone I might meet would not see my stricken face, and set off for home, my steps slow despite the cold, for in my mind I heard a small voice saying, "What will become of me? What will become of me?"

All through November my misery grew. There was no word from John. Polly let slip to my mother that we were no longer walking out together and, while it explained away my pale face and red eyes and thereby eased my burden of pretence, my mother's sympathy and attentions were hot coals heaped upon my head.

She set about trying to distract me from "pining". She invited neighbours to visit to provide entertainment, but their talk of other pairings and weddings, deaths and births was like pins stuck in my sides. She bought me trifles, brooches and ribbons and made tentative mention of *other fish in the sea* and a certain shoemaker, at which I turned my head away in case she should see the panic in my eyes. She baked pastries and pies to tempt my appetite and was at her wits' end when I could not stomach them. Finally, my father got wind of John's departure and announced his intention of renewing our acquaintance with the family of the shoemaker and I could no longer stay quiet.

As he sat down to write the letter, I asked Polly to fetch Mother to me in my bedroom. There, sitting together on the edge of my bed where once I had lain with my heart abuzz and with my head full of romantic dreams of John, I told her the truth of the matter. It was worse then ever I had imagined, for instead of rebuking me she held my hand and comforted me, saying all would come right, but there were tears on her face as she pressed her cheek to mine.

At length she told me to stay in my room until she sent for me and she went downstairs to talk to Father. The quiet mutter of her voice was soon followed by the bellow of Father's as he questioned her. "How could you have let this happen? Did you not realize the shame that it would bring on the family? Is that why Patty has been mooning about, whey-faced, this past few weeks?" A stream of questions with no pause to let Mother answer, then a bang as he closed the lid of his bureau in the study and a bad-mouthing of John such as I had never heard my father utter, nor ever thought he knew such words.

Mother remonstrated with him but to no effect; he continued, raising his voice to drown her out. I brought my feet up on to the bed, curled my arms round my knees and rested my forehead upon them. I heard Polly come into the house but there was not let-up in Father's tirade, so I guessed that she had had the sense not to go into the parlour. Then there was the creak of the stair and the tap of fingernails on my door. She slipped round the door and closed it behind her.

"Whatever is it?" she said.

"Mother and Father know," I gulped.

Polly sat beside me and put her arm round me. "They'll come round," she said, but now there were two raised voices coming from downstairs and their tone belied it.

"Father's never going to forgive me for this," I said. "It will be all round the parish."

I felt Polly shift slightly and looked up to see that her face was grim.

"What?" I whispered. "What's the matter?"

She squeezed my shoulder harder. "Only Sarah Eaves's gossip. No one will pay any mind to it."

"Tell me," I said, my hand gripping Polly's.

Polly dropped her eyes from mine as if she couldn't bear to see the pain that her news would bring. "She has been saying that you are with child and that neither the poet nor the shoemaker knows which of them is the father."

"But I never . . . Why would she do such a thing?"

"I feel I am to blame," Polly said miserably. "It's the bloody nose I gave her at the grocer's that's made her rise to this new spite."

My knuckles whitened as I gripped Polly's hand still tighter. "How far abroad has the rumour spread?" I said, the full import of it now hitting me like a blast of icy air. "What if John hears of this and doubts me?" I began to rock to and fro, hugging my knees, saying, "What have I done? Oh, what have I done?"

At length the voices downstairs lowered and then, a little later still, Father went out. Mother came upstairs to us, her eyes red, and told us to come down to the kitchen to take some dinner. We sat together, but it was a silent affair and I could scarcely eat a bite, for my feelings kept rising in my throat to choke me. She told us that Father had agreed to write to John, making no mention of the circumstances but simply inviting him to visit. Polly nodded encouragement and squeezed my hand beneath the tablecloth, but I feared that the combined weight of John having found another and his hearing the world's rumours about me would overtip the balance of his esteem for me and he would refuse and stay away. Mother passed her hand over her face and said that we must carry on as normal and that sitting about would not get the chores done. She set Polly to washing dishes and sent me out to feed the hens.

I shook some grain into a wide pan and went out to the yard at the back of the house, where the birds pushed around my feet, their tawny feathers brushing my dress and their scaly feet scratching on my boots as they scrabbled for the first dropping of grain. The beaten earth of the yard was hard from the cold and worms hard to find. I threw the grain out further to disperse the flock and they scrambled and gobbled for it. I looked around for the cockerel and spotted him at the far side of the yard, flapping and pecking at something. I waded through the warm softness of the gathered chickens and found that he was atop one of the hens, his beak gripping her neck so that she was unable to move and sat heavy down upon the ground. The flesh of her back showed through where the feathers had been plucked by the cockerel's pecking and clawing, and stubby quills pointed hither and thither where others had been broken off.

Suddenly overcome with anger I took my foot to the cockerel and toppled him off her, holding him back with the toe of my boot, which he pecked to no avail while she limped away towards the food. I let him up and he stalked off, his wattles shaking as he poked his head forward, the very picture of injured pride.

I returned to my feeding, clicking at the hens as I always do. I was beginning to be able to see the bottom of the pan, so I squatted down to tip out the remainder in front of the injured bird. As I scattered it, some fell not on the earth but on a harder surface that made a sharper noise. My father's boots. I looked up at his gaiters, his belt, his work-coat, his face. What I saw written there made me scramble quickly to my feet. I held the pan flat against my belly.

162

He looked down at the pan. "Well may you hide it from view," he said. "You have every reason to be ashamed of yourself."

I looked at him beseechingly.

"I can barely believe what you've done," he said. "Are you happy now?"

I hung my head and made no reply.

"My daughter wed to a jack-of-all-trades! Even if he marries you I shall have red ears each time I go to market. And if he doesn't, no one else will and you'll be hiding at home, afraid to show your face! Do you have no foresight? Didn't you once think of the consequences?"

I stared at the ground, not daring to reply.

"Thank God we live well away from the village or we should be in danger of low belling," he said, running his hand through his hair as if at his wits' end.

At this I looked up sharply, for I was afraid. It had happened to a woman in Maxey who had children by different fathers. The villagers came under cover of darkness, beating their pots and clashing their pans together. The mob surrounded the house and kept on coming every night with their infernal din, until within the week the woman moved on.

Father shook his head slowly. "You could have had a good life with Thomas Butterworth, a respectable husband with a business to inherit, but would you heed your parents' advice?"

"I didn't love him," I said in a small voice.

He snorted. "Love! Who's talking of love! A lime-burner, Patty, a common labourer. You won't talk

163

of love when there's no bread on the table or money for the rent."

"I couldn't help it. Thomas was your choice, not mine," I said, my voice beginning to waver. "You were the one who wanted a good match and money in the bank and never cared to ask me what I thought."

"You think it was for my own good! That I would seek to benefit from your marriage! After the cares I've taken . . . After wanting only the best for my girls . . ." His mouth worked, his beard jutting forward. He took in a long breath. "And if even the lime-burner won't have you, what about Polly?" he said. "Have you thought what your ruin would do to her prospects?"

This cut into my heart, for, being young and thoughtless, in truth I had never thought once of the effect on Polly — and my flush must have showed it, for he pressed his advantage.

"I've promised your mother that I will write and invite him to visit, but there my involvement will end. Let us hope he will marry you," he said. "If he will not, then I'll have to send Polly away in the hope that she meets someone who doesn't know our sorry history."

My tears began to fall then and I held my hand out towards him. He put his own behind him and clasped them behind his back.

"I will have none of you," he said. "You have made yourself a hard bed and now you must lie on it," and he left me and went back into the house, closing the door quietly behind him.

At my feet, the chickens pecked disconsolately at the frozen ground and squabbled over a few stray bits of chaff that blew hither and thither about the yard.

In the days after Mother took the letter to the post office at Market Deeping I swung from hope to despair, back and forth, like the pendulum of our grandmother clock. I imagined John visiting with news of his imminent publication and setting all right by asking my father for my hand. Next minute I would be convinced that he would not answer at all: Father had not made him welcome in the past and John, I knew, was sensitive to the smallest slight. The treatment that Father had dealt him on his visit to our house, accentuating his inferior station and belittling his attempts to raise himself through his writing, smote John hard. He was often tongue-tied in the face of authority and Father had not only the advantage of years and status but also his power as the head of the household to which I belonged. It would not come easy to John to answer an invitation from one who he felt had demeaned and spurned him.

Nonetheless, when Mother next went to Market Deeping she arrived home with a letter and I was sent to fetch my father in from the fields. He was pleaching the end of a stretch of hedge and would not look up when I said that the letter was here.

"Mother says will you come back to the house?" I said, but he didn't even pause in the rhythm of his work, cutting halfway through at the base of the hawthorn, then bending and weaving the slim branches together to make a tough lattice work. I might as well have been air. I walked back towards the house, then stood awhile, unsure what message to return to my mother. Only when he had finished heathering the last ten paces did he straighten and leisurely pack away his billhook in its holster at his belt and his whetstone in his leather apron pocket. I went on into the house to rejoin Mother and he followed on.

The invitation sent to John was to dine with us on Saturday. The reply, when Mother broke the seal and read it out to us, was a single page and there was no separate note for me, which I had secretly hoped for, though I barely knew I had hoped it until its absence disappointed me.

Thank you for your kind invitation to dine on Saturday next. Sadly I am unable to visit at this time but hope to be able to come at some other time to make your re-acquaintance.

Yours respectfully,
John Clare

I looked to Polly. "He doesn't say why he can't come," I said.

"Uncivil pup," Father said, slapping his belt and apron down on the oak dining table, which made Mother wince as the tools struck its polished surface.

"Perhaps he's busy with the gentlemen in Stamford who are to help him publish his poetry," Polly said. "The talk is that there is a London publisher interested."

Mother nodded several times. "That's good, isn't it? He'll be able to look after Patty better as a man of letters, won't he?"

"The letter says he is not coming," Father said drily, "which is no more than I expected."

"But he doesn't say he will not come at all," said Mother. "Polly, fetch the writing paper: we must send again."

"Send again be dammed," Father said. "I'll not chase after him! I've asked him to visit and he has declined. His intentions towards Patty couldn't be clearer."

My heart grew heavy. I couldn't help but contrast the words John had spoken in our courtship with the cold, formal tone of this letter, and though it was addressed to my father, surely, if he felt any warmth for me still, it would have shone through somewhere just as the sun gives a cloud a gilt edge.

Mother said, "Perhaps we should send again to say he may come at his convenience?"

"I will do no such thing," Father said. "I will stand no such condescension! No doubt he feels above us now and that with a brighter future before him he can woo where he will."

I wondered then whether Betty Sells, or one of his earlier loves who had always been far beyond his reach, had his attentions now. The pear on the highest branch is always the ripest and maybe Elizabeth Newbon or Mary Joyce was the fruit he sought to pluck. The thought was so unbearable to me that as Father turned to leave the room I laid my hand upon his arm and uttered one word. "Please . . ."

He brushed my hand away and spoke instead to Mother in a slow, distinct voice. "I said that I would write one letter and I will do no more. Your daughter must reap as she sowed." He went from the room, leaving his damp apron on the table for Mother to lift and tut at the cloudy mark on the shiny wood.

After a few weeks my sickness began to abate, but instead of beginning to bloom, as I had seen other maids do at the third month, I began to decline. My appetite did not return, for anxiety gnawed at me harder than hunger.

My waist began to thicken, so that I had to tie the fastening of my dresses more loosely, but my limbs and face grew thin, as if the growing child were consuming me. When I felt the first quickening of the baby, instead of joy I felt fear, as though the calumny of the world were set at my ears. My skin grew sallow. Half-moons showed under my eyes from nights spent staring at the corners of the eaves in my room and fancying them as dark and deep as the well in our yard. Abandoned by my lover, I was not equal to Father's coldness. I spoke little and smiled less.

Often my feelings rose up too fast for me to quell and I would hurry from the company of Polly and Mother and seek solitude in my room. It was on one of these occasions that Polly sought me out and told me that she could no longer bear seeing me brought to this state and that she intended to find John and tell him how things stood with me. I knew that I should beg her not to go, that if Father found out he would treat her in

168

the same way that I was being treated, but I was brought so low that I could not. Instead I simply rested my head on her apron and wept.

Polly returned late as the afternoon was drawing into dimness and was scolded by Mother for her tardiness. She was weary from long walking, for she had been obliged to offer to do errands for Mother in Stamford in order to find an excuse to travel to Helpstone. Nonetheless, as she and Mother started to unpack the basket, she nodded quickly at me, making my heart stir into hopefulness. I said that I would help her put the purchases away and Mother retired to join Father in the parlour. Polly glanced after her, then pulled up a chair to sit close to me at the kitchen table, which was strewed with packages.

"I saw him," she said, taking my hand. "I found his sister, Sophia, at home at their cottage and she fetched him from the Blue Bell."

"He doesn't believe what people are saying about me?" I broke in. "He knows that the baby is his?"

"I'm sure he must," Polly said. "He knows that we live quietly here and that there's little in the way of society. In any case, he holds you in high regard. Didn't he say that he was first struck by your artless, unworldly ways?"

"Then, why has he not come to see me?" I said with some vehemence.

There was the sound of a chair being pushed back in the parlour, at which Polly got up, took down the pot for storing the sugar against weevils and began to undo the blue paper wrappings of one of the parcels.

"I didn't want to seem to upbraid him," Polly said in a low voice, "so I didn't mention it, nor the rumours we had heard about him rekindling old flames."

I sighed and rested my brow on my hand. "I'm sorry. You were wise on my behalf."

"He said that he had been rhyming hard and had written many new poems," Polly offered, "and that he is now sure of publication of his collection of poetry just after Christmas, and that he hopes to find a patron in Lord Milton or the Marquess of Exeter."

I shook my head at this, amazed at how John's fortunes were reversing. "He will forget he was ever a lime-burner and be too good for a farmer's daughter."

"No, I'm sure he means to marry you, for he said that his publishers' advisers were concerned that no scandal should attach to him . . ." She stopped short, reading the hurt in my face.

"Does he care only for his reputation, then? Is that his only reason for marrying?" I asked, for I felt that I had given all to him freely with no counting of the cost, which is surely the nature of love. All this talk of how the World judged success or failure, fame or infamy, seemed a cold matter like a set of scales with glittering weights. Everyone seemed to watch in both fear and fascination, continually measuring their actions against it and in dread of it tipping out of their favour. "Didn't he ask after me? Or say when he would come?"

"He asked if you were well and I said that you were not, at which he looked uncomfortable and muttered something about fearing a lukewarm welcome."

"But not from me!" I said passionately and Polly shushed me.

"I fear it's as you said. He's bitter at his treatment by Father and now he's stubbornly determined to stay away from the house for a while because his pride has been hurt." She leant nearer to me. "But he will marry you," she said, "I'm sure of it," and she took from her pocket a worn leather purse and slid it across the table towards me. "He sent you this as token of his good intentions."

I stared at it. It sat fat and heavy among the packages. "This is for me?" I said stupidly.

"It shows he's in earnest," Polly said, giving it a little push closer towards me.

Slowly I loosened the ties of the neck. Inside, among the shine of silver, was the golden glint of guineas. "What is it for?"

"I told him that Father was cold and unkind to you and he said that this gift should shore up your independence until you can be wed."

I upended the purse over the table and the coins rolled hither and thither among the packages, paper and string. Polly looked alarmed and reacted quickly to stop those that were rolling towards the edge, but some escaped her and fell to the stone floor, making a great clangour and spinning away under the table and dresser and into the dark corners of the kitchen. I felt inside the purse for a note, a ring, a stone or flower, some

171

token that would mean more to me that this cold stuff, something that would hold a message that came not from the pocket but the heart, nor from Clare to the house of Turner, but from John to his Patty. And it was just as I shook it again and found it quite empty that Mother and Father, fetched by the noise, came in to find me surrounded still by the debris of Polly's purchases, and Polly stooping to gather scattered coins into her skirt.

CHAPTER
TEN

Walk Lodge to Helpstone

It was late January before I finally saw John. Father marked the occasion by his absence, his anger at my fall being exacerbated further by the shame he felt Polly had brought upon the family by seeking John's assistance. He would have nothing to do with wedding plans, but left all to Mother, who was tired and irritable as a result and had to bear alone the task of arranging for the banns to be read at our church, near by at Casterton, and the embarrassment of answering the parson's questions regarding the need for such haste. I was sorry to have brought her such trouble and tried to do as many of the household tasks as I could to ease her burden, but her annoyance with the situation spilt over into annoyance with me and nothing I did was ever to her satisfaction.

When John visited, Mother left us alone in the parlour, all need for propriety being long past, yet we sat with the tea tray between us as proper as if we had never met. He asked me politely if I were well and said that I was looking bonny, which I knew was untrue, but was glad of the compliment. He talked of his book, which had been favourably reviewed in the *London*

Magazine, and gave me a cutting of the review from the *Stamford News* to show my father. This I folded and slipped into my pocket, for it seemed a marvel to me that I was to be married to a real poet whose books people discussed and passed judgement upon. Indeed, this development was one that caused John some distress as, although the printed reviews were good, he heard rumours of criticism in the locality about him exceeding his station or reports of carping at his grammar and use of local dialect. As his face fell when he confided this, I felt for a moment the return of our intimacy and ventured to comment that it was like as not "sour grapes" and that he should pay no mind to it. At this he smiled and said that I was ever the provider of sound advice, which made my foolish heart swell with pride.

He brightened and told me how he had been called to Milton Hall and how Lord Milton had promised a hundred guineas a year in his support, and how this had relieved his mind a little about the difficulty of supporting his household, for it comprised both parents and his sister Sophia already and would soon be increased to include myself and the child.

He had been summoned to Burghley too, where he had been overcome by the grandeur of the place and feared so much that his shoes might dirty the thick carpets that he had been quite tongue-tied before the marquess and unable to converse with any sense about his poems. Nonetheless the marquess had promised him fifteen guineas a year and had sent him to have a fine dinner in the servants' hall.

I questioned him a little about the inside of the house, as I had passed it many times when visiting Stamford and had always been curious to know what the interior was like. He said that there were pictures wherever you looked: huge portraits in gilded frames, tapestries the size of duck ponds and even painted ceilings with naked gods and goddesses that made you crick your neck to look at them. The place was so huge that it seemed a world all of its own, and when he had first arrived and was left waiting in the doorkeeper's room he'd counted eighty-four leather fire buckets lining the shelves, which is more than are kept in the town.

And so, we talked of trifles and I made never a mention of Betty Sells or Elizabeth Newbon or Mary Joyce but went along with the pretence that his long absence had been necessitated by his hard work towards our future. Neither did he mention the baby though I saw him glancing at me, as I leant forward to pour more tea, and marking the way my gown puckered above the slight rounding of my belly.

When it was time for him to leave he asked me whether I had enough money for the things I would require for the wedding. I nodded quickly to pass over the subject and he blushed a little and stammered out that he had put a poem about me, called "Patty of the Vale", in his book. He kissed me on the cheek and said that he would see me in church for the reading of the banns, then went to bid farewell to Mother.

I stood by the window to watch him go. He turned and raised his hand to me as he reached the gate and my heart quickened as I raised mine. I stood on, gazing into the empty garden long after he'd gone, pondering on the news about the poem. The manuscript had been put together some months ago. Surely including a poem that was named after me was a sign that his intentions had always been serious? For it was a love poem, I was sure, and all in the locality would know the Patty to whom it referred. I was aware that this should bring me joy, but beneath this thought was doubt, like a quick undercurrent running contrary to the sliding movement of a broad stream: if he had not meant to marry me, including the poem would have shown complete disregard for my situation and shamed me in the most public way. What was I to believe? It was thus that I learnt the lesson that love and trust are not one and the same, for although my heart was still his I was no longer sure what he would do with it.

I rested my hand upon my belly and felt the fluttering response of the new life within me. Perhaps all would come right with the birth of the child to bind us. A new emotion filled me: tenderness for the tiny creature I carried and had hardly thought of without fear until now. I might never know whether John loved me with all, or only part of, his heart, but I would have to carry the weight of that doubt in secret. I would have to doubt, but love him anyway, rub salve on my bruises and grow strong enough to carry all. I placed my other hand on top of the first, making a firmer cradle for one who knew nothing of love or lies, passion or fear, yet was growing inexorably towards the day when all the confused business of living would begin.

176

The wedding date was set for March. Over the next few weeks we saw each other briefly when we attended church to hear the banns being read. We snatched a few words in the churchyard after, though Mother and Polly stuck close by me. On the last of these occasions John told me that he was to go to London the week before the wedding to meet with Mr Taylor and Mr Hessey, his publishers, and to be shown round the literary world.

London! I had heard of its multitudes, a sea of people thronging the close streets and the huge bridges that spanned the busy river. I thought of the press at Stamford market and tried to multiply it many times, but I found my mind unequal to the task, for I had heard tell of markets spreading for miles along city streets, selling everything you could imagine: old clothes, fruit and vegetables, bonnets and bloaters, walnuts and umbrellas. And at night, it was said, there were theatres, all lit up, where there was singing and juggling and all manner of entertainment, and crowds and carriages filling the streets at all hours. In my mind's eye I saw John and his companions receding into such a crowd, a river of women's bright dresses and men's dark coats and shiny hats moving through acres — nay, miles — of brick and stone. So that instead of congratulating him and asking him to tell me more I found myself touching his sleeve and saying, "You will be back in time?" at which he smiled and said I was not to worry, for he would be with Mr Gilchrist, the editor of the *Stamford News*, and in good hands.

John's prospects as a poet being brighter than his prospects as a labourer, Father became reconciled to the principle of the marriage; however, he still washed his hands of any involvement with the practice of it. Finally, in desperation at his stubbornness Mother laid the matter before her brother, who agreed to stand in Father's place and to give the wedding breakfast. Father agreed to this on condition that I was not to return to Helpstone with John immediately after the wedding but would remain at home until the baby had come.

And so we were wed in Casterton church at the end of March. John had met another patron while in the capital, a married lady called Eliza Emmerson, who had sent me a dress in which to be wed. I was greatly surprised that she should send such an expensive item to someone she didn't know, on the strength of only a week's acquaintance with John, and could but conclude that she was either immensely rich or subject to strange whims and fancies. Nonetheless, the dress was beautiful; the cloth had a fine sheen and the sprigged pattern was not printed but in the weave itself. I have never taken such care with my sewing, before or since, as when I altered that dress to accommodate my changed figure. Though I was seven months heavy with child, like any other girl I wanted to look my loveliest on my wedding day.

When my uncle and I stood outside the church in the bright spring sunshine and all within was dark and quiet, as if holding its breath, I felt suddenly apprehensive. It was not as I had imagined it would be,

178

with my father proud beside me and my schoolfriends chattering in the pews. My uncle, of whom I have always been fond, patted my hand where it lay on his arm. "You look like a princess," he said, not realizing that it was the passing of the days of such childish fancies that I was mourning.

The sound of the fiddles and haut-viol starting to play frightened the pigeons from the roof above us. When I hesitated still, he said, "It's a new chapter, my dear. Shall we see what is writ there?" I clutched tightly on to my posy and gathered up my skirt and we walked inside and up the aisle, our footsteps echoing on the stone floor, the back of the church being empty, as the wedding party was small, with family and a few close friends on my side and on John's only Sophia and a friend or two who had undertaken the long walk from Helpstone.

John stood with his hat in his hand, squinting to see me against the brightness of the open door. As I drew level with him he smiled and, heartened by his admiration, I drew myself up taller and smiled back. I forgot all the people round us and we looked only at each other. As long as our gaze was joined I knew that we would not stumble in our words or fumble in our fitting of the ring, and so we made our vows loud and clear and they were sealed with a golden ring and a kiss.

As we led the wedding party from the church there was the sound of scuffling and giggling from behind the tombstones and then the sound of counting. A group of the Casterton children, raggedy and with tousled hair, came out with their hands full of petals and lined the path where we would walk, all fidgeting and nudging one another. I looked askance at John, but he nodded at me and pulled me on, so we ran down the path between them in a snow of primrose and cowslip petals, pale yellow, violet and pink. We stopped at the lich-gate and John turned and gave them a deep bow, and they ran away, laughing. I reached to brush the petals from his coat, and he to pick them from my hair, and as our eyes met he paused and I knew that he, too, was thinking of that other time, of our first loving. Warmth flooded through me and I felt that all would be well.

We went back to Walk Lodge hand in hand. We had our wedding breakfast and John gave Uncle and Mother each a copy of his book as a thank-you. When all were chattering among themselves I took John aside to the window seat overlooking the garden and said mischievously, as if I were mortally offended, "Are all my relatives to read the poem about me before I have heard it myself?" and John grinned and went to get my mother's copy. He opened the book and showed me the title page. I looked to him expectantly.

"It says 'Poems Descriptive of Rural Life and Scenery, by John Clare'," he said, his face pink with pleasure. I nodded eagerly. He found his place in the book and we both turned towards the window and away from the room, as if to steal a little privacy from the assembled company. In a low voice he read his poem, "Patty of the Vale".

180

Where lonesome woodlands close surrounding
Mark the spot a solitude,
And nature's unchecked scenes abounding
Form a prospect wild and rude,
A cottage cheers the spot so glooming,
Hid in the hollow of the dale,
Where, in youth and beauty blooming,
Lives sweet Patty of the Vale.

Gay as the lambs her cot surrounding,
Sporting wild the shades among,
O'er the hills and bushes bounding,
Artless, innocent and young,
Fresh as blush of morning roses
Ere the midday suns prevail,
Fair as lily-bud uncloses,
Blooms sweet Patty of the Vale.

Low and humble though her station
Dress though mean she's doomed to wear,
Few superiors in the nation
With her beauty can compare.
What are riches? — not worth naming,
Though with some they may prevail:
Their's be choice of wealth proclaiming,
Mine is Patty of the Vale.

Fools may fancy wealth and fortune
Join to make a happy pair,
And for such the gods importune,
With full many a fruitless prayer:

I, their pride and wealth disdaining
Should my humble hopes prevail,
Happy then, would cease complaining
Blest with Patty of the Vale.

When he finished I asked him if it were true that, after all he had seen of fine life in London, he would rather have me than any riches, and he said, "Of course it's true. Isn't it said that a good wife is far above rubies?" Then it was my turn to blush at the first sounding of the word "wife" from his lips and he sat close beside me and held my hand.

Sophia came over to us and asked if I was well and when I replied I was generally well but my back ached a good deal, she said that perhaps I was carrying the baby low. Then, natural as you like, she leant forward and put her hand lightly upon the top of my belly and said that she envied me and that soon I would have a beautiful baby girl, she was sure of it. Apart from Polly, she was the first to touch me or to speak about the baby with any kindness and I knew straightaway that we should be firm friends.

John had drawn back while we were talking, as if such things were women's business, but Sophia said to him, "Come, John, it's your baby too." She took his hand and placed it where hers had been. The warmth and heaviness of his larger hand stirred the child and I felt it turn inside me in a long movement from one side to the other. John looked so startled at this that Sophia and I burst out laughing, and then laughed all the more

182

when a look of both astonishment and delight mingled on his face.

"It won't be long before you meet the little Clare," Sophia said to John. She kissed me on the cheek and left us to say our farewells in private.

The next two months until Anna's birth were hard for me. John was unable to visit often as his time was taken up with both labouring in the fields and working on his poetry. The money promised by his patrons was slow to arrive and his publishers advised that, when it did, the capital must be kept intact and only the dividends used to live on, so our struggles were not over in this respect.

I grew more hot and bothered as the weather became heavy and muggy in May; everything around me seemed to be bursting into flower: the cow parsley in the hedges, the candles in the horse-chestnut trees; only I remained in a state of heavy expectation.

Mother's anxiety unsettled me and Father's continual upbraiding, despite the fact that I was now married and soon to be gone from the house, made me feel very low in spirits. Polly did her best to cheer me and encouraged me to sew and knit tiny garments for the baby. She had more patience with me than Mother did. She would go at my pace when we walked in the garden or would rub my back for me when it was paining me. This, too, made me feel sad, for I was forever speeding time along in my head towards the birth, even though this also meant speeding it towards the day when I should join John and Polly would be left lonely. At the start I had been so scared of the birth that I had wanted to stretch time out, but, as my mother had told me, when it drew close I became so sick of the discomforts — the broken sleep, the feeling that there was no room left to squeeze my meals into, the frequent tensing and hardening of my belly as my body prepared itself — that now I just wished it to be over. Mother nodded grimly when I complained. "The baby will come when it's ready," she said, and that was the end of the matter.

Anna was born on the second day of June, on a bright morning after a long night of labour, and I thought her the most perfect thing I had ever seen. Word was sent to John and in the early evening he came straight from the fields, still dressed in smock and gaiters and with the sweat of his day's labour on him. I lay propped against a mound of feather pillows and he bent and kissed me.

"May I see her?" he said. As he approached the cradle where Anna lay sleeping he ran his fingers through his hair, as though to tidy himself beforehand, and my heart softened as if it were candle wax.

He peeped into the wooden crib and then drew sharply back, blinking. Then he bent slowly over and gazed upon her as if drinking her in.

I said, "She has your fair colouring."

"She's like a little daisy-flower," he said, without taking his eyes from her face. "All white and pink and buttoned up in sleep."

He sat down beside me on the bed and took my hand, so that our fingers were laced together. I leant over to look with him at the baby: only the length of my forearm, her hair pale and downy but her eyelashes

184

dark against her cheek, her sweet nose and mouth and the tiny, sculpted whorl of her ear.

"I feel that a string in me is vibrating that has never been plucked before," John whispered, and held my hand tighter. "The sound of it is too sweet to bear." He turned to me suddenly. "What if some harm should befall her?"

"We won't let it," I said quickly.

"She's too much like me," he said. "I fear for her."

"What do you mean, John?" I said gently.

"Some find the world too harsh a master and feel its trials and disappointments too keenly," he said. "And there are fears and deceitfulness and foolish temptation waiting to snare her. I fear for her, Patty."

"She will have us to stand between her and the world," I said, a fierce feeling rising up in me that was both angry and tender together.

"I hope she will have your disposition," John said. "She'll be the better for it." He pulled me to him and kissed the top of my head, my face resting against the rough smocking of his shirt, so that when, after minutes sitting thus, we parted, a zigzag shape was marked on my cheek. He teased me and we laughed together and so, when Mother came in bringing tea and sweet cakes, she found us joyful again. She talked to John about his poetry, and his plans to make a future for his family, until dusk began to steal over the sill and he had to return to Helpstone before dark should waylay him.

On the first day of the new month, John came with a hired cart and, loaded down with my marriage trunk and such pots and pans as my mother could spare, we set off on the nine-mile journey to Helpstone and my new home. Anna was wrapped in a sling at my breast and her tiny face, still with the yellowish tinge of the newborn, peeped out from the muslin in which she was tightly swaddled. Mother and Polly came out to wave us off, but Father stood in the shadow of the doorway and would come no further. Mother gave me a shawl she had embroidered for Anna all wrapped up in tissue paper, and at the last minute, as John lifted the reins, Polly ran forward and pressed into my hand a tiny silver spoon with the letter A chased upon the handle. Then we were pulling away and the yard, the hen coop, the barns and buildings all slipped away behind me like the turning pages of a child's well-thumbed picture book that must be closed and put away.

Tired out by all the effort of packing, I dozed against John's shoulder, stirring momentarily when the cartwheels hit a pot-hole in the road and jolted me into half-waking. Lulled by the movement, Anna slept too, and was just beginning to fuss a little and root for feeding when we pulled into Helpstone. I looked round me with interest at the village that was to be my new home and wondered about the folk who were to be our neighbours, for Walk Lodge was isolated in its leafy coomb and our nearest neighbour two miles distant.

I was first struck by the church, which was of pale golden stone and had an octagonal tower such as I had never seen before. A few tiny children played on the steps of the Butter Cross and two old women stood talking at a cottage door, but apart from that the village seemed deserted, for all except the very old and very young were out in the fields at haymaking, leaving the place to the sparrows that fluttered in the dust and the dogs that lay in the road, idly scratching themselves.

The horse slowed as we made our way down the broad main street and John pointed out on our right the tall, square house of his dear friends Parson and Miss Mossop, and on our left the Blue Bell, where he used to work as a potboy as a youngster. We drew up outside the small thatched cottage that was to be my new home.

As the sound of the horse's hoofs stopped I became conscious of a different sound, the low burbling coo of many pigeons. Between the cottage and the inn, a huge dovecot stood. Fantails strutted and pecked in the dust at its foot and others went in and out of its arched openings, little doors into a shady interior safe from the fox.

"It's like a giant cat purring!" I said to John.

"You get used to it," he answered. "It lulls you to sleep. Their Lordships may get the squabs but at least we get the lullaby," he added laughing.

John helped me down from the cart, for my legs were stiff with long sitting. He hitched the horse to a fence post and shooed the birds away to make a path to the door, then showed me inside.

The room was darker and smaller than our rooms at home and the empty grate seemed too mean ever to heat the place in winter. A ladder in the corner showed the way to the upper storey, which was gained through a trapdoor. The furniture — a table and a chair and some three-legged stools — was plain, but all was clean and neat. There was a narrow bed built into one wall, closed off from the room by a curtain, and in one corner a spinning wheel with a half-filled spool, as if someone had recently left off spinning. Lavender lay drying on the sill of the window at the back of the house. The window was open and looked out on to a garden of flowers, with an old apple tree in one corner. John went to the window and called, and instantly his mother came bustling in from the garden. She was small and grey-haired and carried a jug in one hand and a bunch of cornflowers and roses in the other.

"They're here!" she called back over her shoulder to John's father, Parker, and Sophia, who followed her in. She set the jug down on the table and the flowers beside it and embraced me and the baby all at once, exclaiming that Anna was beautiful and then that she'd not yet got the flowers in water that were to be for our room. I looked uncertain at this, for there appeared to be only one room up and one down, and I wondered how we were all to be accommodated with decency. Seeing my confusion, she laughed and said, "Did John not tell you? Never fear, you newlyweds won't have to share our bedroom nor Sophia's truckle bed." She tapped her finger to the side of her nose, then she drew me by the hands to the only chair and bade me sit down while she poured me a drink, saying I must be fair clemmed after the journey.

Sophia asked to hold Anna and took her over to the window to quiet her with looking at the nodding flowers, and Parker grasped my hand in his and patted it while bidding me most welcome.

A cup of ale was placed beside me and a piece of bread and dripping handed to me "to keep you going till mealtime". I remonstrated that only John and I were eating and Parker said, "Aye, but he needs feeding up and you be eating to feed the baby."

I bit into the bread. It was coarser than the bread we had at home, and thicker — a chunk rather than a slice — but it was good and the smear of dripping made it tasty. I took a draught of the ale and its warmth spread through my bones in the same way that the conversation warmed me, soothing me and drawing me in. Between mouthfuls, I started to answer their questions and asked some of my own. Anna began to grizzle and no one stalked from the room or frowned at me over the top of a newspaper. Sophia simply passed her to me and carried on chatting away, and I thought again of the dovecot; the warm press of birds in the small dark spaces.

Later, when I had fed Anna, I left her with John's mother and John and I went out to the cart to fetch the marriage chest. John grinned at me and, instead of carrying it into the house, led me towards the door next to it in the row, telling me that he had managed to take on the tenancy of the two-roomed dwelling adjoining his parents' home. This was a great relief to me, as we should have been very throng if our new little family had been thrust into a space that would barely accommodate the existing occupants.

The downstairs room was small and sparsely furnished with a dresser, table and chairs, though John's books were everywhere: some still in the wooden crates in which his publishers and patrons had had them delivered, others in piles at the end of the table lest they get dirty or damp, for the floor was only earth.

From the chest, John unpacked embroidered napkins, tea-table cloths and tray cloths and handed them to me. At a loss where to put them, for there was no other surface than the plain, deal table on which to display them, my armful of linen grew and grew until John started to laugh.

"Soon you'll disappear behind a mountain of doilies," he said. We packed them away in the dresser drawers. "When my poems are on every shelf in the land I shall buy you tables and knick-knacks galore," he teased.

"Then, you'll waste your money," I said, "for I'm perfectly happy as we are," so glad was I that this little home was all ours and private.

"But let me show you this," he said, delving into one of the crates and bringing out a beautiful violin. It was brand-new with never a scratch on it, not like his battered old fiddle with its worn chinrest. "It's a Cremona," he said, "a wedding present from Hessey, one of my publishers." The rich chestnut tones of the polished wood shone out in the cramped, dark room like a ruby discovered in a bucket of coal.

"And these," he said, laying the violin back in its sawdust bed and turning to show me a case of pristine copies of his book, "these are for me to keep or give

190

away to friends as I like." He gave a broad smile. Then, gesturing to the other boxes, he added: "Almost every day a parcel of books or a letter arrives from some new admirer of my poems. I shan't want for reading matter, that's for sure!"

My heart swelled to see him so happy. "I'm very proud of you," I said, wishing that my family could see him now and my father be forced to eat his words.

John began to unpack more from the chest. First came china plates and teacups — these I propped up on the shelves, their painted roses giving colour to the room — then cutlery and pudding bowls, colanders and pans, which I stowed in the cupboards beneath. John took the little brass weights from the weighing scales and whimsically lined them up like chessmen on the narrow dresser shelf, where they gleamed against the dark wood. We stood back to survey the effect and John slipped his arm round my waist.

"There are good times ahead," he said. "Believe me, Patty. A second edition of *Poems Descriptive of Rural Life* is planned and I have a hundred poems in my head just bursting to be let free on to the paper for the next collection. Perhaps I should make a start now?" He looked around as if to snatch up pen and ink, sit down upon the marriage chest and begin there and then.

"Perhaps first we should tidy the chest away upstairs, and you could show me where we'll sleep?" I said. "And the garden, and where you fetch water from?", for my mind has ever had a practical bent and I wished to be a good housewife.

191

"Of course," he said, calming again. "You shall see all and then we will fetch Anna's cradle in and I shall return the cart to its owner and everything will be done in its proper order." There was merriment in his eyes as he added, "Quite right too, Mrs Clare."

The next morning when I awoke I couldn't at first think where I was. The soft burbling noise I could hear was quite different from the shushing of the woods in our little valley at home. It took me a minute to realize that it was the noise of the doves in the dovecot close by and that the bed I lay in, tucked under the eaves of the tiny room, was in my new home at Helpstone. I stretched, luxuriating in the warmth and the heavy, satisfied lassitude of my limbs. John slept beside me, his arm thrown back above his head against the stone wall, and Anna was fast asleep in her cradle. She had lain with me awhile in the night for her feed and then, milky and yawning, had been tucked into her cradle once more.

A sharp clang from outside made me jump. It was followed by the noise of wheels, and I slipped from under the quilt, lifted the corner of the sacking that was tacked across the window, and peeped out. Passing directly beneath was a stranger, a man in a dun smock, pushing a wheelbarrow with a rake laid precariously across it. He was so close under the thatched eaves that I could have reached down and knocked off his hat. I let our makeshift curtain fall and stepped back, my heart beating fast. At home I was used to a view of hollyhocks, foxgloves and roses, and a garden bounded by the woods; I never closed my shutters, for none could see me save for birds or the occasional hedge-pig that trundled slowly across a twilit lawn. As the squeak of the wheelbarrow receded, I knelt down at the side of the window and looked out again into the village street.

Almost directly opposite was a large threshing barn with a steeply pitched roof. Its huge doors were closed. In the bright sun, the weathered blond wood was almost the same colour as its pale stone, so that it resembled a blank cliff face in which little birds must nest, for they flitted in and out of the old airing holes that dotted its face. This must be the place where John had learnt the art of threshing when he was so small that Parker had to make him a tiny flail so that he could lift it.

There were other cottages up and down the street, all higgledy-piggledy, differing in size and style: some roofed with thatch and some with slate, some pale golden stone and others whitewashed or built in red brick. While I watched, a dung cart passed along, dropping clumps of manure and straw as it went. Then three little boys were shooed from a cottage by their mother. They called up a collie dog from the back of the house and went running down the road towards the Butter Cross. I smiled to see them, for I have always taken a special delight in watching children play or dogs frolic: their simple joy in being alive. Their sheer excitement tows my heart with it.

"You look beautiful when you smile."

I turned to find John leaning up on his elbow and looking at me.

As though thinking aloud he said, "Your face is as open as a primrose; I'm sorry I ever doubted you."

"What do you mean, John?" I said, returning to bed and slipping back under the cover beside him.

"I was told lies by false friends who knew folk who claimed long friendship with you. They said that you favoured the shoemaker over me and you had fallen for his child."

I drew away from him. "And how long did you believe it?" I said coldly, for I was affronted that he should have been so untrusting. I looked down into the cradle at Anna's tiny sleeping form, all swaddled in a soft shawl to keep her safe from any draught, and felt doubly hurt on her behalf.

He sighed. "Don't be like that, Patty. I'm trying to make amends." He touched my arm through the sleeve of my nightgown. "I want all to be open and honest between us."

I turned quickly towards him. "Did you believe this ill of me when you left me standing at the stile and didn't come to meet me? And when you would not come to supper? Can you imagine how it felt to be abandoned so heartlessly?" I stopped, surprised by my fierceness, for I had thought this all dead and buried and that, by a wedding and a new start, I had smoothed over the hummock where it lay. Thinking that now we would argue, I expected John to reply in kind and I took a deep breath ready to say my piece in return, but instead he looked intently at me as if willing me to understand.

194

"I know how it must have seemed, but I was so full of anger and jealousy and *hurt*. I tried to write it out of me in poems. I went to Walkherd one evening with the idea of seeing you, but I lost my courage and, instead, said my adieu and vowed never to return. I told myself you were a rosebud turned to nightshade, full of deadly poison. I tried to amuse myself with other women —"

I broke in, for this was more than I could bear to hear. "Why did you send the purse full of money? Was it because Polly had convinced you I was true? Was it guilt money?"

He nodded, his expression miserable. "It felt wrong. I just didn't know what else to do. Then when I saw you again and you looked so ill and worn I felt such true regret but couldn't speak it. For all my prosing on paper I've always been tongue-tied when the situation demands that words be spoken."

Anna stirred and then began to cry. I leant over and lifted her into the bed with us and tucked her into the crook of my arm, where she quieted and looked up at me with her steady gaze.

John reached over and stroked her cheek with one finger. "She is truly perfect, our little girl," he said.

I said nothing, for such a turmoil of feelings was in me that I was afraid to speak.

"Can you forgive me? Shall there be only truth-telling between us from now on?"

"There has never been anyone else for me," I said, but still kept my face bent over Anna so that my hair hung down before it. "And that is the truth before God."

He lifted my hair away from my face and placed it over my shoulder, so that I should look at him. "There shall be no one else for me from now on," he said. "And this is my solemn vow." He put his arm round me and I moved close to him and laid my head against his chest and stayed quite still, listening to his heartbeat, and thought of our marriage vow to be close as one flesh, as Eve who came from Adam's rib.

The chill of the evening returned me to the present, where I stood pondering at the edge of the orchard. The sun had dipped below the straggle of trees on the horizon, leaving a yellow afterglow, and the starnels were quiet and gone to roost in the branches of the ash. I rubbed my elbows, which were stiff from leaning on the fence, and walked back towards the house, my dress hem soaking with dew as it brushed through the long grass.

I returned from my sweet dream of the past to a remembrance of current worries: Anna's health; how to manage John and make him well again; how to stretch ends to meet. As always at such times, I missed Polly sorely. She was ever a good listener and the pair of us keepers of each other's burdens. When I first left my parents' home for Helpstone she had managed to visit when passing to and from Stamford on errands, but soon after, squeezed by a harsher tenancy agreement, Mother and Father had to sell the farm and move away and she must needs go with them.

I pictured her sitting across from me at the fire at home, all those years ago, her face lit rosy on one side and with her hands folded in her lap in her quiet way. When I used to tell her my worries she would always ask me questions when I faltered, or, if I became too passionate, say: "Tell me exactly what is the problem, right from the beginning." Then she would wait until I had control of myself again. Somehow in the telling, my thoughts would straighten and my fears would be soothed away, as if she gathered them up like armfuls of crumpled cloth and ironed and folded them back into an orderly pile for me to carry away.

As I approached the house through the garden I heard the low sound of the men's voices through the open window. Parker and John were still discussing the steam plough with Freddy and Jack, though no amount of discussion would make such things go away once they'd arrived, and what the men in the fields had to say about it would matter not a jot. Freddy and Jack were the youngest of the carters and would be first to go if any of the teams were sold. I sighed as I put my hand to the door, the wood still faintly warm from the day's heat. I entered the dimness of the hall and shut the door behind me, as if I could close it against Progress, trotting along the hedge lines like a fox. I hoped that it wouldn't stop at our gate to sniff and prick its ears.

CHAPTER
ELEVEN

Lords of Misrule

It was September and almost all the corn was in. All of us, except Parker and the boys, had been working in the fields between Northborough and Helpstone for the previous couple of weeks and that day the last of the harvest was to be brought home.

The weather was heavy, the heat trapped below low milky cloud, and the thrips that came off the corn as it was cut tickled my arms and made my scalp itch. The men, John and Sefton among them, worked up front, following two clips behind Mr Turvey, who was chosen to be Lord for the harvest-home celebration. After them came the women and children, Eliza, Anna and I along with them, gathering the cut wheat into sheaves, the children making the bands for us to bind them, then stand them in sixes to form the stooks.

I paused in my work to glance over at the hedgerow where I had sent Charles to rest when I had seen that he was stumbling with tiredness. Billy Wheelright had been overcome with the heat earlier — he had fainted clean away and had to be taken home. Sophie looked exhausted, her eyes half closing, so I sent her over to see that Charles was all right, rather than go myself, so that she could sit with him awhile and have a little shade. Anna, too, looked weary, although she had lost the pallor that had worried me two months ago. It was clear that her dangling apron strings were shorter than before. I wondered when she would tell me what I was now sure of. I had tried to persuade her to rest but she had shaken her head and carried on.

We had been working since first light and now the early evening sun seemed to beat out of the packed earth as it gave back its heat to the air. We worked on and on, too tired to speak, until at last the final square of standing corn was left. Then the boys and younger men, who were nimble on their feet, set down their scythes at the headland and picked up the stout sticks they had brought with them. They ranged themselves round the last stand of corn. Mr Turvey gave a loud "halloo" and a rabbit broke cover and ran, scut bobbing, taking all by surprise. It dodged between Sefton and another man and Jack Beddoes called out, "Not as quick on your toes in the daytime, eh, Sefton?" and all the men laughed.

I looked to Anna. "Has Sefton been rabbiting in Royce's Wood again?" I said.

Anna raised her eyes skywards. Sally Andrews, who stood close by, said, "Jack has a mouth as wide as his legs are bandy," for taking game meant prison and if one man was caught the keeper would look out with a sharper eye for others.

On that day, though, rules were suspended, for it was the end of the harvest and all were allowed to take rabbits for the pot. The mowers began to cut and soon more rabbits and hares broke cover and ran, zigzagging, to try to escape the shouting men. Sefton, perhaps piqued at the earlier laughter, was the first to strike successfully and he picked the creature up by its hind legs and held it aloft, with a look at Jack Beddoes, then threw it down again and clasped his stick and bent his knees ready for the next.

I began to occupy myself with making bands for the final sheaves, so that my hands could keep my eyes busy. I concentrated fiercely, for although we needed the meat as much as the next family there was always something about the way the creatures' hiding place grew smaller and smaller that made my heart beat fast along with theirs and made me look away when finally they ran.

When the last corn was cut, a great cheer went up and I looked up again and hurried back to the gathering. Everyone lent a hand until the sheaves were all set in stooks, each with its open arch facing the prevailing wind, for, although it was still and hot that day, the next might bring a breeze, and wind and sun together are just as good for drying corn as drying washing. When all was done we stood, hands on hips, releasing our tired backs, and I gazed over the field and thought each line of stooks as neat as a row of buttons. Sophie found new life from somewhere and ran with the other children to gather green boughs from the hedges, and flowers from the banks, to decorate the sides of the one stook that stood alone at the field gate. It would be left there after all was gathered in, as has always been the custom.

When all was ready, Mrs Turvey stepped forward to be Lady and her daughter gave her a crown of Michaelmas daisies. She joined the Lord at the front and they led the procession from the field: Lord and Lady, then the horse and cart, with the firkins and baskets that had held our dinner and the scythes that the men had gratefully laid aside, next the men and boys, then women and children. We went at a slow pace at first, for the horses too were tired, but as we approached Helpstone village they picked up their pace towards their oats and straw and the men began to sing of harvest home as we turned into the main street. John was singing along as loud as the rest of them, his face ruddy with heat and his eyes bright with excitement. Eliza nudged me and said, "Father is with the Billings brothers."

Parker had stayed at home as the heat was too arduous, and without his company John had fallen in with his old friends and drinking partners John and James Billings. Both unmarried, they kept late and rowdy hours and their house was known as Bachelors' Hall.

"He'll have a rare thirst after this heat," I said, worrying that the ale would flow too freely at the harvest supper that was to come.

When we reached the Blue Bell, next door to our old home, the women and children stopped and the men carried on through the village towards the rick yard to unload the contents of the cart and stable the horses. From the inn, the pot boys were already carrying out tables and chairs and many of the Helpstone women went off to their houses to do the same and bring them to the threshing barn opposite.

The wide barn doors were thrown open, letting light into the lofty interior, where motes of last year's chaff still hung in the air, having been raised by the recent sweeping.

Betsy Bates and Sally Andrews, who has always been a well-covered body, struggled to step over the high threshold with the long trestle they were carrying and Anna went to help. I stepped before her and took the end of the table, saying quietly, "Don't be lifting these heavy things, my love. You go over the road and help bring food across instead."

Anna lifted her eyes to mine with an enquiring look as I took her load from her, and I smiled and nodded, as if to say I would keep her secret until such time as she chose to tell. She blushed a pretty pink and did as she was bid and went to take the easier task.

Betsy and Sally exchanged a glance.

"Anna's looking bonny these days," Sally said, puffing and blowing between the words as we side-stepped with the heavy table.

"Being married is suiting her, then?" Betsy said to me with a wink, which I ignored.

I put my end of the table down with a bump and shunted it noisily into place.

We set up in two long rows the rest of the tables and chairs, a motley assortment of different heights and sizes of furniture, so that some would sit high and others sit low, but fit for our purpose: to eat, drink and be merry. There was plenty of space left over behind the far row for dancing and a high roof to fill to the rafters with songs.

Plates of beef pies, bacon and cold plum pudding were brought across from the Blue Bell and placed at intervals on the tables. In the midst of the coming and going the men returned from the rick yard and the Lord took his place at the head of the assembled company, with the Lady next to him on his right. At this I called to Sophie and Charles from the open barn door to come away from playing at the edge of the pond. They were chasing the ducks to see them run on to the water with flapping wings, then fold them and float all serene as if nothing had happened to disgruntle them. I took the children to the village pump to wash and we splashed our faces and hands and rubbed away the worst of the dust and grime.

I saw Parson and Miss Mossop approaching, he with his white collar and his prayer-book in hand and she with a large pickle jar clasped in front of her. Behind them, old Otter the fiddler and the fieldworkers who also played in the church band came carrying their black instrument cases. They walked together, brushing the dust of the day from their clothes and straightening their collars.

When we returned to the barn, the buzz of conversation was growing to a hubbub as the blacksmith, the wheelwright and the horse collar-maker and their families joined the throng.

I ushered the children to their places at the foot of the table, then greeted Parson Mossop and Jane.

"Is John here?" Parson Mossop asked. I pointed him out where he stood dividing up a quid of tobacco between his friends and himself. "He looks well," Parson Mossop said, although I privately noted that John was very animated and laughed the longest and the loudest of his company.

Parson Mossop surveyed the rest of the crowd. "We'll start with a Grace and hope that it doesn't get too riotous," he said. "Perhaps the presence of the Church will keep things decorous," he added with a broad smile that gave the lie to his serious words.

When everyone had their places and stood behind their seats, Parson Mossop went to the front and stood with his head bowed and his hands crossed over the prayer-book held before him, until all fell quiet.

"The Lord has blessed us with a good harvest," he said. "We thank Him for this bounty and undeserved kindness and for the strength of our arms that has helped us cut and gather it." He paused and looked along each row of workers. "We thank Him for . . ." he began again, but at that moment the overseer arrived. He was wearing an apron and a woman's mob-cap and carrying a milking pail banded with bright iron hoops and full of frothing ale.

". . . This vision of loveliness," a ruddy-faced youth called out, and all burst into an uproar of laughter, for it was the custom in these parts that the roles of master and servant be switched for just this night in recognition of the toil and goodwill spent by the team in the field. The overseer, who was a large man with mutton-chop whiskers, grinned at the assembled company and said in a high-pitched voice, "Humble greetings to my Lord and Lady," while dropping the ugliest curtsy ever seen.

A small boy pulled at his mother's skirts and said, "Why does she have a hairy face?" at the same moment that Parson Mossop, who had continued intoning his prayer despite the fact that none could hear him, raised his voice to say, "And that concludes our grace. Amen," and the whole ended in a muddle of laughter and mumbled amens.

Parson Mossop gave up the unequal fight and took his seat at the top table while the overseer presented the Lord with the full pail of ale and a jug to dip into it and pass along the tables. From pockets in waistcoats, aprons and breeches came knives and forks that had chinked there all day, and those who had none brought out skewers they'd cut and sharpened from hazel twigs taken from the hedges during the day. At a word from the Lord, all set to helping themselves from the plates that were nearest them.

"Where's William?" I mouthed across at John, who sat diagonally opposite, for I had been expecting him to join us as he'd been employed scaring birds from the crops before the harvest started. John shrugged and turned back to his companions. It was unlike William to miss a horkey as he was of an age for a big appetite. Perhaps it's just as well, I thought, as he's also of an age to try to drink like a man, though only with a boy's stomach and thus with an inevitable result. I took some meat, pease pudding and a pie from the platters and slipped them into my apron pocket for William and Parker when we got home.

Anna and Eliza sat beside me, with Sophie and Charles further down, Charles eating with the single-minded concentration of one who thinks he may never see such food again. The girls were talking of Sefton.

"Why must he take such risks?" Anna was saying. "I tell him that I'll manage with what we have but he won't listen."

"He goes at night?" Eliza asked. "You must stop him."

"A gang of them go together so that some can look out for the gamekeeper."

I tried to hear over the hubbub, for this news disturbed me. If Sefton was caught it would mean three months in jail at least — more, because there was no one to pay the surety for him. What is he thinking of with a new wife and a baby on the way? I thought.

"It worries me," Anna said, looking over at Sefton. "There are rumours of mantraps and dog-spears still left in those woods, even though they're supposed by the law to be all taken out now."

"He's a fool, then, and should have more sense," Eliza said, with such vehemence that Anna looked back at her sharply. Eliza flushed. "He shouldn't speak about it so openly," she added more moderately.

"Is it foolish to ask why a rabbit or a pheasant should belong to one person any more than a sparrow or a blackbird does?" Anna said, then sighed. "That's the argument he makes, but it's not one that the court would take kindly to, I think."

Just then there was a "Whoah!" from the group of young men nearest us where Sefton was and we looked over to see that some horseplay was going on and a tankard had been upset. A stream of beer flowed from it and splattered on to the dusty floor as the men's voices dissolved into laughter.

"He's like some great puppy," Anna said: "always in trouble but impossible to scold."

A bowl of punch and syllabub was brought round and we all dipped our cups in to fill them.

"What is it?" Sophie said, peering suspiciously into her cup.

"It's beer and spice and sugar that's been milked into, that's all," I said, tipping some out of Charles's cup and into Anna's, for the poor mite was so weary I was afraid that if he drank much he would fall asleep and I should never be able to carry him all that way home.

The musicians, who had been served earlier, pushed back their stools and began to tune their instruments. The fiddler played a snatch of a jig and Sally Andrews, who was collecting up the empty plates, gave a little hop and a skip as she went. Sefton wobbled the table as she passed and shouted, "The earth's quaking, Mrs A!" She went to cuff him, but missed, and cursed him roundly but in good humour instead.

The musicians formed themselves into a group behind the tables, where there was plenty of room for dancing, and struck up the tune "Now supper is ended" and everyone joined in to sing a rousing chorus. This was followed by a jig and some of the smaller children crawled under the tables to get through to the open space and started hopping from foot to foot.

Sally gave a cry of triumph, pulled Sefton from his seat and with a broad grin danced him down the length of the row of tables and back again. He made a great show of fanning himself and called out, "It's like dancing with a haystack tied round with a piece of string!", then dodged quickly back to put the table between them as she swung for him again.

Sefton walked round the tables towards us and Sally subsided on to her stool, waving her hand in front of her face just as Sefton had done in mimicry of her, though she was unaware of the fact that he had her likeness so well. Pairs of lads and lasses, men and women, were now quaffing the last of their drinks, scraping back their chairs and squeezing by one another to go and dance.

Sefton took Anna's hand and said, "Will you have the first dance with me, Anna?"

Anna hesitated for a moment, then smiled and said, "I'm not fit for too much jigging about," as she rose to her feet.

"Just one will do no harm."

Sefton led her over to the other dancers, who were moving clockwise round the floor in pairs, hopping and twirling as they went. They paused for a moment on the edge; then, seeing a break in the moving crowd, they launched into the dance, Sefton with one hand holding Anna's and the other at the small of her back, the better to hold her steady as they swung round. I caught glimpses first of Sefton's face as he sang along to the tune and then Anna's smiling up at him. When the dance ended the band started another tune straight away, but Anna was not to be persuaded and they returned to us, she looking rosy and smoothing her skirts before taking her seat.

Eliza had been busying herself with scraping and stacking the plates in a pile at the end of the table, but at Anna's return she looked up and I saw her catch Sefton's eye.

Sefton took a step towards her, then, as if checking himself, turned back to me with a grin and said, "How about you, Mrs C? Would you like to hoof it with me a little?"

"I think my hoofing days arc over," I said. "A slow trot with John is more my mark."

Anna, heated from the dance, was filling her cup.

"Eliza, then," he said and reached across to catch her wrist before she could lift another plate.

"I'm busy," she said rudely and went to pull away, but Sefton held his grasp.

"Come on, 'Liza," he said. "Don't tell me you've given up dancing along with smiling these days." He slid his hand from her wrist to her fingers and lifted her arm to make an arch over the table that lay between them, then walked her down to the end as if about to lead her in a procession.

Anna reached for my cup, refilled it for me and passed it back.

"You're looking mighty bonny, my love," I said. I held my cup up as if in a toast and she caught my meaning.

She hesitated, then touched her cup to mine. "To new beginnings," she said.

". . . And may all your troubles be little ones," I added, and we drank and embraced. I folded her into my arms as carefully as if she was an egg in a cake and she pressed her cheek to mine.

"I'm sorry I didn't tell you before," she whispered. "At first I was afraid it wouldn't stay."

I nodded and smiled as we broke our embrace, full of gladness that the baby was already wanted and loved, her secret hugged to her for a time as a hope too precious to share, rather than the guilty secret that had been my lot.

"You're past the first three months?" I asked.

She nodded.

"Then, all will be well, I know it," I said, squeezing her hand. "Will you tell your father?"

We both looked over to where John now stood with his back to us, watching the dancing. He was clapping his hands in the air and stamping one heel on the floor to the rhythm of the music. Beyond him the pairs of dancers spun like whirligigs, leaning back as they turned round the axis of their crossed hands, the women's skirts billowing out, the men's faces ruddy with exertion, sweat glistening on their brows and at their throats. I caught a glimpse of Eliza and Sefton spinning near the centre of the crowd, Eliza's head thrown back, her fair hair loosed from its bands and streaming out behind her, then the bodies closed round them again and hid them from view.

"Do you think I should?" Anna said. "It's not too early?" and I sensed the tension in her between the desire to celebrate and the superstitious fear that in the telling you risked your joy being taken away from you.

"Are you coming back to Northborough tonight?" I asked.

Anna shook her head. "We're staying on here. Sefton's got some work at the farrier's for ten days or so, then we'll help bring the harvest in and stay on a day or two for the gleaning."

"You'd best tell him now, then," I said. "You're past the worst danger."

Anna started making her way round the drinkers and the elderly still sitting at tables. The band finished their tune with a flourish and straightaway started another and I saw Eliza fall against Sefton, laughing. He steadied her elbow and kept her close as they both moved as one into the next dance.

Anna reached John and plucked at his sleeve, so that he half turned and bent his ear towards her. She beckoned him to come to one side and they moved up the row towards where the Lord and Lady and the Mossops were sitting, looking benevolently on. They carried on behind the top table to where the sacks of grain remaining from last year were stacked. The children were playing round them, some hiding behind and some climbing over the top, a complicated game of tag. Sophie and Charles were among them and I realized that I was sitting alone at my stretch of the table.

The music was reaching a crescendo, the jig played louder and faster, until it seemed impossible that the dancers could keep up. The fiddler's bow moved as swiftly as an old woman's knitting needles as he threaded the melody through the deeper sounds of the wind instruments. To concentrate better on Anna, I put my hands over my ears.

For a moment I felt strangely detached as the music was muffled, as though I were watching a mummer's show and the figures before me were engaged in a play that was already written, its parts predetermined, its ending inevitable.

I saw Anna's hands moving as she explained her news earnestly to John. I saw John clasping her and lifting her up, his face aglow with pride, then setting her down again quickly as if suddenly deciding that she must be treated like cut-glass. I looked round for Sefton, but neither he nor Eliza was anywhere to be seen.

I unclasped my hands from my head and the music rushed back as it galloped towards the high note on which it would end. Parson Mossop had left his seat and was side-stepping between the tables towards the band. As the players paused between tunes to mop their faces with sleeves or handkerchiefs, he reached Old Otter and spoke to him. Otter nodded and turned to talk to the other members of the band. In the lull, a few dancers returned to the tables to drink down a draught or went back to their seats, exclaiming to one another and puffing out their cheeks. The others chattered among themselves, some pairs still holding hands, ready to hop to it once more as soon as the band struck up again.

From the small door at the rear of the barn, Eliza slipped unobtrusively back inside. She blinked in the relative brightness and looked confused, as if wondering why the music had stopped. She moved quickly to the edge of the group of dancers and started talking to one of the other girls. I half rose from my seat to go and fetch her back to sit with me, but I was arrested by the sight of John leading Anna, protesting, out before the crowd to where the musicians were standing. He was waving with the other arm in order to demand quiet.

"I have an announcement!" he shouted. "I have something to say!"

The babble of conversation dropped to a hum and then died out. Those still sitting at the tables twisted in their chairs and all looked towards John and Anna. John's face was red and his hair, where it thinned on top, was ruffled up in a cockscomb.

"Where is Sefton?" John called out. "Where's my son-in-law?"

Anna was blushing and I saw Sally Andrews nudging Betty and whispering, her hands clasped together in anticipation of being proved right in her guesswork. The room fell quiet as people waited for Sefton to step forward and I saw Eliza glance at the little door and then quickly look away. Then, as if summoned like a genie, Sefton appeared at the wide barn door, bearing a barrel and with a wide grin on his face.

213

"Does somebody want me?" he said and, passing the barrel to John Billings, he made his way to the front to stand beside Anna, overtopping her by both head and shoulders.

"I have an announcement," John said more quietly.

"You said that before!" shouted someone in the crowd.

John looked a little confused, then recovered himself. "I would like you to drink to the health of the happy couple, lately wed, who are to have a child!" Someone pressed a drink on John; he raised it, slopping some of its contents over the rim, where it dripped from his hand. "Anna and Sefton!" he said.

"Anna and Sefton," echoed the company, those who had drinks raising their cups and those who had not beginning a round of applause that rippled and took hold of the whole room.

Eliza lifted her hands as if to clap, but then held them there, unmoving. She stood as if a lightning bolt had pinned her to the ground and I feared that at the next moment she would crumble. I willed her to look to me, but she did not. Her hands dropped back by her sides and she looked about her, as if seeking a way out, as her friends began to lean forward to ask questions.

Parson Mossop, who had married them, stepped forward to congratulate Anna and clapped Sefton on the back as Sefton's friends pressed forward round him to shake his hand.

"You be better at catching a maid than stopping a rabbit, then!" Jack Beddoes called out from the back of

214

the room, where he sat with his bandy legs stretched out before him, a pint of ale balanced on his pot-belly.

"That's rare coming from one who couldn't stop a pig in a passage," Sefton retorted, and the crowd gave a roar of laughter that drowned out Beddoes's response.

Eliza extricated herself from the other women at last and began to hurry towards the big doors out into the street. I got up and went to meet her.

"Eliza," I said, "come and sit with me, child."

Her eyes were full of tears and she looked over my shoulder at the darkened street as though she would run into it and not stop until she reached home.

"Eliza," I said again, laying my hand on her arm. "I can't manage your father and the little ones home on my own. I need you to stay."

She took a great swallow as though the words that she would say must stay in her throat, gave a little shake of her head and followed me back to the table.

"Here," I said, "drink this," and I handed her the remains of my syllabub. "It'll put a little heart in you," for truly I had never seen Eliza look such a picture of misery.

She bent her head to the cup to sip and let her hair swing forward so that no one could see her face.

The stir round Anna and Sefton had not abated and I looked back over to see John climbing on to a chair in order to regain the attention of the company. He swayed a little and steadied himself with one hand on Sefton's shoulder before raising his other for quiet.

"My family . . ." he began. "I'm very proud of my family." He paused as though overcome by emotion. The faces turned towards him were smiling, willing him on, but instead of moving into a speech he mumbled, "Save them and keep them, save them and keep them," and gripped Sefton's shoulder again, looking round him as though unsure where he was.

"Go and find the children," I said to Eliza: "your father's unwell," and I got up to go to him.

"I love both my families," John said, "though it's a bit of a job to keep them. You know I have two families?" he said in a conversational tone. He glanced down at Sefton. "Sefton here has one wife and that's all a man needs, for sure; two are too many to keep."

Someone in the crowd laughed uncertainly.

". . . And babies, lots of babies. One more mouth to feed. Lots more mouths to feed." His voice took on a singsong tone. "Always want and need, always want and need."

There was an embarrassed shuffling of feet in the crowd.

Parson Mossop reached up and laid his hand on John's arm as if to persuade him to come down, but John shook him off.

"And what of Mary?" he said. "What of Mary and her family? What has happened to them and when will I see her?"

I had been squeezing by Sally Andrew's stool to get to him, but now I stopped in my tracks as some of the women turned to look at me.

"O Mary mine," John began to sing, "my heart's desire!"

I felt the blood rise to my face as I stood pinioned by the gaze of my neighbours and heard a whispering begin along the tables.

"You told me she's dead," he said to Parson Mossop.

"Come down from there now, John," the parson said. "You've said your piece."

"You're all liars!" John cried out as Parson Mossop and Sefton took his arms and stepped him down off the chair.

Parson Mossop signalled to Old Otter to step up to the front and play, and between him and Sefton they managed John over to the table and sat him down. Anna followed on behind.

Sally pulled her stool in to let me pass, looking up at me with her eyebrow cocked. "Quite a night for your family, eh, Patty?" However, when she read in my face the mortification I felt, she quit her bantering and said in a softer tone, "Come now, it'll be a nine-day wonder and all forgotten."

"I wish it were so for John," I said, "but nothing seems to shake him from his fancies."

"He has other imaginings?"

I swear her eye brightened at the prospect and I wished I'd said nothing as was my usual habit. "It's a private matter," I said, and passed on to where John sat. Anna was squatting down before him, holding his hands and talking to him earnestly. His chin was resting on his chest and he looked at her dejectedly from under his eyebrows. As had happened previously, now that the episode was over he fell into an exhausted torpor and seemed quite unable to move himself to action.

"We have to go now, John," I said grimly, for I smarted from being so humiliated in front of the whole village; it was as though I had been struck on the site of an old bruise and my wincing made clear for all to see.

He made as if to rise, but fell back into his seat. I came to the side of him to take his elbow, but he shrugged me off. "I want Mary," he said, "not you."

"Then, Eliza will have to do," I said shortly and Sefton and Anna took an arm each and brought him outside to the street, where Eliza and the children were waiting.

"Do you think you'll manage?" Anna asked.

"Sophie, Eliza, link arms with your father," I said. "Charles, take my hand."

They did as they were bid and we walked down the street as far as the road to Northborough with Anna and Sefton walking in silence beside us.

Although John wove a little from side to side he leant on the girls and allowed them to steer him on a tacking path along the road. When we reached the parting of our ways Sefton wished us a brief farewell and seemed anxious to return to the festivities, but Anna kissed us all in turn and watched us a way down the road before she turned and followed him.

I took Sophie's arm so that we made one long chain, the better to bolster her efforts to keep John straight, for she watched her feet with the concentration of one who is dropping with weariness.

"I'm tired," Charles said, pulling on my hand. "Can I have a carry?"

"No, my love," I said. "You must be a man and help us find our way home."

A golden harvest moon shone, blurred at its edge, misting the darkness round it to a watery blue and casting a pale light over our way. I saw that Eliza clenched her jaw and that her eyes glittered. "Eliza?" I said quietly over the top of the heads of Sophie and John, but she ignored me and I held my peace, thinking that we would talk when we reached home.

Ahead of us a fox crossed the lane. It stopped and turned momentarily towards us. Its eyes caught the moonlight: two bright points that looked at us levelly and then, deciding we were of no interest, turned away. It passed through the hedge with barely a rustle and trotted away over the stubbly field.

The movement seemed to awaken John to his new surroundings and he looked about nervously as we walked on. When we came level with the field gate there was a humped shape standing just inside it and he jumped and cried, "Who's there?"

"For goodness' sake, it's nothing, John, just a stook of corn," I said, though I could see that in the moonlight it looked like a hunched figure and just the stuff of children's nightmares.

Sophie stopped, drawing us all to a halt. "Why do we always leave one there? Why isn't it in a row with the rest? It's spooky."

"There's always one left there even when the field's cleared. It's a kind of offering, a thank-you for the harvest. It's nothing to be scared of."

"Doesn't anyone ever steal it?" asked Charles.

"No. If any of the gleaners steal just one ear, the others will shake their bundle of gleanings to the ground. It stays there all year."

We walked on. John fell back into a morose silence and Eliza would not be drawn into conversation, so I talked of this and that to the children to keep them awake enough to put one foot in front of the other.

When we reached home, John snapped at us that he could manage and trod heavily up the stairs. At the top he called back, "Are you coming, Patty?"

"Presently," I said tersely, for I was tired and still prickly with the embarrassment of the spectacle he had made of us and smarting from his abrupt dismissal of me.

I sent Eliza to see Sophie to bed and I took Charles up. A stub of candle still burnt in a dish. Parker and William were both in bed, Parker snoring fit to wake the dead and William, quite oblivious, asleep on his back with his feet sticking out from under the quilt. It was chilly now, the night was so clear, so I tugged the cover down, but that left his shoulders bare. I sighed: it was clearly too small now to spread the length of his gangly frame and I had no material to make another.

"Skin a rabbit," I whispered, pulling Charles's shirt up and over his head. His arms were floppy as I fed them into the sleeves of his nightshirt, and as I took off his shoes he put his arms round my neck and leant his head on my shoulder, limp as a raggedy doll. I tucked him into bed beside William and he fell asleep instantly.

I remembered that there was a spare blanket that I had been intending to mend to rid it of its old moth holes. It would be better than nothing. I pinched out the candle and went to our room to fetch it.

As I fumbled at the wardrobe door in the darkness, John said, "Are you coming to bed now?"

I turned and could make out the white of his nightshirt and the sheets. He was sitting up in bed and had turned the covers back on my side. I pulled the blanket out and hugged it to me. I did not feel loving towards him after he'd sung Mary's praises in front of the whole assembly. "John," I said, "how can I lie close with you when there's someone in the bed between us?"

There was silence, then, "Come, Patty, you know you are still my wife." His voice had a querulous tone, as if he said this not to comfort me but to make a demand.

My back stiffened. "I know it, but you seem to forget it," I said sharply.

"I can't help it if I miss Mary!" he said. "I made a vow to her when we were young."

That's as maybe, I thought, but such vows are surely overwrit by those given at a wedding, and even if they remain in a person's heart they shouldn't, for sure, be shouted out abroad to all and sundry.

I crossed to the bed and pulled the triangle of the turned-back covers up across the sheets. "There isn't room for three in a marriage," I said.

"Patty . . ." he said, reaching for my arm.

"I have business with Eliza," I said and walked out of the room, shutting the door behind me.

My heart beat fast all the while I was tucking the blanket in round the boys. That has put the cat among the pigeons, I thought, for straightaway I realized I had said all the wrong things — things that would only get John all stirred up — and though it had been a relief to say what was in my heart I knew that I had mishandled him and feared that it would lead to further trouble.

I tapped on the girls' door and went in. The curtains were open and the moon shone in on Sophie, curled up fast asleep with her pillow between her and the cold wall, and Eliza, lying on her side, wide awake, with one hand under her cheek.

I sat down on the end of the bed and rested my hand on the curve of her hip. Eliza said nothing.

"You must forget him," I said at length.

She made no answer, but stared fixedly ahead at the pale oval of the mirror on the wall, its bevelled edge glinting in the moonlight.

"For both Anna's sake and your own," I whispered, for fear that Sophie might wake. I steeled myself to say what must be said. "Sefton likes to exercise his charm. He's a young man at the height of his powers; he thinks the world is his for the taking."

I longed to take her in my arms, but then she would weep and I would soften and what needed to be said would be left unspoken. I forced myself on. "It means nothing."

Eliza gasped as if holding her breath was the only way of keeping a sob inside.

"Anna mustn't be upset," I said in a softer tone. "She's expecting a child."

"I can't bear it." Eliza wiped her face with the back of her hand.

"You must," I said. "They'll be back in Northborough soon and you'll see them every day. You must decide now to stifle your feelings."

"I've tried. I've been trying," she said.

"Shall I speak to Sefton? Get him to stay away?"

She shook her head. "Everyone would notice and wonder why."

Eliza's long hair was spread behind her on the pillow and I reached over and smoothed it. The strands were a soft tangle, still scattered with scraps of straw, and something round and prickly: a head of clover. I teased it out.

"I'll help you," I said. "I'll make excuses for you, say you're unwell and have taken to your bed, if necessary." I bent to kiss her forehead, and as my breast pressed against her shoulder I felt the shudder of the weeping she was keeping deep inside. "I know it's hard," I said, kissing her again.

I got up and left her to herself, for sometimes tears cried alone offer more relief than words.

There was no movement from John as I came to bed and I slipped between the sheets quietly, feeling unequal to any further talk. I tried to think of everyday things, things to be planned for in the weeks ahead. I thought about the clearing of the fields and the church bells ringing to say that we gleaners could move in. I imagined working alongside the other women, filling the bags at our waists with the short ears and gathering the long to lay on sheets, to be bundled and carried upon our heads, home for threshing. I tried to imagine working happily alongside my girls, and failed.

As I began to sink towards sleep a snatch of John's poem "The Wheat Ripening" drifted through my mind.

What time the wheat field tinges rusty brown
And barley bleaches in its mellow grey
'Tis sweet some smooth mown baulk to wander
    down
Or cross the fields on footpath's narrow way
Just in the mealey light of waking day . . .

Then a picture of the stook in the gateway came into my mind and I thought of the way one pile of sheaves was built on the remains of the last, how winter and weather would turn the bright gold to grey; the rain would moulder it and the wind would thin it to a pile of straw.

John stirred and mumbled in his sleep. Half roused again, I heard him say, "It's the end of the summer," and wondered by what magic his dreams could be so tuned to my thoughts. It made me think of our days of walking out together when at the self-same moment we would stop and exclaim at an object — a tiny flower, half hid along the path; a bird's feather; a colour in the trees — and I felt a sadness settle over me.

I lay wide awake again, counting over the gleanings of my marriage, searching for the precious grains among the wisps of stems that blew, rolling, across an empty field.

224

CHAPTER
TWELVE

Golden Rings

I had chosen the right day to bake: the weather had turned chill. An October wind strained through the yellowing leaves of the apple and pear trees, scattering them, crisp and curled, on the grass. It shook the bunches of keys in the ash tree like a jailer pleased to keep us all indoors.

Inside, the kitchen was warming through as the wood in both the fire and the oven took light from the kindling. The oven, which was set into the wall in the chimney corner, was a tricky thing to manage, for it had to be heated by a fire in the bottom until the stones were hot, then the ashes riddled out and the wooden door put in place to keep the heat in while the bread was baking.

From the sack that stood on a chair in pride of place I measured out flour: the produce of our labour gleaning, threshing and carrying to and from Maxey Mill. I tipped in each measure for three loaves from the brass pan of the scales into my biggest mixing bowl, which is the colour of a brown egg, with a plaited edge round the rim, and I enjoyed the familiar feel of it under my hands. I had brought these things from home

225

when I was married and had used them carefully, so that although the colour had worn off the raised edges of the china plait there was not a chip in the bowl, and the pan and the weights still gleamed from long polishing.

Parker had a cold and had stayed in bed. Eliza and the children were out gathering sweet chestnuts to roast while the oven was hot. The house was peaceful for a while and the only sounds were the sputtering of the logs as the green wood caught and the ticking of the mantel clock.

John came downstairs and went to pass through the kitchen to the parlour. His mouth was a thin line, clamped shut as it often was these days.

"Are you going to write for a while?" I asked gently enough, for I had been trying to humour him out of the dark mood that had overtaken him since harvest time.

"What is it to you whether I write or not? You don't care one way or the other as long as I'm out of your way." He stood in front of the fire, warming his back.

I sighed but refused to rise to his baiting. "There's fresh ink in the drawer," I said, mild as milk. I put my hands into the soft, cool flour and hollowed out a well in the centre. "Which would you like? Bloomers or cobs?"

"I expect you'll do as you like as always," he said.

"Perhaps you could write to Dr Allen?" I suggested, for it had been three months since John had returned from Essex and he had still written no word of explanation or thanks to the doctor who had taken care of him.

He shrugged. "I'm in no mood for letter writing. I've not had one letter since I've been in this godforsaken spot. Friends, publishers, they've all forgotten me and I'm quite, quite alone."

I rested my hands on the rim of the basin. "Come, John, that's not true. It was Mr Taylor who arranged for you to be looked after at High Beech, remember? And you're not forgotten by your family."

He scowled at me. "You forgot me as soon as I was away."

"I had no money to come, John," I said simply, my heart sinking as the argument took its familiar turn.

"A man needs comfort and a wife in his bed and I had none. No doubt you were busy elsewhere."

"John . . ." I said, a warning note in my voice.

"Everyone knows that women are faithless," he said, staring at me.

"You go too far," I said, biting back the other words that formed in my brain about visits to Springfield, the women's quarters at High Beech, and poetry books lent out to all and sundry as an excuse to call on every miss in the area.

"'*Better to marry than to burn*', the Bible says. Better to burn than marry, say I, and if you'll have none of me, then I'll none of you."

"You aren't being reasonable," I said, as calmly as I could. "You should think quietly for a while and you'll see that I've always been true to you." His glare didn't waver for an instant and my resolve to stay quiet began to fray. "Despite provocation," I added. Then I pressed my lips together and began to measure out water and teaspoons of yeast. Not until I heard the parlour door shut behind him did I let out my breath.

There had been no marital relations between us since before the night of the harvest supper. Nor were there likely to be, I thought, if he carries on in this vein. Each night we lay back to back, the space between us filled by the ghostly figure of a woman formed in the ideal image of John's fancy, and I began to fear that even if we were to turn face to face neither of us would be able to see over her to truly meet each other's eyes. And I missed him and I was lonely too. I wanted the old John back again. But I would not be second-best to a ghost any more.

I mixed bread dough, rolling it round the basin until it formed a soft, heavy lump, then shook more flour on to it and on to the table. I pressed the knuckles of both hands into its soft resistance before lifting it and rolling and kneading again, venting my feelings in pummelling and squeezing. John's words had hurt me. I tried to keep in mind Parson Mossop's advice and told myself that I must make allowances for John. I had tried to do this ever since the onset of his illness and must keep on trying.

It had been the year after we started our married life together in Helpstone when our fortunes took a turn for the worse. I remember being heavy with our second child and busy all day keeping house and minding little Anna as she learnt to walk. Keeping up with her and saving her from as many bumps and spills as I could took all my energy and perhaps I didn't heed the early signs that all was not well with John.

There were delays in setting up the trust fund that had been promised by John's patrons. The publisher, Mr Taylor, advised that in any case John should only ever draw the interest on the money and leave the substance intact. There was nothing for it; John must go back to labouring at the same time as pushing ahead with composing *The Village Minstrel and other Poems*, his second collection.

Fame and field husbandry were poor bedfellows, however, and John was constantly forfeiting precious wages to attend to visitors: being called away from his work on the whims of clergymen, ladies with poetical sensibilities and would-be poets who turned up all unexpected at our door. I was often at my wits' end, for they would catch me with an untidy house or in the middle of cooking or washing and with Anna clinging to my apron, half dressed or with a dripping nose. A few were genuine well-wishers and became firm friends with John; the majority came to gawp at the lowliness of his beginnings and were more amazed at the novelty of a man of his class writing poetry at all than interested in the sense of what he had written.

Once, a whole class of girls from a Stamford school was brought by their teacher and gathered outside our door, waiting for some words of wisdom from the peasant poet. None were forthcoming and the girls giggled and whispered among themselves. John would often become taciturn in such situations and it would be left to me to smooth over the awkwardness and manage the social niceties as best I could. On this occasion it came on to rain and there was nothing for it but to invite the whole class indoors. They filled our little room so tight that I couldn't get to the pot to stir our dinner and the stew burnt and stuck to its sides. They fluttered and primped at their hair so affectedly that I was quite out of patience and muttered under my breath that a little shower never hurt anybody. John slipped away upstairs.

The strain of being all things to all people — country neighbour to his fellow labourers, literary gent to poets and publishers, and grateful receiver of patronage from some whose canting views he abhorred — began to tell upon John. He took to drinking with his workmates and once came home with a black eye after falling down. He would stay out until all hours at Bachelors' Hall, until I was forced to the indignity of fetching him home to bed and trying to quiet him as we staggered along in the dark. "I'm my own man! Let no one forget it! I am my *own* man!" he would proclaim to the street, but this bravado would be replaced in the morning by terrible low spirits.

There were quarrels between two of his patrons and his publishers, Lord Radstock and Mrs Eliza Emmerson on the one side, Mr Taylor and Mr Hessey on the other. Disagreements flared about the nature of his contract, his patrons insisting on a better deal on his behalf, though he had never asked them to and, indeed, felt mortified by their actions.

His various supporters demanded that his poetry be in this or that style. He was urged on by his publishers, but reined in by patrons who disapproved of anything radical. Lord Radstock threatened to cut off his financial support if passages that criticized the wealthy landowners who had benefited from the enclosures were not removed. I still remember some stirring lines: ". . . every village owns its tyrant now, And parish-slaves must live as parish-kings allow." John's motto was "Blunt is best" and despite added pressure from Mrs Emmerson he said that he was damned if he would be censored. I admired him for standing his ground, but he found constantly resisting such pressures an emotional and wearing business.

In May, a month before her first birthday, Anna took a fever. We were beside ourselves with anxiety to hear her wheezing after each cough and to see her so hot, her skin flushed all over and her hair dark with sweat and stuck down in strands against her head. The doctor had only a mixture to offer and it seemed to do very little to help. I dampened her brow with cool cloths and fed her water by teaspoons, as the croup would not let her take it from a cup. In the day, John's mother and Sophia brought round dishes of food for us and honey for Anna's throat and took turns to sit with me while John was out in the fields. In the night, when Anna cried with tiredness but could not fall asleep, John and I took turns to walk up and down our tiny kitchen, carrying and soothing her as we did when she was a tiny baby and couldn't settle.

After four days the fever finally abated, but the cough stayed with her right up to her birthday, wearing her out and making her want to be held on my knee and cling close until she finally fell asleep at the end of the day through sheer exhaustion. Even when she was fully recovered, John's nerves were strung out tight as a result of the constant fear for her health, for the fens are near by with their damp and vapours and dangers from malodorous ditches and biting insects.

One evening, as I sat sewing while John wrote, he suddenly put down his pen. "I'm harried in every direction," he said. "It's making me unwell."

"Tell me how you're feeling," I said. "Could you not rest tonight and start afresh tomorrow?"

He leant his forehead on his hand. "The truth is, I feel constantly fearful, as if some great calamity is hanging over us and I must be on my guard at all times and ready to fight it off."

I put down my work and went to him. "Perhaps it's the thought of another mouth to feed," I said as he laid his head against my belly and I stroked his hair.

He pulled away and shook his head. "'Tis how I felt last time before the fit came on me."

At first I thought that he referred to his writing, for when he wrote for days on end and late into the night, producing tens of poems at a sitting, he would say that he was "in the fit".

"The next thing was a feeling of terrible cold and pains in my chest and head," he continued, "and then I became insensible."

"When did this happen? Why have you never told me before?"

"The worst was the April before we were wed, when I was passing over Lolham Bridges," he said. "The last

232

I remember was the sound of the rushing water below growing louder and louder, then the ground came up to meet me."

"You forget to eat enough, John. I'm always telling you," I said, giving him a serious look. "If a body doesn't eat, even a man can faint clean away."

"It wasn't that," he said, "for, when I woke, the sun was bright in my eyes and I found my coat all dirtied, as if I had been rolled in the mud, and my hat was some way off and lying in the road."

"Oh, my poor dear!" I said, and took his hand and rubbed it between my own as if I would even now warm him back to sensibility. "Did no one help you? How did you get home again?"

"No one came by," he said. "When I felt a little recovered I just got up and walked again. But I felt so . . . alone, so fragile, Patty, as though I was a bubble on a river that could be dashed against a stone and disappear in an instant, as if it's never been." He rubbed his brow with his palm, to and fro, to and fro. "And though Mother and Father had Dr Skrimshire out to see me, that feeling has never fully gone away."

His voice became hoarse as he continued. "I have dreams, not just at night but waking dreams of fathomless falling and horrible faces mocking me and telling me that all hope is lost and that I must despair." At this his head began to nod and I realized that he was sobbing, though without a sound. I put my arm round his shoulders and cast about for what I should do, for although I had seen John affected before by another's sadness or a sight of beauty so that his eyes would fill I

233

had never seen him, nor, indeed, any man, cry so that his body shook.

The part of me that was still a young girl was a little frightened, but the part that was a woman was stronger. "Come, come to bed, my love," I said, and closed his notebooks and helped him to his feet. "You have been doing far too much; you must leave it now," I murmured. "You're overwrought, you need to rest. Come and lie down and I'll lie next to you," and I helped him up to bed and undressed him, for his hands trembled too much to do it for himself. I lay down beside him and whispered, so as not to wake Anna, sweet things and endearments and held him in my arms until he fell asleep.

The new baby, who was born in June, was a fine little boy, but he was taken from us after only a night and a day. I can barely think on that terrible time even now and try to turn my inner eye away when the memory rises in my mind. We wept together and John said that the babe had gone home again. For comfort he would repeat like a catechism that the infant had gone back to his Maker, where he would be even better loved than here, but I know that no one could have loved that child more than we and I'm sure that this was not what he truly felt. He tried to hide from me that he was sorely afflicted with doubt and could not understand how religion could encompass such a cruel occurrence. His strange fantasies of devils and demons worsened and he dreamt of moon-washed churchyards and open graves.

In the weeks that followed, John had days when he couldn't drag himself from his bed, far less put words on paper. Sophia, despite being busy with her wedding preparations, for she was soon to be wed to William Kettle, came round whenever she could. She would busy about the chores I had neglected and would put Anna upon my knee and tell me to sing to her, knowing that the best comfort I could have was closeness with my living child.

Although John lost all interest in his poetry for months after our loss and didn't believe that his second collection would ever come to fruition, eventually he began writing again. Once he had started, he buried himself in it as if to shut out all else. On the days when the fit was on him he would not even stop to eat until the end of the day, and in a week he would write enough to fill a book. I had no strength to stop him or try to govern these excesses. He would sit muttering over the words as he committed them to paper. It was in these mutterings that I first heard the phrase "keep them from evil", a prayer that seemed to intrude upon his thought at random as if it were a charm he turned in his fingers without knowing he did so.

This was the first time the states of torpor and mania grew extreme and it set the pattern for the malady that was to return to plague him at intervals ever after.

The remembrance of this time of trouble had stopped me in my kneading and I came to myself with my hands resting on the table and the outside of the dough fast drying to a floury crust. I blew out a long sigh, for such memories when they assailed me tightened my chest and puckered my forehead, so that I felt like a cord that has been knotted and cannot be got smooth again. I picked up the dough and began to roll and stretch it, but this time at a slow, methodical pace, making my mind go blank and letting the feeling of the soft, heavy stuff in my palms and the regularity of the movement comfort and calm me.

I heard someone enter the cottage, then Anna's voice greeting John and his replying cheerily, and was glad that Anna wouldn't think for a minute that anything was amiss.

She came into the kitchen with her shawl still wrapped tight round her. "The weather's really turned," she said as she came to kiss me and I held my arms up and away from her to save her clothes, for I was floury up to the elbows and morsels of dough were stuck to my hands.

Anna took off her shawl and hung it on the peg on the back of the door, then stood next to the fire while she unbuttoned her cuffs and rolled up her sleeves. Side on, the curve of her belly was unmistakable now and I tried a smile and said, "The bread's not the only thing rising, I see."

She laughed and looked down at her figure, resting her hand at the waist seam of her tartan dress where the gathers spread rather than lying flat and neat. "Sefton's convinced it's a boy because I'm carrying high, but I don't know. It could be a girl; I just have a feeling."

236

I nodded. "I felt sure that *you* were a girl, though it was only through dreams that I knew it." I divided the dough into three and pushed one of the lumps towards her. "I had a great desire for crab-apple jelly," I said, "the sharper the better. In fact, after that it was easy to know the girls, for every time with them it was something sharp — jellies or pickles or suchlike — and with the boys it was always cheese."

"Well, it's pickle for me," Anna said, looking astounded, "that or apple chutney, so perhaps my feeling's right." She dusted her hands with flour and began kneading.

"Has Sefton found work?" I asked.

She nodded. "Over at Barnack, hewing stone to help out with a big order."

"Not permanent, then?"

"A few weeks," she said, and our eyes met for a moment, for we both knew the difficulties I had had sometimes in keeping a meal on the table and I heartily wished that she should have better.

I changed the subject. "Have you started stitching baby gowns?"

"I've cut some out. Sefton got me some cotton and calico, and I've bought some flannel for napkins. I've not started sewing yet. Sefton laughs at me being so mole-sighted. He says when I sew I hold the cloth right under my nose."

"Bring it all round next time," I said. "Eliza and Sophie will help with the finer work and having company will make hemming all those napkins less of a chore."

I had formed two loaves into chunky ovals while Anna still rolled and folded her dough. "Dreamy!" I said as I shifted the loaves on to the griddle tray.

She smiled. "Sorry. I seem to find it hard to concentrate these days." Deftly she shaped the dough and passed it to me.

"It's all right. You're allowed to be a little distracted." I put the tray on the hearth to make it rise and fetched a bowl of water for us to wash our hands and the baking things.

"There," I said when all was dried and put away. "Now, shall we do the ring test and settle once and for all what this child is to be?"

I sat Anna down by the fire and she held her hands out to the warmth. From under Parker's chair I fetched my sewing box and took out some thread, teased out a length and bit it off with my teeth. I tried to slip off my wedding ring to tie to the end of it, but it wouldn't come. I tugged at it. It was no good; my fingers were no longer the long, slender fingers of the girl I was when it was placed there. They had more flesh on them than once they'd had and, as I pulled the ring up the skin gathered at the knuckle, making a barrier it could not pass. I showed Anna and pushed it back into its place. "Well, I'm not likely to get thin again at my age," I said with a wry smile, "so I expect you'll bury me in it."

Anna nudged my arm. "Don't say such things. How could we all do without you?" She slipped her ring off, easy as butter, and handed it to me. "See, mine's not even bedded in yet," she said, holding her hand out, and sure enough there was the faintest of pale lines where the skin had not browned with the sun but no dent in the flesh as with mine. I held the ring in my palm; shiny and new, with no wear or thinning, it was still a perfect circle.

I tied it to the thread. "Here, put your feet up," I said, pulling a three-legged stool from the chimney corner. "Lie back as best you can."

She put her feet up on the stool and smoothed her dress tight over her stomach. I held the thread between my thumb and forefinger over her, running my other hand down its length to still it. "Back and forth is a boy and round and round is a girl." The ring hung virtually motionless, with perhaps the slightest tremor communicated along the thread from my hand, which was a little unsteady.

The door banged and I heard children's voices raised in excitement, and Eliza shushing them and saying that Father might be working. Sophie burst into the room, carrying a bucket that was half full of prickly brown chestnuts, and Charles and Eliza followed behind.

I looked up but didn't change my position. "Now, don't make a rumpus," I said. "We're in the middle of something ticklish here."

Sophie put the bucket down and came closer.

Charles looked uncertain. "What are you doing to Anna?" he said.

Eliza remained standing at the door.

"Hello, 'Liza. We're trying to find out boy or girl," Anna said.

"You'd better come in and shut the door," I said, "otherwise we'll get a draught ruining it."

Eliza shut the door and stood with her back to it. "You're looking well, Anna," she managed.

"Now sshh, everyone," I said, "and keep very still." I ran my hand down the thread again and pinched the ring between my thumb and forefinger to still it. All of us peered at the ring; despite herself Eliza couldn't look away.

"Nothing's happening," whispered Charles.

"Just wait," Sophie said.

Slowly the ring began to swing, at first so slightly that it was impossible to tell the shape of its tiny movement, then you could see that it traced a minute circle, then bigger, then unmistakably a circle the size of a saucer was being described over Anna's belly.

"It's a girl, my darling," I announced triumphantly and leant forward to kiss her. "Congratulations."

"It's a girl, it's a girl!" chanted Sophie, jumping up and down.

I put my arm round Charles. "Just fancy," I said, "only eight years old and you're going to be an uncle!" Charles looked unsure about this. "You'll have a little baby to play with," I coaxed.

"A boy would have been better," he said, pulling a face, and went off to tip the chestnuts on to the table and find a knife to start splitting the nuts from their cruelly spiky shells. Sophie, no doubt afraid that he would put all the biggest ones on his pile, pulled up a chair and joined him.

Anna was trying to untie the thread from her ring but having no success. "Can you do it, 'Liza? You're the one with the lace-maker's eyes," she said, holding it out to her.

Eliza took it and carried it over to the window. She turned her back on us and picked at it with her fingernails.

"I should have a look for Charles's baby clothes," I said, "though I know some of them have ended up as wash rags. There's only so many times things can be hand-me-downs."

Eliza came over and handed the ring and thread to me. "Do you want me to look in the clothes chest?" she said. "There might be some things there."

She started upstairs and I called after her, ". . . Or in the wardrobe in my room."

I sat and talked to Anna while the children gathered up the sweet chestnuts into a bowl and put the cases back into the bucket to take out for compost.

"Eliza is taking a long time," Anna said, glancing at the clock. "I should get back and get on. I can't sit at your hearth all day, comfortable though it is."

I went to the foot of the stairs and called up.

"Coming," Eliza's voice came back muffled.

She clattered back down the stairs carrying two or three napkins and a parcel done up in paper. "Sorry," she said breathlessly, "but this is all I could find." She hesitated, then passed the napkins to Anna and gave the parcel to me.

"Ah, I know what this is," I said, sitting down and placing it on my knee so that I could open it where all could see, for it was the christening gown I had made for Anna and that all my children had worn in turn for their baptism. The wrapping was rough sugar paper saved from many purchases, but it was folded as carefully as tissue paper. I remembered last putting the gown away after Charles's christening. I ran my finger over the intricate smocking embroidered with daisies, their centres neat French knots, the material a fine cotton lawn with a scalloped edge at the hem and tiny pleats at the cuffs. I lifted it by the shoulders from the paper and the smile collapsed on my face. The body of the gown was patterned with holes and thinned-out patches where moths had eaten through the fine threads and shredded my careful work.

"Oh!" I exclaimed, for I had so wanted Anna's baby to wear the gown that I had carried Anna to church in so proudly. My hands fell back into my lap, crumpling the tiny garment on to the paper. "I should have thrown that blanket away," I said miserably, for fast on the heels of my disappointment came the realization that, with winter coming on and the rent due, there was no money to buy fine linen for another.

Sophie came and put her hand on my shoulder and Anna took the gown from my hands and peered at it. "Perhaps we could save the collar and the pretty hem," she said, "and add them to a new gown?"

"Maybe," I said, patting Sophie's hand where it rested on my shoulder, for she has ever been able to tell when I'm upset, sometimes even before I know it myself.

"It won't be needed immediately at least," I said. "We will just have to try to put a little away each month."

242

Anna took the paper and folded it away again, then levered herself up from the chair by its arm. "I must go," she said. "Thank you for the napkins."

Eliza took down Anna's shawl from the peg and handed it to her, and Anna kissed her on the cheek and then took her farewell of the rest of us in the same fashion.

"I'll have to go to Market Deeping for new camphor," I said abstractedly. "The stuff I have must have lost all its strength."

I saw Anna to the door, then returned, meaning to put the bread in the oven.

"Can we do the chestnuts first?" Charles asked.

"Oh, very well," I said, thinking that it would keep Eliza busy supervising the children and stop her from brooding, and soon there were cracks and explosions behind the oven door, then burnt fingers and tears, and the christening robe was forgotten by all except me. It stayed in the back of my mind and I mourned it, not just for the sake of a future joy lost but for that little one who was our next-born after Anna and was christened in haste, wrapped in a gown that was far too big, snatched away untimely, leaving me with only empty clothes to touch and hold. And later came the tiniest of all, who was born too soon and was buried at dusk outside the wall of the churchyard, with only the sexton and the midwife in a black shawl to see him on his way.

CHAPTER
THIRTEEN

Beggar's Market

In the afternoon, when the baking and all my other chores were done, I fetched some coins from the tin and put them in my purse, so that I would be able to buy the camphor we couldn't do without. To make further use of my trip to town, I took a basket out to the orchard and filled it with apples. I planned to sell them to the grocer at Market Deeping who would sometimes take them from us, there being little opportunity to sell them at home: nearly every cottage in Northborough had a garden and at least a fruit tree or two of its own, and folk had no need to buy apples and pears that they could harvest or exchange among themselves.

I put my head round the parlour door to ask John if there were anything else that he needed, for, in times of trouble, it is on such civilities that relationships rest. I found him surrounded by notebooks and papers, some spread over the surface of the desk flap where he wrote and some loose sheets that had floated to the floor. When I came in he bent to gather them up and tucked them inside the book he was writing in.

"There is something," he said. "I've written to Dr Allen. Perhaps you could post the letter, if you're going into the town."

"Of course I will," I said warmly and took the folded sheet from him, for I was mightily pleased and heartened that he had taken my advice and I thought that in doing as I suggested he meant to make some kind of amends.

As I passed out into the garden the wind nearly took the letter from my hand. I put it into the basket and weighted it down with an apple, then covered my head with my shawl and wrapped it round my shoulders. With the basket over one arm and my hand at my chin to keep my shawl in place, I set off down the lane, with the wind pushing me on like a hand at my back. It thrummed in the hedges where the thick foliage had thinned out to leave places where the sky, in chinks of white and blue, showed through the thorny twigs.

I met with Sam Dawes, who was coming the other way. A widower, he lived alone at the other side of the village and generally kept himself to himself. He was returning to Northborough with a billhook over his shoulder and he told me that he'd been over at the estate, taking down branches that the wind had split, to make the woods safe for His Lordship's sport.

"Is there much wood down elsewhere?" I asked, for no one was allowed to gather wood in the estates any more, on pain of a brush with the courts, and so we must scour the trees in the hedgerows and all compete among ourselves for a little warmth in the winter.

Sam pointed across the fields towards Maxey. "There be an elm with a branch perilous close to falling and plenty of kindling already brought down," he said. "It'll be too much for me on my own. Perhaps your lad might help, for a share?"

"I'll send William round to you tomorrow if the wind drops," I said. I gave him my thanks and we said farewell and passed on our way.

This encounter, though brief, made me uncommonly happy, for Northborough had not been a friendly place, in my experience so far. I had grown tired of greeting neighbours only to receive a curt nod in return, or, if I managed to engage someone in conversation, feeling that they listened with the merest politeness and did not offer any response or opinion in return. We were still not forgiven for getting the cottage over the heads of those who had expected it. I had overheard the mutterings when we moved in: *Helpstone folk. Lord Milton's pet poet. Incomers.* Even now the talk was that we paid no rent. It made my heart sore when I thought how in reality I must scrimp and scratch to find the money, but I would not discuss my business abroad. That much of my parents' pride had rubbed off on me and reticence was stamped upon my character as clear as my memories of our house at Walk Lodge, secret among the trees.

I glanced back at Sam's retreating figure and at the village beyond: a cluster of houses round the tiny church, then cottages strung out along the lanes, with wide spaces between, until they petered out and met the flat, open fields. In the winter, sometimes wind and weather drove across those fields like a cavalry charge and hit the village so forcefully that the very houses seemed to hunker down and huddle together. Perhaps Northborough people are bred to close their ranks, I thought; perhaps it comes from living on the edge of the fens. I was greatly heartened, though, that one of their number had, for a moment, dropped his reserve.

This lifting of my spirits, however slight, led me on to think more hopefully about John, despite the words that we had exchanged earlier in the day. At least he has listened to me and written to Dr Allen, that's something, I thought. I began to wonder whether he had expressed his feelings in the letter about being home or given any indication of whether, despite his irascibility and fits of agitation, being with us was helping him or making him happier. No sooner had these thoughts struck me than my fingers began to itch to open the letter. I could hear my mother's voice saying *Eavesdroppers hear no good of themselves*, but another voice whispered that I might find out something that would help me gain a better understanding of John's malady.

Ahead lay the Great Oak, a place to get out of the wind. It used to stand a good thirty feet high and in the summer it dried the ground beneath it in a circle as wide as its canopy of green. Cattle used to shelter there when the sun was fierce and many a time I sought refuge there myself and watched as tiny tree-creepers, looking for insects, ran up its grooved trunk, then fluttered back down to start their search anew.

It was felled when the field was enclosed and the wood sent off to the timber yard. By now it would have been dried, sold and built with: beams propping up roofs and lintels topping windows and doors. What remained was a hollow stump, waist high and wide enough for a man to stretch his full length within.

I picked my way across the tussocky grass until I reached it, then scrambled along one of the roots that protruded round it, all polished to a shiny grey by weather and boys' feet. Perching my basket on the rim, I climbed over the edge. The earth inside was bare and packed hard and the charred remains of a fire spoke of gypsies or passing journeymen.

I put down the basket and sat down on the dry earth and immediately I was out of the noise and fuss of the wind. Tucking my knees up within the tent of my dress, I leant my back against the wooden shell of the tree. I lifted the apple from the letter and placed it aside. The page was folded in three and sealed with a dot of wax that had only just caught the edge. When I ran my thumbnail beneath it the stiff paper sprang apart. As I opened it out, it crackled.

I glanced up at the O of the sky above me with a sudden fancy that a face might peer in at me. The small clouds passed across the chilly blue as they had done all day and nothing broke the emptiness but the odd crow, buffeted by the wind. I opened the letter and spread it flat against my thighs.

My first feeling was one of relief that John had written in a proper manner, beginning "My Dear Sir" . . . I read carefully, my eye following my finger as I ran it across the smooth, creamy paper. He started politely by apologizing for having departed from High Beech in such a hurry, but then became querulous, complaining of the lack of visits from his literary acquaintances and the over-zealous attentions of the keepers.

He asked that Dr Allen recover some books for him: further copies of Byron that he had lent to sundry ladies round the forest and who he implied were company that would get him into trouble. Though hurtful, none of this surprised me in itself, for I had suspected it before. However, I had not expected the doctor to be quite so much in John's confidence and, as I read on, my dismay grew.

Of his return home to Northborough he said that he found neither home nor friends but merely a lodging with "one of my fancies and her family", which I took to mean myself, while his "poetical fancy", Mary, though lost, was always in his thoughts and the subject of his every song. I gripped the edge of the paper and felt my familiar indignation filling me like a boiling pot. He appealed to the doctor's sympathy, detaching himself from all of us and describing himself as a widower or a bachelor. He asked that the allowance granted to him by a patron be sent on so that he could be independent and pay board and lodging. My cheeks burnt at this. How could he refer to me, his wife of over twenty years, as if I were no more than a landlady, a housekeeper paid to cook his food and do his washing! My hand moved as if to crumple the paper, but I stopped myself and determined to read to the very end.

The letter finished in a rant in which all control was lost. He blamed women in general as faithless and deceitful from the very first and cited Eve, "who cuckolded Adam with the help of the Devil". "A wife is not so much use as a good cow," he wrote.

I shut my eyes and tears of anger and frustration welled up behind my closed eyelids. I pressed my knuckle against first one eye and then the other. I would not let one more tear fall on his behalf, I told myself, and blinked at the paper until the words that swam before me resolved once more into their unavoidable meanings.

He wrote that he wished to lead the life of a hermit and be left alone to dream of Mary. I felt as though I was sinking into a cold lake, falling through its freezing lower waters into its weighty dark.

I do not know how long I sat there. At length a gust of wind found its way into the hollow trunk and stirred the charred wood, spreading the ashes and waking me from my sorry reverie. I began, very slowly, to refold the letter.

I would have to send it, despite the hurt and shame it would cause me that a stranger would read it and think me cold, John vengeful and our marriage loveless. If I hid it or destroyed it Dr Allen was sure to send after word of John again and all would come out; and I couldn't tackle John about his betrayal both as my husband and as my friend. I had read what was not meant for my eyes and was trapped by my own misdemeanour.

I smoothed the fold of the paper down, then licked my finger, ran it underneath the dob of wax and pressed it to the surface. It wouldn't stick. I would have to ask the post mistress to re-seal it. Then I would watch her do it. It was one thing having a doctor privy to John's disordered feelings, but I would not risk our linen being open for inspection to any clerk or delivery boy who cared to look.

I buried the letter under the pile of apples, then wiped my hands on my dress. I passed my sleeve over my forehead as if to iron out the lines that writ my feelings on my face and set off on my journey once more.

People moved quickly along the High Street at Market Deeping, bustling into the shops to get out of the blast. The men turned up their coat collars and the women held on to their poke-bonnets and clutched their flapping shawls round them. They hurried from stall to market stall like leaves drifting against a wall, only to be stirred again by the wind and moved on.

When I came out of the post office, a coach-and-four was turning in through the arch of the Bull Inn, the horses' hoofs slipping and clattering on the cobbles as the driver reined them in. Their flanks were dark with the sweat of a long journey. I imagined the passengers descending and the boxes and mail sacks being unloaded. I imagined John's letter in its mail-bag and how the bag would be thrown into the mail coach like a sack of potatoes, the hands that would sift and sort the wishes and dreams, the thoughts and sorrows, of so many people, all unknowing, just so many pieces of paper to move from one town to another. How I envied them their ignorance and wished that I had never peeped into John's mind, for, as with Pandora's box, the things I had learnt were free in my world now and would rise up to fly around my head and never be captured again.

I crossed the street and bought mothballs and camphor, then set a more cheerful look upon my face and went into the grocer's shop. Mr Darnley was at the counter, weighing sugar into half-pound bags. A rule, a pencil and a pair of scissors protruded from the breast pocket of his coat.

"Good afternoon, Mrs Clare," he said. "What can I do for you?"

"Good afternoon, Mr Darnley . . ." I started.

The corners of his mouth turned down as he saw the basket I was carrying and its contents. "I see you've brought apples, but sadly I've no need of them at the moment." He gestured to the baskets of fruit ranged along the sides of the shop and the tiers of apples stacked rosy side out.

I thought of the long winter to come and the butter and cheese, the lard and bacon, that we would need to keep the cold out over the months ahead. Taking my courage by the scruff of the neck, I stepped forward. Mr Darnley held up his hands as if to stop me in my tracks.

"You have no russets," I said boldly, picking one out of my basket to show him, "nor Bramleys for fruit puddings now that the weather is turning chilly."

252

He leant over the counter to peer into my basket. "I have room for only a certain amount of stock . . ."

I placed one of each type on the counter. "They're masterly fine apples," I said. "You'll not find better."

"How old are they?" He took one in his hand.

"Picked today," I said, sensing some progress. "By myself."

"Very well." He sighed. "I'll take the russets and the cookers but *not* the pippins." He pulled out two trays from under the counter and I sorted the apples into their varieties. I placed each carefully to make sure that it wouldn't bruise, for I hoped to return in a week or so with more and wanted him to be impressed with the produce.

"Thank you very kindly, Mr Darnley," I said as he counted the coins into my hand. They were fewer than last time but that was the way in a good harvest year.

He looked round the shop for a place to put the trays down and could find none. I moved towards the door. "Now, don't bring me any more," he said to my departing back.

I took my leave as if I hadn't heard him and hurried down the steps from the shop and out into the street. In my rush I didn't see the drayman, rolling a barrel across the street towards the inn, until it almost ran over my toes and I had to pull up short to avoid it. The couple behind me on the pavement bumped into me so hard that the basket was jounced from my grip and part overturned, so that some of the apples went rolling away into the street. I gave a cry and reached to retrieve those that were scattered round my feet. Before I could get my hands to them, there was a dart and a dash and a raggedy child had snatched them up. As he ran harum-scarum down the street, another jumped down from a doorway and ran forward to copy the first. The man behind me had recovered his breath and pounced on the lad, catching him by his collar.

"Call your brother back!" he said. "You thieving beggar!"

The woman picked her way round them and went to recover the apples that had rolled away. I looked down at the boy, who still gripped the apple fiercely and would not give it up, far less call his brother, who was by now probably several streets away. His clothes were scant: a coat from which his wrists stuck out like a scare-the-crow's and, underneath, no shirt but a dirty vest, all open at the neck without collar or neckerchief. Judging by his size, the lad was no more than five or six years old, but Want had left his face thin with no hint of baby cheeks. His eyes were dark and quick as he glanced from side to side, searching for his best chance — an alley to disappear into or a passing cart to catch on to and ride clear away. Something in the way he hesitated, tension in his every muscle, made me think of the rabbits in the last stand of corn.

"I know these boys," the man was saying. "They're from the Boswell's crew. Gypsies." He gave the boy a shake. "I know their thieving ways; they're into every hen-house between here and Stamford. They'd have the turnips from your garden."

"He's just a child," I said. "He's close to starved. Look at him."

The man looked up at me, speechless, and in that moment the boy dropped the apple, slipped from his jacket and took off, running, weaving between the stalls and dodging round ladies' skirts, so that he was soon lost from view. The man threw down the jacket with a curse and I picked it up along with the apple.

"Now he will be cold as well as hungry," I said, for my heart was sore at his skinny elbows and the way his shoulder-blades had stuck out as he ran.

"Never fear," the man snorted. "He'll soon filch another coat from someone's washing line." He took his wife's arm and bade me good day with a look that said quite the opposite.

I walked across to the doorway that the boy had been standing in and laid the coat down, then tucked the apple into the pocket. What if he were my boy? The thought came uneasily to mind, that all that lay between us and the gypsies' state was a set of walls and a roof and finding the rent to keep them around us. I hesitated, then put another into the other pocket for good measure and went on my way.

When I returned home, John called out to me from the parlour. I took off my shawl and folded it away wearily. The parlour was in worse disarray than when I had left it and John was surrounded by open notebooks and slips of paper covered with scribbled notes, drafts crossed through and verses with tiny drawings in the margins. His fingers were ink-stained and there was a dark mark at the corner of his mouth where he had been sucking the end of his pen. He twisted in his chair to speak to me.

"Did you get more paper?" he asked.

"You didn't ask for any," I said.

A look of annoyance crossed his face. "You know I always need a good supply."

"Paper will have to wait," I said. "While there are only coppers in the rent tin and nothing to put on the bread when I've baked it, paper is the last of my worries." I fussed about, sweeping the loose sheets that were strewn over the mantelpiece into a pile and weighting them down with a candlestick.

John put his palm to his forehead. "I have new poems in my head . . . new cantos of Don Juan . . . and sonnets and songs. I must set them down."

An image of the letter came back to me, my hands gripping it as the words hurt me as surely as if the nib had scratched them on my skin.

"Why would I want to waste our last pennies on paper?" I said. "So that you can write more poems to Mary?"

"What do you mean 'our last pennies'?"

I wished that I had bit my tongue, for I had been keeping the extent of our difficulties secret and now I knew what would follow.

John began twisting the pen tightly in his fingers as if he would wring something from it. "I won't see us in the poorhouse! We'll not be paupers! Where is my annuity from the trust fund, the money from Earl Fitzwilliam?"

He stared at me as though I should have the answer to the tardiness of lords. I opened my mouth to say that it was difficult to see how one could remind someone directly of their charitable intentions, but that perhaps writing on another subject might remind them of one's existence and thereby jog their memory about the other matter. I had no chance to voice this advice, however, before John started off again.

"I've written to Dr Allen asking him to send on directly any money he holds for me, but I have little hope of ever seeing it. The world is full of unkept promises and friends who fall away. No one is to be depended upon." He turned his back on me.

I took the apple basket into the kitchen, where Parker was sitting by the fire.

"You sold some, then?" he asked. "That was well done."

Most of the remaining apples had survived the journey well and could be stored, but since there were a few that were bruised I picked those out and gave them to him to peel. He took his paring knife from his pocket and began to run it round an apple towards his thumb, which was all bent backwards with the stiffness of age.

I heard the outer door open and thought that it would be William, but it was Jack who came in, though he wasn't expected until the evening. He went straight to the fireside, sat down opposite Parker and bent over to unlace his boots.

"What's wrong? Are you all right? Where's Freddy?" I asked. I could see that the poor boy was frozen to the marrow of his bones and couldn't make his fingers work to unpick his wet laces. When he looked up at me his face was pale as whey.

"Don't worry, he's well," he said quickly, reading in my eyes the fear that his early return might signal that some disaster had occurred. "Freddy's still at work." He shrugged. "I, as you can see, am not."

"They've not turned you off?" I said.

Jack nodded. "They're selling a team. Master thought he'd do it now and save feeding them all winter."

I sat down hard at the kitchen table. There was no point asking why it had been Jack and not one of the others: he was the youngest of them, only fifteen, had been there the shortest time and that was the way it always worked.

"They didn't even give you a week's notice?"

Jack fished in his pockets and brought out a handful of coins. He cupped them in one palm and held them out to me. "They paid me when they told me this morning." He tipped the money into my hand.

"This morning?" I echoed.

Parker broke off momentarily from his careful peeling and held the apple as if weighing it in his hand. "Bad time, with winter coming in," he said. "Was it those new ploughing engines? Was that it?"

"Those and the threshing machines," Jack said. He pulled a wry face. "You know how they measure the head of steam those engines get up? Horse power. They do, they really do — they measure it as the number of horses the engine can replace." He snorted. "As if all horses were the same, like stamped metal, like cogs and wheels."

"But where have you been all day?" I said and pushed the money on to the table so that I could take his hands and chafe them between mine. As I leant towards him I noticed that beneath the scent of fresh weather that he had brought indoors with him was still the smell of the stable: oat straw, old wood, horse.

Jack stared at his half-unlaced boots. "I tried for work over at the quarry where Sefton got a place, and at Burghley, in case Father's name might be remembered by the Head Gardener and still count for something, but I had no joy." He looked up at me. "I didn't want to come home with all bad news."

Parker shook his head. "Not even decent notice. Things aren't done as they should be these days. No sense of responsibility for a man's livelihood; all they care about is writing a profit figure in the ledger with noughts like a line of fat raisins." He picked out another apple and made a sharp incision in it.

Jack said, "Horses are all I know. I won't get another job until the hiring fair in the spring."

A glum silence fell upon the room, broken only by the scrape of Parker's knife against the crispness of the apple. He reached the end without breaking the peel, but instead of holding it up with his usual exclamation of triumph he dropped it into his lap and rested his hands upon his knees.

I thought about my raised hopes at selling some fruit to Mr Darnley. The money was a drop in a bucket compared with Jack's earnings. Even if I sold off the entire orchard's crop I would replace only one month's worth of a grown man's wage. And Sophie and Charles were due to go back to school next week. Sophie needed a new slate and Charles, new shoes. I chewed at the side of my thumbnail while I calculated how long the rent money I had saved would last us and wondered how I could postpone the paying over of the rent. Thoughts of bacon and meat stew had better be forgotten: it would be thin soup and kettlins, and what kind of food is that to keep out the cold?

The silence proved too much for Jack. He rose and went upstairs. Eliza quietly put on water to boil for tea. I listened for sounds of Jack moving overhead and when none came I feared that he was even more bothered than he had let show. I said to Eliza, "No tea for me, my love," and went upstairs.

The boys' bedroom door was ajar and Jack was sitting on the end of the bed with his head in his hands. I sat down beside him on the saggy mattress and gave his shoulder a squeeze. He didn't look up and so we sat in silence for a while.

"There will be other work eventually," I said, putting a brave face on it.

"Not with such horses," he said into his palms.

"Ah, you'll miss them," I said, suddenly understanding that this was much more than money worry and hurt pride, for the bond between a carter and his horses is a strong one. To the horse, the man is hay and oats and water, he is the brush that takes away the itch and the warm blankets over flanks chilled with sweat. To the man, the horse is the follower of his will, he pulls when the man says pull, hastens at the click of the tongue on teeth. He is the instrument between the man's hand on the plough and the furrow in the earth, and the man, through him, wields ten-fold the power of his arm.

Jack passed one hand across his face. "They were already gone when I got there," he said to the floor. "I should have liked to lead them out. I should have liked to send them out with their coats glossy and their brasses shining and their manes braided as they were for Stamford Show."

"They were beautiful, Jack," I said, "and they couldn't have had a kinder, better master." But I knew from the hunch of his shoulders that nothing I could say would be nearly enough.

He shook his head. "When I think of leading them it's as if I can still hear the creak of their collars and feel their breath on my neck."

I took his hand. "Come and help me store apples," I said, and led him from the room like a child. We went down to the scullery, where the apple trays lay stacked one above the other on the high shelves that ran along one side of the room. Our winter's logs were stacked beneath, along with a sacking bundle that Parker had placed there and said no one was to touch.

I made Jack hold a chair steady while I climbed it and then asked him to pass the apples up to me one by one. I spread them on the willow slats of each tray in turn, being careful that none should touch and spoil. They glowed in the dim light cast by the one tiny window and filled the cool room with their sweet smell. I carefully replaced the wooden blocks that separated the trays to let the air pass between them. I looked around at the rows of trays that were still empty: what I had stored seemed pitiful few. But better than nothing, I thought as I climbed down.

Jack took my arm to steady me. He held on to it and said, "Those horses served me well. I should have been there, Ma." He laid his head for a moment on my shoulder and I laid my cheek against his hair and marvelled at the strong springy curls that once had been wispy baby hair, soft as a handful of skeins of silk.

CHAPTER
FOURTEEN

The Wayfarer

November was a month for chill rains and fog. The clouds seemed to descend upon us so that the very air became water and the sound of geese calling would build up eerily out of nowhere, only to pass overhead and fade again into the distance. The fens to the east of us flooded. Deeping Mere brimmed over, leaving its reed beds stranded in the centre of a new lake, water stretching its silvery arms across the fields in a cold embrace, fingering the hedgerows. The landscape was shaped anew: drainage ditches filled and overflowed and low land hard won from the marshes was reclaimed by its natural element. Pools and lakes of standing water appeared overnight where pasture used to be and cows lowed piteously from the hedge banks and had to be rescued and led to drier ground.

John hankered to be back in Helpstone, where the landscape did not betray you and change to something new and unknown and where there was no danger of waking to find water lapping at your threshold in the morning.

It was on just such a dreary afternoon that I returned home from visiting with Anna to find Eliza in a state of consternation. She met me at the door, saying that John had gone walking, striding over the fields with no hat, his head down into the wind. He had been gone all afternoon.

"It's not much of a day to be walking," I said, unwrapping the damp shawl from around my head and pushing back behind my ears the strands of hair that had come loose. "What brought this about?"

"He was walking up and down in the parlour. Reciting."

"Did no one think to go with him and keep him company?"

"We had no chance to ask if we might go," Eliza said. "He was walking and muttering and then he just banged his papers down on the desk and set off."

"Without even a coat?"

Eliza nodded.

I lifted his coat from the peg. "William!" I called out, then louder, "*William!*"

William came shuffling out from the kitchen in his stocking soles and with his mouth full of something, which I suspected was one of my new-baked scones, meant for tea-time.

I thrust the coat at him. "Go and find your father and take him this," I said.

"Where's he gone?" said William, spraying crumbs.

"If I knew that I wouldn't need to send you looking," I said. "And tell him to come home for his tea while there's still some to be had." I gave him a pointed look.

Eliza and I settled down to some sewing, but I made slow progress as I kept glancing at the window and listening for the door. At last I heard Parker letting someone in, but instead of William and John it was Parson Mossop arrived to visit us. Eliza and I quickly moved to tidy away the sheets that we were hemming.

"You find me all at sixes and sevens," I said, tucking one folded end of the sheet under my chin while I brought the other up to meet it. "If you'd like to wait while I put more wood on the fire in the parlour . . ."

"No need at all, Patty," the parson said. "I shall do very well here," and he sat himself down at the table that was still spread with all our needles and scissors and pincushions, leaving the fireside to Parker. I must admit that I was relieved as our log store was not as full as it could be. Eliza began to make tea and find plates for the scones.

Parson Mossop glanced round. "You are very quiet at home today?" he said.

"John is out and the children are upstairs resting after helping with the Potters' pigs."

"Not at school?"

I blushed, for we were so short of money I had had to take them out of school. William had been mending the gaps left by the gleaners and the labourers in the hedges and the farmer had needed someone to mind his pigs and stop them slipping through the holes. So, for a couple of days, while William stuffed brushwood into the thin places, Charles and Sophie herded the swine for pennies and threw sticks up into the oak trees to get acorns down for them.

Parson Mossop looked thoughtful. "Forgive me if I'm being indelicate," he said, "but has John had all the annuities promised him by his various patrons?"

I shook my head, for the interest on the annuities that we depended on had still not been sent and even the half-yearly five pounds that we had been promised by Earl Spencer was overdue and we feared perhaps forgotten.

"Then, John must write and ask," the parson said.

"His pride won't let him," I said quickly.

Parson Mossop tapped his teeth with his nail. "Maybe I could ask on his behalf?"

"I doubt he would agree to that," I said, remembering a time when a well-wisher had written to Lord Milton asking that John be given employment. John had then himself written to Lord Milton, a letter full of apology and regret that His Lordship had been so bothered. The offence he had felt at being treated as a charity case had shown between the lines just as if it had been writ there in ink.

"Will he be back soon? I could at least put it to him as a proposition."

I glanced at the window. The thin drizzle that had been falling all afternoon persisted and the afternoon would soon begin to draw in. "He should be back before too long," I said. "He has only gone for a walk."

Eliza handed out the tea things and offered round the scones, which I noticed thankfully she had cut in halves to make them go further. Parson Mossop bit into one.

"Very good scones, Patty," he said. "You have a light touch with your baking." We pressed him to have another but he refused and sipped his tea. "And what of the rest of the family?" he asked. "Jane would have come with me but she has a dreadful cold and I thought the weather too damp for her to venture out."

I started to express my sympathy that Jane did so poorly, but Parker broke in gruffly. "Jack lost his job and has had to go away to work on the other side of the county and board with a wagoner's family."

Parson Mossop looked from Parker to me, his eyes full of concern. "This must make things very difficult. I dare say if he's boarding he only has a pittance to send home."

As always, his sympathy undid me and all my worries came tumbling out. "It's true," I said, "but, worse than that, we all miss him something awful. Ever since Jack went, John talks of the family being split up and imagines it the first step to the poorhouse. He tells Eliza that she must stay with us in the house and seems convinced that she'll go off into service, even though she has no idea of such a thing and knows I cannot do without her here." I had to stop and catch my breath. "He can't rest until the children come home safe at day's end, thinking William might be tempted to take wood or game that he shouldn't or the young ones may venture too near the water and fall in. He worries until he exhausts himself and falls into muttering, fancying he is someone else entirely and safe from all these troubles."

"Why have you not sent for me before now, Patty?" Parson Mossop said at the end of my outburst.

I blinked and set about picking up the loose pins on the table and returning them to the pincushion. "I tell myself that at least Jack will be well fed. He writes that the wagoner's wife gives them butter for their bread and onions with boiled bacon."

The parson shook his head. "A sorry state of affairs. As soon as I'm home I'll have a basket of food made up and sent over to you." He lifted his hand to quell my protest that we would manage. "And like it or not, I must speak to John about pursuing the money that has been promised." He nodded vehemently. "There must be an intervention. He may not like it, but for the family's sake it must be done."

We sat in silence save for the ticking of the clock and the sound of the parson drumming his nails restlessly on the boards of the table. I pondered that I had not told him the half of it, not about John's letter to Dr Allen, nor how unpredictable John had become, swinging from being half crazed with worry on his family's behalf to extremes of irascibility when he would berate me with imagined faults and failings.

Into the silence dropped the sound of the house door rattling as it opened and John's voice exclaiming, followed by the scuff and shuffle of shoes being taken off. "It's preposterous!" John was saying. William's voice was low in reply, placatory, a murmur that I couldn't make out.

John strode in, pushing the door so hard that it bounced off the wall and shuddered a little on its hinges. He looked round at all of us but didn't pay any heed to the fact that we had a visitor or to our sombre silence: his face wore the expectant expression of one checking that his whole audience is attentive.

"There has been a mistake," he said. "What has happened to the old path? Someone has planted a hedge across it — not even a stile! And the way is all nettles and brambles either side, so you can't follow it without being snagged at every step."

"Where did you find your father?" I asked William.

"In one of the cow pastures."

I raised my eyebrows as if to say "And?"

"On the way that used to run across the fields to Glinton." He flushed.

I let out a long sigh. I had thought that William, having been absent from the harvest home, would be unaware of his father's renewed fancies about Mary Joyce, but this was evidently not the case. It made me wonder if the children talked among themselves of John's odd behaviour and whether the younger ones were as unaware as I had assumed, for Eliza wouldn't have discussed it with William. Sophie, I thought, Sophie is so quiet that you almost forget she's there, but those big eyes see everything and what's beyond her understanding she stores up to worry at like a dog with a bone.

"Hedges everywhere!" John raised his voice.

Parson Mossop half rose from his seat. "Calm yourself, John," he said.

"We are all hedged about with hawthorn that you can't push through. William tried but he couldn't make a passage."

I glanced at William's hands, all covered with scratches, and couldn't help but tut and frown. "Whatever were you thinking of?" I said to both of them, reaching down to get the iodine from the cupboard under the pot shelf. "William, for someone who won't do as he's told you have a strange habit of doing whatever damn-fool thing your father thinks up. Sorry, Parson," I added. I tipped a little iodine on to a rag and held on tight to William's hand so that he couldn't pull it away while I dabbed it.

Parson Mossop sat back down, watching John closely.

"A gamekeeper came," William whispered to me. "I was trying to get us away before he caught up with us."

John looked at him sharply, as if he would tolerate no interruptions. "'There's been a terrible mistake,' that's what I told the man, 'this hedge is in the way,' and he had the audacity to laugh and say that we had better go back the way we'd come as we were on private land, unless we wanted to be taken for poachers, the both of us." John banged the door frame with his fist. He glared round at us and began to mutter to himself.

"Was it Curtis?" I asked William.

William nodded and my heart sank, for Curtis was the keenest of the gamekeepers and desperate to make an impression on his master. William drew in his breath sharply with each dab of the blue-stained cloth. "He turned us back," he said, "and we got some way down the path, but as soon as we were well out of range Father started talking about High Beech and madhouse keepers and people following him, and he was all for us going back to take him on and said that between us we should box him well."

At this Parson Mossop pinched the bridge of his nose between his thumb and forefinger. "This is not good, Patty," he said, "not good at all."

"Do you think Curtis will take it further?" I asked William.

He shrugged. "Father turned back to face him up and said he was Jack Randall and why didn't he step up like a man, and Curtis stood with his hands in his pockets, scowling, while Father stared at him."

"Tell me it didn't come to blows," I said, glancing at the parson and imagining the constable coming at any minute to hammer on the door.

William shook his head. "I just kept walking and calling to Father that it was time we were home and eventually he came away, though he's been like this ever since."

"You did well," I said.

"Maybe Father's angry that I walked away," he said. "Is it my fault? Should I have done different?"

"No, you did well."

Parson Mossop patted William's arm and said, "Thank the Lord you were there, William."

John looked up on hearing the parson's sonorous voice. "You should be able to walk where you want; a free man should be able to walk to the edge of the world!" he said. "They have no right, no right, to catch the land in parcels and tie it up in green thorn!" But despite the anger in his words I saw that his hand against the door jamb trembled.

Parker, who had been nodding as though listening hard to all that John had to say, motioned to him to take a seat by the fire. "Come and warm yourself, son," he said. "You look half-starved with the cold."

John took a step into the room and looked about him uncertainly.

Parker patted the arm of the chair. "There's no one here but your family and our good friend the parson. Come and sit in your own fireside corner and share some baccy with your old father." He fished into a pocket, took out a folded paper, unfolded it and began to pull off a plug of tobacco for John to chew, talking to him quietly all the while.

I finished tending to William's hands. "There," I said, and kissed him roughly on the top of his head.

"There are other places to walk," Parker was saying. "There are some marvels to be seen in the fens. Do you remember, when we first moved here from Helpstone, showing me the yellow flags that grew all along the banks of Cross Drain?"

"Everywhere has its beauties in the summer," John said grudgingly, "but the fens are dreary in the colder months: so grey and bare." He rubbed his arms. "The wind can blow right through you," he leant forward as if telling Parker a secret, "until you feel you're hardly there at all."

Parker looked at John with puzzlement. He rubbed his bristly chin. "Well, it's true that flat fields and flat sky can make for dull walking in the winter, but we must count our blessings and walk while the weather lets us." He beckoned Eliza over. "'Liza, make us another strong pot of tea, one you could stand a spoon up in, there's a good girl."

John said no more but sat gazing into the embers of the fire. I gave quiet thanks for Parker's straightforwardness and practicality.

Parson Mossop took a small book from his pocket and put it on the table. "George Herbert's verse," he said to me in a low voice: "always an inspiration. Perhaps you would pass the volume on to John? Now is not the time for him and me to have our talk, I think." In a louder voice he said, "I must take my leave," and stood. He shook everyone by the hand and when he came to John he told him not to get up but clasped his hand warmly, John's fist disappearing entirely between his large palms. "I'll visit you again soon," he said to John.

"Very well," John muttered, "for we're in sore need of true friends." He looked up at him with dark eyes. "Soon the water will be at the door and we will all float away."

"We'll not let that happen; I'll come again soon, never worry," he said.

I showed the parson into the hall and shut the door behind us. "You must forgive John; he's not been well . . ." I started.

"I fear for him, Patty," he said, looking at me directly. "I fear that he'll harm himself or that unwittingly he'll bring the family to harm."

"He isn't as bad as this all of the time," I said.

He kept up his level gaze. "Nonetheless, I should like Dr Skrimshire to see him."

I was glad of the dimness of the late afternoon in the ill-lit hall to hide the tears that came to my eyes, for I knew what calling the doctor would mean. Dr Skrimshire would say that John was no better than when he was sent to High Beech and he required care that his family couldn't give him.

"He has some better days," I said, but as the words were spoken I knew that in truth there had been few good days since before harvest and, in the three months that had passed, John had become violently changeable and his misery more pronounced. "It's always harder in the winter," I said. "If I can just wean him through to spring . . ."

Parson Mossop put his hand on my arm. "I hope that will be possible, Patty, but it does no harm to be prepared in case the illness continues to worsen. I can write to Earl Fitzwilliam for support: perhaps he might find a place for John at the asylum at Northampton."

"There is Christmas coming soon," I pleaded. "No one should take a man from his home at Christmas."

Parson Mossop sighed. "Very well," he said, "let us reconsider about the doctor after Christmas, but I'll write to the earl as a safeguard, just in case. Hope for the best but prepare for the worst, eh? That's always been my motto." He opened the door and a chill blast of damp air swept in. "Take care, Patty," he said. "Mind, I've not forgotten about the provisions. I'll send them over tomorrow."

274

I stood at the door to see him down the path, but he waved me in. "Don't catch cold," he said. "Go on inside."

Unable to face returning to the family, I went into the parlour. The fire had burnt itself out. I pulled up the little three-legged stool and sat down, then stretched out my hands, but there was only the faintest warmth. The cinders had fallen through to the tray beneath and the grate yawned, black and empty. "I'll set a good fire tomorrow and keep it well banked up," I said to myself. "John shall have his writing if he has nothing else." My harsh words that he should have no more paper came back to me and I regretted them bitterly, for in truth I had no quarrel with his writing, only with the words he had written that had hurt my feelings and my pride. At least he will be occupied again and able to retreat into work and hide away from the world, I thought, though at a deeper level I felt troubled and uneasy about this as a solution.

Outside, the day had worsened and a squall of rain blew down the chimney, bringing with it a spatter of grit and soot. I shivered. *The wind can blow right through you until you feel you're hardly there at all,* he'd said.

I thought of the letter to Dr Allen, in which John had said he would like to live like a hermit. The parson would argue that retreating to an asylum, where he would want for nothing and would have the peace he craved, would be the best way to achieve his desire for Trouble to leave him be. It all made sense, yet it seemed like giving up. I couldn't, *wouldn't*, accept it.

I thought of the way that John had written of us, as if he sought to sever every tie with his real, living family. Surely such bonds were the guy ropes that would tether you against the wind and keep you in place, sure of who you were and where you belonged? But for John, unable to cope any longer with being the head of the household, a place where there were only his poems for company felt safer. Poems that re-invented a simpler time . . .

A place where he could be peaceful, yes, but lonely, too, surely: a place where a person would feel thin, transparent as the honesty in the hedgerows that the wind blew through with the dry rustle of paper.

CHAPTER
FIFTEEN

The Holly and the Ivy

The day before Christmas I took Sophie and Charles out in the lanes to gather greenery to bring into the house, leaving Eliza at home making pastry. I climbed the hedge bank and sawed through the tough stems of ivy with Parker's paring knife and pulled the strands away from the bark in long twining strips.

"See how it holds on so tight," I said to the children, who climbed up beside me, holding open the old grain sacks we'd brought to hold our booty. "The tree will do better without it."

"They look like centipede legs," Charles said, pointing at the suckers on the underside of the stems.

"But the leaves are pretty," Sophie said, "and we can drape the long pieces on the mantels and window-sills." She held a piece out like a banner. "Will everything be just like last year with a big fire and candles set by the mirrors so that everything is bright? And presents and games and a pudding?"

"Will there be a thruppence in it?" said Charles.

"I don't know about that. Sophie nearly swallowed it last year, do you remember?" I said. "Let's try for mistletoe down Fox Cover." I changed the subject quickly as, without Jack's wage, money was so tight I feared that Christmas would be a sparser affair than last year with plums the best thing in the pudding. I remembered magical Christmases past at Helpstone, when John's poems were the toast of the town and publishers and patrons sent gifts along with compliments: silk neckerchiefs and eau de cologne, spinning tops and toy hussars. And there were boxes of books with gilt on the covers: as well as story-books for the children there were volumes of poetry, religious treatises and all manner of learned things for John. My favourites were those with pictures inside. I loved the natural histories of birds and animals and the botanical volumes with plates showing strange flowers with long stamens or fleshy petals such as are never seen in these parts. John used to gather the children round the fire and read to them from the new story-books they'd been given. I would lean on the back of his chair, looking at the pictures of George and the Dragon or the Genie of the Lamp, in colours that glowed even brighter than the fire, forgetting the steaming pot or the dishcloth in my hands.

Even after such times had fallen away, John and I had always managed sixpenny chap-books for the children. The presents I had this year were all simple, home-made things. At least they shall have something, I thought fiercely, and we'll all be together except for Jack. A familiar pang shot through me as I thought of him too far away to travel home for Christmas Day, and I hoped he would be warm and well fed and treated as part of his employer's family in the spirit of the season.

278

John had not been persuaded to write to his patrons and Christmas festivities had doubtless put a penniless poet even further from Their Lordships' minds. He had received a reply from Dr Allen, which he had read out to me. It was full of good wishes and told John that there was a place for him at High Beech with bed and board any time he wished to come, as long as he did nothing to make himself unpleasant as a visitor, and that he would be free to come and go as he pleased. There was no mention of money.

John had sat over the letter, gnawing on his knuckle, then picking it up and putting it down and reading it again. When I had suggested that Dr Allen was probably holding the money to use as future fees should he ever return to High Beech, he flew into a rage at me and said I wished him back there. When I told him that I did not but only wondered whether writing to Dr Allen to say that he intended to stay home for good might then elicit the money, he said that on the contrary he wouldn't be staying very long in this hellish fen and would soon be with his other family. He said that, in any case, his Byron poems would soon be out and he would have no need of the money.

"What poems are these, John?" I asked.

"George Gordon, Lord Byron," he said, and smiled and patted my arm as if all was well after all.

Finally he screwed the letter into a ball, saying in a perfectly conversational tone, "I won't go back to that shithole. Leopards Hill is nothing but a prison and Springfield a whore-house full of pox." He dropped the letter on the floor and returned to his writing, muttering imprecations upon "Dr Bottle-Imp" and all his keepers, and I thought it prudent to creep away and make sure the family let him alone until he should be calm again.

The children and I walked on together through the frost-bound country. Where the fields had flooded, they had turned to ice and the reeds and bull rushes were decked with icicles like pennants where the fog had dripped and clung, to be blown horizontal and turned to glass by the bitter east wind. The ploughed fields of the higher ground were dusted all over with rime. The furrows were hard, their tilth that once turned crumbling at the ploughshare now set like iron waves in a rutty sea. Winter had the land in its fist.

Charles set his heel to a puddle, trying to break through the ice. With each blow you could see the dark water moving beneath and the ice whitened and powdered on the surface but wouldn't break.

"I hope it snows tomorrow," Sophie said.

"It's almost too cold for snow," I replied as we stopped to take some holly from the hedge.

"We could skate on the mere," Charles said, giving up trying to break the puddle and sliding to and fro on it instead.

"The ice might not be thick enough," I said. "It has to be thick right through to the middle to be safe, you know."

"There aren't many berries on this," Sophie said, pulling the holly branches apart.

"The birds have had them already," I said. "Never mind, if we take some of the newer branches we'll get some lighter green. The leaves are softer too." I took one and pinched it, showing Charles that the sprigs with the small yellower leaves could be picked without prickling.

"I can't fit much more in," he said when his sack was almost full. Sophie pulled her sleeve down over her hand and pushed the contents of her sack further down.

"Still more room for mistletoe there, I think," I said, and we walked on towards the oak, its own leaves all but stripped, save for a few brown tatters holding fast, but its trunk twined about with thick, ropy stems and its branches draped in green.

"That one's the best," Sophie said, pointing at a huge ball that hung just out of reach.

"We only need a little bit," I teased.

"You could lift Charles up: he could get it."

I stooped down and Sophie helped Charles to climb up on to my shoulders and then steadied me as I got back to my feet. She passed Charles the knife and he held on to the branch while cutting the knotty stem. The clump of foliage fell and Sophie caught it, a look of triumph on her face. I let Charles down gratefully and rubbed my shoulders.

"I'm going to put this up," Sophie said, teasing out a piece and running her finger over its long round-ended leaves, its white berries like a cluster of pearls. She twirled it in her fingers.

"Where will you put it, then?" I asked.

"In the doorway for visitors," she said promptly, then flushed.

Aah, the whole world loves Sefton, I thought to myself.

When we got home, Sophie and Charles wanted straight away to deck the house out in green finery. We laid yew and box on the window-sills and draped ivy round the mirrors and along the mantel above the fire.

Sophie dragged a chair into the hall and stood on it to reach the top of the door and fix a bunch of mistletoe there. Charles, in a sulk because she would give none to him, began to wobble the chair, making her squeal and grab on to its back. She jumped down and gave him a shove.

"Come now," I said. "There's a deal more to do; everyone shall have a turn."

Charles picked up the second sack and took it into the parlour and I followed. John was sitting at the desk with his chin on his hand, staring fixedly through the window and across the garden as though waiting for his next words to walk towards him across the field. Sophie came in, dragging the chair behind her; it scraped horribly on the flagged floor and John blinked but remained determined to ignore our presence.

"We've come to decorate the room, John," I said as I helped Charles up on to the chair so that he could tuck sprigs of holly round the picture frames. He draped a great garland of ivy atop John's portrait, but one end immediately came loose and flopped over the painting, falling across the yellow waistcoat and olive-green coat

282

like a sash. Charles went on tiptoe to try to lift it back, overbalanced and knocked the painting crooked, just as Sophie took a huge armful of greenery from the sack and dumped it down on the window-sill right in John's line of vision.

"Oh, for God's sake!" he roared. Both children froze: Charles with his hand upon the bottom corner of the painting and Sophie in the act of spreading out the twigs. "Is there nowhere I can get any peace?" He slapped his palms down on to the desk, then began to mutter as he tapped the fingers of each hand in turn: "Boxer, Byron, Boxer, Byron, Boxer . . ."

"Hop down," I said to Charles, who was staring at John with a face as long as a fiddle. "I'll do this." I straightened the picture and jerked my head towards the door to signal to Sophie that she and Charles should go. They picked up the chair together and very carefully carried it from the room.

"I'm sorry we disturbed you," I said to John and, leaving the ivy trailing at a crazy angle across the painting, crossed the room to pick up Charles's sack.

John put his head down upon his arms as if to block out sight and sound. I could hear the children whispering in the hallway.

"We're finished now," I said, and tiptoed out, closing the door gently behind me.

Charles, his lower lip stuck out, was pushing Sophie's sack with his toe and Sophie was picking the leaves off a mistletoe sprig, rolling them between her fingers and dropping them on to the floor.

"Your father's feeling a bit unwell and out of temper," I said, and hung the holly sack from the coat peg. "Come with me. I've got an idea for a present for him for tomorrow that'll cheer him up."

I took them to the kitchen, where Eliza was filling pastry cases with sugar and currants. I settled them beside the fire with Parker and brought out all the paper wrappings from our purchases over the last few months: brown paper that had wrapped cotton and flannel, blue sugar paper and white paper bags that could be slit open and laid flat. I gave Charles the pair of scissors, saying, "Cut all the sheets to the same size, as big as you can make them, with nice straight edges." Then I gave Sophie a needle and thread and told her to sew the pieces into two little books to give to John, one from her and one from Charles.

"Do you think he'll like them?" Sophie said.

"I know he will," I said with all the warmth I could muster.

"Should we draw a picture on the front, like a cover?" she asked, her brow wrinkled.

"That's a good idea," I said. "You could draw your favourite animal or one that Father has written about like the hedge-pig or the wagtail. Do you remember the poem about the hedge-pig rolling in the crab-apples? It went:

'The hedgehog hides beneath the rotten hedge
And makes a great round nest of grass and sedge
Or in a bush or in a hollow tree
And many often stoops and say they see

Him roll and fill his prickles full of crabs
And creep away and where the magpie dabs
His wing at muddy dyke in aged root
He makes a nest and fills it full of fruit . . .'"

The children having settled to their tasks, I took out the ham that Parson Mossop had so kindly sent over, along with spices, raisins and butter for a pudding. I began to make incisions in the good thick layer of fat and to press cloves into them, in studded rows.

There was a knock at the door and Charles jumped up to answer it. He returned with Sefton, who was carrying a pail. Sophie scrambled to her feet and Eliza rubbed her sticky hands on her apron.

"Happy Christmas, one and all," he said, handing the pail to Eliza.

"Eggs," Eliza said to me.

I smiled. Now we had all we needed for a pudding.

"Anna has sent me to find out what time we should come tomorrow for Christmas dinner."

"Is she well?" I asked.

"Just a little tired, I think. She has to take a nap in the afternoon or she's nodding over her tea these days." He cast his eye over the food spread before us and then winked at me. "I see it will be a banquet."

"Come between noon and one o'clock; that'll give us plenty of time to prepare after morning church," I said.

Eliza had put the pail on a chair and had started to take out the eggs and put them into a bowl so that Sefton could take back the bucket.

"I packed them in straw," Sefton said, "so none would get cracked. Look, there are more beneath," and he put his hand into the bucket to lift the straw.

Eliza dropped her eyes quickly from his and muttered that we should have a grand pudding.

Charles pulled at Sefton's hand to get him to look at the books they were making and Sefton squatted down and talked earnestly with him and Sophie about what pictures they should draw. "What about the Turkish Knight?" he said to Charles. "Like in the mummer's play."

From the corner of my eye I saw Eliza take something from the straw and slip it into her apron pocket, then she picked out the last egg and placed it in the bowl.

"And for Sophie," Sefton was saying, "Christmas bells and ribbons, pretty as a picture . . ."

Sophie was looking at him with eyes like saucers.

"I need to steam the ham," I said. "Excuse me." I came over with my pot of water and stood so that they must clear a path for me to reach the fire. Sefton rose to his feet and I hung the pot on a hook above the flames. "We'll expect you after noon, then; tell Anna," I said to Sefton.

He moved towards the door. "We'll see you then, for feasting and fine times, eh, Charles?" Casually he picked up the bucket. "I'll see myself out," he said, with a nod to us all, and left. The sound of whistling, *We all want some figgy pudding*, reached us as he regained the lane and set off for home.

The children returned to their snipping and stitching. Eliza picked up the bowl of eggs, saying, "I'll put these in the scullery to be cool." I dithered for a moment, picking up the stray wisps of straw that had been scattered, unsure what to do, then followed her.

She was standing with her back to me, facing the small high window, looking down at something in her hands, and didn't hear me come in.

"Eliza," I said softly.

She spun round with a gasp, dropping a slip of paper wrapping, which floated to the floor, and closed her hand around its contents.

"Is it a gift?" I said.

She opened her hand, which held a glint of silver. I stepped closer to look. A tiny oval locket, no bigger than a fingernail, lay at the centre of a tangle of fine silver chain.

"Where . . . ? How . . . ?" I exclaimed in spite of myself, for I had never seen such a delicate piece of jewellery. "Is it stolen? You must give it back!"

"Sefton wouldn't give me something stolen," she said indignantly. "He . . ."

"Eliza," I said, a warning in my voice, "you must give it back not because of where it might have come from but because you have no right to accept it, and nor is Sefton free to give it."

Eliza closed her hand round the chain, and the locket dangled, catching the light. Her eyes filled with tears. "It's Christmas," she said.

"What? A Christmas gift from a brother-in-law is given after dinner round the fire with the rest, for all to see, not secretly, the day before!"

I picked up the piece of paper and handed it back to her. "You must wrap it back up and find a private time to return it. Anna must know nothing of this and, so help me, if Sefton carries on with this folly, never mind telling Freddy, I'll lay hands on him myself."

Eliza placed the locket on to the crumpled paper and trickled the chain round it, then folded it and returned it to her apron pocket. She kept her hand upon it as if even there it might get lost.

I put my arms round her shoulders, gave her a squeeze and said, "There now, it will be best for you, too, in the long run."

I turned back to the door, thinking to leave her a little while with her thoughts, and there was Sophie, peeping round, her face pale and her lips open. She started as I turned. She said quickly, "Charles has dropped the needle and it's stuck between the flags and I can't find another."

I stepped in front of Eliza so that Sophie shouldn't see she was upset. "In the pincushion," I said. "I'll come in a minute."

Sophie stared at me for a moment as if about to speak, then tipped up her chin a little and went back to the kitchen.

"Bring some logs when you come," I said to Eliza, trying to soothe my jangled nerves by a return to normality. "The fire needs building up a bit for all this boiling and baking."

CHAPTER
SIXTEEN

Starnels

When I awoke on Christmas morning the room was dim and I thought at first that snow had fallen in the night. I got out of bed, wincing as the soles of my feet met the cold boards, and found that the window was covered with feathery, ferny shapes. I breathed on the frost on the inside to melt a hole and tiny crystals came away as I rubbed my finger against the glass. The ice on the outside remained, though, and I remembered how Polly and I used to heat a penny in the stove to press it against the window to make a peep-hole. I lifted the iron latch and pushed the window until its icy seal gave way. I opened it a crack to find a bright, clear sky as brittle as the icicles that hung a foot long from the thatch. John grunted as the keen air cut into the room and I quickly shut the window as he pulled the quilt up round his ears.

I went downstairs and found the fire lit and the kitchen warm. I stretched my hand out and felt the heat, just as Freddy came in, dressed and carrying a bucket of water with his sleeve wrapped round the handle to stop his hand from sticking to it.

I gestured towards the fire. "Thank you. I thought you would sleep in on your holiday," I said.

"Happy Christmas, Mother," he said, setting the bucket down and enveloping me in a cold, fresh embrace. There were two plates on the table with crumbs round them. "Who else is up?" I asked.

"William," Freddy said. "He had breakfast, then went foraging for nails and a length of rope, and then the Astley brothers called for him and they all went off together."

"Hmm, that'll be one less of us at church, then," I said.

"But back again in plenty of time for dinner," Freddy said, and we both smiled.

When we all got back from church we were frozen to the marrow from sitting in the damp vaulted space, our breath mingling white as we sang the carols and our fingers and noses pinched red by the raw air. Parker and John had stayed abed when we left, but now Parker was in his chimney corner and John retired to the parlour. William had still not returned.

Eliza and I set to, boiling potatoes and stewing apples for a sauce for the bacon. The pudding, which I had wrapped in muslin before we went out and set to steam slowly, filled the kitchen with the warm, sweet smell of cinnamon and all-spice. Charles and Sophie, released from the stillness of church and excited by the thought of treats to come, grew rowdy and began a game in the hall, lining up the boots and shoes and trying to throw pebbles into them. Such a clattering

290

and banging, such a squabbling and quarrelling, they made about it that at length I heard John's chair scrape on the floor and then a pounding on the parlour door. Into this mayhem Anna and Sefton arrived. Anna picked her way carefully over the boots that had fallen on their sides, one hand placed protectively upon her belly, and Sefton, with a wide grin, followed, carrying a firkin of ale and a handful of penny whistles. I ushered them all into the kitchen except for Charles, who I told to tidy up the boots, and I endeavoured to get everyone seated round the table by sending Freddy to get extra chairs from the bedrooms. Parker shook Sefton's hand and gave his compliments of the season.

I helped Anna to a seat. "You're looking really well, Anna," I said.

"I'm fine apart from my swollen ankles," she said, smiling. She lifted her skirts and stuck out her feet to show me.

"You should lie with your feet raised. Sefton told me that you're taking a nap in the afternoons. I'm glad he's looking after you," I said in Sefton's direction.

"Of course, of course," Sefton said, taking Anna's shawl from her. "Her wish is my command." He shook the shawl out with a flourish and draped it over the back of her chair. Then he turned to me.

"Are we to have a tune?" he said, cocking his eyebrow and holding up the whistles.

"Not until after we've eaten," I said firmly, and he inclined his head and put the whistles up high on the mantel, then pulled a grimace at Charles and Sophie in mock misery.

"Pour everyone some ale, 'Liza, while I fetch your father," I said.

"It's very noisy," John said as soon as I entered. He put both hands to his temples.

"Dinner is ready, John," I said. "Will you come and have some?"

"Can people not celebrate quietly? I see no necessity for such a furore."

"It's just that we are delayed, waiting for William. Won't you come and have some ale with us?"

"Dr Bottle-Imp says, 'No Barleycorn broth,' though I say it does no harm," and he began to sing to himself: "*John Barleycorn, will keep you warm, Your love's forsworn, John Barleycorn.*"

"A little will not hurt," I said. "It's Christmas Day and Parson Mossop has sent us good vittles. We have a great deal to be thankful for."

"Very well," he said, slapping both hands down upon the desk. "I shall come and Jack Randall and Nelson and Byron and all, with gloves and my eye patch and pen."

Taking his arm, I led him in to dinner and seated him at the head of the table but next to Parker, so that he should have conversation that would be quiet and calm.

As I lifted the ham on to a plate I heard William come in. Although he tried to slip into his seat at table without my noticing, I saw that his breeches were wet to the thighs and he was shivering.

"What have you been doing, William?" I said. "How on earth did you manage to get so wet?"

Everyone turned to look at William and he muttered quickly, "We made a sledge and went out on the mere, me and the Astleys, and it fell through the ice."

"Are you completely out of your wits?" I said. "You could have been drowned!"

"I was all right. The sledge got wedged and they pulled me out."

"William! You could have gone right in and got trapped under the ice!" I felt sick at the thought. "How long do you think you would last in that freezing water?" John put his hands to his head and began to hum loudly. I glanced at him and then bit back my words. I would have to talk again to William later. "Go quickly and get dry clothes on," I said.

Eliza poured some ale for John and set it down in front of him and Parker asked him if his morning's work had gone well. He answered with no more than a nod, but he ceased humming and drank a little ale. I took a deep breath and turned my attention back to the dinner. I was soon taken up with how best to carve the meat so that everyone should have some and in ensuring that the potatoes were just right, neither hard in their middles nor falling apart. William returned to the table and I served the meat, then left Eliza to serve vegetables and sauce while I lifted out the pudding and, after unwrapping it from its muslin, transferred it to my mother's mixing bowl, the only container I had that was big enough to hold it. It looked very fine against the shiny white interior and with the rope decoration round the rim, and as a final touch I reached down a holly sprig from the mirror and pushed it into the soft, dark, treacly mound, then placed it on the table in the centre to a cheer and applause from the family.

Parker said the grace and all was silent for a while as everyone ate steadily and with great appetite, for this was food such as we hadn't seen since harvest time. William ate fastest of all, the cold having lent an urgency to his need to fill his belly.

At length conversation recommenced and toasts were drunk to the parson for his generosity and to "absent family" for Jack, at which I felt sad and filled my cup again.

Parker pushed his plate aside and rubbed his stomach. "I'm full to bursting," he said. "I'll have to pass up the pudding, though it hurts me sorely to do it."

There were more groans and heavy sighs from others, so that I suggested we break off from eating for a while and rest our overtaxed constitutions.

Charles straight away tugged at my elbow. "Can we do the presents? We've finished making them."

I nodded and Sophie and Charles got their little books, Sophie's with a fine picture of the rowan tree in our garden and Charles's with some big uneven stitches and a picture of a robin. They took them to John and delivered them with a kiss.

"For me?" John said. "You're very kind." He turned the pages of first one and then the other, smoothing his hand over each page. "Mr Byron will find these very useful." He tapped the side of his nose with his finger and Sophie began to giggle. He put the two little books side by side. "People are very kind," he said, "though the robin is very big for the tree." Charles looked back at me as if to know how he should respond.

"Come here to me," I said to the children and gave them the things I had made to hand out to the family: embroidered collars for the girls, mufflers for Freddy and William, a pen-wiper for John and a foot-warmer cover for Parker to save his feet from chilblains. For Charles I had made a glove puppet from an old sock, with wool twist for hair and a magician's cloak with yellow stars. Straightaway he put it on his hand and crawled under the table, holding the puppet up over the edge and making the spoons and forks dance with its antics.

Anna unbuttoned the cut-work collar she had on and, with Sefton's help, replaced it with mine, embroidered with stems of running stitch and French knots for roses.

"Thank you. It's beautiful," she said to me.

As Sefton straightened it for Anna, I noticed that Eliza put her hand to her own throat and pressed her palm against her dress just below her collar-bone, as if checking for something or feeling for a shape beneath, then she smoothed the collar she was wearing. She thanked me for the new one but folded it back into its wrapping and tucked it into her pocket.

To Anna I said, "Have you and Sefton exchanged gifts already?"

"He had a new pocket watch from me that I saved all year for."

"And you?" I prompted.

"Oh, I had mine far in advance: the material I told you of — for the baby's things."

"That's very practical." I looked hard at Sefton, who I saw at least had the grace to blush.

She laughed. "I'm very practical now I'm to be a mother." She nudged Sefton. "Show Ma your pocket watch," then said to me, "It has a copper case, just like a gentleman's."

"I didn't bring it," Sefton muttered. Anna looked disappointed. "It's safest in my weskit pocket and I didn't wear that today," he ended lamely.

Sophie and Charles were whispering in the corner. "We'll both take it," Sophie said, and they brought me a little book of folded paper.

"We made it from the leftovers," Charles said. "You have to hold the ends," and he took my hands and opened it out to reveal a string of dancing ladies all artfully cut so that they were joined by their raised hands and their stiff skirts. I danced them up and down, then pulled both children on to my knee and hugged them tight.

"I have nothing to give." John's voice was low and hoarse. "Not even a chap-book." He looked up at the mantel where the whistles lay. "Not even a penny whistle." He shook his head mournfully. "I have nothing for the children."

I loosened my hold on Sophie and Charles. "The gifts I made come as presents from us both, John," I said in a neutral tone.

"There used to be toys and fruit-cup and sugar plums . . . the *Arabian Nights*, paisley shawls, silks and paintings, a cornucopia . . ."

Parker put a hand on his arm. "Fortunes ebb and flow, my boy, and a boat must move with the tide and be thankful that it floats."

John shrugged off his hand and jumped to his feet. "I have something. I do have something!" he said, pushing his chair back hard against the wall. He turned and rushed from the room.

I passed my hand across my face. "Go after him, Freddy," I said, but before Freddy could rise from the table John returned, waving a sheaf of papers.

He held the pages out to face us and showed them round the table. "My next collection," he said reverently. "*Don Juan* by Lord Byron, soon to be published by Messrs Taylor and Hessey of Fleet Street, London, purveyors of poetry and saviours of the poor."

He put the papers up close to Parker's face and gave them a little shake. I opened my mouth to speak and John held up his hand to stop me. "The fact that neither party has been near in five years is neither here nor there, for who would remember to call on a madman, eh? eh?" He stared round the table as if daring us to challenge him.

Sophie made a funny sound in the back of her throat and I held her a little tighter.

"John," I said "now is not —"

He pointed his finger at me. "Don't you 'John' me," he said. "What better time than Christmas to celebrate a finished piece of work? Jack Randall's in the ring, step up, step up . . . The book is all but finished and we shall have Victory! We shall have Victory, the admiral says, and sail home in her and all will be well!"

He rifled through the papers, throwing some down regardless of the dirty dishes and plates, from which they soaked up grease and smudges of sauce. I told the children to hop down and I rose from the table, but we were so many that we were packed in and I could not make an easy passage to him.

He held up a page and began to read:

"Poets are born — and so are whores — the trade is
Grown universal — in these canting days
Women of fashion must of course be ladies
And whoring is the business — that still pays"

"Enough, John!"

All around me the faces were full of consternation. Anna's hand flew to her mouth in alarm and Sophie shrank behind my chair as if trying to put a barrier between her and what she was hearing. Charles, though not understanding the words, at the sight of everyone's faces began to cry.

John stared me in the eye. "You people," he said, laying down his papers. "To hell with you, then," and with one movement he put his hands under the edge of the table and lifted.

I pulled Charles towards me out of the way. Anna cried out and pushed herself back as plates, cutlery and dishes came sliding towards her. Sefton and Freddy moved to stop it from upending completely but were too late; with a clatter of metal and a smash of pottery, the dinner slid from the boards. With a thud the solid oak hit the flagstones and everyone scrambled back except for Parker, who sat as if transfixed, unable to move his old bones. I gave a cry at the sight of my pudding bowl, now reduced to shards of fawn and white china mixed in with a treacly mess, while ale frothed in a puddle round it and bacon fat and vegetable leavings were scattered among chipped and upturned plates.

Sefton, brushing down his breeches, which were splashed with beer, began a long stream of swearing and Anna tried to shush him. Charles joined Sophie behind the chair and Eliza went to them.

John stood with his fingers still resting on the edge of the table and with his mouth working with emotion. Freddy gave him a long look, then said in a quiet, precise voice, "Will you help me right the table, Sefton?" and he and Sefton took an end each, so that John had to step back. They set the table on its feet again.

I bent and picked up a piece of the rope-twist rim of the pudding bowl and put it back on the table.

"Oh John . . ." I said, in sorrow rather than anger, for he bent to pick up the two books of coloured paper that were now sodden and spoilt, their pages blotched and their ink drawings run into streaks and blobs.

"Oh no," he said and looked up at me like a child. "Where is the tree? Where is the bird?" Then he shoved them into his pocket. He crossed the room and climbed the stairs.

"I'm taking Anna home," Sefton said.

I nodded, took up her shawl and wrapped it tightly round her. I kissed her on both cheeks and felt them cold. "You're not to worry," I said. "It will be all right," though I could not see how. Sefton took her hand and led her away.

"Parker," I said quietly, forcing myself to sound calm, "would you take the children into the parlour and tell them one of your stories?"

Freddy brought a bucket and began to fill it with the food and broken china and William went to fetch water from the pump. Eliza stood with a plate in her hand but made no move to do anything with it. "That one is good," I said gently. "Look." She nodded and put it by.

I left them and went upstairs. John was sitting on the floor, squeezed into the space between the bed and the wash-stand. As I came towards him he brought his hands up to cover his face. "Leave me be," he whimpered, "leave me be."

I bent down to him but he turned his face away. I squatted down beside him. "You're not well, John," I said. "Won't you come and lie out on the bed? You'll feel better for a sleep."

At the sound of my voice he curled himself round his knees and started a low moaning cry. I inched forward and put my hand on his shoulder. As each keening came to an end I felt his body shudder under my hand. I stayed like this until at last he became quieter, his hunched shoulders dropped and his hands that clenched the fabric of his sleeves grew limp and let go.

"You're worn out and now you must rest, John," I said. I slipped my hand down to his elbow and supported him as he struggled to his feet. He sat on the edge of the bed, his face blotchy. As I eased off his jacket memories of the many times I had done this before, when he was groaning and dog-tired from a hard day's labour or laughing and garrulous from too much drink, came flooding into my mind; times when he was comfortable with my touch and such intimacy seemed natural. Now he sat unmoving and unmoved, letting me undress him as if barely aware of me. I folded the coat and hung it over my arm. John laid down his head on the pillow and I lifted his legs up on to the bed and took off his boots. I lifted the counterpane and quilt from my side of the bed and folded them over him.

Tucking the covers round him as I would with the children, I said, "What is it, John? What's the matter?"

"I can't get back," he whispered. "Spring and love are gone." He closed his eyes and furrowed his brow as if trying to push away evil thoughts and summon sleep.

I tiptoed towards the door and was met by Parker coming to find me. "I can't interest them in a story," he said. "Sophie's upset and Charles keeps asking what the matter is and why his father didn't like the books they made. I've left them with Eliza."

"I'm coming," I said. "John will sleep for a while now."

Parker looked over at the humped shape beneath the covers, his old face suddenly collapsed and fallen in, the lines round his mouth downturned and deeper. In a low voice he said, "This can't go on, Patty. There must be something the doctors can do." He took out a large handkerchief and blew his nose loudly.

"I'll watch over him tonight in case he wakes and goes wandering," I whispered. "You mind he used to do that last time, before High Beech? Out into the night in nothing but his nightshirt?" I let out a sigh. "And in the morning I'll send word to Parson Mossop." I was still carrying John's coat over my arm, holding it tight against my front. I smoothed my hand over the silky lining and hung it carefully over the back of a chair before following Parker downstairs.

The boys were still putting things to rights in the kitchen. Freddy had set about washing the floor and William was scrubbing the table. When he saw me, William broke off and came over. He stood still before me with his head bowed and I realized that, thirteen or no, he wanted me to put my arms round him. I drew him to me and he put his head down awkwardly upon my shoulder, for he overtopped me by a good head's height.

"Was it my fault, Ma?" he said. "It was only a prank on the ice; I didn't mean to fall through."

"It was no one's fault," I said, my voice thick in my throat.

"I swear I won't do it again. Nor climb up into the kites' nests like I did last summer, nor any other tomfoolery, if only Father can be well again."

302

I patted his back with the palm of my hand. "I'm glad that you'll be careful, for your own dear sake," I said, "but I fear no bargain you or I could make will help your father, for what ails him is beyond our influence." I leant back from him to see his face and found it pale with misery.

Parker sat down in his fireside chair with a heavy sigh. "You're doing a grand job on that table, William — better than I could do with my old creaky joints."

I squeezed William tight, then let him go. Without speaking, he nodded and went to pick up his scrubbing brush again. His shoulders were bent over his task as though a milk yoke was on them. In that moment I wished with all my heart that he could be the carefree boy still, however foolish his pranks, and not have to play the man before he was ready to put childish things behind him.

In the parlour, Eliza had set out a little table and was building a house of cards for the children. Charles sat on the floor beside her, looking sulky, while Sophie sat on a stool opposite and pulled her thumb across the top of the rest of the pack again and again, leaving the cards bent and dog-eared. As I opened my mouth to remonstrate, Eliza looked up at me and gave a little shake of her head.

"I've started with diamonds. Shall we use black next or use all red?" Eliza said.

"Red ones," Charles said.

"Don't care," Sophie said.

"Give me some hearts next, then," Eliza said.

Sophie flicked through the cards and picked out a handful, then cut the remainder into two piles and began shuffling them together roughly on her knee. Eliza delicately placed a card flat on to the points of those already balanced to make the first row of arches. She added another, saying, "Look, Charles, this is where it begins to get ticklish."

Charles knelt up to see. "Can I put one on?"

Eliza passed him a card, saying, "Go gently now," and he held his breath while he placed it carefully next to its neighbours.

"Why did Anna and Sefton have to go home?" Sophie said to me abruptly, tapping the pack of cards, first one side then the other, on her knee.

"It's important that Anna isn't upset," I said levelly. "Because of the baby."

"Are they not coming back again, then, so we can have supper and games after?"

"Not today, I'm afraid."

"Christmas is over, then," she said, pulling a mutinous face. "We never even played charades or anything."

Charles looked up, pausing with his hand outstretched to place another card.

"Come, Sophie, we can still entertain ourselves," Eliza said. "Why don't you do the next tier of the house?"

"I was going to show Sefton how I can play a carol on the penny whistle." Tears welled up in Sophie's eyes. "I don't want to play stupid cards!" She threw the pack of cards on to the table, where they spilled across the surface, knocking the foundations of Eliza's carefully arranged construction and bringing all down in a heap together.

Charles jumped to his feet, his face red and angry. "You've ruined it!" he shouted.

Sophie scowled back at him. "Well, Christmas is ruined anyway."

"I hate you!" Charles lunged across and gave Sophie's hair a sharp yank, making her yelp and push him hard by the shoulders.

"Charles! Sophie!" I said, catching hold of Charles as he stumbled back and pinning his arms by his sides as he tried to pull away.

Sophie stood up and Eliza put out a hand to stop her. Sophie glared at her: "It's your fault they've gone, you and your horrible secrets!" She pushed between Eliza and the table and ran from the room.

Charles gave up struggling, turned his head to my skirts and burst into tears.

We heard the door to the girls' room upstairs slam, then the sound of bed springs as Sophie flung herself down. Eliza bent and slowly began to pick up the cards that had fallen to the floor.

"Shh, shh, now," I said to Charles, rubbing his back. "All will come right again, you'll see," but my words rang hollow even in my own ears.

The next day John withdrew further from us to a place where none of us could reach him. He ate little and took no care over his appearance, refusing to let me help him shave, for he said that Boxer Byron had nowhere to go and no visitors expected. When Parson Mossop came he would not converse and instead the parson read to him: verses from the gospel to uplift his spirits and from Revelation. Only when he read the words that had comforted us so when we had lost our babies did John rouse himself: "And God shall wipe away all tears from their eyes; and there shall be no more death, neither sorrow, nor crying, neither shall there be any more pain: for the former things are passed away." He replied with a text from Job: "Man is born unto trouble, as the sparks fly upward." And the parson shut up his book and simply sat with him awhile, looking deep into the embers of the fire. Afterwards he sent word to me of the day that the doctor would come.

John slept late into the day and then was wakeful at night, and I would wake to find he had lit a candle and pulled the chair up to the window, where he would watch the flame mirrored in the dark glass. He would not be persuaded back to bed, saying that he must keep watch, and he would sit up with the counterpane wrapped round him until morning came or the candle burnt down to a stub.

The night before the doctors were to come I must have fallen asleep at my vigil, for I woke to find John standing at the open window, and I jumped from the bed, fearing that he meant to climb down. The counterpane had fallen from his shoulders and his body struck cold through his nightshirt as I put my arms round him. He stared out over the frosty garden to the orchard, where the trees were grey wraiths, their branches outlined in rime. "The starnels have carried the ash tree away and left a skeleton," he said.

On an afternoon just before New Year, Dr Skrimshire, who had treated John in the past, arrived with a surgeon called Dr Page from Market Deeping. At first my heart lightened, for I wondered if this might be to seek a second opinion and I tried to nourish the hope that some new insight or treatment might have been discovered in the four years that John had been away at High Beech. Then the thought struck me that two signatures were needed on the paper that had sent John away before and I was filled with misgivings. The doctors gave me their high hats of shiny black silk and I didn't know where to put them, for the kitchen table was floury and the hall coat pegs not long enough to hold them. I gave them to Parker to keep on his knee as he sat in the chimney corner. I showed the doctors into the parlour, where they talked with John for the quarter-hour and then called me in to ask me for pen and ink. With this, like the last swallow of summer, my final hope flew away and I knew that, just as last time, they had no treatment for John other than confinement and that he would be taken from us to Northampton Lunatic Asylum.

With heavy hands I opened John's desk. Dr Page raised his eyebrows at the piles of notebooks and paper that slid forward as I folded down the lid; he and Dr Skrimshire exchanged a glance. I lifted the papers aside and pointed to the pen and ink-well, finding myself unable either to speak or to pass the object over and make my hands play traitor to my heart.

"He'll do very well at Northampton, Patty," Dr Skrimshire said. "Earl Fitzwilliam has been very generous with the arrangements and he'll live as a gentleman. You'll see; his comfort is assured."

Still no words would come. Dr Page looked up from his writing. "I think it just as well that Mrs Clare should not visit," he said with a meaningful glance, "given the patient's history of absconding." Dr Skrimshire inclined his head.

It was pointless to make demur as the four pounds required for the journey by stage-coach was as far beyond my grasp as the moon would be if I tried to pluck it.

The coach that came for John was black and shiny as the doctors' hats. It put me in mind of John's journey to London when his poetry was first published and our hopes were high. I had to stare at the ground and empty my mind again before I could take a step down the garden path towards it. Now as then, the small boys of the village followed the coach and stood a little way off, whispering, when it stopped.

Two men got out of the carriage and politely shook my hand. They were both dressed in smart, townish clothes and of stocky build. One had a bowler hat that he removed before greeting me; the other was bareheaded and had thick brown hair that he smoothed constantly as if he didn't know what else to do with his hands. The driver remained seated, wrapped about with rugs and with the horses' breath rising in front of him. I asked him to put away the horse switch that he had propped in front of him in case it should frighten John.

Parson Mossop fetched John's bag from the house and put it down beside the gate. Then he brought John out and all of the family followed. Each of the children embraced him in turn. Anna and Eliza wept afterwards and clung together.

"Keep them safe from ghosts and devils," John said to Parker. "It's safest to keep them indoors," and he started his familiar muttering, a litany of "God bless them" and "Keep them from evil".

Parker grasped John's hand and passed his other arm round his shoulders. "Come home to us soon, son," he said. "You'll be in the best hands and come home hale and hearty."

Parson Mossop asked Freddy to take the children and the girls inside.

One of the hired men took up the bag and stowed it on the roof of the coach and the other approached John and stood beside him with his hands clasped behind his back. I stepped forward to say my farewell. When I embraced John, he stood stiffly with his arms by his sides. I took his hand and closed his fingers round the little volume of George Herbert's verse.

"Come along now, sir," one of the men said. He took his arm and began to walk him towards the coach.

John's eyes widened in alarm. "Patty?" he said. "Patty!" as the other man closed in on his other side.

Parson Mossop grasped my arm firmly to stop me following. The men moved John towards the open door of the coach and one took his elbow to help him up the step. His small figure hunched between their bulky frames looked slight and frail and, though I knew that he would have a good place at Northampton, suddenly his fear of the keepers at High Beech returned to me and his feelings became my own. I stepped forward, but Parson Mossop was at my side and all I could do was to hold my hand out towards John and feel the tears come, warm against my cold face.

John looked back over his shoulder and called out, "You are no wife to me!" He shook himself free of the man's restraining hand. "You are not my wife!" he shouted.

Parson Mossop put his arm round my shoulder and half turned me away, as if to shield me from John's words.

As John was bundled inside he shouted, "See, they are in cahoots, the priest and his whore!"

One of the men pulled the door shut behind him, the driver flicked the horses and the coach started to move away. Disturbed by the shouting, further down the road neighbours came out into their gardens.

"What are you looking at?" I shouted at them. "Is it enough of a spectacle for you? Is it?" and I made to break away, but the parson held on to my shoulders, saying urgently, "Patty, Patty! It's all over now. Come indoors, it's all over."

The village boys who had been staring all the while ran forward to follow the coach again. One of the Hawkins boys picked up a pebble and flung it at the departing carriage. It struck the varnished wood a glancing blow and skittered off over the frozen ruts in the road. The man with the hat leant from the window of the carriage and peered back at them and they turned tail and fled.

"That's right," I yelled at them. "Go and tell your mothers what a show you've seen!"

The carriage rounded the bend in the lane and disappeared from view. I turned my head into the parson's shoulder and wept without stop. John was gone from me and I had failed. I had utterly failed.

Part II — Spring 1842

CHAPTER
SEVENTEEN

Stork Beak Marks

Gradually the pattern of our days fell back into the order that we had followed when John was at High Beech. We sat at our old places at the table. In the evenings, Freddy sometimes used the parlour to sketch in and I often retired there to be quiet by myself. I would run my fingers over the spines of the books in John's bookcase, feeling the roughness of board or the smoothness of leather and the indentations of the tooled lettering. I would pick one out and labour over reading a little or fall into deep thought and just hold the book on my lap. The sound of Parker's fiddle would reach me from the kitchen: he had taken up playing again now that he was no longer able to reminisce with John. The children asked him for jigs and reels and he chose the tunes to please them, but left to himself he played ballads and mournful airs. Despite the milder weather, I put an extra blanket on the bed, for I felt the cold now there was only me to warm it and woke each morning anew to John's absence and my loneliness.

There had been letters over the past few months but John's were very brief. He told us that he had a slight cold or reported that he was well again and enquired after our health. He asked to be remembered to our old Helpstone neighbours. He gave us no description of the place or how he spent his days or what acquaintances he had made among the other patients. The letters were all similar, and if you had dropped them and then sought to put them back in order you would have been hard pressed to say how they should run, for all were written in much the same vein, almost as if he had copied one from another.

Parker and I spoke together about our concern to know more and to be reassured that John was well looked after, and we shared our frustration that we had no means to visit. Northampton was at such a distance that it might just as well be Essex and at four pounds the fare for making the trip by stage-coach was still far beyond our means. The only hope was that Freddy might be able to make use of a rare opportunity. He was friendly with Mr Potter's driver, who had told him that the master was planning to buy some land adjoining the farm and that he would need to go in the trap to attend to the legal side of the purchase in the county town. Freddy was hopeful he might be able to sit up front with him on the bench, with the master's permission, and travel as far as the centre of Northampton. It would then be a mile or so to walk to the asylum and he could return to take the trap back at the end of the day. Freddy was working extra hours whenever he could in order to convince the master that he deserved such a favour and in the hope that his day's wage would not be docked if the opportunity to make the trip arose.

Earl Spencer's five pounds had arrived two weeks after John's departure, enabling us to pay the rent and allowing me to buy shoes and slate and return the children to school. Nonetheless, I knew that I must still plan ahead for a lean year with Jack away and now I needed to get seeds, potatoes and onion sets in the ground to make sure that we would eat. Eliza had offered to help, but I had asked her to go and visit Anna and sew napkins with her. Anna's time was near and having company not only helped to relieve her anxiety but also mine, for I didn't like her to be left alone.

There was a great deal of work to be done. As I began digging over a new bed I looked at the yellow and purple crocuses that flamed in the grass and lit the garden's shady corners: at the foot of the bushes and round the rain barrel beside the door. I sought to draw their vividness into me, to read their hopeful message of spring, but I could not feel it. John had seemed to improve at High Beech; he had recovered his determination and feeling sufficiently to walk the eighty miles home and, having achieved his goal, had relapsed and suffered worse than before. Any doctor would now say that home was what brought on the malady: that the trouble of too many mouths and not enough money weighed on him too heavily. The thought that being back with us had thrown him into a worse state, and the knowledge that he blamed me for "sending him away", were hard to bear. *You are not my wife*, he had said, unwilling even to share himself between me and his memories of Mary. No longer even half a wife, I was now shut out. I cannot banish you so easily, I thought sadly, for I worried how he did at the new asylum despite the note I had received assuring me that the superintendent, Dr Prichard, would make John his special concern.

In the deepest recesses of my mind I still harboured the hope that by some miracle the doctors would return to me the man I married, the ardent, loving, hopeful John, and believed that somewhere within the carapace of false identities he'd built for himself lay the one true person, sleeping, hidden. It was too cruel, this illness that could so change a personality: that turned a man against his wife and erupted into violence that scared his own children. It unpicked the cloth of his mind and worked it through with random threads, leaving it flawed and altered, so that the portrait of his true self was obscured, a faint outline that even he could no longer discern.

I turned up a spadeful of soil and bent to pull out the long tap roots of plantains and the white roots of dandelions. I threw them on to the steadily growing heap at my side and chopped the spade through the earth to let in some air, seeking release from my feelings in the sharp strokes until my breath came quick and short. I left the shovel sticking upright in the ground and stood with my hands on my hips. The ground I had cleared was a brown tablecloth spread on a picnic field of green. It would take me days to clear it and replant. I'll get William to do some of this, after work, now the days are getting longer, I thought. He seemed to see more easily when I was struggling these days and was more ready to lend a hand, for he had been shaken by events at Christmas. I felt my earlier determination to clear a good-sized plot ebb away as the frustration that had fuelled it turned to sadness. Nonetheless, I returned to work, seeking a slower, more methodical pace in the hope that I might lose myself in the monotony of the movement: dig, push, lever, turn; dig, push . . . I set my eyes upon the earth and concentrated. First and foremost, I must feed my family and keep them in good health. All else depended on that. I had done it before without John and I would do it again.

I had been digging for an hour or so and was thinking about stopping to find something to eat for myself and Parker when Eliza came running to the gate, apron strings flying. She leant across it, unable to find enough breath to get her words out, but I knew immediately what had happened. I dropped my spade and hurried over.

"How often are the pains?" I said.

"A hundred counts apart," Eliza said, still red in the face from her exertions.

"Is there a fire lit?"

Eliza nodded.

"Then, go and put the biggest pot you can find on to boil and I'll bring the other things we need."

Eliza hesitated as if she would rather wait for me. I gave her arm a gentle push.

"Go! Comfort Anna until I come. I'll be there in just a minute." She picked up her skirts and ran back the way she'd come. I called after her, "Find old sheets, towels, newspapers — anything you can think of — to put on the bed."

I went first to the pump and drew a half bucket of water and took it to the kitchen. Parker woke with a start as it thumped down on the table and he looked round in alarm.

"Anna's baby is coming," I said. "Can you get me scissors and strong thread? There . . ." I pointed to my sewing box in its place under his chair and Parker pulled it out and began to hunt through the contents.

I scrubbed my hands red to get rid of the dirt from my digging. In my head a panicky voice was saying, "Please, God, let Anna be all right," again and again, but I pushed it to the back of my mind knowing that I must stay calm and think, for my dear girl's sake.

Parker held up the things I'd asked him to find and I said, "Yes, yes. Oh, and the shawl — the baby shawl I made!" He got it from the box and I snatched all up together and set off, Parker calling out good luck and blessings behind me.

Sefton's cottage was smaller than ours, having only one main room and a back-kitchen downstairs and one bedroom above. The door stood open and I went in to find a big iron pot unattended, bubbling fiercely over the fire and filling the room with steam. The boards creaked above me and there was a swish of skirts. I climbed the steep stairs and emerged through the trapdoor into the bedroom, where Anna was pacing to and fro across the room, between the wash-stand and the window, with both hands clasped low under her belly, her expression as if she were far away, intent on dealing with the pain.

Eliza was standing by helplessly. "She won't lie down," she said. "I didn't know what to do."

"That's all right. Let her walk," I said. "It's best to be ruled by what the mother feels natural."

At that moment Anna stopped and grabbed the rail at the foot of the bed, bending over and resting her forehead on the cold iron.

I went to her. "There's my brave girl," I said. "Where is the pain worst?"

"It's everywhere," she said, closing her eyes tight. "My belly, my back and my thighs."

I began to rub her back with a slow, circular motion.

"She was sick in the garden," Eliza said. "I dug soil over it."

"You did well." I noticed too that she had prepared the bed with plenty of newspaper covered with cloths. Her face was almost as ashen as Anna's and I sent her downstairs with instructions to boil the implements I had brought. "I'll call you when I need you," I said firmly, for I felt I needed to turn all my attention to Anna and couldn't afford to deal with Eliza if she fainted or gave way in tears.

For half an hour or so Anna alternated between pacing and stopping at the foot of the bed to support herself until the pain had passed. Then the time came when she became distressed. She moved from side to side as she leant on the bed rail, as if unable to find relief; she began to moan and there was sweat on her upper lip. Afraid that her legs would give way beneath her, I took her firmly by the elbow to lead her to the bed. I coaxed her from her clothes, all except her shift, but when she lay prone against the pillows she cursed and gripped the sheets as though it hurt her worse to lie back.

I remembered that I had always found the pull of the earth a great assistance and helped her to move to her hands and knees on the bed. Her waters broke and I called for Eliza to help me and to bring cloths. While Eliza took away a layer of the bed coverings I talked all the time to Anna.

"Everything is going well, my darling," I said. "It'll be soon now."

The room was very plainly furnished but above the bed there was a sampler. I remembered Anna sewing it, the time it took her to sew the whole alphabet. Her eyes were never good even as a child and I recalled her pride when she finished it and embroidered her name and the date at the foot. I pointed to it. "Look, Anna." She looked up, her face pulled into a grimace of pain. "Say the letters, my love. When the pain comes, say the letters as slowly as you can," I told her, for I didn't want the baby to come too quick and make a wound that would delay her recovery. She started to say her alphabet through, keeping her eyes fixed on the sampler and breaking off to moan or curse when the pain overcame her.

Eliza returned and stopped, transfixed, at the end of the bed. "Ma," she said, "you can see it!" She bit her lip as if it pained her to see it but she couldn't look away. Sure enough, the crown of the baby's head was showing and I began chanting the letters along with Anna, making her slow down. I led Eliza forward and showed her how to support Anna, then gathered up the sheet in readiness and began to ease the head as gently as I could. Anna left off speaking as all her breath was needed for pushing and the noise she made deep in the back of her throat as she did so. Eliza lifted her hair away from the sides of her face and bunched her shift above her back so that she could look down between her arms towards her belly to see her baby being born.

The head was almost fully out and as it came the forehead and nose turned towards me. A big baby, I thought, but had no more time to think further, as Anna let out a long cry and I caught up the sheet in both hands ready to catch the infant as a shoulder, then the body, followed the head in a slither and slip and a safe landing into my hands.

"Is it all right?" Anna was saying and Eliza stood staring at the sheets as if she had never seen blood before. The tiny creature made a choking, gurgling sound and I hooked my little finger inside its mouth to clear it and tipped it upside down as I had seen my midwife do. It let out a wail and Anna began to laugh and cry at the same time.

"It's a girl," I said. "It's a little girl."

The baby kept up a jerky wail, her little legs kicking in helpless protest at the indignity of being forced out into the cold. I laid her down on the bed so that I could look at her properly. It was then that I began to have misgivings. I knew that it was common for a new-born's head to be misshapen by the birth —

Freddy's had been pointy, almost pixie-like, but had returned to normal within a few days — but this was different . . . There was something wrong with the proportion of the head in relation to the little face . . . There was too much forehead and the skin was too tight and shiny, so that the shape of the temple bones was clearly marked. Quickly I lifted her head and felt the soft spot. I was right: instead of a soft dent where you could feel a pulse beating it was hard, stretched taut beneath her downy hair. My heart missed a beat.

Eliza helped Anna on to her side, her legs trembling as the tension in them was relieved. She lay limp and exhausted, strands of her hair stuck to her face with sweat and tears.

"Can I see her? Can I hold her?" she said urgently over the baby's cries, although she lacked the energy to sit up and reach for her.

"Stay still for a minute," I said, casting about in my mind for ways that I could soften this for Anna.

"It still hurts," she said in surprise, clutching at her stomach.

"The afterbirth is coming, that's all," I said.

When it was delivered and all was in order I deftly tied the three threads and cut the lifeline between mother and infant, then wrapped the bawling child in the sheet, bringing a swathe of the material up loosely round her head. She quieted as I swayed with her, shushing her. She opened her eyes. They were the bluest blue I've ever seen, clear as an April sky; they took my breath away. With a corner of the sheet I dabbed her face gently before passing her to Anna.

"Put her to the breast, Anna," I said.

Anna was looking strangely at the baby. "Her head . . . Is it right . . .?" She trailed off, looking to me with eyes full of such fear that, God forgive me, I couldn't say what I suspected, couldn't bear to shatter her happiness like a glass that had not even been sipped from.

"It was a difficult birth," I said in a matter-of-fact tone. "Such things are common. Feed her. See if you can get her to latch on." I helped her to guide the baby's cheek against her breast so that she would turn and root towards her.

All this time Eliza had been staring at the baby with a puzzled look. As I turned away from Anna she caught my eye and must have read the concern in my face. She glanced back at the baby. The folded cloth had fallen back and the shape of the back of the head was clear, too fully rounded and unnaturally swollen. She put her hand to her mouth and, without saying anything, hurried from the room.

"Where's Eliza going?" Anna said.

"To get soap to bathe the baby when she's fed," I lied. "I'll fetch the water." I took up the china jug that stood inside the basin on the wash-stand and carried it carefully downstairs.

Eliza was gone, the door left wide open. I tutted, annoyed that she was so unable to hide her reaction, thinking that she had recoiled from the oddity of the baby's appearance. Surely she could overcome her emotions, for Anna's sake, I thought, feeling disappointed in her. The baby couldn't help her misfortune.

325

Such a sweet little thing! I felt my eyes begin to fill and blinked the tears away. I had thought Eliza more tender-hearted. I filled the jug with a mix of hot water from the pot and cold from the pail until it was pleasantly warm.

When I returned to Anna she was cradling the baby's head in her hand. She looked up as I came in and I saw that she was crying. I set down the jug and went to her.

"What's wrong, my love?" I said, sitting beside her on the bed.

She traced the baby's cheek with her finger, and the baby, who had fallen into a milky sleep, moved her mouth a little as if dreaming that she still sucked. Anna looked at me, "It's too late," she whispered. "I love her already. It's too late to go back," and she lifted the baby and put her lips to the infant's poor, misshapen head.

"We'll find money for the doctor," I said helplessly. "Maybe the swelling will go down," and I squeezed her hand tight.

The baby stirred, opened her eyes, and contemplated Anna with a deep-sea gaze that seemed to know mysteries we had grown too old to remember. I took Anna's forefinger and placed it within the child's palm. The tiny fingers curled and gripped and Anna let out a gasp of surprise.

"Try to pull away."

Anna attempted to withdraw her finger but to no avail; the baby kept it in her fist, the tiny half-moons of her fingernails whitened with the tightness of her grip.

"See," I said, "she's strong. She's going to be a battler." I smoothed Anna's hair away from her brow. In my heart I fervently blessed them both, but couldn't trust my voice to speak my feelings. I turned and busied myself pouring water into the basin and laying out soap and towels beside it. I splashed water on to the soft inner part of my arm. "Shall I bathe her and then fetch you some tea and bread-sops?" I asked. Anna nodded and I took the baby from her. Moments later when I turned to speak to her again, she had fallen fast asleep.

By late afternoon I had helped Anna to wash and put on her nightdress, stripped the bed and remade it with fresh sheets. I had lined with folded blankets a drawer that I took from Anna's wardrobe and made a snug place to lay the baby down. Anna had taken some bread-sops with a mite of butter and salt and pepper and some very sweet tea, and a little of the colour had returned to her cheeks. I had decided that I would send William for the doctor the next day to look at the baby. I would ask Jane Mossop if she could supply some meat, maybe a little piece of veal or mutton, so that I could make Anna some broth, and that from somewhere I would find money for half a pint of stout a day to build up her strength.

I was just sitting downstairs for a few minutes to eat a haunch of bread and sip my own tea while Anna fed the baby again upstairs, when Sefton arrived from the quarry. His jacket, trousers, work boots, hair and all were covered with stone dust so that his sudden appearance at the door made me start. He was no less surprised to see me, but the realization of the likely reason for my visit clearly dawned on him at once. A wide grin spread across his face.

"Sefton!" I put out my hand to stop him, so that I could speak to him first about the child, but he was past me in an instant and taking the stairs two at a time, calling out in his deep voice: "What have we here, then? Boy or girl? Does the child favour me? Are his features as handsome as mine?"

I half rose, then sat back down again, wanting to help but not wanting to interrupt such an intimate moment between man and wife. I heard Anna's voice, quiet and serious as though she was explaining something, but I couldn't make out the words, then questions from Sefton, getting shorter and louder as if in disbelief, until his final words were loud enough to hear.

"Is it because it was too early?" he was saying.

I took up my courage with my skirts and climbed the stairs. Sefton was standing at the end of the bed, his hands resting on the rail where earlier Anna had rested in her labour. I didn't think that he had even approached Anna and the baby, for he had the look of a man who sought to keep his distance and he stood behind the foot rail as if to keep a barrier between them. Silently I held out my arms for the baby and Anna let me take her. She was swaddled tight with her two tiny hands up by her chin and her fingers curled, delicate and perfect.

"I don't care what she looks like," Anna said. "She's ours; she's part of us, you and me."

"Of course she's ours!" Sefton said. "But that's the pity of it, for we won't have her very long."

"What do you mean? She's strong, she'll get better, or grow out of it, or . . . or something."

Sefton shook his head. "I've seen beasts born with things like this, swellings, malformations. They nearly always . . . They don't survive," he finished.

Anna brought her hands up as if to cover her ears. "Don't say that," she said.

"There's no point in doing anything other than calling a spade a spade," he said. "I don't understand it any more than you do, but it's clear the baby's not right and it makes sense to expect the worst."

"She's a girl," Anna said. "The baby's a girl. Won't you look at her again? Won't you hold her?"

Sefton looked alarmed. "There's nothing I can give her."

I took a tentative step towards him, turning so that he could see her all tucked in the crook of my arm.

"She has the dearest little rose-bud mouth just like Anna's was," I said. "See? And your blue eyes." I tilted her towards him so that all he need do was reach out his arms, but he retreated, leaving go of the foot rail and clasping his hands behind his back. Despite the size of him the look in his eyes was that of a frightened little boy.

"I don't want her to look like me," he blurted out. "That means there's something wrong on my side. It's not my fault. There's nothing like this in my family."

The baby, roused by the loudness of his voice, began to cry and I clasped her close again, holding her up to my shoulder and walking her round the room, shushing her as I went. She filled the room with her sharp, indignant cries, and with a jolt I remembered my two lost babies, one who had barely strength to make a whimper and didn't last out a day and a night, and the other, born blue, whom neither blankets, nor cradling arms, nor our warm breath, nor tears, could save.

When she quieted I turned back to her parents and words came unplanned. "You have a living child with a lusty cry and, believe me, there is much to be thankful for in that." I thrust the baby into his arms so that he had no option but to take her. He held her awkwardly away from him as if afraid to smudge her with dust. I settled her more comfy in his arms, saying, "Go on with you — it's clean dirt not muck."

"Where's your rent tin?" I asked Anna.

"On the dresser downstairs, but there's not much in it."

"We'll put it together with ours and tomorrow we'll get Dr Skrimshire and see what's to be done." I nodded, my lips set firm together.

Sefton turned towards Anna as if looking for a place to put the baby down.

"You hold her a while," I said to him. "Sit with Anna and comfort her, for she's laboured longer and harder than you today."

I went downstairs and quietly began to tidy up, thinking that I would go home soon and leave the new family together to get accustomed to one another. However, before long the little one began to cry again and within a minute Sefton was clomping downstairs. He went straight to the dresser, lifted down the flowered jug I had given them as a wedding present and took out a tin from behind it.

330

He tipped the contents out on the table and I thought that he was offering it to me towards the doctor's bill. Instead, he slid some of the coins towards him and caught them in his other hand as they came to the edge of the table, then put them in his pocket.

"I'm going out," he said, scooping the rest of the money back into the tin. He looked at me as if daring me to challenge him. "I'll be at the Exeter Arms," he said.

I kept my tone neutral. "Does Anna not need you here to help, perhaps?"

"A man needs a drink after a day's thirsty work," he said.

From upstairs the baby's crying continued in a series of hiccupping, jerky sobs.

"Sefton!" Anna called. "Can you bring a clean napkin?"

Sefton hesitated, clinking the coins in his pocket.

"Sefton, have a heart," I said.

"I said I'd meet my workmates. It's women's business here," he said.

"You're newly a father, just as Anna is newly a mother," I said, as a gentle reprimand, "and if it were me I should value my husband's company tonight."

"Well, I will value John Barleycorn's company." He put his hand to the door latch. "Isn't that what a father's supposed to do, drink a toast to the infant? Isn't that what they say, 'Wet the baby's head'?" he said bitterly and walked out, shutting the door behind him.

Later, when I had made both mother and infant comfortable, I sat on the edge of the bed to talk to

Anna while she nursed the baby. "Does Sefton go often to the Exeter Arms?" I asked.

Anna shrugged. "He often goes out in the evening but he rarely says where. Sometimes he comes back with rabbits or something for the pot, so I don't ask him where he's going. That way if I got asked where he is I wouldn't have to lie."

"He shouldn't be taking such risks these days," I said. "And too much ale is an expensive habit. You should find a new place for your rent tin."

"Is there enough in it to fetch the doctor?" she asked.

"I've taken what there is and I'll make up any shortfall," I said. "Sefton will have to stay home tomorrow whether he likes it or not."

Anna smoothed the baby's cheek with her thumb, then gently laid her in the makeshift crib beside her. She yawned and I said that if she felt weary she should rest because the baby would need feeding in the night.

"Lie down with me, Ma, like you used to when I was little," she said.

So I swung my legs up on to the bed and leant back against the pillows, holding her hand as she slid down under the covers. Her eyes were heavy but she still seemed loath to sleep and I said, "You sleep. I'll watch the baby for you. Never fear, no harm will come to her while I'm here."

I watched over both of them as they slept, Anna's breaths slowing as she fell into a deeper sleep and the baby's breathing steady, though faster and lighter. I wondered what the baby would be called. I felt sure that Anna would already know her by name, for a woman's closeness with her baby starts earlier than a man's. We know when they sleep while we walk, lulled as if by the motion of a rocking boat, and we feel them startle and throw up their hands when we trip and almost fall, or when a pan is dropped and makes a clatter.

My lost babies had secret names. Long before they saw the world for so brief a time, I knew them as Samuel and Edward, guessing their sex from my appetite and the way I carried. And I had let myself imagine on, into their lives; their baptisms, the clothes I would stitch, their first steps, then words, slates filling with letters, trees climbed, birthday gifts given, kisses exchanged. I knew that when a baby dies the parent loses them at all ages; they lose not just the acquaintance of a few hours or days but all the edifice of their future that they have painstakingly built brick by brick, a home for them to live and grow within.

Both times, I couldn't speak to John of my grief, for he was in no fit state even to help himself. I hid it. I hid it deep along with the shape of my baby, his weight in my arms, the life I had planned for him, his secret name. I carry it still inside me, this locked box that, opened, still has the power to wound as it did then. It is a burden I will never lay down because it is all I have left of that child.

As I watched my girl sleep I prayed that the little one would survive and that Anna would not have to close that hard weight into her heart.

The evening grew dim. A blackbird chattered its alarm call in the garden and I rose to find a candle. Anna stirred and woke. She sat up in bed and stretched, then as if suddenly remembering all that had taken place she turned quickly to look at the baby.

"You've both slept soundly," I said. "It's getting late." I lit the candle and held it above the sleeping infant, shielding it with my hand so that its brightness wouldn't wake her. "What is her name, Anna?"

"I suppose I must decide that with Sefton," she said, reluctantly.

"What will you suggest?"

"Anne Maria," she said promptly. "Anne is close to my own name but just a little different, as I hope she'll be close to me but also be her own self."

"I'm sure Sefton will like the name anyway," I said, smiling.

Anna rested her hand gently on the swaddled form of the baby. "He went out without even saying when he would be back," she said, "and he wouldn't hold her for more than a minute. I think he's missed his chance to name her, hasn't he, little Anne?" she murmured. She unfolded a blanket to add to the baby shawl as the cool of the evening crept through the draughty window.

I looked at the darkening pane. "I hope Eliza has fed the family," I said absently.

"You don't have to go, do you?" Anna said quickly. "I don't want to be here with just my own thoughts."

"No, no, of course I'll stay until Sefton's back," I said. "Don't be too hard on him," I added. "He's had a shock and it's made him angry." I went over to the wash-stand and set the candle in front of the glass to double up the light. "You're tougher than you realize," I said. "Your feelings for the baby will give you the strength to face with fortitude whatever is wrong. We must will her to be well." I thought again of Sefton's bitter tone. Better to be angry than hopeless, I thought to myself. There is power in anger that can be harnessed, whereas despair gives up the fight.

CHAPTER
EIGHTEEN

The Doctor's Visit

By the time I heard Sefton return I was bleary with tiredness and stumbled downstairs to meet him at the door. Anna and little Anne were sleeping soundly and I put my finger to my lips. Although the smell of ale on him was strong, the long walk home seemed to have sobered him up and he nodded and moved quietly, taking off his boots before going upstairs in his stockinged feet.

As I let myself into my own house I expected everyone to be abed, but in the glow from the embers of the fire I could make out Parker nodding in his chair. I touched his shoulder and he woke with a snort, then collected himself and said, "Ah, there you are. Is all well? How is Anna?"

"Anna is well," I said. "Did Eliza not tell you how things stand with the little one?"

"Only that it is a little girl," he said. "She was very subdued and I thought it likely that the birth had been a bit of a shock to her, so I asked her nothing further."

I took up the poker and proggled the fire, breaking open the biggest remaining log until it flared and threw out a little more light and heat. I sat down opposite

Parker. "Well, the baby is strong and feeding well, but her head is larger then it ought to be and we must have the doctor."

Parker rubbed his chin with his bony hand. "Have we got the necessary?" he said.

I took down our rent pot and emptied it out into my apron. I stared at the handful of coins. "I thought there was more than this," I said.

"There were Charles's shoes and the new slates came out of it, remember?" Parker said.

I dug into my apron pocket and added Anna's money, then counted it all together into my hand.

"Not enough," I said, flatly.

"How much are we short?"

"More than half," I said with a horrible sinking feeling in my belly, for the only things of value in the house were John's books. I looked across at Parker, expecting him to be smitten by the same thought, and to be cast low as I was at the prospect of selling those hard-won treasures that had given him such pride in his son, but instead he was wearing a broad smile and almost clapping his hands together.

"I have something," he said. "I've been saving them for just such a time as this and now it has arrived."

I looked at him askance. He lit a candle at the fire, then levered himself up from the chair and went out to the scullery, returning with a long bundle under his arm, all tied up in sacking. As he sat back down with it across his knee, I took the candle from him so that he could undo the knots. His thumbs were stiff with the rheumatism, bent back from the top joint, but I knew better than to offer to do it and waited without hurrying him. At length he freed the rough cloth and unfolded it, to reveal a dozen or so shiny walking sticks. The shafts were straight and ended in a metal tack, and the handles, which described a neat right-angle, were beautifully shaped and polished, the pale wood buffed to a fine shine.

"Parker!" I gasped. "How have you come by these?"

"I grew them with Freddy's help and William has learnt to shape and finish them," he said quietly. "These are what the ash grove is for."

I jumped up and embraced him, the sticks clicking together as I did so.

"Steady, steady," he said, smiling, "we don't want any scratches on our handiwork."

I picked one out and leant my weight on it. It was firm and solid and the handle sat comfortably in my palm. I took a little turn round the room as if I were a fine gent and the tack made a tap, tap, on the flagstones as neat as any dandy would on a city street.

"They should fetch good money," Parker said. "And so they should, for they've been years in the making." He tapped the side of his nose. "Forward planning, you see. As I always say, take the long view and plan ahead."

"How ever did you make these beautiful handles?" I asked, bringing the stick closer to the fire to inspect it. "I can't see the join; they seem to be all of one piece."

"Well, that's the clever bit. That's why you have to dig them up and replant them. The old trunk becomes the handle and the new shoot becomes the shaft." He

338

picked one out and ran his hand along the wood. "I shall keep this one," he said, "but tomorrow 'Liza will take the rest to market and sell them and we'll have enough for the doctor and some left over."

I bent over and kissed his leathery cheek, then laid my own against it. "You are a good man," I whispered.

In the morning, rather than scolding Eliza for leaving me with all to do at Anna's, I spoke mildly to her and thanked her for cooking for the family the night before. I hoped that then she might voice her feelings about the baby.

While I set plates and bread and dripping on the table for breakfast she riddled out the ashes from the fire in preparation for laying it anew. Her fair hair was still tousled from sleep and hung down, obscuring her face as she bent to her task, the cold morning light from the window catching it and picking out the strands of lightest gold.

"I must eat up quickly and go round to Anna's to make her some tea and kettlins," I said. I waited to see if she would offer to visit too.

Eliza said nothing.

"The baby is to be called Anne," I said.

The ash pan grated along the floor at the mention of the baby.

"The baby can't help how she looks, you know," I said, beginning to lose patience with what I took to be Eliza being overly fastidious. "If you look closer you'll see she has a lovely face." I passed her the brush to sweep up the ashes that had spilled. "Poor little mite,

339

she's going to need all the love she can get — including her auntie's."

Eliza bent over her sweeping, keeping her face turned from me. "It's not permanent, is it?" she said in a small voice. "She will be all right?"

"We'll have to see what the doctor says," I said.

She put down the ash pan and the brush, sat down in Parker's chair and put her face in her hands.

"Whatever is it?" I asked, standing over her.

"It's my fault," she mumbled from behind her fingers.

"Don't be silly! How could it be your fault? It's an unhappy chance, that's all. The sad truth is that not all babies are born fit and well and we must make the best we can of it and be grateful she was at least safely delivered."

"It's a punishment," she said, her voice growing smaller still so that I could barely hear. "On me and Sefton."

"Eliza!" I said. "How can you say such a thing? God doesn't afflict the innocent to pay off old scores for the sins of their elders."

Her hand went to her collar and with her thumb and finger she felt at the thin material of her dress in the gesture that had become familiar to me since first I noticed it at Christmas. Close up I saw, just visible through the cotton, the glint of a silver chain. Before I could speak to berate her for not returning the locket to Sefton as I'd told her, she rushed on.

"I've behaved very ill towards Anna," she said. "I couldn't help it; I've loved him since he first came calling and used to make up to both of us."

340

I squatted down beside her among the spilt ashes, my skirts raising a little puff of powder into the air.

"Are you sure it's love, Eliza?" I said. "Are you sure you aren't just flattered by an older man's attentions? Perhaps it's hard to see an elder sister courted and wed and feel you have no follower and are being left behind?"

She began to cry then and laid her head against my shoulder. "It feels like love," she said. "I wouldn't have done it, else."

In my head I cursed Sefton roundly for playing so with my girl's affections and for the vanity of his desire to follow every pretty face and conquer every silly heart. I took the corner of my apron and wiped her eyes. "Now listen, Eliza," I said, "and tell me the truth. Did you lie with him?"

She turned her head away and my worst fear was realized. "Only once," she said. "It only happened once. I was coming back from wood-gathering and I met him on the road by chance . . ."

"How long ago was this?" Immediately, without thinking, I glanced down at her waist. She shook her head. "Months ago. I wouldn't let him after that." She took my hand in both of hers. "I have tried, Ma. I've tried so hard, what with Anna and the baby."

"And you want to make amends?" I said, as calmly as I could.

She nodded.

"Anna must never know," I said. "It would break her heart." The look that passed across Eliza's face was like a cloud passing over water, turning all to grey. I said more softly, "Once is a mistake and not wilful and will surely be forgiven. But you must carry the burden of this knowledge yourself, for Anna will need all her strength to care for little Anne and you must make your amends by helping her to do this in any way you can."

"Shall I go to her now, while Sefton is at work?"

I rose and said, "I have another task for you this morning, just as important and one that will help us all," and I explained to her that she was to go to market and raise the money to fetch Dr Skrimshire.

"I shall set off directly," she said, smoothing her hair back and twisting it into a knot at the back of her head. Then she stopped, one hand holding her hair in place. "I must get pins," she said and clattered up the stairs, treading the spilt ashes everywhere.

"You should eat breakfast first," I called up after her, "and you must talk to Grandfather about the price of the sticks and how best to sell them."

I finished my own meal, and leaving the rest of the family to serve themselves, went quickly on to Anna's to see what kind of night she had had and to make her some breakfast.

It was afternoon before Eliza returned and found me at Anna's, but she came with the news that the doctor would follow very shortly, as soon as he had finished visiting his regular patients. We busied ourselves in tidying up the room downstairs and banking up the fire, for it was a cold, wet day for spring. Rain dripped from the eaves of the thatch and fell steadily over the small patch of untended garden where couch grass and white nettles grew among the cabbages.

It was warm enough downstairs, but the bedroom, with its open rafters, struck very chill in wet weather and there was a damp smell like mouldering straw. When I had come in at breakfast time I had heard Anna coughing, so I had brought her and the baby downstairs and settled them in the chimney corner, where Anna now dozed in a chair and little Anne slept in the makeshift crib beside her.

Hearing the clatter of hoofs in the lane, we peered out and saw Dr Skrimshire dismounting. He tied the reins to the gate and unbuckled his black bag from the saddle where he had carried it before him. As he picked his way along the overgrown path we moved back from the window. Eliza touched Anna's hand to wake her and I took off my apron and smoothed down my skirts in readiness to answer his knock.

The door being low, in order to enter he had to take off his tall hat, and as he bent below the eaves water drops fell on his shoulders, making him wetter still.

"Come in, come in, you will be soaked to the skin," I said, forgetting my formal greeting.

Dr Skrimshire smiled. "Indeed, it is most inclement weather," he said. "How are you, Mrs Clare? I trust John is faring well at Northampton?" and he swung off his coat, dotting the earth floor with dark drops.

"He writes that he's in good health but remarks on little else, so it's hard to tell how he is in spirits."

The doctor patted my shoulder. "It's bound to take him a little while to get used to another change of place

343

so soon after High Beech," he said. "He will settle in time, I'm sure of it."

My heart sank to hear words that spoke to me of permanence rather than hope of a cure but I held my tongue, for I was anxious to know his opinion of little Anne and how Anna did. I stood aside to let him speak to Anna and he asked her some questions about how she felt now and about the birth: how long was her labour, in what position did the baby deliver, had she fallen or injured herself in any way beforehand. While Anna answered them all, her serious eyes never left his face.

"Was the infant early?" he asked, and tapped his chin with his forefinger.

"Twelve days, sir."

"Hmm, a little premature," he muttered to himself. "Would you lift the infant and lay her on your knee, so that I can examine her?" He rubbed his hands together to warm them.

Anna gently lifted little Anne, who woke with a startled cry and then gazed up at the new face bending towards her.

"She has a bonny little face," the doctor said and I silently thanked him for his kindness, for Anna's expression was hard to behold, as if she feared how others would respond and was taking a great leap of trust in showing her to the world.

He ran his hands over little Anne's head, feeling the ridges of the soft plates of the skull, then took out a metal instrument with two long arms and a little notebook with a shagreen cover.

I saw Anna stiffen and he said, "I'm only going to take some measurements of the head. She will just feel it a little cold, perhaps, but will come to no harm." He placed the instrument like a pair of tongs first across the temples, then further back, then front to back, and each time wrote down words and figures that were indecipherable to me. Little Anne made never a murmur, seeming fascinated by the doctor's gold fob watch, which hung across his waistcoat and dangled forward each time he bent across her.

"Is she feeding well?" he asked and Anna nodded.

"And she does not vomit it all back, nor cry a great deal?"

"No, no more than any normal baby."

"I need to look at her back," he said. "Could you turn her on to her front?"

Anna lifted little Anne over so that her head was resting on her knees and her feet were towards Anna's stomach, then undid the little bows tied at the back of the tiny nightgown and lifted it aside to reveal her, naked but for a baggy napkin, from which her legs stuck out, skinny and pinky-brown. The doctor ran his finger down her backbone from her head, then pushed back the top of the napkin to check right to the end of her spine.

"Vertebrae intact," he muttered. "No lesions."

Without her covering, little Anne must have begun to feel cooler and she started to kick like a little swimming frog and to cry, so that her ribs moved in and out as she gulped at the air.

"Oh, there, there," Anna said, her hands hovering above her.

"Well, no need to ask my next question about whether the baby has normal movement," Dr Skrimshire said, for she was kicking so hard that she had flushed red from her feet to her head and the wrinkles of skin at the back of her neck were turning puce. "Best wrap her up again before we have the neighbours in, complaining," he said with a smile.

Eliza had drawn closer and was peering over the back of Anna's chair.

"She's very cross," she said.

Anna started to do up the ties again, then gave it up as hopeless; little Anne wriggled and jerked so much she simply wrapped her in a blanket and put her up against her shoulder, where her sobs subsided to gulps.

Eliza and the baby came eye to eye for the first time. "There are tears!" she said. "Oh, poor little soul!"

Anna twisted round. "Would you like to hold her?" she said.

Eliza looked uncertain.

"Take her, 'Liza," I said. The doctor had gone back to his notebook and was writing furiously, so that I hoped he had reached some conclusions.

Eliza came round and took little Anne, copying exactly the position in which Anna had held her, as if trying to transfer her to her own shoulder without the baby noticing. She was not to be hoodwinked, however, and started to cry once more, jerking her head back against Eliza's supporting hand.

"Walk with her and hum to her," I said, so Eliza paced slowly round the table, jiggling her a little with every step until she settled again.

The doctor sat quietly with Anna, asking her more questions about her own health. "I notice you have a cough," he said. "Is it an old one on the mend or a new one just beginning?"

"It's mainly at night when I lie down," she said. "It's just a cold."

The doctor took out something that looked like a small ear-trumpet and listened to Anna's chest. "I'll give you a tonic," he said. "I fear the damp in these parts at this season is not good for the health." To me he said, "Be sure to air the bed before they sleep. They must have warm, dry sheets."

He returned to his notebook and continued to write until he came to the end of a page and finished it with a flourish as if signing his name. He tore it out and gave it to me.

"For the baby we will try rhubarb and jalop first for their purgative effect and calomel as a diuretic. You must take that to the chemist and give the child two teaspoons daily."

"You know the condition, then?" I said. "It is treatable?"

"There are treatments but it is a serious matter," he said. "It's dropsy on the brain: a build-up of fluid, which is causing swelling and expanding the soft bones of the head."

Anna was looking from one of us to the other. "But she will be all right?"

The doctor looked down at her. "I can't say for sure. There can be complications — problems with vision or movement, sometimes fits."

Anna looked over to where Eliza was standing by the window, holding little Anne and pointing to the raindrops falling from the thatch like silver threads. "Fits . . ." she echoed as if not wanting to believe her ears.

The doctor continued, forcing a more cheerful note into his voice. "She is otherwise in good health; we must concentrate on that. She has a lusty appetite and a cry to match, which are both very good signs."

"And the medicine will help?"

"If it doesn't we will try something else," he said. "She'll need warmth and feeding: meat and milk once she is weaned. Building her strength up is the thing and you must call me again if there are any changes in her condition."

He took up his hat and coat from the chair and said to Eliza, "You know where my practice is? The chemist's shop is in the same street. If you wish, you could ride with me now and save the walk one way."

Eliza nodded and gave little Anne back to Anna, who held her tight and kissed her again and again.

I gave money to Eliza for the mixture and she wrapped her shawl round her head and shoulders and pinned it there against the rain.

"Would you be kind enough to walk with us to the gate?" the doctor said to me when he had taken his leave of Anna.

"Of course," I said, and with my arms outstretched, holding my own shawl over my head as a makeshift umbrella, I mouthed to Anna that I would be back soon and we set off into the drizzle outside.

When we reached the gate the doctor paused. "I didn't want to upset the mother further; another shock may be too much for the system so soon after a confinement."

"There's something more that we should know?" I said, pulling Eliza to me and taking her arm in mine. "How should we care for the baby if she's taken with a fit?"

"You must simply watch over her to make sure that she doesn't injure herself in the spasms and hope that it will pass."

"It may not pass?"

The doctor paused, then said, "The older the child is, the better the chance of survival, should such a thing happen." He sighed. "With a young infant, particularly one born prematurely . . ."

"You are saying that we should christen the child early," I said more boldly than I had meant to, for I was shocked by the news and blurted out my worst fear.

The doctor gave the slightest inclination of his head to me, then, seeing Eliza's face, added, "A precaution, a precaution only."

"There must be something we can do!" Eliza said. "If we can keep her safe from the fit, she will get better, won't she? Surely she will get better?"

"There are other things that we can try, such as head-wrapping and blood-letting, when the baby is bigger," he said, "but once the bones of the head fuse and harden the fluid must be released or it will press more and more upon the brain."

"This is why the child must be strengthened?" I said.

"In preparation for a surgical procedure to the skull known as trepanning," he said, his face grave. "We must hope that it won't come to that, but it's crucial that the child thrives in this early period and builds up her strength, you understand?"

I nodded, immediately determining that little Anne should want for nothing.

He strapped his bag to the pommel and mounted, then drew the horse parallel to the gate so that Eliza might use it as a mounting block. He held out his hand and helped her into the saddle, then tipped his hat to me and clipped the horse with his heels. Eliza's face as they rode away was pale and the folded paper for the chemist was clutched tightly in her hand.

I stood watching them go, composing myself to rejoin Anna, then walked slowly back to the house, my skirts brushing the cabbages where drops of water lay like beads of quicksilver between the leaves. They trembled and rolled a little way as I passed, each one a fragile, momentary perfection.

Anna was rocking with the baby in her arms when I came in. "What did he say?" she asked straightaway.

"Oh, it was just about the matter of his bill — how it was made up . . . that sort of thing," I said.

"I'm worried about fits," Anna said. "When Father used to suffer them I've seen him lose consciousness and fall to the ground, they happen so suddenly. And the muscles become rigid — how could a tiny baby survive such a paroxysm? And what should I do if she fell into a fit?"

"There's not much to be done except wait for it to pass," I said, for I knew that John had only ever come out of a fit in his own time and remembered nothing afterwards of what had taken place, except for a numb sensation and falling.

"I'm afraid it could happen when I'm out of the room," Anna said, rocking all the time, back, forth, back, forth, in her seat. "And how will I dare to sleep?"

"Here, let me take her," I said. "Why don't you go and rest now while I'm here to watch her?"

I lifted little Anne and Anna stopped rocking and slumped back into her seat.

"I think she should be christened," she said, "in case . . . I think it should be soon," she finished.

"Eliza fetched the cloth for the christening gown today," I said, thinking aloud. "The service would have to be here at Northborough, not Helpstone, though; you're not yet fit to travel."

"Well, it would ease my heart if it were soon," she said, "and Eliza shall stand as godmother after all the to-ing and fro-ing she's done on little Anne's account while I could not."

I glanced down at the baby. "She's sleeping," I said. "We shall make the gown and hold the christening just as soon as you'd like, my darling, but look at her, did you ever see a baby more content?" I laid her down in the drawer. Her tiny limbs were relaxed, her weight slack as I lowered her, one hand beneath her bottom and the other supporting her shoulders and head. Her eyelashes rested on a cheek as smooth as china. "See," I whispered, "she's warm and fed and cared for and can fall into a sleep as deep as a feather bed. And so can you," I said, helping her to her feet. "You go on up and I'll sit right here in your place and watch over her as keenly as you would yourself."

Anna climbed the stairs. "You will stay awake?" she called back to me.

"I'll watch until Sefton comes home. You rest while you can."

While the baby slept, I planned the christening gown, trying to concentrate on something that was within my power, rather than be overwhelmed by the future, which was not. I wished that John was here and just as he was in the old days when he would listen to my worries about the children. We would talk of ways to solve a problem or how to endure it and, in the talking, halve the load.

It will have sleeves gathered at shoulder and cuff, I determined, and a yoke with smocking, done in the white silk thread left in my sewing box, though maybe just at the front, for speed. The shawl, we had already. There would also be a bonnet, I decided: a generous shape that gathered into a flat panel at the back and a frill at the front, so that after the water had been tipped upon her head she would wear her bonnet and look like any other baby being brought from church and Anna should carry her home as proud as any other mother. I couldn't stop her fears or even mine, but I could at least give her this.

The baby stirred in her sleep, then settled back to stillness, lulled by the thrumming of the rain.

CHAPTER
NINETEEN

Holy Water

The next day I went to visit the curate to arrange the date of the christening. Finding that he was not at home, I walked down to the tiny church. Smaller than St Botolph's at Helpstone, St Andrew's has no great tower. Instead, two bells hang from masonry arches beneath a steeply pitched roof and a high and a low note ring out to call folk to service or to the fields at harvest when gleaning can begin.

I found the curate on his knees in the churchyard, scraping at one of the old gravestones with a spoon. I gave him good morning, then asked what he was doing.

"It vexes me to see the monuments so untidy," he said, gesturing to a pile of weeds that he had grubbed up from the foot of the stones. "Then I found I couldn't read the inscription here and felt that I should know all my parishioners, past or present."

I peered at the letters, their shapes smudged by grey and yellow lichen. *In loving remembrance* was all that I could make out. "Folk don't move about much in these parts," I said. "You'll find the surnames are familiar to you already, I expect." I touched the rough surface of the stone, picking at the dry flakes of lichen with my fingernail. "I've come to ask when you can christen my granddaughter," I said.

He looked up. "Ah, yes. Congratulations," he said. "I heard there was a new addition to my little flock. Have you received the baby-garment box from Mrs Harper?"

"I didn't know that such a thing existed," I said.

"There's a collection of baby clothes that's passed hand to hand, paid for from the poor box. You should have had it before now."

Seeing my doubtful expression, he added, "I'm sure Mrs Harper has no need of it: her youngest is crawling now. Is the infant a boy or girl?"

"A girl. Anne Maria, after her mother," I said, "but she's not . . . robust. I wondered if the christening could be sooner rather than later? To put Anna's mind at rest."

He rubbed his cheek, leaving a smudge of dirt upon it.

"Bring all to church on Sunday for morning service and we'll baptize her then. That's only two days away. Will the mother be strong enough to bring her so soon?"

I nodded, for although Anna wasn't well I knew that she was determined on this course of action.

"Sunday it is, then, and I'm sorry for all your troubles," he said kindly, and returned to his scraping. The noise of the spoon rasping against the stone followed me as I let myself out at the wooden gate and walked along beside the churchyard wall.

I went straight to Anna's to tell her the good news and it cheered my heart to see her take out her Sunday dress and the collar I had given her at Christmas to try which brooch she would wear. I pressed the dress for her, as much to air it as to iron out the creases, and hung it from a hook in one of the beams downstairs, to keep it dry and perfect until the christening. Her cough was no worse and little Anne seemed unaffected by it and continued to feed with an appetite.

In the evening, when I had finished at Anna's, come home and fed the family, Freddy had still not returned. After a while I began to fret and, it being a light spring evening, decided to walk a little way along the road out of the village to see if I could catch sight of him coming.

A breeze blew from High Borough fen as I walked out of the village towards the Glinton road. It shivered the catkins in the cob-nut trees in a neighbour's garden, making them tremble prettily. The rain of the last few days had formed puddles in the ruts in the road and I picked my way round them with my skirts bunched in one hand.

When I reached the Glinton road and left the shelter of houses and trees on either side, the breeze stiffened and swept across the flat fields like a broom, bringing with it the smell of earth and water from the dykes. A group of tinkers passed me, a family with three dark-haired children and a babe in arms. The man asked if I needed any ribbons or thread and made ready to undo his pack, but I was anxious to meet Freddy and said no, not this time. I hurried on, knowing that now spring had come all manner of trades would be passing through the village along with the knife-grinder, the barber and the toothpuller.

At last, when I was near the crossroads that led to Etton, I spied a lone figure in the distance and knew from his walk that it was Freddy. I hastened on and saw him raise his arm as he recognized me. When we met, I turned back for home and he fell into step beside me, slowing his pace to accommodate my shorter step.

"I've been to see Father at Northampton," he said. "That's why I'm so delayed. We set off soon after four this morning; it's a long trip. I feel my bones have been shaken loose in their joints." He shrugged his shoulders up and down as if to click them into place.

"How did you find him? What is the place like? Is there any chance he might be let home?" I put my hand up to my mouth after this last question and my eyes filled up with tears, for I had had no idea that I would ask it. Freddy looked at me with concern. I said "It's only . . . the last few days have been difficult."

Freddy placed my arm through his own. "It's a very grand place," he said, "quite new, all white Portland stone. It's huge, quite the grandest place a Clare is ever likely to live in, but when I arrived I found that Father wasn't there."

"Not there! Don't tell me he has run away again? For pity's sake!"

"No, no, all turned out to be well. The asylum is a mile or so's walk from the town, but when I arrived I was told I must turn tail again, for Father is free to wander as he wishes and had gone into the town to buy tobacco."

"But you did find him?"

"I must have followed in his footsteps, for when I reached the tobacconist's he told me I would more than likely find Father sitting on a stone seat beside the door of All Saints church, having a smoke, and so I did."

"Did he recognize you?"

"Ye-es — he recognized me straightaway but his memory wasn't quite right in other respects. He asked about all the family, even Grandma, and when I said, 'Have you forgotten that she passed away?' he was distressed and said I wasn't telling him the truth."

I took a moment to digest this before speaking again. "So what did you do?" I asked. "How did you comfort him and persuade him back to the asylum?"

"A young man turned up, nothing to do with the asylum, and Father forgot all about our conversation and brought out a piece of paper with a poem on it and the man read it, then gave him the price of a glass of ale and seemed well pleased."

"Did you see what manner of poem it was?" I asked, intrigued.

"It was one where the first letter of each line makes up a girl's name, Verity or Charity or suchlike — yes, Verity it was. I assumed it was the young man's sweetheart."

At this I tutted out loud, not because John wrote yet another love poem to some other woman, for this was an act of generosity on some young lover's behalf, but because of the waste. That he should be writing these ditties, rather than his verses rejoicing in the glory of nature or even mourning its passing, filled me with disappointment on his behalf.

"It was very hard to know what to do for the best," Freddy said. "The young man asked Father if he wrote poetry for a living and Father told him that when he was Shakespeare he wrote plays, but that he had written poetry as Byron and Keats and Clare and that all were the same man."

Despite myself, I laughed at this, imagining the young man's confusion. "I dare say he beat a hasty retreat after that," I said, and Freddy smiled, relieved to see me in better cheer.

"I walked back with him to the asylum and several people seemed to know him," Freddy said. "I believe he goes to sit in that niche most days and so folk have grown accustomed to finding him there with his notebook in hand and they ask him to write their Valentines."

"But it worries me, Freddy," I said. "Not everyone will be well disposed towards a man who says he is who he is not. Even worse, when he thinks himself Jack Randall, what if he were to meet someone who takes up his challenge? I don't understand the superintendent allowing him to wander: what if some harm were to come to him?"

Freddy nodded. "He asked me to take him home, Ma. What if he were to try to set off home again not knowing the way?"

I sighed, for, far from relieving my mind, this report of John had worried me further and I could see no way to speak with Dr Prichard, the superintendent in person, and get answers to all my questions. "Perhaps I can ask Parson Mossop to make some enquiries?" I said. "I'm still glad you went. At least you found him in good physical health and in good spirits. It was kind of your master to let you go."

"He was kind on the journey out but ill-tempered on the way back," Freddy said. "His land purchase couldn't be fully completed, so he'll have to make the trip again next week to finalize the deal. As a result of his ill humour I'm to fodder up and supper up the horses tomorrow, so I shall be out before dawn and not back until dusk," and he rubbed the back of his neck as though the ache sat there already.

I squeezed his arm. "I've kept you boiled potatoes, onions and spring greens," I said, "and you shall have the last of my baking."

As we passed a drain, cut deep through the rich soil and running straight as far as the eye could see, Freddy spotted the bright yellow of marsh marigolds and jumped down to pick some for me, calling out: "Look! Mollyblobs." Quick as a glint on water I was transported back some twenty years to John holding out a flower from the hedge to me. The lift of Freddy's face towards me was so much his father's that I was undone and had to pretend an interest in the sky, where a hawk hovered high above us, until my voice could be trusted once again.

He scrambled back up the bank and put the flowers into my hands. "What's the matter, Ma?" he said.

"I was remembering your father picking me scarlet pimpernel and calling it 'poor man's weather-glass'," I

360

said. "He showed me how its petals were all closed and, sure enough, a half-hour later it was raining. We had outrun the weather, though, and were safe and dry inside a shepherd's hut." I made a wry face. "I wish all troubles were as easily avoided."

"Would it help to see Father in the flesh?" Freddy said as if something had just struck him. "Maybe I could ask if you could travel next week, as I did today?"

I gasped. "Do you think your master would hear of it?"

"When I've done my extra work tomorrow and he's got over the frustration of his plans being thwarted, I shall approach him," he said.

"But would I find my way?" I said. "The crowds . . . I've never been further than Stamford, you know, and what about Anna and the baby?"

"Someone would direct you — everyone knows the place — and once you're on the right road you can see it from far off as it sits atop a hill," he said. "Eliza could help Anna."

I hesitated. "I feel I'm needed here: Parker, the children, the baby . . . What if something goes wrong?"

"We could manage, Ma."

"I don't know. The doctors said not to visit in case it made him try to walk home again, and who knows what dangers that could lead him into when he's not in his wits?"

Freddy was silent and the thought of John's long walk was accompanied by the sound of our boots crunching on the gravel.

"He didn't show any sign of following me home, though he said he was homesick," Freddy said. "I walked right back to the asylum with him and he greeted a fellow patient and went inside with him." He gave me a searching look. "The master is a farmer not a property speculator: this is likely to be the only time his business will take him to Northampton."

I hesitated.

"The chance isn't likely to come again," he said.

I nodded, hardly able to believe that such a chance had come and half afraid of taking it. "Ask the master," I said. "No harm in asking, just to see what he says."

Later in the evening, after Freddy had given all the family what news he had of John and passed on his love and greetings, Eliza and I sat together to make the baby's christening gown and bonnet. I cut the soft white material using one of the tiny nightgowns as a pattern and adding in fullness at shoulder and chest to allow for gathers and folds. Eliza worked to make a lace collar. She slipped easily back into the art she had learnt at such an early age and, seeing how engrossed she became in its intricacies, I heartily wished that the new machines that destroyed the demand for handmade pillow lace had never caught on.

When the light faded so far that her face was bent low over her cushion, she carefully laid it aside and fetched the candle stool that had been stowed away in the scullery long ago.

"Shouldn't we leave this until tomorrow?" I said.

For answer she showed me her work and I saw that she had chosen a Buckinghamshire point lace, a complicated fretwork pattern. "There won't be time before Sunday, what with all the napkins to wash, unless I stay up and get it done," she said.

I looked at her face, all pinched by anxiety and guilt. "Anna will be very pleased," I said gently. "You know she would like you to be godmother?"

"I don't feel fit," she said.

"You'll do very well," I said firmly.

She lit a candle and fixed it into a candlestick, then stood it in the socket in the centre of the round stool. "Where are the flashes?" she asked. "I hope none have got broken."

"They're packed in straw in an apple drawer," I said, "the one at the bottom on the left that has nothing in the drawer above."

Eliza went to the scullery and returned carrying two spherical bottles of the thinnest glass, one in either hand like silver moons. She filled them from the water pail and stoppered them, while I fixed the supports into the remaining holes in the stool, each one with a cup into which a globe would fit.

Eliza wiped each bottle dry on her apron and set them in their wooden hollows. The candle flame reflected in the glass wobbled and trembled as the water level settled, then Eliza took up her work on her knee again and drew close, so as to set it beneath the lenses, and the light, as if by magic, was concentrated on it, strong as a burning-glass. She gave a little noise of satisfaction and patted the edge of the cushion. "It will be my best work," she said, the frown she always wears when she is concentrating appearing between her eyebrows. She bent again to her work, lifting and placing the brightly coloured bobbins with dextrous fingers.

In the fainter glow I sat and stitched a running thread round the shoulder of one sleeve to make the gathers. The simple stitching needed no close attention and I pondered instead on my feelings about maybe being able to visit John. Hopes rose like blades of grass that have been trodden down; perhaps I should see some improvements in John's condition. I imagined myself speaking to a doctor, maybe even Dr Prichard himself, finding out that there were treatments and plans for a cure, daydreamed that I might hear some loving words from John's lips and longed for him to remember himself.

No sooner had I convinced myself that all would be well than doubts assailed me anew. What if he were worse? What if he failed to recognize me as he had when I met him on the road from High Beech? My heart was so bruised and battered from worry about my girls and little Anne that I didn't feel it would survive a direct blow. I realized that up until now I had longed to see John, safe in the knowledge that it was impossible to do so; now that it was a possibility I feared going in case I should lose my last hope and be rejected again. I thought of the rancour he had shown me at our last parting, insisting that I was not his wife, perhaps blaming me for his having to go away from home again and feeling betrayed and vengeful.

I pulled the thread tight at the last stitch, sewed a knot to secure it and bit the loose end off with my teeth. I paused to watch Eliza, her head inclined, her golden hair coiled heavy at the back of her head, save for a few escaped strands at the nape, the long line of her neck and her pale fingers moving among the pins and bobbins. For a moment I imagined unburdening myself to John, telling him of my worries about our girls, the predicament Sefton was causing, the moments of fear about little Anne when thoughts of the worst sidled like a cat at a dairy door and slipped into my mind. Such conversations were no longer possible between us, everyday life at home was already a load too heavy for John to bear, and if I visited I would have to guard my tongue for fear of placing one more stick upon an almost broken back.

I must have sighed out loud, for Eliza looked up and, as if reading my mind, said, "Will Father come home soon or will it be years like last time?"

"I don't know," I said.

"You must go, Ma, if you have a chance to visit. I can look after the family while you're gone."

I nodded my thanks. "I think I'll go on up to bed. Will you be long?"

"I'm not sleepy," she said, though there were shadows under her eyes like pennies.

I folded the small pieces of the garment and put them into the dresser drawer. As I went towards the stairs, Eliza said, "How do you bear it?"

I half turned. "What, my love?"

"The loneliness." She held my gaze for a moment and then turned back to work on the tiny collar.

On Sunday morning I rose early to make sure that the children were up betimes, properly washed and tidily dressed for church. Anna and Sefton were to bring the baby to be clothed in her new gown and we would all walk down to the church together.

In the event it was Anna who knocked at the door with the baby in her arms. I took little Anne from her, scolding Anna for carrying her all down the lane when it was barely a week from her confinement. "Where is Sefton?" I said crossly as we went through to the kitchen, where Parker sat in the chimney corner, polishing his boots with an end of rag.

"He wouldn't get up," Anna said. "He was at the alehouse again last night and got into a brawl with a drover."

Eliza looked up quickly from the table, where she was pressing little pleats into the front of the christening gown she had laid out on a thick blanket. "What has happened?" she said.

"He's split his knuckles and he has a lump on his head the size of an egg."

Eliza's hand went up to the side of her own head.

"He says that he'll follow on and meet us at the church," Anna added. "I asked him to endeavour not to be late for his own child's christening." She walked to the mirror and fussed at her hair, then unpinned and re-pinned the brooch at her neck.

"Come," I said. "Look what Eliza has made."

Eliza laid out the bonnet and the robe, the collar delicate as cow parsley.

Anna took the hem between her thumb and forefinger and felt the fine fabric. "It's beautiful," she said. She bent close so that she could see the lace. "This is far finer than machine lace; surely London ladies would pay for such delicate work for christening robes or bridal gowns if you could only find a factor?" She touched the edge of the collar with her fingertips. "'Liza, this is fit for a princess," she said and embraced her sister.

Eliza held her arms stiffly for a moment, then clasped them round Anna and hugged her tight, her face pink.

"Quick, quick, time is short," I said, starting to unwrap baby Anne from her shawl. "We must dress her in her finery and go." I sat Anna down opposite Parker and put the baby in her arms.

"William! Sophie!" I shouted upstairs. "And where has Freddy got to? We can't go without the child's godfather," and I busied around like a shepherd moving a flock from field to field.

As we walked down to the church together, Freddy carried little Anne most of the way, her white bonnet and shawl bright against his dark coat. She looked so tiny in his arms that I needs must see him as a man and not a boy, and I thought what a fine husband he would make one day; he was so gentle with the infant and carried her so proudly. It was a fine day, the blue sky smiled from ear to ear and the chiff-chaff called in the hedge. Ahead of us the Hawkins family walked towards the church, the three boys made to go in front under the eye of their parents, and behind us came a trickle of others as doors shut and gates clicked and all made their way towards the sound of the tolling bells.

As we reached the churchyard, Freddy handed the baby back to Anna so that she could carry her in. We passed into the dim interior, the tone of the bells muffling through the thick stone walls. We sat at the back and filled the whole pew, with Anna at the end to save a space for Sefton and to be ready near the font, but she thus became prey to all the curious glances of those who followed us in. She held the baby tight against her, plucking at the bonnet frill, drawing it further down over her face, and snapped at Charles when he tried to peer round to look at her. "I want to see her. I haven't seen her properly yet," he said in a loud voice, and I told him to be quiet and set him on to finding the hymns and lessons from the numbers hung up above the pulpit. Sophie sat with her hands folded over her prayer-book, gazing straight ahead, overawed by the solemnity of the occasion, for she was to be the second godmother.

It was chilly in the church, for the sun wasn't yet strong and even in high summer little warmth penetrated the weighty walls. The stained-glass windows cast a murky light. I shivered and wished that I had brought a thicker shawl.

The curate emerged from the vestry wearing his surplice, all starched and clean but with his hair ruffled up on end where he had pulled the garment over his head, no doubt in a hurry as he served three such tiny churches in the area. He smiled and nodded at his small congregation and gave the notices, including the announcement that there would be a baptism. At this there was a stir and a craning of necks as folk turned round to look and whispered among themselves. The curate climbed the steps to the pulpit and started the service. He rumbled his way through the prayers and the first lesson, at the end of which Sefton arrived, making old Mrs Spicer jump with the clunking of the iron latch on the church door, and making all heads turn. Sefton was pale and ill shaven but otherwise tidy. He nodded his apologies to the curate and slipped into the aisle seat next to Anna. I smelt a whiff of ale and wondered if it was from the night before or a fresh drink this morning to sustain him through the occasion.

Despite the modest size of the congregation we made the responses loud and clear and sang the hymns with gusto in order to get warm; Parker and Sam Dawes's old voices softened to a tenor pitch, whereas Sefton and Freddy's bass notes boomed out.

After the last lesson the curate announced that all should witness the promises made on behalf of the new addition to his flock and asked the family to gather round the font. I gave Parker my arm, as it was difficult for him to edge between the narrow pews, and he leant on it and shuffled along as best he could. We pressed close to the ancient font and I rested my free hand upon its stone rim, worn smooth by many other hands, and thought of all the babies who had been brought here to be blessed and then returned with children and grandchildren of their own. I missed John sharply then, imagining how we would have exchanged a glance and a smile to be witnessing this ritual as grandparents rather than parents, and hung on all the tighter to Parker's arm.

Eliza, Sophie and Freddy were on my other side, then William, then Charles, standing on tiptoe to see the holy water. Anna and Sefton stood opposite with the curate; Sefton fidgeted, smoothing his hair and pulling at his coat collar. While Anna jigged the baby to quell her first murmurings, Sefton glanced covertly at Eliza, but she fiddled with her purse and would not meet his eyes.

"Hath this child been already baptized, or no?" intoned the curate, holding up his open prayer-book, from which a piece of silk dangled, marking his place.

"No," answered Anna and Sefton together.

"Dearly beloved . . ." the curate began his request that we call upon God to grant the child baptism with water and the Holy Ghost so that she might be made a lively member of the Church. Then we all knelt on the cold floor, bar Anna and Parker, who could not get down so low, while we prayed that as God saved Noah and his family so the child might pass through the waves of this troublesome world until she come to the land of everlasting life. Charles's eyes grew round at this and he looked at the baby as if wondering how she would manage a journey in the ark.

Gratefully, we scrambled back up from our knees to hear the reading from the gospel, how Jesus said, "Suffer the little children to come unto me, and forbid them not: for of such is the kingdom of heaven." This verse always brings a lump into my throat no matter how many times I've heard it, perhaps because it holds out such promise that my two lost ones are with Him that my doubting heart finds its hope too painful to bear.

After this there was a pause from the curate to allow everyone in the congregation who had been stifling coughs and sniffles to make themselves comfortable and there was a deal of nose-blowing and throat-clearing while he stood patiently waiting for all to be quiet.

He turned to the godparents and explained in the words of the prayer-book how they were standing surety for the child to keep God's commandments until she should come of age to be confirmed. At this the church became so quiet that you could have heard a mouse squeak and Sophie looked so serious that I wished I could have reached over to give her hand an encouraging squeeze.

"I demand, therefore," continued the curate, "dost thou, in the name of this Child, renounce the devil and all his works, the vain pomp and glory of the world, with all covetous desire of the same, and the carnal desires of the flesh, so that thou wilt not follow, nor be led by them?"

I saw Eliza, who had lowered her eyes to gaze at the glassy surface of the water in the font, blink at the mention of the desires of the flesh. Freddy and Sophie gave their response quick on the heels of the curate's words, so that Eliza's followed on after and rung out. "I renounce them all," she said, lifting her head as she said it.

Sefton stood stiffly beside Anna, his hand under her elbow.

The curate continued through the creed and prayers, then filled a little silver dipper with water. He took the baby from Anna and Anna untied her bonnet strings and slipped it off.

Charles, seeing her properly for the first time, said, "She has a very big head!" then, realizing he should not have spoken, went bright red and hid his face.

"Perhaps she will be very clever," said the curate softly, relieving the awkwardness. The baby lay quiet in his arms, looking up at the new face above her. The curate turned to the godparents, saying, "Name this child," and in unison they said, "Anne Maria Clare." He held her over the font and poured a little water on to her forehead, naming the trinity with each tip of his hand: "I baptize you in the name of the Father, and of the Son, and of the Holy Ghost."

Little Anne looked surprised at the first coldness, scrunched up her face at the second and opened her mouth and wailed at the third. Anna raised her hands as if to take the baby back and said in a loud whisper to Sefton, "It's too cold. It's hurting her head," but Sefton looked away and said nothing. The curate dabbed the baby's forehead gently with the shawl and gave her back to Anna, who wrapped her up, stilling her little arms that stretched and grasped in consternation, and murmuring to her with her head bent low.

The curate read again from the prayer-book, then asked all to kneel for the Lord's Prayer. Then there was the exhortation to the godparents to see to their duties to teach the child her prayers and the Ten Commandments in the vulgar tongue and themselves to die from sin and mortify all evil and corrupt affections. Through all this the godparents listened attentively, Anna rocked the baby and Charles came round to Parker and began to tug at his sleeve for attention. Only I marked how Sefton watched Eliza, his eyes narrowed as if willing her to turn to him. So effectively did he shut out the words of the prayers and the collects that followed that, when they ended and a babble of chatter began in the congregation as folk collected up their belongings to leave, he remained stock still for a moment and only came back to himself when Eliza turned smartly away and returned to the pew to recover her gloves.

The curate shook hands all round and offered his congratulations, and Sefton was drawn into conversation like it or no. There was a scatter of nods from the other villagers as they filed out, though only Sam Dawes came over to speak to me and say he wished the baby health and happiness. Anna interrupted to say the baby needed feeding and she and the others would go on ahead to their house, and all departed except for Eliza. She hovered at my shoulder, as if she wanted to speak to me, all the while that Sam told me of his recent ill health and his nephew's visit and his garden.

At length he too set off for home and I gave the curate a little money for the collection, in thanks for his trouble and kindness, and Eliza and I came out into the churchyard.

"Did you want to tell me something?" I said. "I'm sorry to be so long, but old Sam's on his own and so he likes to talk when the opportunity presents itself."

Eliza rubbed her finger across her brows. "Only that I have a terrible headache after all the sewing and would like to be excused from the celebration at Anna's," she said.

"You've done well, Eliza," I said quietly. "Very well. Go and rest now and I'll bring you some food back later."

We parted at the churchyard gate, and she hurried away, her step quickening almost to a run.

I walked alongside the churchyard wall and could hear children's voices shouting and laughing round the corner. The Hawkins boys letting off steam after an extra half hour in church, I thought. As I rounded the corner I saw them up ahead, the youngest walking along the top of the churchyard wall, his arms outstretched for balance, while the older two sat on a tombstone, egging him on. When they saw me coming they jumped to their feet and ran, and I felt a pang of guilt remembering how I had bellowed at them when they threw pebbles at John's carriage. The youngest boy, startled by his brother's speedy departure, twisted round to see what had frightened them and, missing his footing on the lichen-covered stone, slipped and fell into the lane, scraping his arm down the side of the wall as he went. He let out a piercing cry and I ran to him and took his other arm to help him up.

"Don't belt me, missus," he said.

I stared at him in amazement. "Are you hurt?" I said. "Let me look."

He stood still, blinking, his lower lip stuck out.

"That's right, be brave and we'll see if we can bandage you," I said, for there was a nasty cut on his forearm with scratches either side and yellowish smears of lichen dirtying the wound. I took out a handkerchief and dabbed away the worst of the dirt, then folded it clean side out and tied it round his arm, more for a comfort than to give any practical support, for already the elbow was swelling. "Can you bend it?" I said.

He tried it a little way and winced.

"You know, it's better not to climb where it's slippery," I said.

He lifted the corner of the makeshift bandage and poked at the swelling experimentally.

"Ask your ma to wash it and put a cold compress on it to bring down the swelling," I said, but he looked at me vacantly as though he had never heard of such a thing.

"Here," I searched in the corner of my purse and found a halfpenny left over from the collection, "from the baby on her christening day."

He almost snatched it from my hand and turned and ran, as if afraid I might change my mind and ask for it back again.

I closed my purse and shook my head, then carried on along the lane to join the family.

When I reached Anna's, Sefton answered my knock and I saw him look beyond me down the path as if expecting to see Eliza.

"Where is she?" he said rudely, without even greeting me. In the room beyond I heard chatter and laughter and the sound of china being laid out.

"If you mean Eliza, she has a headache brought on by sewing your baby daughter's christening gown," I said pointedly. He made as if to step past me but I didn't move aside. "She is indisposed," I said. "Should we go in?"

Sefton turned his back on me and went into the house, leaving the door open. I followed on and shut the door, fiddling with the latch to provide a moment to compose myself and put a smile on my face.

I kissed Anna. "Well, the christening went off very well," I said. "Clare babies always bellow when the water is poured on them. It's nothing to worry about; it shows they've got a good pair of lungs."

She looked over to where Parker held little Anne fast asleep in the crook of his arm. "I'm glad she's properly named," she said.

I had helped Anna to prepare food the day before so all was ready. We had a bite and a drink and then drank again to the baby's health and happiness. Once they had eaten their fill, Charles and William began to get restive in the cramped quarters of the tiny room and started arm wrestling among the debris of the meal, making the plates jump each time a fist was forced down to the table. I sent them off, telling them to go home and change out of their Sunday best so that they could then go fishing or nesting or suchlike. Sefton made a comment to Anna about preferring to take one's Sunday leisure in the open air and I looked at him sharply.

While I washed the pots, Anna showed Sophie how to sit and hold the baby on her lap and the menfolk talked of the weather and the crops and the coming railway. I began to fret about Eliza and think that she might have more need of my company. Sefton drank steadily with the concentration of one who knows his measure and is determined to exceed it as quickly as possible.

I told Anna that I would take some dinner to Eliza, packed some food for her and said goodbye, patting Sophie on the head and telling her she would make a proper little mother one day.

When I got home I found that Eliza had gone to bed. The curtain was pulled across to dim the room and her best dress was thrown anyhow across the chair. She was lying on her side, with her hair still pinned up, as though she had not even had the energy to undo it.

I knew she was awake as I saw the glint of her eyes and I whispered, "How are you feeling?"

She sat up in bed and at the open neck of her petticoat I saw the silver locket swing as she moved. "I can't sleep," she said. "I wish I could. I wish I could sleep for years until I was old and didn't care any more."

I sat down on the end of the bed and patted the hump of her knees. "Believe me, it doesn't get any easier just because you're older," I said. "The heart is an organ of fire: it can warm us or consume us and, like a fire, it's hard to control."

"Then, it is consuming me," Eliza said, "and I wish that I could put it out."

I took her hand. "No, never wish that," I said. "You're young, young enough to master this disappointment and love again."

She laid her head back against the pillows and closed her eyes. "I'm so tired," she said, "like a fox that's run too long and must go to ground."

I stroked her hand, rubbing my palm over the back of it, then straightening and rubbing each finger as she used to like me to when her hands were aching from lacemaking.

A loud banging on the door made us both start. "Whatever is the matter?" I said, half rising to my feet.

"Eliza!" Sefton's voice rang out. "Eliza! I want to see you!"

Eliza gripped the edge of the blankets and shook her head.

"He's been drinking," I said. "I'll go down and tell him that he must go home to Anna." I stood up, sucking in a deep breath.

The pounding on the door began again, a hollow thump of fist on wood. "I know you're at home. I only want to speak to you," he shouted.

"Wait," Eliza said. "Give him this." She reached behind her neck, undid the clasp of the locket and thrust it into my hand. "You must give him a message for me; I can't do it face to face."

I listened carefully, my face sombre. As I went downstairs I gathered into my palm the ends of the chain that trailed between my fingers and closed my hand on it, so that it was hidden, for this would be a difficult matter to complete with any delicacy.

I opened the door and Sefton stood with his hand raised, ready to knock again, the other hand resting on the door frame.

"No need to have the door down, Sefton," I said. "I'm not as sprightly as I used to be. What is it you want?"

Sefton lowered his arm and put his hand in his pocket but remained leaning against the door frame, which brought him uncomfortably close. I could smell the beer on him and saw a nick upon his cheek where he had cut himself shaving and the unmatched line of his whiskers where he had hurried the job this morning. He looked down at me and said, "I just want to see 'Liza, Mrs C. There's things I want to tell her." His words blurred into one another and he stared intently at my face, as if determined to keep his eyes clearly focused.

"You can't see her today," I said firmly. "She isn't well and has gone to bed."

"Gone to bed be damned!" He leant his head for a moment against his outstretched arm. "Have you told her I'm here?"

"She sends you a message by me," I said, speaking slowly and carefully. "She wishes me to return something that should never have been hers." I held out my closed hand.

He took his hand from his pocket and held it beneath mine. I put the necklace into it and it sat in his palm, a tiny pool of glinting chain and silver drop against work-hardened skin and creases ingrained with stone dust. He stared at it for a moment, then picked up the locket and opened it, as if expecting to find within a message that would make more sense. A tiny curl of hair lay in each side, both fair, though one was soft and shiny, the other coarse and thick. Sefton moved to shut it again, but his large fingers fumbled with the delicate object and upended it so that the tiny snippets fell. With a curse he bent to retrieve them but, released from the shell-like curve of the casing, each curl fanned out into individual hairs that the wind caught and whisked away.

"It's for the best, Sefton," I said, for he watched the contents of the locket go as if it were a golden guinea rolling away from him over the grass.

"Why has she done this?" he said.

Now that it came to delivering the rest of the message I wished myself anywhere but here. "She wishes you to put a lock of the baby's hair in it and to give it to Anna," I said, my voice getting quieter and quieter, "and that from now on you must love her as a sister and no more."

He nodded slowly, as though digesting what I had said, then quickly slipped the necklace into his waistcoat pocket and laid his hand over it.

I waited for him to give me an answer, but he didn't speak and half turned away. "I'm sorry, Sefton," I said and closed the door gently, slipped on the latch and leant my back against it. My heart was beating fast, for I fancied I saw something in his eyes that belied his muted actions. Sure enough, there was no sound of retreating steps from outside and I went quickly into the parlour, taking care to approach the window along the wall where I couldn't be seen.

Beside the door Sefton stood with both hands and his knee against the rain barrel, which was full of water after the days of wet weather. Like some latter-day Samson he set the whole of his strength against the weight of water, oak and iron band, and with a groaning cry heaved it over. Then he bent, as if snapped in the middle, his hands on his knees and his head hanging. A river of green water gushed over the garden, combing the grass down flat and swamping clumps of celandine and speedwell. The barrel itself shivered from the impact and lay curiously flat against the ground, which told me that the shock had stove in the bands and broken the staves on the underside.

I saw Sefton straighten and look up at Eliza's window. Then he walked away down the garden path and left the gate swinging.

CHAPTER
TWENTY

County Town

The master and mistress sat tucked around with rugs in the trap. I sat up with the driver and, despite the hardness of the bench seat, the jangle of the harness and the unevenness of the road, I found my head nodding and my chin dropping on to my chest.

I had started out at four in the morning while it was still half dark, walking with Freddy to the stables, where I had waited while he foddered the horses. I had held my elbows against the early-morning chill and listened to the horses' regular pull and champ at the oat straw and tried to prepare myself for the day's undertaking, drawing strength from their dogged munching and their calm, sad eyes. When the driver came, he and Freddy readied the trap and helped me up on to the bench so that I was in place before we drove round to get the master, lest he change his mind and all our plans come to nothing. "Possession is nine-tenths of the law," the driver said with a wink, and he and Freddy shook hands. We had travelled without incident to Thrapston, where we had changed horses at the farm belonging to the master's cousin. The master and mistress took a little breakfast in the house and the driver and I shared the potato farls that I had brought before we all set out again.

Despite my tiredness, as we entered Northampton I roused myself and gazed in wonder at the many tall buildings, some crammed together with barely a passage between them, some joined up altogether so that a building extended the whole length of a street. We jounced along over the cobbles in a stream of other traffic, traders with barrows and gentlemen in fine coaches all mixed up together in a river of folk all running towards the centre like filings to a magnet. In front of us was a cart with baskets of earthy potatoes and frilly spring greens and behind us a group of men on horseback, each one leading another horse alongside as we made our way towards Marefair. A little way ahead a wagon stopped outside a butcher's shop to deliver some sides of lamb, the man shouldering each carcase with an easy, practised movement. Never in my life had I seen so much meat. Our driver pulled the horse's head round and skilfully manoeuvred the trap down a smaller side street to avoid the delay. "See, I know all the best short cuts," he said to me.

We emerged again in a grand square, where folk crossed and recrossed the wide space: gentlemen with earnest looks, intent upon their business, ladies in full-skirted gowns and fine bonnets walking daintily to avoid the dirt and the street-sweeper, and a group of clergymen deep in conversation gathered outside an imposing church. Recognizing Freddy's description of golden stone and huge portico, I touched the driver's arm. "Is that All Saints?" I asked. He nodded and I craned my neck to look as we passed in case John might be sitting in the niche where Freddy had found him and I would need to jump down here instead of waiting until we reached our final destination.

This morning, though, the niches on either side of the huge double doors were empty. Their hollowed shapes and rounded arches seemed embrasures within which statues should stand and I wondered at John choosing to sit there in such public view. Perhaps the crowds held no fear for him after his visits to the capital city, I thought, and I remembered him describing how he would sit in the window of his publishers' offices in Fleet Street. He would watch the street for hours, marvelling at the strange fashions and picking out the town beauties in their silks and bright colours with cheeks that were pink indoors or out, not rosy with fresh air like a milkmaid's complexion.

We passed on through narrower streets until we reached the solicitors' office, with its shiny black front door and painted railing, where the master was to conduct his business and conclude the purchase of land. The driver handed me the reins and stepped down to help the master and mistress down from the trap. They arranged to meet at the same place in the afternoon and, without a look to acknowledge my existence, mounted the steps to the front door, knocked and were immediately admitted.

The driver took his place again and urged the horse on, saying, "I can take you as far as the coaching inn and put you on the right road from there."

"That would be very kind," I said, for I feared getting lost in the warren of streets and felt that the closer I could get to the edge of the town before being left on my own the better.

"Tessie here will need a good rest," he said, nodding at the horse's dappled back, "so master and mistress will take their leisure over lunch and expect me to pick them up by three o'clock. You come and find me at the inn a quarter of an hour before."

I nodded and thought that I must follow the clock carefully at the asylum and be sure to allow plenty of time for the walk back to town.

We pulled up at the entrance of the coaching inn and the driver pointed with his whip to the place where the street curved left. "A little way beyond the bend you'll meet with the road you need," he said. "Turn east and before you've gone a mile along it you'll see the asylum. You can't miss it; it stands on its own, high up, overlooking the Nene Vale, a big white place, virtually brand-new."

I gave him my thanks and scrambled down, then paused to watch him turn into the yard, loath to lose sight of my last contact with home.

There was not as much coming and going on the street as in the centre of town, yet I jumped at the sudden noise of a window sash being lifted and the flop of a rug against the brickwork as a maid began to beat it. A man with a florid face and the garb of a groom spoke to me and held out his hand as if to accost me, but I bent my eyes to the ground and slipped past him. I hurried along, keeping close to the buildings, as if the dun colours of my dress could merge with the stone and become invisible.

When I came to the road that led out of the town, I turned along it with relief and was glad to find that the houses soon petered out and gave way to fields and orchards on either side. Apart from the odd cart making its way tardily to town, not a soul was afoot on the road and I could walk on unmolested. Small insects brought out by the spring sunshine flew and crawled among the wayside flowers and bees hovered between primula and forget-me-not, their leg-sacks full to bursting. I wondered if John would have forgotten me this time as he had when he walked home from High Beech and how my heart would hold out if he had. I picked a yellow cowslip and pinned it at my breast, for it was one of John's favourite flowers.

At length, up ahead I could see a large pair of wrought-iron gates on the right-hand side of the road, with a mixture of deciduous and evergreen trees within them. Peeping through beyond were grey roofs with chimneys widely spaced. My heart began to beat harder as I approached the gates and I wondered if I would be challenged by a keeper at the gatehouse, but as I turned in at the cobbled entrance no voice rang out and no one appeared, so I followed the drive through the trees until I emerged in front of the asylum itself. It's not as big as Burghley, nor as grand, was my first thought, as it lacked all the ornamentation and curlicues of that palace, yet it had a grandeur and stateliness born of its symmetry and simplicity, for everything about it was equally matched. Built as a quadrangle, it sat four-square on the high ground, its white stone pristine, its tiers of windows perfectly spaced and proportioned. The central section, which had a porch supported by columns, was topped by a pediment with a single round window, and the whole looked out over a wide lawn that sloped gently away to end in bushes and trees with open countryside beyond. The overall effect was of moderation rather than show, measure and reason rather than artistic display. Nonetheless, its size and elegance made me feel very small and suddenly the cowslip with its gay yellow face seemed frivolous and foolish. I wondered behind which of the many windows John sat and whether he would see me approaching, and that made me think of other windows and other eyes and I quickened my step, wishing to enter as soon as possible.

I passed under the porch and tapped as lightly as I could with the great iron knocker on the door. It opened almost immediately and a balding man with a corpulent figure bade me good morning cheerfully, introducing himself as the steward. I told him my name and my business and, screwing up my courage, asked if it would be possible to speak with the superintendent, Dr Prichard, after seeing my husband.

"Dr Prichard is away at present," he said, "but I will be very happy to discuss your husband's case with you. I believe John will be either in the airing court or the men's parlour. I'll take you to him."

We passed through the grand entrance hall, then through a door into the open space at the centre of the quadrangle: a large courtyard. It somehow put me in mind of what it must be like in the belly of a ship. The walls were high all round me and it was further darkened and enclosed by them being fashioned not in the white stone of the façade but of red brick. The area was cobbled and the flat rectangle of grey stones seemed matched by the flat rectangle of blue sky above, giving the impression of a box within which disturbance could be contained. Small-paned leaded windows of intricate design looked into the courtyard. A quick movement at one window caught my eye and at another a face was pushed against the glass, the nose and mouth flattened into a grotesque shape. In one corner a man was on his knees, apparently in an act of prayer, for he would one minute clasp his hands before him and bend his head and the next throw his hands up and mouth words to the sky as if in supplication.

Two others were playing quoits in what appeared to be an orderly fashion, until one finished his turn and on going to collect his rings from the pole was struck on the back of the head by the other man, who made his throw regardless of the first being still in the way.

"That is my point," the thrower called out, while the first turned with a glare, rubbing his pate and cursing. "I cannot help it if your head is too big for the ring to pass over," he added. "You shouldn't be the pole if you can't do the job properly."

I tried to stifle the urge to laugh, for I didn't want to seem cruel, yet it was very funny.

"Excuse me," the steward said to me and went to talk to the two men. After a while he took them to a bench where a table was laid out with a box of dominoes and, having settled them there, went quietly to tidy the game of quoits away.

"They seem to have settled their differences quickly," I observed on his return.

"Oh, yes," he said. "They sometimes forget they are the best of friends and fight each other, but we find it more efficacious to distract patients from their aberrations than to take issue with them. We hope to keep returning them to reasonable behaviour and reward it with privileges until it becomes a habit once again. This is the new method of moral treatment espoused by Dr Prichard."

"What of the poor man who seems to be calling on the Almighty?"

"Aah, his delusion is very advanced, I fear. He thinks himself Pharaoh and is in constant fear of plagues and misfortune befalling him."

"The method doesn't work as well in some cases?" I asked.

"It *is* more difficult to displace delusions that have become firmly rooted, it's true. We never refer to the strange fancies, as that would reinforce them. Instead we distract the patient and hope that in time they will let them go themselves. Sometimes they do and are returned to normal life; sometimes they don't and continue to need expert care here." My face must have fallen as I thought of the number and frequency of John's strange fancies, for the steward added, "Rest assured that they are very well looked after and all is done with kindness."

He glanced round as if to find something with which to distract me, then pointed up at the larger, grander, first-storey windows behind us, saying, "That is the Great Hall where our patrons meet."

I imagined the Worthies, sitting at their deliberations for the good of the patients, looking down on them as they took their exercise as if looking into a beehive and marvelling at the strange ways of an alien society. "What a gap there must seem between the aldermen and the inmates." Without thinking, I spoke aloud.

"Not as wide as you might suppose," he said. "The men and maids who wait at their table are patients who are soon to leave us and we have had aldermen as well as doctors and priests as patients here. Madness is no respecter of persons."

He led on and we passed through a little door at the far side of the yard and into a wide, oak-panelled corridor that gave on to rooms on one side and looked out into the courtyard on the other. The place was warmed by fires that were lit in fireplaces between the windows, with seats in nooks either side. I wondered at the luxury of lighting fires in this mild spring weather; it seemed a sin to waste so much good wood. Then I saw that in one of the nooks a young man, dressed only in his nightshirt, had climbed up and curled up as tight as a hedgehog with his hands over the back of his head, and I was glad that such a poor soul shouldn't be cold.

We came to a heavy oak door and the steward opened it and peeped inside. "There he is and no one else is here," he whispered. "He is taking a nap." I followed him into the room and he showed me to a

390

mahogany chair placed opposite the couch on which John reclined. "I'll leave you now," he said quietly. "You'll find me just next door when you've finished," and he left me alone with John, his retreating footsteps soundless on the thick rug.

The room was silent save for the hiss of logs in the fire beneath the carved mantelpiece and the faint sound of birdsong in the grounds beyond the tall windows. A polished table with a pile of books stood between the windows, fine paintings of ladies and hunting scenes were on the walls and a gilt clock ticked lightly on the mantel. A proper gentleman's parlour, I thought.

Truth be told, I was glad that John was sleeping as it gave me some time to gather my thoughts and order my emotions, for I was very afraid that he might fail to recognize me as he did on the road home from High Beech, a hurt my battered heart could not bear twice, and I didn't wake him. In the quiet room I became aware of his soft, regular breathing and I was relieved to see him thus, peaceful and at ease. His head was tipped back against the back of the couch, his mouth open a little way, his chin having dropped down. His clothes were new and unfamiliar: a double-breasted waistcoat, breeches with gaiters and well-polished black shoes. A fustian jacket lay over the arm of the couch and from its bulging pockets protruded a newspaper, the corner of a small volume and a notebook with slips of paper spilling from it.

After a while a log split with a crack and a flare of sparks and John stirred and woke.

"What . . .?" he muttered as he passed a hand over his face and focused on me.

"It's Patty, your wife, come to see you," I said quickly to avoid any doubt or awkwardness.

"Patty," he repeated wonderingly, then seemed to wake fully and sat more upright in his seat. "How is all the family? How do the children do?"

"They're all well," I said. "Jack is still working away and we miss him, but we hope he'll be home again before long. You remember the ash grove Freddy planted under your father's direction? He and William had a scheme to make walking sticks and we've made good money selling them at market." I broke off there before my nervous tongue should run away with me. I didn't want to be drawn into telling of the new baby as I feared I wouldn't be able to hide my worries about her health. John would not be able to assuage them and it would only give him pain and cause him concern about Anna. "How do you fare here, John?" I asked instead. "All seems very well appointed."

"Oh, it has no end of modernities," John said. "Hot water whenever you want it! And there is a big kitchen garden I work in sometimes. The food is very fresh — they have their own glasshouses, you know." He leant forward as if he would confide in me. "They are feeding me up for a big fight," he said, "though I haven't been told yet who is the challenger. They give me meat to eat and tobacco to chew and as much paper and ink as I require. Nothing is too good for Jack Randall and I'm known here as King of the Forest!" he finished triumphantly.

"And you are allowed to walk into Northampton too, I hear?" I said, gladly catching his enthusiastic tone.

He beckoned me forward so that our knees were almost touching. "It is a good thing that I can walk a little way, for the reason I'm here is that too many words in my brain are pressing to get out and that has made me mad." He nodded at me as though I would find it hard to believe this. "Oh, yes," he said, "I am quite unable to keep my mind quiet and I wish it could be still as it used to be when I simply walked the furrow with my hand on the plough."

"You are happy here, though? You don't stray too far?" I said, thinking that if his old ploughing days had such appeal he might set out to find the fields he loved and come to some harm along the way.

"One mile. Exactly one mile radius: that is all my range. Dr Prichard has the 'fluence on us and we are like tethered goats," he said.

This puzzled me. "You mean the superintendent has some power over you?"

"Indeed. He has a strong power and demands obedience. And also armies, as I said, guarding the one-mile boundary." He took a quid of tobacco from his weskit pocket and got up to poke it into the embers of the fire to roast. "Even when I'm Nelson I have no chance of defeating him," he said with a satisfied smile, "for he is unbeatable on land just as I am at sea."

"Come now, John," I broke in, ignoring all the tenets of the asylum, "you are not Nelson; you have never even been to the sea!"

He looked at me as though he were dealing with a child or an idiot. "I am he," he said, "and Byron and Jack Randall too; they are all the same man and I have been them, though now I am John Clare." He squatted beside the fire and retrieved the tobacco with the poker, picked it up, then swore and dropped it again.

"You are none of them neither," I muttered, but too low for him to hear, for I found it hard to know how to deal with these preposterous claims that credited the superintendent with mesmeric powers and took my John even further away from me.

"Your father is well and sends his fondest love," I ventured, then would have bitten back the words because John immediately said, "And how is Mother?"

"Do you not remember, John?" I said gently. "She passed away some years ago. Freddy visited you just a few days ago and you talked of this."

"Aah, Freddy! I was very glad to see him and have his company on the road as I did in the old days. My mother . . ." He looked confused. "I believe I do remember . . ." He dusted off his tobacco and popped it into his cheek. "No, I do not," he said and started chewing furiously, his eyes filling with tears. "We all must die," he said, "I know that, but my dear mother . . ." He walked over to the windows and pointedly turned his back to me.

"She was a good woman . . . very kind to me when first we moved to Helpstone," I offered, but he said nothing. I sat feeling quite miserable, wishing to take him in my arms but afraid to do it because of the harsh words he had said at our last parting. The clock chimed

394

a single note for the half-hour. I waited as minutes ticked away, then at last John blew his nose and returned to his seat.

He gazed into the fire for a while, his hands on his knees. Suddenly he brightened and said, "If you are from Northborough you must know Glinton?"

With a sigh born of knowing where this was leading, I agreed that I did.

"How is Mary, who lives there?" he asked. His face softened. "I hope she's well and still likes to walk."

The moment stretched between us until, in pity, I said, "She does very well, I believe," and let out the breath I had been holding.

His face relaxed into a smile, which was a reward for telling this falsehood and a sting to my heart at the same time.

"I have a plan to make some money from the orchard at home," I said swiftly, moving us on to a safer subject. "I shall visit Mr Darnley early this year, before the season starts, and remind him of the quality of the apples I took last year and ask him to send his man with a cart and take the whole crop. I can offer him a good price if he takes them all."

John didn't comment but rose and spat into the fire, then sat again.

"The spring flowers in the garden are all coming out now," I tried again to interest him, but although he looked at me as if following my words I could see that his thoughts were far away. "Like this one," I said, showing him the flower at my breast. "Do you remember how we used to walk for hours together? The flowers we used to find?" Something urgent in my tone caused him to stop chewing and look at me afresh. "Do you remember when we picked lilies-of-the valley in the woods for my garden at Walk Lodge?"

"Of course, I know you are one of my wives," he said, "and mother of my children."

"But the flowers, the smell of them when we carried them home? You had brought a little trowel and a pot to carry them in, because I loved them so, and we had planned to collect them. Do you recall it, the green wood and me kissing you for your trouble?" I took one of his hands in mine and looked into his face. "We were so happy then, our life together all before us."

"I remember a blue dress," he said, and I had to be content.

I loosed his hand and sat back again in my chair. The clock chimed the hour.

"I have to go now, to be able to get home," I said.

"Will you come again?"

"It's difficult," I said. "We haven't got the money for the stage-coach and the luck that brought me here today is unlikely to be repeated." I touched his sleeve. "You must concentrate on getting better."

I stood up, but John made no move and remained seated. "I have a skylark in a cage in my room that they gave me for its song," he said. "We are allowed plants and birds in our rooms."

"Does it sing?"

"It sings all the sweeter in closed quarters," he said, "but I wish it had a mate to whistle to."

"I'm sorry that I have to go," I said.

"I remember you in a blue gown, playing hide-and-seek," he said.

Tears came into my eyes and I laid the little yellow flower down upon the couch beside him as I bent to say goodbye and kiss his cheek.

I closed the door behind me softly and paused to dab my eyes with the corner of my shawl.

The door to the next room was open and, as I approached, the steward rose to his feet and came out from behind his desk to meet me.

"I'm sorry, I must rush to get back in time to catch my lift with the trap," I said.

He nodded and picked up a ring with keys. He led me through the building towards the main door. "How did you find him?"

"Quite calm, but a little . . . confused," I said.

"Indeed." The steward nodded and worked through his keys until he found the correct one, then unlocked and opened the door. The bright sunlight made me blink. Before he could say farewell I found myself touching his arm.

"Please, now that you have had John here for a few months, do you have a better understanding of his malady or how to cure it?"

The steward frowned in concern. "I'll walk with you to the gate, Mrs Clare," he said. We set off together along the gravel path that skirted the wide sloping lawns, smoothed and rolled to a green carpet with never a thistle or nettle in sight. "Fenwick Skrimshire wrote on the admittance papers that the cause of your husband's illness was 'too much poetical prosing', but in my experience there is usually more than one pressure on a mind before it breaks," he said. "Thwarted hopes, loss of loved ones, sudden unexpected changes in fortune, powerlessness to effect change in one's life, all these and more can put the sensitive mind under intolerable strain."

"Do you think his writing more a symptom than a cause, in that case?" I asked. "For at times it was beyond all bounds of reason and I have known him write a hundred sonnets in a fortnight."

"That is certainly a mania," the steward said with interest, as if this cast additional light on the case. "Tell me, did torpor often follow?"

"He would become exhausted, almost mute, and often then be physically ill," I said.

"Mmm, and his first delusions began when? Just before his sojourn at High Beech?"

"No, some years earlier; he would imagine faces at the window and devils in the ceiling."

He looked thoughtful and lowered his eyes to the path and we walked on in silence as I waited for his verdict. As we passed under the trees that led towards the gatehouse he said, "Sadly, we have no sure way of undoing these tangles and for this I am truly sorry. We must hope that a life of safety, plenty and order will allow an older pattern to return." He paused, then asked me, "Do you have a large household to care for?"

"I have five of my children still at home and John's father, who is now quite aged."

I saw him take in the plain nature of my dress, with its clean but threadbare cuffs, and my serviceable boots.

"One consolation is that he will want for nothing here," he said gently. "Already his physical health is greatly improved, whereas Worry and Want will exacerbate the mildest of conditions."

We reached the wrought-iron gates, which stood open to the road stretching in either direction as empty as when I had come.

He shook my hand. "I hope that you will visit us again. I'm sure we can accommodate you if you'd like to make an overnight stay."

"You are very kind," was all that I could mutter and I took my leave before I should disgrace myself with tears, for I feared that I had no way to take up his offer and that I was not likely to see my husband again.

I walked along the straight white road between the green fields. I thought of how John's over-busy mind was like a loom worked at speed in which a thread can come unhitched and unravel. It makes the pattern incomplete and parts are changed from their first intentions. To cure him of his misapprehensions of being Byron or some other person would be no easy task, for these were no shadowy shapes to be banished at a doctor's say-so; they had become fixed in his mind, woven into the cloth.

Later, as the trap bumped home through the lanes, lamps swinging to light our path and beat back the twilight, I thought with sadness how my heart had leapt when John remembered the blue dress, only to find that his memory was of Mary, for I never played hide-and-seek with him in our courting days: my heart was always there for him to take at will.

CHAPTER
TWENTY-ONE

Fit for a Lady

Apart from Freddy, who had waited at the stables to accompany me home, I saw none of the family until the next morning. All were abed when we came in.

At breakfast, the children said little and seemed intent on cramming as much bread as possible into their mouths, William and Charles even squabbling over the last piece on the plate.

"Did Eliza not feed you yesterday?" I asked in jest, but when William's eyes slid away from mine and Sophie and Charles stared down at the table as though the knots in the wood held some great fascination, I knew that all had not been as it should be.

"I don't think she felt very well," William muttered.

Once the children went off to school and William off to bird-scaring, Parker, who had been eating some breadsops in his fireside corner seat, put his bowl down on the hearth and explained. "Sefton came round first thing before work and upset 'Liza."

"Did the children hear? What was said?" I asked.

"They went out in the garden but we could still hear them shouting."

"I knew I shouldn't have gone," I said to myself.

"Then 'Liza came in and ran upstairs and wouldn't come out of her room all day, no matter how much I entreated. The children went off to school with no breakfast and no package for dinner time neither."

"No wonder they were half-clemmed."

"Sophie and I made a bit of soup for supper, but it was thin, dish-watery stuff and not a bit like yours," Parker said, with a mournful face.

I let out a sigh. "That Sefton . . ." I said, then pressed my lips together tight and picked up the kettle to fill it, clattering the lid. "Did Eliza eat at all, even at supper?" I asked.

"Not a mite," Parker said. "Sophie took soup up to her but she wouldn't sit up."

I made the tea and used up the last of the milk to make bread-and-milk with a little sugar to tempt the appetite, then took it up to Eliza on a tray.

The sunlight was streaming into the room, showing the motes of dust that hung in the air and misted the mirror. Only the top of Eliza's head was visible, her body curled up under the covers, turned away from the light.

"Eliza, I've brought you some breakfast," I said. "It's after eight and a beautiful day."

"I'm not hungry," came from under the blankets, followed by a stifled sniff. "I just want to be left alone."

I pulled a chair over to the bed and sat down on it, with the tray on my knees, so that she would know that I wasn't going to give up. "It's no good turning your face to the wall," I said. "That won't help anything.

Come, now, try a little bread-and-milk; everything will seem more bearable with food inside you."

Reluctantly she heaved herself up and sat with her head against the headboard. Her hair was dishevelled, as if she had been turning in her bed all night in restlessness, and her face looked small and pale.

"Here, my love," I said, placing the bowl in her hands. "Eat."

When she made no move to lift the spoon I put it into her hand and she took a small spoonful, though she chewed and chewed it as if she were taking a horse-pill rather than a sugary confection.

"There," I said, once she had swallowed. "Now try another."

She ate a few more spoonfuls, then gave the bowl back to me.

"What passed between you and Sefton yesterday?" I said.

"We quarrelled. He said that all that had happened was my fault, that I'd bewitched him like a siren." She wiped her eyes with the back of her hand. "Well, look at me; I don't look much like a siren now, do I?"

"Shame on him," I muttered.

"I told him it was over and that he must stop pursuing me, then he said I must promise not to find anyone else and that even if we couldn't be together he couldn't bear the thought of another man touching me."

"I hope you gave him no such promise."

"I didn't give him an answer. He seemed half out of his wits and I didn't want to make him angrier. I tried to be calm and said that it wasn't proper to discuss such things with my brother-in-law, but it didn't work and he got angrier still . . ." She covered her face with her hands and hunched her knees up to lay her head on them.

"You'd best tell all," I said. "It'll be nothing I can't guess or don't know already."

"He said that we were being punished for what we had done but it was worse for him as it was his flesh and blood that had been visited with the affliction." Her voice came muffled through her fingers. "He said that he felt sorry for any other man who ever set eyes on me and that I should think about what disasters I would bring on any followers I might have in the future. And he said that I had betrayed my own sister . . ."

I put my hand on her back as she broke into sobbing. "He blames you for everything to salve his own conscience," I said, and I took her in my arms and rocked her until the crying fit was over.

"There now," I said, tipping her face up to look at it. "You've worn yourself out with crying. You sleep for a while. Sefton will be at his work by now so no one is going to visit, and by the time he returns home I will be back from Anna's and won't give him entrance." I plumped up her pillows and straightened the covers. "I have a few words I wish to say to that young man." I pushed her hair back from her forehead and kissed her there. "Sleep now," I said, and went downstairs to clear up the breakfast debris.

★ ★ ★

When I went outside to throw away the dirty water from the plate washing, I noticed something sticking out from a bush beside the doorstep: a wooden box, its lid half off its hinges, tied round with string. I put down the basin and bent to find out what it could be. I unpicked the knot and lifted the lid, holding it carefully so that it didn't fall back and break the one remaining hinge.

Inside was a pile of tiny baby garments and napkins, all clean and neatly folded, and on top of them a package of sugar with something written on it. I lifted it out and squinted my eyes at the spidery writing. It read: *To the Widdow Clare with thanks from Mrs Hawkins*. I picked up the box to carry it inside, but the package with the message I put into my pocket, for despite the generous intention of the gift and the pleasure of a body being neighbourly the word "widow" cut me so sharply that I had to hide it away. Nonetheless, I saw it in my mind's eye in the dark of my pocket, a scrawl of pencil on sugar paper, innocent as a child's first letters and, like the blunt sayings of a child, showing me what everyone in the village thought: that John wasn't coming back.

When all was tidy in my own home I took the box round to Anna. She opened it as though it were a treasure chest, then touched the tiny white knitted socks and flannel nightgowns, the material creamy and soft with use and washing. She held each garment up in turn, exclaiming in delight.

I said, "It should take us up to her sixth month. When you've finished with it you just wash everything and pass the box on to the next new mother or return it to the curate. It came to us through Mrs Hawkins, with good wishes."

Anna blushed with pleasure. "I'm glad little Anne was christened here," she said, picking out the clothes that would fit the baby now. "We may all be from Helpstone but Northborough will be Anne's native place."

"Is she sleeping well?" I asked.

Anna nodded. "She feeds just after first light, then goes back to sleep until about nine o'clock."

"And feeding well?"

"Oh, yes. She has a grand appetite; the tonics that the doctor sent are strengthening her, I'm sure." She began to fold the clothes that were too big for the baby as yet and place them carefully back into the box.

"Is Sefton more reconciled to the idea of her condition?" I asked. I chose my words carefully: "He seemed not quite himself at church on Sunday."

She shook her head. "He's not himself at all, Ma. Yesterday he came back early and I found out that he hadn't been to work at all but had gone into Stamford, drinking. I'm worried he might lose his position."

"He went off in good time today?"

"Yes, and he said he would play the contrite to the foreman and charm him round." She fetched a bunch of lavender from one of the hooks above the chimney corner and teased out some sprigs to scent the baby clothes.

"But . . .?" I said, sensing that there was more.

"He didn't take his lunch." She pointed to a paper package tied up neatly with a string handle.

"Perhaps he just forgot," I said, though I had misgivings and thought that he might well be at the Hole in the Wall or some other inn by now.

A wail from the corner of the room signalled the waking of the baby, and Anna brought down the basin from the wash-stand upstairs and poured in some hot water from the pot on the fire and some cold from a large pottery jug, ready for her bath.

"What can I best do?" I said, rolling up my sleeves.

"Napkins?" Anna said. "They're in a bucket outside, soaking, and the tub is in the corner there."

By the time Anna and I had finished the chores and had something to eat, it was noon. I showed her how to make herself more comfortable when feeding the baby, by folding a pillow and resting her arm on it, for little Anne was beginning to gain weight now and was heavy to cradle for the length of time that she wanted to suckle. I left Anna nursing her, with her feet up on a stool, and looking at mother and baby, each so caught up in the other that they hardly noticed my going, felt that I had done a good morning's work.

I started off for home but was delayed first by the knife-grinder, who was passing through the area, looking for trade now that the good weather was here, and then by Mrs Hawkins, who was returning to the village with her boys, all with armfuls of withies for

407

basket-making. I hurried over to thank her for the baby clothes and her gift.

She smiled. "I asked Mrs Harper for the clothes box and some others put a few things in. Is the baby doing well?"

"She seems to be thriving for the moment and we're hopeful the doctor may be able to do something for her in the long term," I said. I turned to the youngest Hawkins. "And how is your arm?"

Despite the fact that he was carrying a huge bundle of willow sticks and the arm was obviously fully recovered, he said, "'Tis still painful. Have you got another half-penny, missus?"

His mother opened her mouth to scold him, but he pulled such a woeful face that we both burst out laughing.

"I have no half-pennies," I said, "but next time I make drop scones you boys shall have one, that's a promise."

I said goodbye and went on along the lane, where the gardens seemed to be bursting their boundaries with branches in full leaf hanging over the way, white blossom sprinkling the pear trees and flowers that had seeded out into the verges and twined through the hedges. Thinking that I would bring something home to cheer Eliza, I paused to pick a handful of periwinkle and wood anemone, for the hedgerows are known as "the long acre" in these parts and still belong to everyone.

As I walked up the garden path I saw Parker down in the orchard, shuffling along the lines of ash saplings and pausing to inspect each one. I noticed that the house door was open to let in the fresh spring air and felt glad that Eliza must be up and about and maybe feeling a little better. I bent to pick some jack-in-the-hedge and add them to my bunch of flowers, but straightened again quickly at the sound of a stranger's voice, a man's, coming from inside the house.

"This is very good quality and a fine colour too," the voice was saying.

For a moment I thought it was a haberdasher or draper come to call and sell his wares but something about the tone seemed wrong: he spoke as if he was admiring something he was being shown rather than showing his own goods. I hurried inside.

The dimness after the bright outdoors made me pause while my eyes grew accustomed to it. As if time itself were slowing I took in what was in front of me. Eliza sat on a chair in the middle of the room, while a small man with a neatly trimmed white beard, his shirt-sleeves rolled up, held the tresses of her hair out from her head and with a pair of silver scissors cut them off.

Laid on a piece of black cloth on the table beside him were long strands of hair like hanks of golden thread, fresh spun and shining.

"It will make a very fine hairpiece, good enough for one of my London ladies," he was saying.

I let out a gasp as if the scissors had cut me and the flowers dropped from my hand as another snip severed more and left it hanging in the man's hand.

Eliza turned towards me, her face with a dreamy smile. "Look, Ma," she said. "I'll soon be free of it. Then no one will come near me."

I moved towards the man as if I would stay his hand as he lifted the last strand away.

A look of alarm passed over his face and he cut quickly and almost threw it down with the rest. "I was saying, your daughter has very fine hair, madam," he said. "I can pay two shillings for hair like this; two shillings is a very fair rate," he babbled as he folded the hair into the cloth and placed it quickly into his knapsack.

"Please leave my house," I said.

Eliza raised her hand to her head and smoothed it over the back, down towards her neck, feeling the shape of her skull where heavy coils and curls had been. She ran her hand back up to her crown, making the cropped hair stand up on end in random spikes, like a cat with wet fur. She looked smaller and frailer, her eyes huge in a thin face. Then both hands went up to her head and she began to run them through the short hair, combing it and patting it as though looking for what was no longer there.

"Leave my house," I said again, my voice shaking.

The man rummaged quickly in the pouch tied round his middle and placed two coins on the table where the hair had been. He slung his bag over his shoulder and made a small bow to Eliza, saying, "I bid you good day, miss."

I led the way to the door and watched him scuttle down the path.

410

I returned to find Eliza staring into the mirror above the mantel. "I was sick of myself," she said. "Now I am somebody else."

I turned her away from the mirror to face me. A few long hairs still lay on her shoulders, stuck to her grey gown like glistening threads against the dark material. I led her to the seat in the chimney corner. Her hands were cold and I fetched my shawl and wrapped it round her. I thought my heart would overflow unless I found an outlet, so I busied myself picking up the strewn flowers and finding a jug for them.

"Are you feeling any warmer?" I asked. "Are you hungry?" Then, "Aren't they pretty?" as I set them down on the hearth beside her, but never a word did she answer. She sat with her hands clasped in her lap, staring straight ahead.

From the garden came a heavy tread on the path, uneven, as if pausing for balance, then a banging on the door. Eliza made no response at all, as if she were deaf to the outside world and had gone somewhere else entirely.

Like a rope that has been strained until it frays right through, something inside me snapped. I marched to the door, knowing exactly who I should find there. At the sight of my face, Sefton took a step back. He stood with his hands in his pockets, swaying.

"Ah, Sefton," I said. "You've come to see Eliza. Well, come. Come and see her." A look of surprise crossed his face as I took hold of his sleeve and led him into the kitchen.

He stood over her, blinking, as if uncertain about what he was seeing.

"There!" I said. "Are you satisfied? It is you who have done this with your harsh words of yesterday."

Eliza looked straight ahead.

"Oh, 'Liza, what have you done?" he said and moved towards her.

I pulled sharply at his arm to keep him back. "Leave her be!" I said. "Do you see where your greedy fancy has led?"

He looked down at me as though working to understand my meaning through his ale-befuddled haze, then said, "A man's not to blame if a girl's more than willing."

"Don't tell me that! You're older and supposedly wiser and you played with a young girl's affections. *You* are the prime mover in this, Sefton."

"A man can't help his fancies, 'tis natural. Your own husband had a roving eye," he said bluntly.

"A man can and should keep his desires in check and you have no illness or madness to excuse you."

He shook my hand from his sleeve. We stood, glaring at each other, but I would not give way. "Go on," I said. "Go back to your family."

He stepped back, looking from me to Eliza and back again. Eliza said nothing, her eyes dark and vacant.

I moved forward. "Go back to your wife, Sefton," I said, holding his gaze. "You can only have one of my girls. One. And you've already made your choice."

He turned round and lumbered from the room, bumping into the corner of the table as he went and jarring its feet along the floor. I heard the house door creak and his footsteps receding down the path.

I knelt down by Eliza and rubbed her hands between my own. "This must stop, Eliza. Here and now," I said.

CHAPTER
TWENTY-TWO

World Enough and Time

All through May and June the spring sun passed across the fens, warming the earth and drawing leaves and shoots after it to bend and flutter in its wake. Men worked to clear the dykes, digging out the mud from the bottoms and turning it up on to the banks, where it gave off a vegetable smell and served as a rich base for a new crop of yellow flags and kingcups.

The roads grew busier still and strangers passed through the village: gypsies looking for a new encampment, tradesmen in search of sales, day-labourers in search of work, and drovers with cattle that filled the narrow lanes, tearing mouthfuls from the hedges as they went. All was flux and change, in keeping with the season.

One June day, I took my mending basket and sat outside under the ash tree. Eliza used often to join me and bring her sewing outside too, but these days she was a late riser, staying in bed even longer than Parker, so I sat and sewed and watched little Anne, who lay on a blanket at my feet in the dappled shade. I often looked after her for a while in the day so that Anna could get a little rest. She had still not returned to the

414

robust good health that she used to enjoy before the birth and was troubled by coughing, particularly at night, which disturbed her sleep and made Sefton irritable about getting up early for his new job at the flour mill. He had got employment easily enough, for there will always be work for a man who can shoulder a meal-sack as if it were a feather pillow. I was mightily relieved, for as well as the housekeeping there were tonics and tinctures for the baby to pay for.

Little Anne, in a faded pink dress and a napkin, lay on the blanket, kicking off her knitted shoes. Her arms and legs were more rounded now and her hands, once so delicate and frail, had a soft, pudgy look that made you want to kiss them, and little creases like bracelets at the wrist. She gurgled and sucked her fingers while I sat and darned.

All round me the birds called from the bushes and trees and I thought of John and hoped that he too was somewhere outside on this fine morning and not listening to his sad skylark. I imagined him walking across the smooth lawns of the asylum grounds, then down towards the river with its water-cress beds, and sitting on a grassy bank to write a poem. A memory of watching him write when we were courting, and used to sit beside the little River Gwash, came back to me and I wondered if he still rested his paper as he used to, on the crown of his hat.

The baby stilled for a moment, her attention caught by the movement above her. I watched her looking up into the leaves. Where I saw spring growth, black buds and the pale brown remnants of last year's ash keys, she, unaware of time and its effect, saw only shapes and patterns.

I laid aside my darning needle and the shirt I had been mending and picked little Anne up on to my lap. I held her warmth to me and brushed my cheek against the top of her downy head. The plumpness of her body had made the swelling less noticeable, her proportions closer to normality, but I still feared for her future. I remembered the doctor's warning that by the age of two the bones would fuse and a desperate problem would require a desperate remedy.

I kissed her and searched in my basket for the little wooden rattle that John made for Anna so long ago. I put it in her hand and shook it gently. She stared at it, then moved it to her mouth as she does with everything she's given to hold. I put the darning back into the basket and sang to her, "O darling child", knowing as I sang that I would store this moment for safekeeping: her face, her soft weight, the intensity of my feeling.

As I sang the last verses of the song, Eliza came slowly down through the garden and into the orchard, bending under the low branches where the trees are planted close together. She was wearing her grey dress again despite all my persuasion that the warmer weather warranted a cotton print. Her hair had grown a little in the passing weeks, enough to show its gold shades clearly once more, and it glowed in the sunshine, the dark dress serving to set off its fine colour.

When she reached me she sat down on the grass, saying, "I wondered where you were." Her face, though still pale and a little thin, seemed to me even more beautiful than before, for her hair, smooth to her head save for some wispy curls tucked behind her ears, accentuated the slight hollows at her temples, her high cheekbones and the delicacy of her features.

"We've been having a happy time singing, haven't we, little Anne?" and I bent close to the baby, shaking my head so that her mouth opened into a smile.

Eliza knelt up to get a better look. "She's growing," she said and gently squeezed her forearm between her finger and thumb. "She's getting quite chubby." She looked to me for confirmation and I smiled.

"She's doing very well," I said. "Here, take her."

Eliza stood and took her into her arms, looking earnestly into her face. The baby gave a little cry in protest at being dislodged from her warm spot.

"Quick, quick; pull a face as Charles does to make her smile," I said.

Eliza glanced at me, then pulled a comic face at little Anne, who stopped mid cry, stared for a moment, then made a gurgling, hiccupping sound and scrunched up her eyes.

We looked at each other.

"Is she laughing?" Eliza said.

"Do it again."

Eliza pulled a face again, this time widening her eyes and sticking out her tongue. The baby laughed again.

"She's laughing!" Eliza said, catching the baby's expression as if it were reflected.

I smiled too, for I hadn't seen such animation on Eliza's face for months. "Take her round to Anna's to show her," I urged.

Eliza faltered. "I don't know . . . I'd rather stay here with you."

"Go on, take her, my love. It's nearly time for her feed anyway, so Anna will be expecting her home."

"What if I see anyone? I look as though I'm straight from the poorhouse with my hair like this — they'll think I must be lousy."

"Nonsense," I said firmly.

She hesitated still and made a little move, as if to hold the baby back out to me. Little Anne, her entertainment removed, began to grizzle.

"Quick, quick," I said, and Eliza did it again with exactly the same result.

"She likes me doing it," she said, her face once more alive.

"Then, nip along now before she gets too hungry and can't be distracted."

Eliza, cradling the baby so that she could talk to her all the way, turned and went back through the orchard, ducking carefully under the branches.

I stooped and picked up the blanket, then folded it. As I did so I looked out beyond the ash tree to the pasture that was also part of our plot. It was full of thistles and docks and it was a constant rebuke to me that we hadn't put it to good use because we couldn't afford to buy a cow to graze it. Every year we hoped to put a little by towards getting one, so we could have good milk for the family, but there was never enough money. We had to make do with the skimmed leavings that some farmers let you buy, others, to their shame, preferring to feed it to their pigs rather than bother to market it to labouring families for their children. Suddenly, an idea struck me and I placed the blanket on top of my sewing basket, picked up both basket and stool and hurried back to the house to discuss it with Parker.

Over a dish of broad beans, potatoes and onions, I put my idea to him. "I know it would be a labour but we should cut that field for hay rather than leaving it as idle pasture," I said. "We're never going to have the money for a cow, so we should just accept it and try to get rid of the weeds to give the meadow grass a chance to grow."

Parker rubbed his stubbly chin. "There would still be some expense," he said. "We would need scythes to cut it."

"We could use some of the apple money from this year to buy them for next."

"We would need an implement to root out all those docks — a spud, it's called."

"Perhaps we could borrow one?"

Parker snorted. "The farmers round here make the threshers empty out their shoes in case they've taken a little grain for their chickens," he said. "Do you really believe they'd let you have anything for free?"

"Well, we'll buy a spud and just one scythe, then," I conceded. "We could manage with one if we worked shifts to cut the hay."

"We haven't got the apple money yet," Parker said.

"No, but I shall go to Market Deeping and I won't come back without an agreement," I said stubbornly. "I will haggle like a fishwife if I need to, but I am *not* having us go hungry this winter."

Parker grinned. "If you visit Mr Darnley with a face as fierce as that one he cannot gainsay you," he said. "You'll make a fearsome marketeer."

I laughed then and shrugged off his teasing, but I was never more serious. There was no man at home to be head of the household but only men who could do it in parts, for Parker was too old but could give me his advice, William was too young but could give me the strength of his arm, and Freddy, who was our main breadwinner, was too tired to do more after the long hours of his work. So . . . I decided that I would plan for our family's future and would have to be mother and father all rolled into one, for John was not there and I must manage alone.

As I washed and dried the plates, Parker began to nod and all was quiet in the house save for his breathing. I took the basin of dirty water outside and threw it on to the nearest vegetable plot. Here, too, all was silent in the early-afternoon heat. No one passed by in the lane and no sound of neighbours' voices carried from other gardens. The only sound was the buzz of a honey-bee that hovered before a foxglove, then disappeared inside a flower, only to emerge dusted all over with pollen. Left alone with my thoughts I felt my enthusiasm begin to drain away and the old ache caused by John's absence returned. I propped the basin against the wall to dry and decided to sit in the parlour for a while.

★ ★ ★

The bright sunshine through the parlour window warmed the rich colours of the wood and books in the room. John's desk glowed red-brown as a polished conker, the grain of the huge oak bookcase showed its fine lines and the lettering on the books glinted against spines that were every shade of brown, tan and green.

Above me the light picked out a cobweb, laden with pale dust, that sagged between one corner of the ceiling and an old holly sprig that still remained tucked behind the corner of John's portrait. I stood before the portrait, searching for the John I knew. It was a watercolour copy of the oil painting that the publishers had commissioned; John had had it done as a present for Parker. The original was painted when John went to London just before our marriage, and although it caught his likeness — the long, straight nose and thoughtful, serious expression — it seemed to record a person I scarcely recognized. The fine cravat and waistcoat, the wing collar buttoned up tight and the pose, seated on a chair with the face at half-profile, spoke of a gentleman used to indoor pursuits. It had nothing in common with my John, walking in the fields or sitting by the brook, his shirt unbuttoned at the neck and sleeves rolled up, his face full of expression as he explained or questioned or bantered with me. The John in the painting was unknown to me, a version from another world, where I had never set foot.

In my thoughts of John, I mostly remembered the days of our courtship. Pictures came back to me in all their vivid colour, as pebbles turned often in the hand

421

will shine bright and polished. That spring day I thought of him, young and ardent, protesting his love as we met or parted at field stile or garden gate. I thought of him offering me a poem for a kiss or bringing me his found treasures, a piece of Roman pottery he said was Time made visible, a rare orchis from the woods to plant in my garden, a love knot plaited out of grass. Our love was open-handed then.

Standing in the empty room, these thoughts seemed more real to me than the present, or maybe I only wished that they were. Sometimes I think that I am doing the very thing that John does when he retreats into his past with Mary, for the past is a safe harbour to return to when the present becomes too hard to bear.

I turned to the bookcase, looking for solace, and ran my finger along the spines at eye level . . . Burns, Gray, Tennyson, Thompson, Crabbe, Spenser . . . volume after volume of poetry, and in among them John's own volumes: *The Rural Muse*, *The Shepherd's Calendar*, *The Village Minstrel*. My hand passed over them, for they too were for public consumption and I longed for something more intimate.

On the shelf below, between *Moore's Almanack* and *The Natural History of Birds*, were the slim spines of some exercise books. I put my finger on top of one and as they were tightly wedged in, wheedled it out. It was an old school book. I waited for the familiar feeling of dread to overcome me, the fear of finding poems to Mary or love notes slipped between the leaves, but nothing came save a sense of things past and gone, dry as a trickle of sawdust, harmless as leaf fall.

I sat down at the desk and flicked through pages of geometric drawings, long multiplications and explanatory notes. The lines for the sums were all neatly ruled and the headings written in a beautiful copperplate script. I smiled to think of my own school books with their blots and painfully executed letters. I turned to the very front of the book, where I was wont to doodle birds and flowers, and found instead a serious inscription:

Steal not this book for fear of shame
For here doth stand the owner's name
John Clare

I felt tenderness then for the boy as well as the man and thought of how as adults we had shared the secrets of our childhood. I told him of my fear of the group of girls at school who called me dunce and said my head was full of sheep's wool, and John told me of all his strange childish fancies. He used to believe that the last swallow left behind in autumn flew down through a lake, clean through the bottom, to where he thought heaven lay. He imagined that it overwintered there to burst back through the water and into the air in the spring. As a boy, he had believed that at the edge of the horizon was the world's end, like a huge pit, and had once walked all day, clear across Emmonsales Heath in search of it. His schoolmates thought him mad.

Perhaps that was where it started, the feeling that he was different, the rumour that he wasn't quite in his wits. John told the things he thought of, whereas others would keep quiet, for people are often afraid to let their

423

inner worlds show and turn away in alarm or confusion when others do so.

I thought of myself standing for hours in hope by a winter stile, of Sefton fighting the rain barrel and Eliza cutting off her hair. Perhaps we are all a little mad. Perhaps the infant is the only sane one among us. She doesn't yet have the inner worlds that we create, where we live out most of our lives, unknown, unshown to others. She lives in the moment of a tree's leaves moving, a glittering shard of light, a pang of hunger, warmth or cold.

I put the book back in its place, lining it up carefully with the rest. I sat down at the desk and opened it for the first time since John had gone. The papers and notebooks spilled forward and I began slowly to tidy them, putting like with like, dividing the notebooks into foolscap, quarto or octavo and standing them up in the pigeon-holes, and smoothing out the sheets and scraps of paper and dividing them between the little drawers. I felt as though I was at least doing him some small service. I read none of what I touched, for I knew that some of his writings in the weeks before he went were coarse and strange and it was not his true self speaking. His familiar handwriting passed in front of my eyes as I closed and folded, and the shape of the letters was dear to me.

When all was done I sat with my palms flat on the desk flap and my fingers spread, touching the places where he had leant his arms as if I would soak up his very essence from the wood. I felt his absence so keenly that I breathed out long and slow. I thought about my

424

visit to the asylum and how I had talked but said nothing at all of any real importance. I began to think that maybe the chance would not come again to see him and that I would never say what needed to be said. I decided that I would write to him.

As soon as I had decided, my spirits lifted a little. I would write that very afternoon and then walk to Market Deeping to catch the post before the coach left the town. I saw myself stepping out into the bright afternoon and hurrying along the way, past the last of the houses, past the old oak where I had read another letter in what seemed now another time, past the mistletoe trees and out along the straight road through the open fens.

I would write then, and walk with a light step along the road, because John would have the message from my hand that he should have had from my lips when I had visited him.

Between my thumb and forefinger, I took the corner of a clean sheet of creamy writing paper and drew it towards me from the pile. The heavy metal lid of the ink-well, squeaked on its hinge as I opened it. I picked up the pen, dipped it and began to write.

I wrote at first without care in my haste to spill my feelings on to paper, then went back and crossed things through or wrote them down another way. I pushed the first sheet aside and started again, only to strike through the whole. I stopped and stared into the ink-well. I looked at the small dark pool and felt that the words I needed to write to John were hidden within it and that I must only open my heart as wide to find them. At length I began again more slowly and deliberately, though still with some crossings-out; then, as I had seen John do, I made a fair copy. In my best hand I added at the top: *To my dearest John from Patty.*

Love is a dream
That does not pass
As dew that, with the risen sun,
Burns from the grass.

It clings, as does
The imprint left behind
On walls where vines are torn away,
Each leaf kept clear in mind.

I have sought comfort
There myself: hands placed
On long-lost leaf prints
Where joy is faintly traced

And tried to find
Your dear, once tender face,
Though you have lost your old self
In a dark, beleaguered place.

I hope you dream,
Whoever holds you there
Upon the mossy bank beside the stream;
As I do, may you dream.

With this, I over-step my hurts
To reach you at the end
And lay my hand once more in yours,
My oldest, dearest friend.

Historical Note on John Clare

John Clare never returned home. He remained at Northampton General Lunatic Asylum for twenty-three years. His worsening mental condition can be seen in the letters he wrote to Patty and the family: in one he says, "I am in the Land of Sodom where all the people's brains are turned the wrong way." Yet he continued to write poetry and his poems are lucid and full of feeling. They were collected and transcribed, in the main, by William Knight, a superintendent of the asylum, whose careful forethought saved some of Clare's best work for posterity.

One of these poems, *An Invite to Eternity*, written in 1847, shows Clare's continuing concern with the idea of loss of identity and his desire for a soul mate to share his journey with him. It is a wonderful, mysterious poem that leaves room for interpretation but perhaps shares something of Tennyson's consternation in "In Memoriam" at the idea of an afterlife in which the individual is subsumed into one amorphous spirit.

An Invite to Eternity

Wilt thou go with me, sweet maid
Say, maiden, wilt thou go with me
Through the valley depths of shade,
Of night and dark obscurity,
Where the path hath lost its way,
Where the sun forgets the day,
Where there's nor light nor life to see,
Sweet maiden, wilt thou go with me?

Where stones will turn to flooding streams,
Where plains will rise like ocean waves,
Where life will fade like visioned dreams
And mountains darken into caves,
Say, maiden, wilt thou go with me
Through this sad non-identity,
Where parents live and are forgot,
And sisters live and know us not?

Say, maiden, wilt thou go with me
In this strange death of life to be,
To live in death and be the same
Without this life, or home or name,
At once to be and not to be —
That was and is not — yet to see
Things pass like shadows, and the sky
Above, below, around us lie?

The land of shadows wilt thou trace,
And look — nor know each other's face;

The present mixed with reason gone,
And past and present all as one?
Say, maiden, can thy life be led
To join the living with the dead?
Then trace thy footsteps on with me;
We're wed to one eternity.

John Clare died of apoplexy (stroke), aged seventy, on 20 May 1864. His body was brought back to be buried at Helpstone, his "home of homes", as he had wished.

Back in 1824, aged only thirty-one and in one of his depressive phases, he wrote down instructions for his own tombstone and drew a picture of a simple headstone inscribed "Here lie the hopes and ashes of John Clare". On his death, initially no stone was erected and it seems likely that this was due to the family's lack of money: Parker, too, had been buried without the addition of an inscription to the shared gravestone that marked the resting place of his wife. However, three years later a fund was raised to provide a low, coped stone. It has biographical details on one slope and on the other the bold statement "A POET IS BORN NOT MADE" — a fitting assertion of genius over social class.

Each July, on his birthday, a festival is held in his honour and the local schoolchildren listen to his poetry and place midsummer cushions of grass and flowers around his grave.

Acknowledgements

My greatest debt is to Clare scholar, Jonathan Bate, for his thorough and very readable biography of the poet. I recommend it to any reader who wishes to find out more about John Clare. Details of this and other resources which I found useful are below:

Life and Remains of John Clare by J. L. Cherry (2008)
The Letters of John Clare edited by J. W. & Anne Tibble (1951)
John Clare Major Works edited by Eric Robinson & David Powell, revised edition (2004)
John Clare The Shepherd's Calendar edited by Eric Robinson & Geoffrey Summerfield (1964)
The Village Minstrel and other poems by John Clare. Published by Taylor and Hessey (1821)
John Clare A Biography by Jonathan Bate (2003)
John Clare A Photographic Journey with Peter Moyse DVD produced by the John Clare Society
John Clare By Himself edited by Eric Robinson & David Powell (1996)
The Life of John Clare by Frederick Martin (2004)

Edge of the Orison: In the Traces of John Clare's "Journey Out of Essex" by Iain Sinclair (2006)

The following books helped me to recreate the world of rural Northamptonshire in 1841:

Saga of the Steam Plough by Harold Bonnett (1972)

Traditional Country Craftsmen by J. Geraint Jenkins, revised edition (1978)

The Rural World 1780–1850 Social Change in the English Countryside by Pamela Horn (1980)

The Victorian Country Child by Pamela Horn (1985)

Life and Labour in Rural England 1760–1850 by Pamela Horn (1987)

Like Dew before the Sun — Life and Language in Northamptonshire by Dorothy A. Grimes (1991)

The Good Life. An Anthology of Working Life in the Country edited by C. Henry Warren (1946)

I would like to thank the following people who helped me:

Laura Longrigg, Katie Espiner and Jane Lawson for their inspiration, astute comments, support and faith in the project, also Judy Collins, Aislinn Casey and all at Transworld who had a hand in the making of this book;

Crispin Powell of the County Records Office, Jon-Paul Carr of Northampton Central Library and Emma Marigliano of the Portico Library for their assistance in researching John Clare's manuscripts and other historical resources;

Dr Philip Sugarman and Mel Whitehall for their hospitality and knowledgeable comments when showing me around St Andrews hospital, formerly the Northampton General Lunatic Asylum;

Peter Moyse of the John Clare Society for providing invaluable information and for an unforgettable tour of Helpston, with readings from John Clare's poetry;

Grace Kempster, Caroline Bates, Gill Howe, Nick Garrod, Kate Wilkinson, Peter and Deirdre Newham, Margaret and Richard Graham, Lucy Anderson, Peter O'Malley and Keith Large for their interest and support;

My family, near and far, for their steady encouragement and invaluable help with research, and for "doing without me" on occasion when I was engrossed in writing;

And finally, a huge thank you to my friend Janet Lambdon for stalwart help in turning my handwritten work into a readable manuscript and for all her unstintingly generous support.

Also available in ISIS Large Print:

Nethergate

Norah Lofts

Forced to flee Revolutionary France after the brutal guillotining of her beloved father, Isabella de Savigny arrives at Nethergate, the Suffolk house of her cousin, hoping for sympathy and succour. Instead, as a poor relation, she is forced to live the life of a servant and suffer the casual cruelty of lady's maid Martha Pratt. When she is seduced and abandoned by the son of the house, Isabella is forced to marry Martha's brother, and her struggle to survive truly begins. However, her misery is lessened when her daughter is born, and for her sake she decides to fight back against a hostile world.

ISBN 978-0-7531-8562-9 (hb)
ISBN 978-0-7531-8563-6 (pb)

Last Train from Liguria

Christine Dwyer Hickey

In 1933, Bella Stuart leaves a restricted life in London to head for Italy and become a tutor for the wealthy Lami family. Her pupil, Alec, is the "not quite right" child of a beautiful Jewish heiress and an elderly Italian aristocrat. When Alec's father dies, Signora Lami sends him to live at the family's summer residence in Bordighera, to be cared for by Bella and Maestro Edward, his reserved and enigmatic music teacher.

These three misfits find unexpected solace in each other's company. As the decade draws to an end and fascism begins to take an ominous hold over Europe, Bella and Edward are eventually forced to flee Mussolini's Italy: to protect themselves and the little boy they have come to love.

ISBN 978-0-7531-8596-4 (hb)
ISBN 978-0-7531-8597-1 (pb)

The Madonna of the Almonds

Marina Fiorato

Bernardino Luini, favourite apprentice of Leonardo da Vinci, is commissioned to paint a religious fresco in the hills of Lombardy. His eye is caught by the beautiful Simonetta di Saronno, a young noblewoman who has lost her husband to battle, and whose fortune is now gone.

Captivated by her beauty and sadness, Bernardino paints Simonetta's likeness, immortalising her as the Madonna in his miraculous frescoes in Saronno's church. As the sittings progress, artist and model fall in love, and Simonetta reciprocates Luini's genius by creating a work of art of her own. She makes a drink for her lover from the juice of almonds — the famous Amaretto di Saronno.

As the frescoes and the liqueur near their completion, the couple's affair distils into a heady brew of religious scandal which threatens their love, and ultimately their lives.

ISBN 978-0-7531-8492-9 (hb)
ISBN 978-0-7531-8493-6 (pb)

The Sonnets

Warwick Collins

This vivid fictional account begins in 1592 when the young playwright William Shakespeare was prevented from earning his living on the stage by the closing of theatres due to the threat of plague. In the three turbulent years which followed, Shakespeare is widely believed to have written the majority of his great sequence of sonnets.

Shakespeare was forced back on the patronage of the youthful Earl of Southampton, to whom Shakespeare dedicated his long poems *Venus and Adonis* and *The Rape of Lucrece*. Southampton had been orphaned at the age of eight, and his appointed guardian was the formidable Lord Burghley, a brilliant but Machiavellian politician and Queen Elizabeth's effective chief minister. Rivalry soon appeared between the older Burghley, who considered the theatre both subversive and seditious, and the maturing Southampton, who loved the arts.

ISBN 978-0-7531-8448-6 (hb)
ISBN 978-0-7531-8449-3 (pb)